THE
WARRIOR

ALSO BY SARAH FINE

Adult Fiction

The Immortal Dealers Series

The Serpent
The Guardian

The Reliquary Series

Reliquary
Splinter
Mosaic
Mayhem and Magic (graphic novel)

Servants of Fate Series

Marked
Claimed
Fated

Young Adult Fiction

Guards of the Shadowlands Series

Sanctum
Fractured
Chaos
Captive: A Guard's Tale from Malachi's Perspective
Vigilante: A Guard's Tale from Ana's Perspective
Stories from the Shadowlands

Of Metal and Wishes Series

Of Metal and Wishes
Of Dreams and Rust
Of Shadows and Obsession: A Short Story Prequel to
Of Metal and Wishes

The Impostor Queen Series

The Impostor Queen
The Cursed Queen
The True Queen

Other Series

Scan (with Walter Jury)
Burn (with Walter Jury)
Beneath the Shine
Uncanny

THE
WARRIOR

THE
IMMORTAL
DEALERS
SERIES

SARAH FINE

47NORTH

Text copyright © 2019 by Sarah Fine
All rights reserved.

Published by 47North, Seattle

www.apub.com

Amazon, the Amazon logo, and 47North are trademarks of Amazon.com, Inc., or its affiliates.

ISBN-13: 9781542043519
ISBN-10: 1542043514

Cover design by Blake Morrow

Printed in the United States of America

For Debbie Simpson, my favorite Spartan and one of the strongest women I've ever known

CHAPTER ONE

Ernie's breath whooshed from her mouth as she sprinted for the barbed wire. She'd just heaved herself over a seven-foot wall and landed too hard, and now her legs felt like jelly. Dread pulled at her like a riptide, drowning the strength she desperately needed to survive what lay ahead. The low-slung grid of spiked metal ahead of her glinted under the pale-yellow February sun. Ernie threw herself to the ground and rolled the first few feet, then shoved up to a bear crawl, keeping her head low and her sore legs moving. Her sneakers were already filled with mud, and she was now coated in it up to her shoulders. Grit crunched between her teeth.

I am having fun, she thought. *This is fun.*

Even her inner voice was out of breath.

"Come on, Ern," Marcus shouted from about twenty yards ahead of her. She suspected he was hanging back just to make sure she stayed in the game. Unlike the rest of their team, he'd chucked his Bear Creek Spartans jersey and was racing shirtless, with his number scrawled across his chiseled chest and back in permanent marker. "Get that ass down before it gets snagged!"

Ernie dropped her butt and continued her scramble under the wire; the last time she'd done this, the rusty metal barbs had raked their claws across her skin. That had been Gabe's doing, a simple flip of a few cards with the intention of trapping her, but back then she hadn't known about the cards, or the powerful Immortal Dealers who played them, so it had just seemed like crappy luck. Back then, she'd thought the world was simple. Back then, she'd had no magic in her life whatsoever.

Heck, back then, she'd believed the world, her world, was the *only* world that existed. Ignorance had been bliss.

Focus on the race, she reminded herself even as her thoughts took a hard left into a swamp of anxiety. Things had been too quiet, as had the new Forger—the being in charge of creating the chaos that made the universe tick. Nearly six weeks ago, Virginia, the former Dealer of the Chicken deck, had vanquished Andy, the former Forger, and taken his place. Ernie had expected everything to go to hell after that, but all Virginia had done was inexplicably restore Gabe's deck to full capacity, and they'd heard nothing from her since. No attacks, no ambushes, and certainly no assignments.

The world had continued to turn, with no obvious intervention from the Immortal Dealers, but Ernie didn't trust the peace for even a moment. She was determined to be ready when Virginia made her move, no matter how relaxed everyone else had become, no matter how much Dealers like Minh and Alvarez and even Gabe had begun to assure her that no apocalypse was on the horizon, that all her fears about someone as evil as Virginia taking the crown of the Forger were unfounded, and that Ernie was the Chicken Little of the story.

But still, she was starting to wonder. Maybe the sky wasn't falling after all. What if Virginia wasn't the enemy Ernie had believed her to be?

"Bullshit," Ernie grunted. She reached the end of the barbed wire and shoved herself up, grimacing as two other Spartan racers whipped past her and Marcus disappeared over a rise, maybe having decided that getting a decent time was more important than coaching a prodigal racer like her through every obstacle. Ernie could hardly blame him— they'd all paid extra to be part of the competitive wave of this race, and even though Spartan competitions were usually individual, her club had a "friendly" bet with a few other local groups to see which team was the leanest and meanest. But while her other teammates had worked their asses off to prepare, Ernie had been MIA for weeks.

On her arm, Legs tingled sharply, from her forked tongue all the way to her large rattle, almost as if she wanted to peel herself from Ernie's body and complete a few obstacles herself. "I don't think this next one is for you, babe," Ernie muttered to the living tattoo as she picked up speed, her feet thumping on the muddy grass. "You'd need arms."

The monkey bars were now in sight, a perfect antidote for her churning thoughts. Ernie clenched and unclenched her fists as she ran. Her arms were toast from the rope climb a few obstacles back, and she'd need all her concentration to make it through. Marcus was on the other side, charging for the final obstacle, but he let out an encouraging "Ah-roo, ah-roo!" over his shoulder.

Ernie swiped her palms down her sides as she ran the last few steps to the bars and sprang up to hang from the first, trying to get some momentum from the swing of her body. She flew forward and grabbed the next rung, then the next, then the next, her hands cramping and sliding on the warm metal. Only a few more, a few more . . . She lunged to grab the final bar, and her fingers slipped, sending her to the ground with a splat. Muddy water soaked her from the waist down.

"Thirty burpees," shouted one of the coordinators, pointing at her.

With a groan, Ernie dodged out of the path of another racer and made for the sideline, where she jumped up, dropped to the ground and did a push-up, and launched herself up for another jump. Burpees were usually no big deal, but she was already running low on fuel, the last obstacle was always the hardest, and she hadn't been training regularly, so stuff that used to be easy was hard as hell.

Which seemed unfair, considering that Ernie was *immortal* now.

"Pick it up, Ernie! You can do it," shouted Devi, the only other female Bear Creek Spartan, as she gracefully sailed through the monkey bars and landed on the other side, just a few feet from where Ernie was burpeeing her heart out.

"Hit the finish hard," Ernie huffed. "We can do this!" Their Bear Creek team had had a real chance of winning their running bet against the other clubs, but Ernie was slowing them down; this was the fifth time in nineteen obstacles that she hadn't made it and had had to do burpees. Shame trickled hot in her chest as she dropped and did her twenty-fifth push-up, arms shaking. She had to go big with the last obstacle, or she wouldn't even be able to look her teammates in the eye.

As soon as she'd paid her dues, Ernie pushed off and ran for the hill that stood between her and the finish line. She skidded to a stop in front of a huge pile of gravel, grabbed one of the large buckets stacked next to it, shouldered herself in next to a few panting racers, and plunged the pail into the loose rocks, trying to fill it to the top as quickly as possible. Then Ernie heaved it up, locking her hands at the front, and made for the path to the top of the hill, trailing behind the other bucket-carrying competitors. Her breath whooshed from her throat, and her heart felt as if it were about to explode. Her muscles were mush. Her deck, safely stowed in a waterproof pouch strapped low on her back *just in case*, flashed hot. "I'm not cheating, if that's what you're suggesting," Ernie whispered to Legs as she started hiking the hill.

"You used to be faster, girl," joked Connie, a member of a rival Asheville club—the Plantation Street Rogues—as she marched past. "Looks like you're gonna be buying the Rogues a round later."

"You're back here with me," Ernie grumbled as she tried to pick up her pace, but her body had little left to offer. She'd been an Immortal Dealer for only four months or so, but her duties—which at first had been officially assigned but lately had been freelance only—had kinda cut into her training time. Her eyes stung—with sweat, she told herself—as she watched Connie put even more distance between them. The cards throbbed against her skin, and Legs tingled on her bare left forearm, offering an easy way out. Ernie could sense the cards the powerful diamondback was suggesting.

Strength. Endurance. Accelerate. If Ernie played those three cards, Connie would be buying the beer. The Bear Creek team could win its bet, and Ernie would be golden.

And also a cheater.

Ernie felt the bucket start to slip from her grip, her numb hands unable to heft the fifty-plus pounds of gravel. Her toe caught on an upturned divot of earth, and she stumbled, a handful of scree sliding over the top of her bucket and scattering in the grass. She sighed with relief to see she still had enough rocks to reach the bucket's fill line, because otherwise she'd have to head back down and refill, losing time she couldn't afford—she was dead last among her teammates, and more racers from other teams were passing her with each second. But now the bucket was sliding down her body, her arms unable to heft it.

Despair rolled through Ernie. Was she really this weak? If she couldn't even do this, what *could* she do? She'd found confidence in her physical strength and fitness for years. She was supposed to be a freaking Spartan warrior, for Pete's sake! It was a key part of who she was. She just had to find that part now.

She whimpered as her bucket tipped again, pouring another few pounds of gravel onto the ground.

"Is that still full enough?" barked a race coordinator who had seen her falter.

Ernie carefully angled the bucket to show the woman that she still had enough gravel, knowing one more stumble would probably mean the end of her race. She was so out of breath that she was wheezing. Her legs shook. When dizziness began to turn the edges of her vision black, Ernie paused, resting the bucket on one of her thighs and trying to catch up with her racing heart. She bowed her head and rested it on the bucket's rim. "Come on," she whispered. "No surrender." She owed it to her team.

She looked up the hill as a few more stragglers lurched past her, hauling their own buckets. Assuming she even made it across the finish line, she might be the very last one to do it. How freaking humiliating.

Clenching her jaw, Ernie jerked the bucket up with an abrupt surge of energy and determination, surprised at how easy it suddenly felt. She planted her foot and took a giant step up the hill. Yeah. This was more like it. No surrender. Second wind. Finish strong. There was no way in hell she was going to come in last.

With her hands locked and her muscles firing, Ernie powered up the hill. She smiled when she crested and saw the finish line ahead, with people crowded along the gauntlet, cheering. She'd struggled through, and now she felt great as she picked up speed, the weight of the gravel barely registering. She broke into a jog, passing an annoyed-looking Connie and several other racers struggling not to drop their loads. When she reached the bottom of the hill, she dumped her burden into the already-huge pile of gravel there, stacked the bucket, and flat-out sprinted for the finish, feeling as though she could run for miles.

As she hit the gauntlet, with cheering racers and supporters on either side, a flash of something in the sky caught her eye, and she glanced up to see a very familiar bird of prey dive toward the ground. Her heart skipped, and she plunged across the finish with a grin. She was immediately surrounded by her mud-caked teammates. "Damn, Ernie, you made the Bucket Brigade look like a cakewalk," crowed Marcus as he embraced her.

"You saved your best for last," said Devi with a laugh. "I ended up crawling across the finish line!"

"I'm a little out of shape," Ernie said sheepishly as she gratefully accepted a towel from Ray, a city cop who was another of their teammates.

"What you just did with that finish shows you've still got what it takes," he said with an approving nod. "Just hit the training hard, and the Rogues'll be buying next time."

It was the most she could have hoped for. She congratulated all of them and promised to meet them later for a beer if she could. After slipping a twenty to Devi to buy their rivals a round, Ernie made an excuse about her parents needing her at the shop and wove her way through the crowd to the spot she'd seen the kestrel heading for.

Gabe leaned against a tree several yards from the parking lot, and Caera, the kestrel in question, perched on a branch nearby. Gabe laughed when he saw Ernie soaked and covered in mud, bruised and walking gingerly, but smiling proudly anyway. "Looks like things turned out all right," he said, his Irish accent never failing to send a thrill down her back. "Despite your fears."

"I'd hug you, but I wouldn't want to foul your finery," she said, gesturing at his usual outfit: scuffed boots, worn jeans, and a T-shirt, with a canvas motorcycle jacket gripped in one hand, as if he was about to whisk himself away to cooler climes.

"I wouldn't mind letting you dirty me up," he replied with a wink.

Her stomach did a little flip. "Maybe . . ." She cleared her throat. They'd been dancing around their relationship for weeks, and she'd found herself pulling away every time Gabe hinted that he'd like more from her, mostly because it felt like the world might explode at any second—it had been kinda hard to relax. "I should probably get cleaned up. Do you want to go out tonight?"

He gave her a good-natured smile. "Can't. I got an assignment."

Her glowing mood went dark. "From Virginia? Tell me."

"Nothing much to tell. Our Forger appeared to me, told me to protect a guy who needed protecting, and I'm off to get to work."

Ernie's eyes narrowed. "She wanted you to . . . protect a guy?"

He nodded. "Seemed altogether decent. I warned her that I wasn't going to take any assignment that involved killing, and she said she already knew that and wanted to respect my wishes."

"Sorry, what? Are we talking about the same Forger? Virginia the Nazi?"

"She's not a Nazi," Gabe chided, reaching out to tuck a stray lock of wet hair behind Ernie's ear. "And I'm wondering now if she's a shade better than Andy."

Ernie snorted. "Because he was so great." He'd been trying pretty hard to slaughter Ernie and her allies just before Virginia ambushed him with a magical knife to the gut.

"I've decided that I'm going to give her a chance."

Ernie supposed it was better than the Gabe of December, who'd been ready to give up his deck rather than use it to cause any more chaos and suffering. "Forgive me for questioning your life choices, but come on. She's a stone-cold killer, Gabe. Protecting people doesn't seem like her thing."

"But it's my thing." He shrugged. "Maybe she gave the job to me as a measure of good faith. And if these are the assignments I get, I'll take them gladly, especially because she said she's upping our compensation so we don't have to take freelance work." Gabe hadn't been around much the past few weeks, as he'd been doing jobs for some billionaire in Dubai, greasing the wheels of a few business deals by using clever plays of the cards. Negotiate. Deceive. Discern. Wisdom. With the right combination, a Dealer could make just about anything happen for a client, for better or worse.

Ernie had pulled a few of those jobs herself, just to make ends meet. While some Dealers took any job for pay, with no thought for the grief they might cause, Ernie and Gabe were ready and willing only as long as the gig didn't involve contract killing or unnecessary bloodshed. That had never seemed like Virginia's style, though. "You really believe this isn't some kind of trap?"

"I guess we'll find out after I make sure this bloke is safely delivered into the arms of his family."

Suspicion ran thick in Ernie's veins. "What kind of bloke are we talking about?"

"Already Googled him up. I do have some Internet skills." He looked comically proud of himself. "He's some academic. Immunology, I think."

"Why would he need protecting?"

Another shrug. "Because someone wants to kill him, I assume."

"Why you? Why now? Are you sure he's not about to unleash some terrible virus on the unsuspecting populace?"

"Give me some credit, love." Gabe gave her an aggrieved look. "I already thought of that. He's a cancer researcher, doesn't work with nasty germs. Why all the questions?"

"Because *Nazi*," Ernie snapped. "And because she killed Trey." The Raccoon Dealer had been a loyal ally and a friend. He'd thrown himself between Ernie and danger—and had paid the ultimate price. "Unlike everyone else, apparently, I'm not about to forgive and forget!" It had to have been a cruel death; Virginia had trapped Trey in a splinter dimension with less than half a deck.

Gabe's easy smile turned hard. "You think I've forgotten that?" he asked quietly. "As if I don't think about Trey every single day?"

Ernie scowled and turned away. "Just saying how it looks."

"Ernie, you know I'd be the first person to oppose her if she took a step out of line. But what good does it do to seek revenge? She's bearing a big responsibility now, and maybe it's changing her."

"Try telling that to Tarlae."

"If I could find Tarlae, there are a few other things I'd say to her, but not that." The Dealer of the Coconut Octopus deck had gone underground since Virginia had murdered her lover. Ernie had tried in vain to use the cards to look for her, but like the spirit of her deck, Tarlae obviously knew how to hide. "But this is our reality now."

"I'm never going to trust Virginia."

"No one but an idiot ever would." He curved a finger around her chin and gently turned her face to his. "If I can preserve life, I always

9

will, and that's what this is, so I'll go along. Yeah? I don't see the harm in it."

Ernie sighed and nodded. "You can't stay for just a few hours to grab that drink with me?" She hitched a smile onto her face. "Come on—did you see what I just did? I don't think I've ever finished that strong in all the Spartan Races I've done."

Gabe gave her a sly look. "Hefting a bucket of rocks as if it were feathers? Maybe that does deserve a bit of a celebration. Even if it's a quick one."

Something in his tone made Ernie pause. "Wait. Wait. You didn't help me, did you?"

"Why would I ever do such a thing?"

"Oh my god. You did." Ernie took a step back, shaking her head. "You used the cards. That's cheating."

"How is putting a bit of wind in your sails cheating? You looked like a walking corpse! Your face was *gray*. Excuse me for worrying a bit."

"You were watching me in your cards!" she shouted.

"Is that a crime?"

"I was supposed to be doing this on my own!"

"It's not like I carried you over the finish line."

Ernie put her hands up. "I'll see you when you get back from your assignment, okay? I need to get home and shower."

"Don't be like this, love."

He seriously didn't seem to understand what he'd done wrong, and that pissed her off even more. She closed her eyes and sucked in a deep breath. "I just need to get home and clean up. I'll feel better after."

"Later, then."

When Ernie opened her eyes, both he and Caera had disappeared. Ernie gritted her teeth and turned to look out at the parking lot, where happy, clueless racers were headed out to celebrate or recover with their friends and families. Ernie had planned to be one of them, but now she felt like she didn't even deserve to be in their presence.

She'd thought she'd pushed through. She'd thought she'd finished under her own power. But it hadn't been her at all—it had been a play, Gabe's cards supplying her with strength and speed none of the other racers had. Strength and speed she didn't deserve.

Her own cards pulsed at her back, as did Legs on her arm, reminding her of their presence, but right now, Ernie didn't feel worthy of them, either.

She reached behind her and unzipped her waterproof pouch. The Transport card slipped from the rest of the deck, easy as breathing. Ernie waved and smiled as Marcus drove by, honking and pumping his fist, still cheering for her strong finish. But Ernie knew the truth. She was no warrior. Not anymore. It shouldn't have mattered so much—she was an Immortal Dealer! She had unbelievable power at her fingertips; all she had to do was deal the cards.

Being able to wield that kind of magic should have been heartening, but right then, it was the opposite. Ernie shoved her cards back in their pouch. Shoulders slumped, she trudged toward her car.

CHAPTER TWO

After a brief stop at her apartment to shower, Ernie drove to her parents'
house. Terwilliger Antiquities was open for business, and there were
a few customers' cars parked out front. In the weeks since Ernie had
rescued her dad from the hellish splinter dimension where he'd been
banished by Virginia for the last eighteen years, Redmond Terwilliger
had seemed determined to make up for lost time. He'd sanded and
repainted the front and back steps, cajoled Mara into a thorough clea-
nout of the basement, and reorganized the shop's offerings of antique
books, magazines, newspapers, and postcards. Bags of topsoil had been
stacked as high as Ernie's waist next to the porch, signaling that spring
landscaping was imminent.

The chime at the front door signaled Ernie's entrance, and her
mother looked up from the display case of pre–Civil War powder horns
and flasks, bullet molds, cartridge boxes, and leather shot bags. Mara
finished setting out a few items for her potential customer, a middle-
aged guy with droopy hound-dog eyes, before scooting around the
counter to greet her daughter. "How did it go?" Mara asked.

"I'm out of shape. Next time will be better."

Her mother's face fell. "Oh. I'm sorry."

Ernie knew her mother was assuming she didn't finish, and she
didn't bother to correct the mistake. She wouldn't be able to stand it if

her mother congratulated her. "It's fine. I just wish I could have been more helpful to my team."

Mara squeezed her arm but pulled back when Ernie winced at the pressure on her sore muscles. "Any team you're on is lucky to have you." She winked.

Ernie smiled as she accepted the encouragement, especially happy that it was coming from a mom who looked so much steadier on her feet than she had at any point since Ernie's childhood. "Is Dad here?"

"In the back." She waved her hand in the direction of the hallway that led to the solarium, kitchenette, bathroom, and bedroom. "He's decided he wants to refinish the floors."

"Do you need any help?" Ernie glanced at the customer fondling the powder horns and then at a couple huddled over by the collection of hand-bound journals.

"If you could make sure your father's not about to sand his foot off or bring the ceiling down on his head, that would be wonderful," Mara replied, giving Ernie a little push toward the hallway.

Ernie trod gingerly down the hall, her muscles feeling like over-cooked noodles. In her pocket, the deck throbbed, and with a roll of her eyes, she reached in and drew the two cards Legs suggested: Healing and Endurance. She pressed them to her body, letting the cards do their work, as she stood in the corridor and listened to strains of eighties synthesizer music coming from the bedroom. When she entered, she discovered her father surrounded by long strips of old wallpaper. Dust coated the blue comforter of the bed and floated in lazy swirls through slants of light coming through the window blinds. He cast a guilty look in her direction. "I may have jumped the gun on this project."

Ernie surveyed the damage and held up her deck. Her father nod-ded. With a quick play of Repair, the wall was soon restored, the strips rising from the floor to knit themselves back together over the patched plaster and wooden walls.

Perhaps recalling the powerful Dragonfly deck he'd long ago given up in his efforts to get back to his family, Redmond Terwilliger looked a bit wistful as his daughter played her Nourishment card for two glasses of sweet tea to appear on the bureau. "Sure does make life easier sometimes."

"Maybe too easy," Ernie grumbled, wondering whether she'd become overly reliant on her cards.

"No such thing." Her father ran his hand over the smooth wall covered in a brown, yellow, and tan pattern straight out of the seventies. "You could make a pretty penny just helping people with their home renovations."

"There are a billion and one things I *could* do with my deck, Dad, but probably only a few things I *should* do. And one of them is to be ready when Virginia comes calling."

"She hasn't made a move against you or any of the other Dealers, has she?"

Ernie shook her head. "She's been sweet as pie, but she also made it clear that she considers us her enemies." The last time Ernie had seen Virginia, the woman's white hair floating around her head like a cloud, her gauzy dress looking out of place at Wedge brewery's parking-lot beer garden, the new Forger had hinted that she was completing Gabe's deck not as a favor but as preparation for a longer, deadlier game. "Despite that, everyone else seems to think she's changed her ways."

"Could she be influencing them somehow?" asked Redmond. "Bribes? A relic that gives her the ability to control Dealers' minds?"

A chill ran down Ernie's back. "She could do that?"

Her father shrugged. "Somehow, the Forger creates whole decks of cards, along with relics that connect one dimension to another, cut through anything, and forcibly merge a Dealer with her deck. Seems to me that Virginia's power is only limited by her creativity."

"Where does the power of the Forger come from, though?"

"All I can tell you is what's in the myths, Weed," he said, dusting off his palms on his pants and plopping down on the bed with his tea. "And there I'm only guessing, because it's all dressed up as fairy tale and legend."

"Like the one about the djinn," Ernie murmured, running a fingertip down her glass, stroking away beads of condensation. She and Gabe had traveled to Morocco to collect a fabled relic her father had uncovered by following the trail of a supposedly magic genie—but the Sunrise relic had been snatched away by Virginia's allies before she and Gabe could figure out what it could do.

"All sorts of legends talk of deities' power to mold life out of clay, or of offering humans some sort of divine knowledge and connection to the infinite. I've always wondered if those myths didn't come from stories of a Forger or the Dealers. As far as I know, no one but a Forger has ever entered the Forger's domain—"

"The center of the universe?" That was what the former Forger, Andy, had called it. "Santa's workshop" was more how Ernie thought of it, with Virginia playing the role of a demented, evil elf in chief.

"It's not clear whether anyone but the Forger can enter that place," said her father. "So I'm not sure we'll ever know what it contains and where the power comes from."

"But a Forger is killable," Ernie said. "If she can be drawn out of her spider hole and caught by surprise."

Redmond Terwilliger paused with his glass halfway to his mouth. "You sure you want to go down that road? I'm not suggesting you run and hide, but trust me when I say that woman is capable of pretty much anything."

"I've seen her handiwork firsthand, Dad," Ernie chided. "Including how she can turn on anyone, including her allies, without even blinking. I can't believe anyone would trust her."

"That doesn't mean you have to fight her single-handedly."

Ernie turned to see the source for that comment—her mother—standing in the doorway, horn-rimmed glasses hanging from a delicate chain around her neck, a steaming mug in her hands. "You could keep your head down," Mara continued. "More chance you won't miss another Christmas with us." She offered Ernie the mug. "Ginger-and-turmeric tea. Good for muscle aches."

Ernie set down her sweet tea and accepted the mug even though her cards had left her feeling refreshed. Her mother had been trying extra hard to take care of her lately, maybe to make up for all those years when Ernie had taken care of *her*. Ernie took a careful sip and coughed as the fumes hit the back of her throat. "You forgot to mention the hot pepper," she said hoarsely.

"It's a wonderful pain reliever," Mara replied.

"Only because it's hard to focus on what ails you when your tongue's on fire," joked Redmond.

"Better your tongue than the rest of you," said Mara, her eyes narrowing as she beheld her husband, who looked badly in need of a haircut and a shave. "Don't encourage our daughter to cling to a lost cause."

He put his hands up. "I'm not doing a thing, dear. Only lending an ear."

"Dad basically gave me the tools to bring her down before," Ernie explained. "If I'd been a little faster and a little wiser, Virginia wouldn't be Forger at all." And Trey would still be alive. Instead, Ernie had lost her best weapon—the Cortalaza blade, which had helped her escape the splinter dimension and had helped her father separate himself from the Dragonfly deck, ending his run as an Immortal Dealer—when Virginia took the blade to kill Andy and ascend his throne. The only hope they'd had to stop her was the Sunrise artifact they'd almost snagged in Marrakech, but now Virginia had that, too. All Ernie had was the key to the damn thing, which at least meant Virginia couldn't use the Sunrise—but Ernie couldn't, either.

"The past is the past," said Mara. "And now I think you have to make the best of it and be glad she's not targeting you." She tossed a nervous glance at Redmond. "Or us."

"That's not fair, Mara," he said gently. "Don't guilt Ernie into abandoning her principles for us."

"What principle says she has to fight a vengeful god when no one else is willing to step up with her?" Mara asked.

"Guys, it's complicated," Ernie muttered, sticking her nose into her teacup and inhaling the stinging fumes. Even if she did want to fight Virginia, she didn't have much of an idea where to start.

"The Forger is supposed to cause chaos," said Redmond. "And honestly, Virginia seems up to the task. She'll settle in, and you'll get used to her."

"You too, Dad?" Ernie rolled her eyes and set the mug on the bureau with an apologetic smile for her mom. "She destroyed our family."

"She actually helped me save it, in some ways," said her father. "She warned me of how vengeful Andy was, which kept me from running back to the two of you. She's not all bad—and she's the reason you made it to adulthood."

"She helped you because she was trying to get you to support her so she could start a mutiny!" Ernie threw up her hands in frustration. She'd thought for sure her dad would be on her side, would maybe point her in the direction of some relic or wisdom that could help her oppose Virginia. But the more she thought about it, the more she had to admit it was a lost cause. Virginia was the big boss now. End of story.

"You'll feel better once she gives you an assignment," said Redmond. "It'll keep you busy."

"Gabe just got one. I think the others have as well. Not sure about Kot—he's been focused on taking care of Nuria."

"How is she?" Redmond asked. Ernie didn't think she was imagining the shadow of guilt behind his eyes, and no wonder—her father had been the one to curse Nuria and the spirit of her deck, by using a relic he hadn't fully understood in a foreign dimension both of them had been banished to by none other than Virginia. Nuria and the Grasshopper had been forced to share one body and mind for nearly two decades, much of it as a hybrid monster that Ernie still shuddered to remember.

"She's learning how to speak again, but it's slow going." After Andy had separated Nuria from the primal spirit of her deck, Ernie had thought she'd return to normal, but apparently the years had taken their toll. "She's still working on rebonding with her deck, too."

"That's too bad." Redmond rubbed his knuckles along his stubbly jaw. "Wish I could help."

"I should probably go visit them," Ernie said, the thought of talking with allies livening her spirit. "We haven't been in touch in the past few weeks."

"That sounds like a good idea," her father replied. "Get a fresh perspective. And I can delve a little deeper with the research if you like."

Mara glared at him. "*Don't* encourage her."

Redmond got to his feet and sauntered over to his wife. "She's all grown up," he said, putting his hands on Mara's shoulders. "And if I can help my daughter, even a little, that's what I'm going to do."

The fearful look on Mara's face almost made Ernie want to promise to lie low. Ernie couldn't blame her—she'd lost her husband, and now that she had him back, she was terrified of losing her daughter. "It's okay, Mom. It's not like I'm looking for a fight for its own sake. But I want to be ready when Virginia shows her true colors."

"If she ever does," Mara said quietly. "Why can't you just enjoy the peace?"

Ernie sighed. "I am, okay? And I think I'm going to head out." She turned to her father. "Unless you need help?" She gestured at the wall.

"Nah," said Redmond. "You've helped enough, and I think it's time for a little study break."

Ernie hugged her parents and trudged back out to her car. Virginia easily could have attacked Mara and Redmond, as both of them were mortal and fragile and perfect as leverage to keep Ernie in line, but she hadn't. Once again, doubt crept in.

She unlocked her car, slid into the driver's seat, and screamed.

"I probably should have anticipated that," said Virginia, wincing and rubbing at her left ear.

"What the heck?" said Ernie. "Why are you in my car?"

"Because I have a job for you," the Forger replied. "One that I hope you'll take."

Ernie shifted in her seat to eye the older woman. Virginia's hair seemed thicker and shinier, and her skin, still wrinkled but less fragile looking than it had been, had taken on a dewy glow. "Why are you making it sound like I have a choice?"

"Because I'm giving you one," said Virginia. "I know you don't like me, Diamondback. And I know you don't trust me. But I'm hoping that over time, we can work together to achieve the universe's purpose."

"And what would that be?"

"I know I said some crummy stuff to you before," the Forger said, looking almost contrite.

"You did a lot more than saying crummy stuff, lady. You killed one of my friends."

"I was too focused on my goal," Virginia said. "I regret some of the things I did." Her pale eyes were riveted on Ernie's, and she looked almost haunted, such a change from the maniacal glint Ernie'd grown accustomed to seeing. "But now I've seen things that altered my perspective."

"Like what?"

"I can't describe the secrets of the Forger's realm," she said. "But it's shifted my lens."

"Okay," Ernie said slowly. "What does that mean for me?"

"There's going to be a robbery. A bank in Munich. I want you to stop it from happening."

"You want me to stop a bank robber? Why?"

"Stealing is wrong," Virginia answered.

"You are shady as hell."

Virginia groaned. "My word, you are a suspicious creature. But I suppose I can't fault you for that. Look—this money would be used to do some very bad things—"

"How do you know that? Can you see the future?"

"I can see . . . parts of the future. How do you think a Forger selects assignments for her Dealers? Unlike when you use your Foretell card— the most dangerous card in the deck, in my experience, but certainly the most tempting—things aren't locked up when I take a peek."

"A peek at what? You've got a relic? Some cards? A magic mirror?"

"You want me to invite you over for tea sometime so you can case the joint?" Virginia's deep South Carolina accent had turned tart. "You do have a history of taking things that don't belong to you." She looked over at the shop with a peevish twist to her lips. "Runs in the family, as I recall."

"Right, right. Stealing is wrong. Says the lady who sent her minions to steal the Sunrise from a defenseless old man."

"You don't know the half of that story," Virginia said. "If you did, you might have a little sympathy for me."

"Dude, the half I know is bad enough. The Brahman Bull Dealer, a guy who seemed to love and admire the heck out of you, stole that relic for you. And you thanked him by stealing his deck right when he needed you most."

Virginia scoffed. "I didn't steal it. You cut poor Cecil right off his arm, which meant Lawrence wasn't a Dealer anymore. The old dear had a coronary on the spot. *You* killed him, Diamondback. Not me."

"Yeah, you just coldly took advantage while he begged for your help. But whatever lets you sleep at night." Ernie had actually had more than a few sleepless nights, thinking of that fight. "You kicked him when he was down, too. Told him he'd failed you. Twice."

"It was the truth," Virginia grumbled.

"Whatever. You killed Trey and took his deck a few minutes later, so I'm not giving you a pass."

"I do feel bad about that, and I intend to set it right."

"How?"

"You do understand that we're not equals and that I don't have to explain all my decisions to you? I know we come from different times, but surely you were raised to respect your betters."

It took all the restraint Ernie possessed not to roll her eyes. "I'd feel better if you could just be honest."

"I'm the Forger, young lady. I've come to give you an assignment. It could have been any assignment, but I'm asking you to be a hero and stop some criminals from robbing a bank. I'm not sure what you think the downside is here, but I promise you, the pay will be good enough to support your . . . *dependents.*"

Ernie turned to see her mother staring out at them from the front window of the shop. Any sign of ruckus might draw her out or at the very least upset her, so Ernie smiled and waved. "I'll take it, Virginia. But if you even try . . ." She paused as she looked over at Virginia, who was chuckling and shaking her head.

"Are you threatening me, Diamondback?" Her words crackled with power.

Ernie needed to keep her powder dry and her thoughts to herself. Threats were stupid—right now she couldn't back them up. "No."

Virginia nodded. "Good. I'm glad you're taking this one. You'll make sure it's done right and that no one *innocent* gets hurt."

"Since when do you care?"

Virginia looked haunted again. "Chaos is overrated. I think we could do with a little less of it."

"Wait. Isn't that what makes the universe tick?" That was certainly what Andy had told her.

"Of course, but the more dimensions that exist, the more people there are out there, making decisions every day, and I thought . . ."

Virginia sighed. "I've done a lot of wrong in my long life, Ernestine. I'd like to set a few things right. And I know that you and the Kestrel, along with several of my other Dealers, have a craving to do some good. So I'm providing an avenue for that."

Ernie searched the Forger's expression for some hint of malice or mischief, but all she saw was that haunted look, like whatever Virginia had learned since becoming the Forger really had changed her. And it made Ernie feel like a jerk for even thinking of refusing the assignment. "Okay. I'll get it done."

Virginia smiled. "I know you will. The payment will be on your Coin card when you succeed. Just peek at your Revelation card to get you going." She paused and then put her bony hand on Ernie's shoulder, causing the cards in Ernie's pocket to flash with blinding heat. "Thank you for being part of the team."

She vanished, leaving Ernie with a stinging burn and a head full of questions.

CHAPTER THREE

Ernie packed an overnight bag. She'd learned that conjured clothes could fade and disappear at awkward moments, so it seemed best to pack some supplies just in case the job took longer than she expected. It'd save time and energy if she didn't have to use her Transport card to go back and forth to her apartment. She did, however, make her supplies easier to carry with the play of a few cards: Amplify and Inverse. That shrank the bag down to something that could fit in the pocket of her coat, and using her Case card, she contained the bag so that it wouldn't re-biggify itself at exactly the wrong time.

Next, she pulled her Revelation card, focusing on her first mission from her new boss. It felt wrong and weird to take an assignment from the woman who'd wreaked so much havoc in her life, but she didn't think any of the alternatives were better. If she refused, it would spark an open confrontation with the Forger. For all Ernie's talk, she wasn't ready to do that yet, not when it seemed like most of the other Dealers—including Gabe—were going along to get along. That didn't mean she'd do anything Virginia asked, but the Forger had been right when she said stealing was wrong, and Ernie guessed it wasn't so bad to foil a robbery, even if she'd been told to do so by an evil maniac.

The image that appeared beneath the card's omega symbol was, indeed, of a bank, one called Münchenbank, specifically. Ernie played

Transport crossed with Conceal so she could arrive on the sidewalk outside the bank without scaring the bejesus out of local pedestrians. Shivering at the icy wind trying to pull her hair from its ponytail, Ernie turned in place to orient herself while stepping out of the way of a few people clutching their coats tight around their bodies and bustling down the street. She stood at a large intersection across from a park, one block of which contained a dense copse of trees and an ornate fountain decorated with a shirtless dude on a horse-serpent thing and a topless lady on a bull. The bank was on a block with several other businesses, including a golf supply store, a clothing store, and a coffee shop. It didn't seem like anything more than a local branch, just a small outpost.

The sun was already setting, and the branch seemed closed, which was a relief, as it meant there wouldn't be a lot of customers and bank staff around when the attempted robbery went down. Assuming it would go down soon—Virginia hadn't been specific about that.

Ernie's Conceal card was losing its warmth as she pondered her situation, so she headed across the street, making for the trees. Once she was there, she slid the card back into the deck and peered at her Revelation card again. This time, it showed a guy's face: a dude with buzzed dark hair, intense eyebrows, dark stubble, brown eyes, and pale skin. With an expression fraught with concentration and maybe concern, he was looking down at something, but she couldn't see what. This guy was the thief, she assumed. Now, at least, she knew whom to look for. She just didn't know where or when to look for him.

Hoping for a little boost in the smarts department, she played Wisdom, its symbol reminding her of two headless stick figures grasping hands, and saw what appeared to be the roof of the building she was surveilling. With another flip of her Transport card, she made it up there, noticing immediately that the wind was worse. She was maybe four stories up from the street, and the only shelter was the large heating and ventilation units, which she squatted next to as she peered at her

Wisdom card yet again. All it showed was the roof. Again. And it didn't exactly make her feel wise.

How was she supposed to stop this crime if she had little idea how the robbers would strike? Was she up here for a better vantage point, or would they actually try to breach the bank's security by entering from the roof? She got up and strolled over to the roof's edge, where a waist-high wall provided a spot for her to duck down and observe. This didn't seem to be a super-busy part of town, but there were pedestrians on the sidewalks and one young couple sitting near the fountain, having a seemingly romantic moment as it lit up for the night, making the white water glitter like ice.

Movement of something or someone in the trees to the left of the fountain drew Ernie's gaze away from the lovers, in time to see a tall, lean guy with dark hair scan the street before stepping into the shadows. Her heart lurched. She supposed he might've been the robber—same color hair. But his skin was a shade darker, his face more angular.

He had looked a hell of a lot like Trey.

Ernie blinked. Trey was dead, and his body lay in the splinter dimension she'd barely escaped with her life and deck. He wasn't even in this world, let alone this city, let alone on the very block where she happened to be at this moment. And she hadn't really gotten a good look at the guy, so it was probably her mind playing games to pass the time.

Maybe.

Maybe.

Ernie was able to resist for only a few more seconds before she used her Transport card for the third time in half an hour to get herself back down to street level, to a spot on the far side of the fountain. Once there, she played Conceal again and jogged for the trees, pulling her Light card to show her the way. The crack of a twig several yards ahead suggested the guy's location, and she made for it.

But when she got there, all she found was a still-smoldering cigarette butt, hastily stepped on but not quite extinguished. She turned in place, trying to spot the smoker. Nothing but silence. She pulled out her Revelation card, focusing on the question of whom exactly she'd seen.

It displayed nothing but fog, which set her heart pounding. The only time her cards wouldn't show something like that was when another Dealer was cloaking him- or herself. "Trey?" she whispered, staring at the swirling gray nothing in her card as if it might clear and reveal his face. Trey had died defending Ernie. If he hadn't stepped in front of her, *she* would have been the person trapped in the splinter dimension. She would have been the Dealer who lost half her cards. She would have been dead, but Trey had taken her place and paid the price.

She couldn't possibly have seen him just now. It was wishful thinking. And a distraction.

The sun had set and the streetlights had come to life, but their glow barely penetrated the patch of trees where Ernie stood. She needed to actually do her job instead of chasing a ghost, so she played Transport yet again and returned to the roof of the bank. Her Light card provided a bit of heat and illumination, and her Nourishment card provided her with a large pretzel—still warm, crunchy on the outside but satisfyingly chewy inside, so delicious that Ernie wasn't sure how she'd lived this long without one—and a mug of beer, which Ernie only sipped. Legs was relatively accommodating when it came to furnishing her with food, but alcohol and vigilance didn't exactly mix. The moment Ernie had this thought, a cup of espresso appeared on the ground next to where she sat.

"You're amazing, lady," she said, rolling up the sleeve of her coat and gazing at the tattoo of the diamondback sprawled along her forearm. "I'd invite you out for a visit, but it's freaking cold up here, and I don't think that's so good for a reptile such as your fine self."

Legs tingled happily on Ernie's skin, sending a wave of affection running through her. If everything else fell apart, she'd be okay if she still had her diamondback. She couldn't imagine losing her and grimaced as she pictured Trey, who had been equally close with the spirit of his own deck—Terrence the raccoon. Andy had said something about how he'd planned to give the Raccoon deck to another Dealer, but Ernie knew nothing beyond that and Virginia's vague statement that she hoped to set things right. Had she managed to resurrect Trey somehow? Had she given him his deck back?

Ernie tried to find him in her cards again, giving up only when a blast of wind nearly ripped them from her grasp. A quick glance at her phone told her hours had passed and midnight approached. Had Virginia sent her here to stall her? Was something going on somewhere, something Ernie could stop if she wasn't stuck here on some dead-end assignment?

For a moment, Ernie considered summoning Gabe. They'd parted badly, and that had been her fault. She hadn't seen him much lately, and she'd missed him more than she was willing to admit. Except . . . they were great together when their backs were up against a wall, but she'd begun to wonder how they really fit when things were quiet.

Why was she pondering all this stuff when she needed to be doing her job? Gabe had his own assignment, protecting that immunologist from whatever threatened him, and Ernie didn't want to distract him, nor did she want to admit she was struggling with her own mission. She'd contact him in the morning if this turned out to be a nothingburger, but until then, she'd try to figure out how to succeed on her own.

She didn't need Gabe helping her cheat again.

And that meant she had to figure this out. She had seen the would-be thief and this location, but he hadn't shown up yet. She pulled out her deck. "Legs, a little help here. I have to stop this guy, but I have no idea who or where he is." She fanned her cards in her hand and ran her other palm over them, feeling what they could do, thinking about the combinations she could play.

Her fingers lingered over one she had never played but that might give her answers now: Foretell. Its symbol closely resembled an eye, an oblong shape with a diamond in the center. In addition to Virginia, other Dealers had warned her about using it, because whatever she beheld would be locked in. But all she was trying to do right now was to see how she could find and stop the thieves. Either she was going to succeed or she wasn't. Compared to other things—like her father's decision to use the Cortalaza blade to cut the spirit of the Dragonfly deck right off his arm, changing his life forever—this seemed somewhat safer, with lower stakes.

"Beats sitting out here in the freezing cold all night." She whipped out the card and peered at its face, thinking of the guy she'd seen in her Revelation card, the would-be thief. Her diamondback tattoo tingled and stung. Ernie gasped, her eyes riveted on the card as a blinding light seemed to reach right out from underneath the eye symbol, pulling her consciousness down. A flash of unbelievable heat blazed against her face and blew back her hair as her ears filled with a deafening roar. Ernie tried to scream, but she had no voice, only terror.

The vision ended almost as soon as it began, and Ernie collapsed against a heating unit, spots crowding her sight, the wind knocked out of her. She reached up with trembling hands to wipe her face, which was streaked with tears. Sniffling, she sat up. Her cards had scattered around her, and she clumsily scrambled to gather them up, stunned at the horrifying power of what she'd seen and her body's response.

She'd just seen the future, and it looked like the apocalypse. And if everything she'd ever been told about the Foretell card was true, that future was definitely going to happen. "No," she whispered. "No." Virginia had said that bad things would happen if the bank robbers succeeded—was *that* what she'd just seen? Did it mean she was going to fail?

Ernie shot to her feet and swayed as dizziness nearly sent her to the ground. Determination surged inside her. She didn't care what the card had foretold—if that was the result of failure, she was going to fight until her last breath to succeed. She didn't have it in her to do anything different.

As soon as the thought entered her mind, the building shook and rumbled, forcing her to brace herself against the heating unit. Piercing alarms split the night air. Smoke and dust billowed up from the street. Ernie lunged for the low wall around the edge of the building and leaned over to see a set of headlights zooming up the block toward the bank. Within the cloud below her, shouts echoed from inside the building, reaching her through the shattered front doors.

The headlights she'd seen pulled to a stop right in front of the building, the driver honking frantically. Anger beating in her temples, she transported herself down to the street a block away as the moan of sirens added to the din. The police were coming, which was a good thing, but three gun-toting thieves in dark clothes had loaded into the getaway car with their driver. The black compact car lurched from the curb and accelerated straight past where Ernie was standing. Her brain still reeling from what she'd seen in the Foretell card, it took her a full second to pull her next course of action together, something she'd practiced in her training sessions: Air, Sharpen, Accelerate, Strike, and Strength. Concentrating hard and praying this actually worked, she raised her arms as a swell of air caught her body and propelled it up and over the street. She flew on the current of that almost solid river of air, quickly catching up with the fleeing car just before it whipped around a corner.

Ernie jerked herself around, barely avoiding a collision with the side of an office building, and ended up directly over the speeding vehicle. "Legs," she barked, thinking of the cards she needed to play next. They flew from her pocket and into her open hand as Ernie dropped onto the roof of the car. The Strength card she'd played would last for another few minutes at least, and it allowed her to hold on tight enough to stay aboard when the driver, obviously having noted the heavy object that had landed atop his vehicle, began to swerve from side to side, nearly clipping a city bus and causing onlookers to gawk. Of course, they might have been staring at Ernie, who was holding on for dear life while riding on the roof of an automobile doing sixty on a city street.

Time to stop these losers. She focused her gaze on the hood of the car and played her Rend card. The engine fell to the street with a clattering crash, and Ernie flew into the air as the car's rear jerked up with its sudden stop. She hit the sidewalk so hard that she heard her bones crack even before the pain hit her. Her deck pulsed hot against her thigh. "Healing," she croaked, even as a few bystanders pulled out their phones to film the carnage and a woman knelt beside her, chattering in German while checking her pulse. Perhaps sensing that Ernie couldn't understand a word, the lady paused briefly to pat her own chest and say, "Doctor," which would have been reassuring if Ernie had been a normal person.

Ernie managed to turn her head as the sirens came closer. The getaway car lay wrecked in the middle of the road, and other vehicles had pulled to a stop all around it, having barely avoided becoming part of the calamity. The four thieves were struggling to get out, but the doors had been crushed inward. Through one of the windows, Ernie spotted a familiar face—it was the guy she'd seen in her Revelation card. Wearing a look of desperation, he was trying to break the window to escape.

Gritting her teeth against the pain, Ernie opened her palm and mentally commanded Legs to bring her the cards, which slipped from her pocket and into her grip immediately. Healing first, because her body had been wrecked and she needed to get the hell out of there. With that one pressed to her torso and doing its work, Ernie played Deceive and Mirage, imagining a few other victims for the doctor to go help, and sure enough, the woman patted Ernie on the shoulder and ran toward the illusions, giving Ernie the space to shove herself up to sitting. Agony lanced through her not-yet-healed body as another of the thieves pulled a gun and began shooting out the windows of the car, causing the bystanders to scream and flee. The dark-haired thief was still pounding on the window, which was now webbed with cracks. The police hadn't arrived yet.

Legs read her mind and intention easily, and a few cards jumped into Ernie's hand even as others zoomed back to the deck. The doctor screamed and clutched at her shoulder—one of the bullets had struck her. Rage building, Ernie slashed her Shield card toward the woman and a group of terrified pedestrians. She smiled grimly as bullets bounced off the clear dome that appeared around them. Then she played Conceal, Draw, Weapon, and Enemy, and the guns came smashing through the car windows and landed in a pile at her feet, invisible to everyone else.

Or almost everyone else. The thief she'd seen in her Revelation card looked at her with round, terrified eyes. Ernie glared back, remembering the horror she'd seen in her Foretell card. This guy was the source of it—she was sure. He was going to be the author of enough suffering to end the world.

But only if he lived. With the echo of that terrible explosion, that devastating heat, still reverberating inside her, Ernie drew the only card that seemed right. She slashed it through the air once. Quickly. Before she could change her mind.

Death. The card flashed hot against her fingertips.

The thieves collapsed like rag dolls inside the car, their shouts cut off. Their hearts silent.

Ernie spun around, jaw clenched, eyes brimming with tears, and shoved her cards back in her pocket. The shield she'd conjured disappeared right as two police cars lurched to a stop, one of them having driven on a sidewalk to reach the scene. She watched the officers run toward the car before she stepped quickly into the shadows of a storefront and transported herself back to her apartment in West Asheville, too shaken to go anywhere else.

She'd killed four men. Everyone in the car. She'd foiled the robbery. Mission accomplished.

Would it be enough to prevent the future she'd seen in her Foretell card? Was it possible?

Torn up inside despite the work her Healing card had done, Ernie lay on her bed and pulled out her Haven card. Her breaths coming in sobbing gasps, Ernie crossed it with her Dreams card, trying to get to the place that would restore her. The moment her feet met the soft forest floor of the eternally spring-kissed clearing that housed her haven in the realm of dreams, Ernie sank to her knees and let herself cry.

CHAPTER FOUR

The tent from her childhood, which may very well have been her father's haven before she'd accidentally claimed it, was stocked with Grumpy Grape Squeezits, Bugles, and Warheads this time. Ernie plopped down on the sleeping bag and slowly placed the Bugles on her fingertips, wishing like hell that she could return to her childhood, to the days before her father had left them, when pretending she was a monster with Bugle claws and a purple-stained tongue was the biggest item on her daily agenda.

Now she wondered whether she really was a monster. She couldn't get the guy's face out of her mind. His wide, scared eyes. Had he seen her? Had he known she was the source of his destruction?

He'd been a bank robber. He and his pals had been firing their guns, not even caring whom they injured.

But she'd disarmed them. And she'd wrecked their car. The police had been on their way.

She couldn't get that hellish vision she'd witnessed in her Foretell card out of her head, though. It all made sense—the bank robbers must have been trying to fund some terrorist plot or something. They were evil, and if she hadn't stopped them, they would've burned down the whole world. She'd done the right thing. The only right thing. She'd had no choice.

She actually was asleep in her bed, but her mind was awake and on fire in the dream realm, and she needed to rest, to clear her head. She got in her sleeping bag and tossed around for hours, but every time she began to relax and sink into oblivion, the fiery memory of what she'd seen would rise once more to torment her.

What *was* that vision in her Foretell card? What was happening in that future? How was it linked to the bank robbers? Because it had to have been—she'd specifically been thinking about their plan and how to stop them when she'd played the card. Unless she'd been mightily distracted, the cataclysm she'd witnessed in that card had to be related to the robbers.

And unless everyone who'd ever told her about the Foretell card had been wrong, that horrifying thing was going to happen, and everything Ernie had done had only pushed the world closer to that future. At that thought, Ernie couldn't lie there anymore. She heaved herself up, wrenching herself out of the dream realm and into the waking world, where she sat on her bed, shivering in sheets damp with cold sweat. Wrapping the duvet around her body, she padded to the living room and switched on the television, clicking over to CNN. It was five in the morning, and the anchor was droning about US economic policy. If there had been some sort of major attack, the anchor wouldn't be gesturing at a chart showing the trends for manufacturing over the last several quarters; no, he'd be covering the terrorism wall to wall.

Just to be safe, she rotated through all the major networks, but it was obvious that nothing catastrophic had happened—at least, nothing outside of the usual chaos and craziness of the world these days. Could that mean she'd prevented something from happening, or did it mean only that it hadn't happened *yet*? Her dad had explained that when he'd used the Foretell card, it had shown him cutting the Dragonfly off his arm, and he'd done so immediately after. It had shown him an answer, and he'd accepted it, but couldn't he have simply chosen *not* to follow through? It didn't sound like the future had been fixed—it sounded like the card had shown him a way out, and he'd taken it.

Ernie still didn't want to bother Gabe, since she knew he'd come to her once his assignment was finished, so she decided to hit up the one other Dealer she'd spoken to about Foretell. She saw him in her Revelation card, sleeping next to Nuria in a cabana on a beach. She smiled at the image; Kot had spent his whole life at the edge of a dead brown sea, and now he could experience crystal blue water and bracing, salty air. He had earned it.

Ernie forced herself to wait until a decent hour to seek him out, and she filled the time in between with an elaborately prepared omelet that she felt too queasy to eat and a trip over to the shop to check on her parents, who seemed so cheerful and happy that she couldn't bring herself to talk to them about what was on her mind. After another check of the news revealed that all seemed (mostly) right with the world, Ernie crossed Transport with Revelation and went to visit the Dealer who'd saved her butt on several occasions.

When Ernie appeared on the beach, a few yards from the thatch-roofed cabana, Nuria was sitting on a towel in the sand, a card aimed in Ernie's direction. She wore a bikini, and the grasshopper tattoo on her left forearm glittered with green-and-blue iridescence. Next to her sat a writing pad and a pencil. As soon as she saw who had invaded her tropical paradise, Nuria lowered her card and smiled. "Eh," she said. "Eeee."

Ernie hitched a grin onto her face. "It's great to see you again, Nuria."

Kot emerged from behind the cabana with two fruity drinks in his hands. His curly black hair had grown a bit, and his dark-brown skin glistened with sweat under the tropical sun. He smiled when he saw Ernie, though it was tinged with wariness. "Welcome to San Pancho. Refreshment?" He offered up one of the drinks.

Ernie shook her head. "How's it going?"

"I will not complain," Kot said, striding over to Nuria and handing her a drink. She made a squealing sound of delight just before her lips closed eagerly around the straw. "She is getting better every day."

Ernie watched Nuria suck down her drink, then reach out and stroke Kot's leg before sliding on a pair of sunglasses and picking up her pad, upon which she began to scribble with the pencil.

"Will you walk with me for a bit?" Ernie asked Kot.

Kot gestured up the beach, which they appeared to have all to themselves. Ernie's sneakers sank into the soft white sand as they plodded toward the whispering waves sliding against the shore. "Is this your home now?" she asked.

Kot shrugged. "Nuria likes the sun, and so do I, so we put our haven here."

"You have only one between you?"

"Being together restores us both, and we saw no need for separate havens."

It reminded Ernie of Trey and Tarlae, who had always been together, and at the thought of what had happened to them, she had a bad feeling in the pit of her stomach. Tarlae was out there somewhere, suffering without her love, but Kot seemed so content that Ernie wasn't about to lecture him on the dangers of being too close to another Dealer—although she had to admit, that might have been one of the reasons she was keeping a bit of distance from Gabe. "Nuria does seem better," she said.

"She is not yet ready for an assignment, though. She works every day to bond with the grasshopper. They were at war for so long." He glanced back toward her. "She has been very focused on drawing lately."

"What about you?"

"I am not focused on drawing. Our Forger has given me one assignment." He turned away from Nuria and looked out at the ocean. "I do not like to leave Nuria alone for too long. She becomes restless."

"But you actually took the job?"

"It was the first time a Forger gave me an assignment," he explained. "Our former Forger acted as if I did not exist at all."

Ernie supposed that made sense. From Kot's perspective, Virginia might not be the ideal boss, but at least she acknowledged him as a Dealer and treated him like all the others. "What did she want you to do?"

"A group of security workers were behaving in an unethical manner, and Virginia gave me the task of ensuring they were caught and disciplined for their violations of rules."

"Security workers," Ernie said slowly. "Was it at a bank, by any chance?"

He shook his head. "Most definitely not. It was at a sort of gathering place for people wishing to engage in recreation. People ride on very odd trains with tracks that seem designed to simulate danger. There is a great deal of screaming involved."

"An amusement park, you mean?"

"It was, indeed, amusing to watch."

"I love roller coasters. Where were you? Six Flags? Disney?"

"It was called Galaxy World."

"Huh. Never heard of it."

"It is a very grand place." He swept his hand over the sun-kissed landscape. "There are several large, enclosed domes that re-create habitats, such as a tropical beach, a jungle, and even a location called Mars. The funny thing is that this park is located in a foggy and drab countryside, like a carnival town. Herestford, it is called. Instead of traveling to places like San Pancho, people come from miles away to spend time in Herestford and *pretend* they are in a place like San Pancho."

"Sounds like Galaxy World is somewhere in England."

"Yes, I believe it is there. And the people who guard the place were engaged in improper practices with the surveillance cameras. I have learned much about technology in this world." He sighed. "It is a very big place, with many things I have never seen before."

"You've had a steep learning curve for sure. I'm surprised your head hasn't exploded."

He gave her a wary look. "That is something that can happen?"

She'd forgotten that Kot and idioms were not friends. "I just mean that this place is different from where you came from, so adjusting to it must be difficult."

"Nuria has had to adjust, too. She was banished from here many decades ago."

"By Virginia," Ernie murmured.

Kot paused to look out at the ocean. "We have not forgotten that. But our Forger has apologized to her. She said she would give Nuria time to recover and said she would like to be a Forger for all Dealers. She said that we might be diverse, but we can work toward common goals, with all grudges forgotten."

"Yeah? She's the one who did the banishing, so why does she get to have a grudge at all?"

Kot lifted his hands in surrender. "I am in no position to go to war with a Forger, not with Nuria vulnerable as she is. I will do whatever is necessary to protect her until she can protect herself."

"It just seems like such a random assignment," Ernie said. "You got a bunch of theme park security guards fired?"

Kot nodded. "It was not difficult—I completed the job yesterday and have already received payment—and I did not have to harm anyone to do it."

"That's good." The feeling in the pit of Ernie's stomach was like a small boulder now, heavy and filled with the weight of her guilt. Should she have stopped those bank robbers without killing them? Or had that been necessary, to stop what was coming? "Hey, can I ask you something?"

"You ask me questions all the time, including whether you can ask them. I do not understand this custom."

"Sorry. I just—you mentioned one time that you'd used your Foretell card and that whatever you saw hadn't come true yet."

"Yes," he said. "It has not happened yet, but I know it will, and knowing that has kept me going."

Ernie swallowed the lump in her throat. "What if it doesn't? I mean, I've heard that if you use Foretell, whatever you see is locked in place, but what if that's not true?"

Kot shrugged. "I do not know if it is true or not, but I hope it is. I played Foretell when I was at my most hopeless, when I had fallen in love with a woman who seemed utterly doomed."

"How long ago was that?"

"Years, I believe. And perhaps I should not have done it, but I had to know."

"Will you tell me what you saw in the card?"

Kot turned to Ernie, a small but powerful smile on his face. "I saw Nuria, and I heard her voice. She was telling me she loved me."

Ernie felt like she'd had the wind knocked out of her. "Whoa."

"At times, I have doubted that either of us would live to experience that moment, but every day, I feel it coming closer."

"I hope it happens soon," Ernie said weakly. For his sake, she wanted Foretell to fulfill its promise, but for her sake, she desperately hoped the card presented only one of many futures. Maybe even the most likely—but hopefully still changeable. She looked over at Nuria, who seemed absorbed by whatever she was drawing. "I won't keep you from her." Suddenly, Ernie wanted to be far, far away. "I'll chat with you later?"

She pulled out her Transport card, her heart pounding. Kot gave her a concerned look. "Are you well?"

"Fine. Just remembered I left the stove on." Ernie played her card before he had a chance to reply, carrying herself back to Asheville. Once at her apartment, she checked the news yet again—nothing terrible had happened. But it didn't comfort Ernie at all. *Years,* Kot had said. What

39

he'd seen in that card had shaped his feelings and probably his actions. He'd refused to put Nuria out of her misery even when she'd asked him to, even after she and the grasshopper had become the scourge of his home dimension, possibly because he'd seen a future with them together, with her able to speak at last.

What did that mean for Ernie? She'd seen what looked and felt like an apocalypse when she'd asked the Foretell card to show her the future related to those bank robbers. She'd do anything to prevent that future, but she had no way of knowing where or how it might come to pass . . .

She turned off the television and pulled out her Foretell card once again. If she played it, she might see—but what if she locked in yet more horror? Bile rose in her throat, and she put the card away as Legs tingled all prickly on her arm.

She needed space to think about this. One wrong move might spell disaster, so she did what she always did when the thoughts in her head were threatening to drive her straight up a wall. She changed into her workout clothes and ran the two miles to the Bear Creek CrossFit gym, which was super basic inside but boasted a tough obstacle course out back. Once there, as the sun began to sink behind the Blue Ridge range, she threw herself into her workout, climbing walls and ropes, doing the monkey bars until her fingers were too shot to grip the metal. Like she had in the race, she fell into the slosh beneath the apparatus, coating herself in the sludge. Unwilling to stop, she did the course once more, dropping to do burpees whenever she failed an obstacle. A few other people came and went, waving to her as they completed their daily exercise, but Ernie acknowledged them with little more than a jerk of her head.

As the lights came on around the course, Ernie still didn't pack it in. Her muscles were screaming. Her legs and arms shook, and her throat ached as her breath rasped in and out. Finally, she stumbled over her own feet as she tried to jump onto the seven-foot wall. Her legs gave out, and she landed on her butt. It felt like she'd been stabbed in the side, and she clutched at her ribs, clenching her teeth to hold in the cry. She couldn't stop now. The vision was still in her head.

"Jesus, Mary, and Joseph," came a familiar voice. "Has the devil himself been chasing you?"

Ernie looked up to see Gabe leaning against the wall, Caera on his shoulder. "I'm . . . working . . . out," she said between pained gasps.

He arched one eyebrow. "And I'm Margaret Thatcher."

"You need to update—" she began, but gave up as he came forward and lifted her from the ground.

"From where I'm standing, it looks like you're punishing yourself."

"Shut up," she mumbled, leaning her head against his chest, relief surging through her as his arms closed around her. "Take me somewhere?"

"Anywhere in particular?"

Anyplace I can leave my brain behind. She shook her head, and a moment later, they were in the void, carried away by Gabe's Transport card. Gabe bowed his head and whispered sweet reassurance against her ear, and when they stepped out of the darkness, they were in his modest seaside cottage in Ireland. Gabe issued a few stern instructions and gave her a light shove in the direction of the shower. Ernie let the steaming water roll over her, and when she emerged, he was waiting with whiskey in hand and a fire in the woodstove.

As the wind rattled the panes and the ocean crashed against the night, Ernie settled into a squashy chair. Gabe wrapped a blanket around her shoulders. He sat in front of her and warmed his whiskey between his palms. "What's happened?" he asked casually.

"Virginia gave me an assignment."

His gaze sharpened. "What did she want?"

"For me to stop a bank robbery."

"Oh." The muscles of his shoulders relaxed. "That sounds like a good thing."

"How did yours go?" She closed her eyes and took a slug of the whiskey, letting it burn.

"I think it went well," he said. "Turns out he was a scoundrel, but I did my job anyway."

"A scoundrel?"

"The only reason he needed protection was that he was . . ." He cleared his throat. "Engaged in a rather passionate affair with a married woman."

"And her husband found out?"

"Spot on. I tried to hide them when he came round, but the wife had left evidence of the affair in her car and in a shared email account, apparently, so the husband showed up drunk, hunting for revenge. With a knife." He knocked back his drink with an abrupt toss of his head, then sighed. "I disguised myself as the immunologist I was protecting, and sent the bloke packing. But he went off pretty upset, so I've got a tracker on him, in case he circles back for another go."

Ernie drained her glass and held it out for a refill, which Gabe provided immediately. "Smart," she said in a choked voice.

She could have done that, couldn't she? Instead of killing the thieves, she could have tracked them, making sure they got caught and didn't make any suspicious moves. She could have done something other than kill them.

"I met up with Alvarez for a drink in Paris, as it turned out we were both there," Gabe said after a few moments of silence. "He'd had an assignment from Virginia, too, earlier tonight."

The Dealer of the Emperor Tamarin deck had nearly died when Virginia had stolen most of his deck in the fall, and it had taken all their efforts to save him. "Did he actually take it?"

"He didn't feel like he had a choice, but I've never seen him so spooked."

"Was it a bad job?"

"Funny thing is, no. All he was supposed to do was make sure a man caught a train from Paris to London."

Ernie frowned. "Why was he spooked?"

"He said he'd seen something in his Foretell card as he tried to locate his target."

She set her glass on a table next to her chair, feeling electrified. "Did he say what it was?"

"He was langered, darlin'. Kept mumbling something about fire. I thought maybe the guy he'd helped was going to get in an accident or something. Not good, but hardly—"

She shot to her feet with every muscle protesting. "I need to talk to Alvarez."

"Tell me what's going on."

"My assignment—" She grimaced.

"We all fail assignments sometimes, love. I'm sure you can clean it up."

"Not necessary." Her eyes met his. "I didn't stop the robbery, but I caught the robbers—"

Gabe grinned. "Of course you did. And—"

"I killed them," she blurted out.

His face fell. "Because they were going to kill people otherwise."

"Maybe? I mean, they were shooting." She held up her hand to keep him from excusing what she'd done. "But that wasn't why I killed them. I did it because I saw something in my Foretell card."

Gabe set his glass down slowly. "A fire?"

"An apocalypse," she whispered.

Gabe pulled his Transport card. "Let's go, then."

CHAPTER FIVE

Finding Alvarez wasn't easy, as he'd cloaked himself again. After they'd visited a few of his usual haunts and the Paris bar where Gabe had left him the night before, Gabe sent out a summoning beacon to the Emperor Tamarin Dealer to see whether he'd return the call. Then Ernie and Gabe went back to the cottage. Ernie was staggering and exhausted, and she fell onto Gabe's bed, unconscious by the time her head hit the pillows.

She awoke to find a mellow sun glowing outside the curtains and Gabe fast asleep beside her, still fully clothed, his boots discarded at the foot of the bed. For a moment, Ernie was able to forget everything else and just stare at his rough-hewn face, the scar on his brow, his unshaven jaw, which was relaxed as he slumbered instead of clenched with worry or frustration. He looked younger like this. He looked more *human.* She smiled to herself, realizing that she thought of Gabe as set apart from the real, normal world, almost immune to basic human needs such as eating and sleeping. But now here he was, snoring softly next to her as if this were their home, as if they had no place else to be. As if they had nothing to do except be together. They'd never had a day like that, and Ernie decided she wanted one.

It wouldn't be today, though. She stroked the hair away from his face, her touch light, and his lips curved into a smile even as his breathing remained slow and deep. Her heart squeezed as she thought about how all Gabe wanted was to protect people, to do right. More than anything, she wanted that for him, and despite her mistrust of Virginia, she hoped the new Forger might actually be allowing them to intervene in helpful, positive ways. A long shot, sure. But Virginia had at one point helped Ernie's father by warning him about the risks of returning to his family, and she had given Gabe and other Dealers the cards they needed to complete their decks. She'd said something about the arc of the moral universe bending toward justice, and how she wanted to see whether Martin Luther King Jr. had been correct when he'd said that. At the time, Ernie had found it ominous, but now . . . ?

She wanted to believe it, but her vision of the conflagration singed the edges of her hope. It had felt like the end of the world. As she swallowed back her dread at knowing Alvarez may have seen something similar in his Foretell card, she realized there would never be a good time for her and Gabe. The world would never stop and clear a space for them, and they'd just have to live with it.

Gabe turned his head toward her, a sleepy smile on his face. "You're awake."

She leaned forward slowly, her heart picking up its pace. "Good morning."

He blinked and rubbed his eyes, then focused on her face, concern furrowing his brow. "Are you—"

Ernie cut him off with a kiss. Gabe groaned as her tongue slipped along his lower lip, and he pulled her toward him. With her hand on his neck, Ernie felt his pulse kick against the heat of his skin, and need rose inside her like a rogue wave. Her leg slid over his, and he shifted her hips so she was on top of him. She was lost in their connection, aware only of his body beneath her. She wanted to claim him, protect him, freeze this moment and hold it forever. His palms were warm as they met the skin of her waist, but his touch still raised goose bumps, desire released after so many months of pushing it away. There would never be a better time than now.

"God, I want you," she whispered against his mouth.

"What took you so long, then?" he asked, and she felt his smile.

"Fear," she admitted.

He paused and looked up at her. "I'm not going anywhere, love."

Their foreheads touched as Ernie pushed away the memory of fire. "I'm so tired of worrying."

"Then let it go, just for now." He ran his hand up her back and wove his fingers into her hair, bringing her mouth to his again. Ernie let him take control, stoking her want with every caress.

As she fumbled with his belt, a blast of heat against her thigh made both her and Gabe flinch. She rolled off him, heart pounding, rubbing at the burn as Gabe pulled his deck from his pocket. "It's my Revelation card, signaling me that my target is on the move," he said, breathing hard. As his long fingers fished the card from the rest, he gave her a rueful look, taking in her mussed hair and flushed cheeks. "Worst timing . . ." His half smile slipped away as he peered into his card. "What in god's name?"

"What is it?" she asked, leaning forward to look and seeing only fog. "I can't see what you see."

"If you're seeing nothing but gray haze, then yes you can," he replied, frowning. "I should be able to see that bloke clear as day." He raised his head. "Unless someone *else* is cloaking him."

"Why would another Dealer even care?"

Gabe shook his head. "I can't clear it up." He cursed. Then he flipped the Revelation card, as if to refocus. "Maybe I can find the Dealer who's concealing him." Gabe hunched over his cards, his gaze riveted. "I don't see anyone I recognize, but I know that street. It's in London."

"We can find him—or her—and get some answers," Ernie suggested.

He sighed as he looked her over. "I suppose we should, but . . ."

"I know." She leaned over and kissed him.

"You're driving me crazy, love," he murmured against her lips.

She grinned. "That doesn't sound too bad."

He got off the bed, grumbling as he headed into the bathroom to shower and change. Ernie took the opportunity to do the same at her own apartment before returning to the cottage to find Gabe waiting, his still-damp hair pulled into a ponytail. "My deck keeps going hot," he said as she approached. "No idea what Caera's trying to tell me."

Ernie's dread, which had been submerged beneath her raw need, was back. "Maybe all this stuff is connected somehow."

"How? Your job was in Germany, and his was in Paris—"

"The world is a pretty big place, Gabe, but your job was in Paris, too. And Alvarez was helping a guy get to London . . . and here we are, looking for the Dealer who's cloaking your target—in London, apparently."

Gabe looked skeptical. "I'm not saying you're wrong."

"I'm not just saying this because it's Virginia—I swear." She paused. "Okay, maybe I am."

"Either way, we can go take a look." Gabe took her hand and crossed Transport over Revelation.

Ernie folded herself against him and followed him into the void. She kept her deck in her other hand, ready to face whatever awaited them. They appeared in an alley off a busy street, next to a place with red shutters and a sign proclaiming itself Bradley's Spanish Bar. "This is where the cloaker was, as recently as a minute ago," Gabe said as he eyed the place. "Funny thing is, I've been here before. Trey and I grabbed a pint after a mission last summer."

"Let's check it out. I need sustenance anyway," Ernie said, heading for the door. She hadn't eaten since the morning before, and as they entered the bar, a clock informed her that it was just after noon.

"Ah, you might find a few crisps and nuts, but food isn't really the thing here," Gabe said as Ernie's eyes adjusted to the dim lighting and the impressive display of bottles behind the bar. A jukebox against the wall sported a collection of vinyl records, and Ernie recognized the current selection as the Clash.

"Holy crap, Alvarez?" she exclaimed as she spotted the silver-haired Dealer slumped over the bar, a cane resting against his stool.

"Looks like he never went home," Gabe said as they walked over to the Dealer, whose head was drooped over his drink.

Ernie looked Alvarez over. "You think he's the one doing it?"

Alvarez turned to look at them, squinting through bloodshot eyes. He muttered something in Spanish. "Leave me alone," he added in English.

Ernie and Gabe sat on either side of him, and Ernie immediately availed herself of a basket of potato chips, trying to look casual but feeling rather desperately hungry.

While she crunched, Alvarez finished his drink and waved for another, but Gabe shook his head at the bartender, who shrugged. "He was waiting at the door when we opened," the man said. "Seems like he got started early."

"Or never stopped," Gabe said, clapping Alvarez on the back.

Alvarez answered with a barely stifled belch. "I can't find him," he mumbled. "Why can't I find him?"

"Who?" asked Ernie.

"I don't like you. I've never liked you," Alvarez said to her.

"Cool. My snake could eat your monkey." Legs tingled on Ernie's arm as if she approved.

"Who can't you see, mate?" Gabe asked Alvarez while giving Ernie a look that said, *Please don't provoke him.*

"My assignment," muttered Alvarez. "I tracked him after what I saw in my Foretell card. But now it's only fog." He groaned and put his head in his hands.

Ernie and Gabe looked at each other behind Alvarez's back. "So someone's cloaking *both* your targets?" she murmured.

"Did *you* get an assignment from that shriveled old hag?" Alvarez scowled at her. "Can you see *your* person?"

Guilt slammed into Ernie once again as she remembered what she'd done to the thieves in Germany, and she shoved a few more potato chips into her mouth as she thought about how to respond. Then it hit her: "Kot had an assignment from Virginia. He was supposed to get a bunch of security guards at an amusement park fired for misconduct. We can go ask if the people he got fired are being cloaked, too, maybe?" Grasping for straws, perhaps, but it felt better than doing nothing.

"Which amusement park?" Gabe asked, reaching for yet another straw.

"Galaxy World?" answered Ernie. "I'd never—"

"Largest theme park in the country," said the bartender as he delivered a round of shots to the three of them.

"We didn't order—" Ernie began.

"That bloke over there said you looked like you needed a drink." The bartender gestured over to the jukebox as the song switched to "God Save the Queen" by the Sex Pistols. Minh, the ever-stylish and centuries-old Dealer of the Pot-Bellied Pig deck, was leaning against the vintage machine, his angular face lit by its glow.

Alvarez grabbed his shot and raised it in Minh's direction. *"Salud."* He tossed it back.

Minh sauntered over to them, a mug of beer in his hand. "I was in the neighborhood. Are we celebrating something?"

"Employment," said Alvarez. "The gilded cage."

"Ah," Minh replied. "She gave me an assignment, too. Nearby. I just finished it."

Alarm bells sounded in Ernie's head. It felt like she was looking at a bunch of scrambled pieces that added up to something, but she had no idea what. "Your assignment was here in London? Did it involve cloaking some people?" That might make sense—maybe Virginia was trying to get them to turn on each other, pitting one Dealer against another?

But Minh shook his head. "I was in Herestford. I had to stop a drunk driver from hitting the road. Most ridiculous busywork I've ever been called to do, but whatever, it paid, and I showed our new overlord that I can play the game, so maybe now she'll leave me alone." He tilted his head as he regarded Ernie, who had jumped off her barstool. "Yes, dear?"

"Herestford," she said. "That's where Galaxy World is."

"Yeah . . . ," he replied slowly.

"Kot had an assignment at Galaxy World," she explained. "Alvarez had one that involved helping a guy get to London from Paris, and Gabe had one in Paris around the same time."

"Who was your guy?" Minh asked the Emperor Tamarin Dealer. "Was he some VIP?"

"He was a twitchy mess is what he was," said Alvarez. "Mumbling to himself about his wife, what a whore she was. Pathetic."

Gabe had gone pale. "Did he happen to have a large mole on his neck?"

"How did you know?"

"I think our missions involved the same guy," Gabe said.

Ernie turned to Minh. "Did the drunk driver you stopped have a mole like that?"

"Nope. And it was a woman. Did you get a job, too?"

"Mine was in Munich," Ernie said, then sighed. "But I used my Foretell card and saw something horrible."

Minh and Gabe looked somber, but Alvarez grabbed Ernie by the shoulders. "What did you see?" he shouted, his eyes red-rimmed, his breath making her eyes water.

Ernie planted her feet and knocked his hands away from her. "I don't know exactly what I saw. It was big and fiery, but I don't know where—"

"I saw a fire, and twisted metal falling as everything burned."

"Mine was like an explosion," she said to the group. "And that's what makes me think my assignment was linked, at least to Alvarez's."

"Minh, can you track the driver you just kept off the road?" Gabe asked. "If we could find out more about her, maybe we can figure out how our assignments are connected."

"Someone's blocked our guy," Alvarez said. "We can't find him."

"Another Dealer," said Minh. Gabe nodded, and Minh pulled his deck, his Revelation card already wiggling free of the rest. "No one's cloaking my assignment. She's right there," Minh said, looking into the card. "Sleeping it off in her car." He grunted. "I didn't even use my deck to stop her. I just gave her keys to the bartender."

"We could go talk to her," said Ernie. "Maybe she knows Gabe and Alvarez's guy."

"That's a bit random." Minh smoothed back a lock of ebony hair that had flopped onto his forehead. "And if you saw something in Foretell—"

"I'm not sure what we saw," she said as the bartender, who had been wiping the counter nearby, leaned a little closer.

Minh gave Ernie a concerned look. "Let's take this out back."

Gabe and Ernie settled the tab, hefted Alvarez off his stool, and marched him to the exit, where they joined Minh in the same alley they'd used as their arrival point. "Just hold on to me," the Dealer of the Pot-Bellied Pig deck said. "Herestford, here we come."

Ernie grabbed Minh's arm just before he pulled them into darkness that evaporated almost instantly as they appeared between the wall of a building and a dumpster emanating the funk of decaying vegetables. As she edged along the passageway that opened on a parking lot in front of a bar, Ernie could hear the sounds of traffic and of distant screaming. She jogged across the lot toward the road and turned to see the source of the screams, perhaps half a mile away—a giant tangle of roller coasters nestled within the walls of what looked like Disney on steroids, a huge amusement park containing several domed structures and a host of other colorful rides. "I didn't realize we'd be so close," she said as she looked over her shoulder at the three male Dealers gathering behind her.

Alvarez's face was gray, and he looked like he was about to puke as he looked in the direction of the shrieks of delight. *"Madre de Dios,"* he whispered.

"She's right over there," Minh said, brushing past Alvarez and striding toward a car at the back of the lot. The parking area and bar lay at the side of a busy two-lane road surrounded by farmland on one side and a string of hotels, restaurants, and businesses on the other. "See? Still in her—"

The flash of light reached them first, but the sound of the explosion was right on its heels, shaking the ground and filling the air with a deafening roar. The shock wave rolled over them, blasting with searing air that tore at Ernie's throat and stole her breath. It threw Alvarez and Ernie to the ground, while Gabe and Minh barely kept their footing. The windows of the bar shattered, as did the windows of the cars in the lot, but even as she felt the slice of glass, Ernie barely heard a thing. Her world was mostly silent, her mind mostly blank, as she looked at Galaxy World in the distance.

It was nothing but a massive, raging inferno.

CHAPTER SIX

With all the power in their cards, they couldn't undo the disaster. They couldn't bring the dead back to life. But with a somber, silent agreement, they left the parking lot and did all they could. Ernie saw each of them—Gabe, Alvarez, and Minh—appearing and disappearing, transporting injured survivors to safety, stifling fire as it crept toward a hotel with a crumbling edifice and blown-out windows, freeing a few people from collapsed buildings near the blast zone.

Ernie's Healing card fizzled out first, after she resuscitated two little girls whose parents lay dead nearby. She realized that fact only when the older girl, perhaps five years old, ran toward the bodies and tried to wake them up. Wondering whether she'd once again made things worse by trying to make them better, Ernie ushered the two wailing children toward a nearby ambulance and transported herself away as quickly as she could. She couldn't watch. She couldn't think about those girls and what lay ahead for them. She had to move, to act, to help, because the alternative was cratering completely.

The entire amusement park had been leveled, and smoke filled the air, blotting out the sun. Ernie's lungs burned, but even if her Healing card had had some juice left, she wouldn't have used it for herself. She didn't deserve it.

She used Strength, though, allowing her to lift a car off a man pinned beneath its dented carcass. She used her Shield card to walk through a wall of fire to get to the source of screams and rescued a couple of families from the burning Information Center at the edge of the park. She didn't even bother to play Mirage or Conceal to hide her obviously supernatural abilities from those people—they seemed too traumatized to process what they were seeing, and she needed all her energy and focus to save lives.

Time became meaningless as she toiled. She didn't bother to count how many people she saved, because she knew the number would be dwarfed by the number of people killed. Instead, she focused on one person at a time, one family at a time, while sirens screamed and first responders did all they could. There were so many fire trucks and ambulances that it looked like they'd come from all over England, and at one point, Ernie spotted Minh controlling traffic lights so that the flow of cars was safer and smoother.

The gray fog of smoke began to darken, and floodlights glowed through the haze, perhaps a quarter mile from the still-burning amusement park. Ernie, who had just played her Nourishment card to pipe oxygen into a collapsed restaurant to give her more time to save whoever might still be trapped inside, paused to catch her breath and found that she couldn't. Her hands tingled, but not with the magic of her deck. Her vision blurred, and then she couldn't see at all.

When she hit the ground, her mind was awake, but her body was in full rebellion, refusing to obey her frantic commands. *Get up. No surrender.* She could hear voices around her, drifting toward her on the smoke. "Bomb," said one person. "Terrorists," said another.

My fault, thought Ernie. Somehow, she'd contributed to this disaster.

"You're no good to anyone like this, love," Gabe said in her ear, and then his arms were around her. The press of the void silenced the sounds of the tragedy. Until it was actually silent again, she didn't realize that she'd been dwelling in a shattering storm of noise—sirens, screams, secondary explosions, the roar of flames, the rumble of collapsing buildings—for hours.

Her eyes fluttered open to soft light coming from a bedside lamp. Gabe laid her on the bed in his cottage and shushed her when she protested at the sight of her soot-smudged clothes and skin. "You can shower when you're actually able to stand up on your own, all right?" he said, but he fetched a bowl of warm water and a cloth, then wiped her hot cheeks and brow.

She breathed in and winced; her lungs were tight and burning from hours of breathing smoke and toxic fumes. Judging from Gabe's appearance—bloodshot eyes, grime-smeared face—he probably wasn't feeling much better. She pulled his hand away from her. "You need to rest, too."

"I'm holding up so far, though my Healing card is down for a bit. I'd use it on you, but—"

"No," Ernie croaked. "I'll be fine." Her body would be, at least.

He sighed. "I should go back."

She tried to sit up but found she couldn't, eliciting a growl of frustration from her throat. "Why am I so freaking weak?" It felt like yet another race she couldn't finish, where she'd needed his help to keep going at all.

"Have you ever heard that saying about putting on your own oxygen mask before helping the person next to you?"

She raised her eyebrows. "You have?"

"I'm old, not ignorant." He stroked her hair off her forehead. "I used Prolong and Nourishment on myself, to give me enough energy to push through." He kissed her gently and stood up. "You might want to save a bit for yourself, hmm? Let me know when you're back in action."

"Seems like you'll know," Ernie replied. After all, he'd found her almost as soon as she'd collapsed.

He drew the blank card that connected them, a gift from the mercurial former Forger, and slipped it into her pocket. "Easier to do when I've got that in my deck, so you keep it for now." He smiled. "I feel a bit stronger when I have it. Maybe you will, too."

Ernie let out a shuddering breath and grabbed his hand. "This is bad, isn't it?"

His smile faded. "I can't think about that right now. We'll figure everything out when the dust settles."

She nodded and released him, closing her eyes so she didn't have to watch him vanish. But when the stillness of the room told her that he'd gone back to try to rescue a few more innocents, Ernie let her face crumple, and she let the tears come. They eventually gave way to a fitful sleep in which she relived the explosion over and over again, but her exhaustion kept her under until she awakened to light filtering through the plain curtains on Gabe's windows. She spent a few moments wondering if it was moonlight or the dawning sunrise, and then decided she was too tired to care.

She dragged herself out of bed and transported herself back to her own apartment, happy that her cards had recharged and were working again. She took a long, hot shower and emerged from the steaming bathroom wrapped in her robe, with a towel around her shoulders and a brush in her hand. She plopped onto the couch in front of the television and, with a sinking feeling, grabbed the remote and caught CNN midstory.

Most deadly terrorist attack in history, blared the chyron. Ernie groaned, then gasped as the image filled the screen.

It wasn't Galaxy World.

The smoke and fire billowed into a city skyline. She turned up the volume and listened to the clearly excited and stressed anchor explaining that the explosion had happened a few hours earlier, right as the International Gamer Alliance had convened its annual conference at Munich's largest convention center. Over a hundred thousand fans and gamers had been registered to attend, and most were thought to have been in the exhibition area when the bomb went off.

Ernie stared at the video taken from a helicopter circling over the city, showing the rubble, the smoke, the still-burning buildings. Munich. It couldn't be a coincidence. And then the story switched, acknowledging that the IGA attack wasn't the only terrorist attack in the last twenty-four hours. Ernie leaned forward, bracing herself for images of the Galaxy World carnage, only to rock back as the screen filled with the sight of a capsized and flaming cruise ship, its cheerfully colorful logo visible on its upturned hull. Before she even had a chance to process that, though, the video changed again, revealing yet another catastrophe, this one at a large conference of aid organizations in Johannesburg. Finally, after brief shots of wailing citizens and emergency efforts, the video transitioned to images of a burning theme park.

But it wasn't Galaxy World. It was Islands of Fantasy in Rio de Janeiro.

Ernie was too shocked to cry. Numbly, she watched the replay of the attack that had happened late last night, surveillance video showing the flash of the explosion, and later one of the giant rides collapsing in flames. Only then, after the anchor announced that at least four thousand casualties were expected from that attack when all was said and done, did the coverage switch once more—this time to Galaxy World, apparently the first in a twenty-four-hour spate of terrorist attacks that had most likely killed over a hundred thousand people.

A hundred thousand people. On three continents. Five separate attacks. No one knew whether the attacks were linked or whether there would be more. But Ernie thought she knew the answers—yes and yes.

What she didn't know was *why*. The how was a little clearer, though, especially as the anchor droned on about what was known so far about the Galaxy World attack, the one that had happened the previous afternoon in England. They already knew who'd done it, because he'd posted a video on YouTube. It was a fellow with a large mole on his neck, and Ernie had no doubt that it was the very same jealous husband that Gabe had been trying to track, the same guy Alvarez had helped catch the train to London. Apparently the bomb had been hidden in a delivery truck that had entered through a supply gate, and she wondered whether Minh had been tasked with stopping a drunk driver who might have collided with the truck, an accident that could have either prevented the bomb from exploding or caused it to go off before it reached the park. And the misbehaving guards Kot had been assigned to get fired—Ernie was betting they might have been able to stop the truck before it entered the park, but instead the park had been shorthanded, leaving a gap in its security.

As for the robbery she had foiled, she had no idea how that had played into the plot, but she knew it must have been one of the gears in this horrifying machine—one of the terrorist attacks had taken place in Munich. And she knew that the Foretell card was one she'd probably never play again. She'd tried to prevent the future she'd seen by killing those thieves, and instead she'd managed to help that future happen. Her decision to kill four people might have even made that future more likely. She'd thought she could play God. She'd thought she could exchange a few lives for many. The consequences of her arrogance were crushing her now.

How many other Dealers had been tricked into causing these attacks, just as she had? How had Virginia done it?

And what would she do next?

Two competing instincts were at war inside Ernie. Part of her, maybe the part that had once been foolish enough to believe she would be the first person to successfully defy the future revealed in a Foretell card, wanted to curl into a ball and hide. There was blood on her hands. So much that she was drowning in it. Virginia had played puppeteer as if she were born to pull the strings, and Ernie wasn't stupid enough to believe the new Forger didn't have a second act planned, maybe more horrific than the first.

What if Ernie did something else to make things worse? She might not know until it was too late. Maybe the best thing to do was nothing at all, seeing as doing *something* had helped make this disaster happen.

But another part of her couldn't stomach sitting back or giving up.

Shaken and grim, Ernie brushed her hair, pulled it back into a ponytail, threw on some clothes, and transported herself to Terwilliger Antiquities.

Her father was out back, turning up a strip of earth around the weedy back patio. Ernie glanced at one of the trees that lined the property back there; that had been the first place she'd seen Trey's face, as he stood guard over her at Gabe's request. Back then, she'd thought he was an enemy, but he'd ended up giving his life for hers. She rubbed away the ache in her chest and waved to her father as he stood up and spotted her.

"How you doing, Weed?" he asked softly. "Bad stuff on the news."

"Yeah," she murmured. "How's Mom?"

"Ah, you know." Redmond squinted toward the sun, then rubbed at his eyes with the heels of his hands. "She's a little sensitive, so I told her to turn off the TV, maybe take a pill and a nap."

Ernie nodded. She supposed it was better than her mom trying to drink her sorrow away. "Virginia did this, Dad. She made it happen."

Redmond's brow furrowed. "I thought she was the Forger. Out of the dealing business."

"And into puppeteering instead."

Her father ran his hand over his head, where a few stubborn hairs still grew. Then he went still and stared at her. "Oh. Oh, no." He swallowed hard. "Did she make you—"

"She didn't ask any of us to cause the attacks directly. None of us would." Ernie thought about all the Dealers she'd met. She had no idea how many there were, actually, as Dealers usually played alone and kept themselves hidden from each other to avoid getting their decks stolen. But she'd encountered several. Some—like Minh and Kot—would never follow an order to kill a bunch of innocents. But others—Ruslan, the Dealer of the Komodo Dragon, and Rupert, Dealer of the Hyena deck—might be willing to cause that kind of mayhem and suffering.

"Well, no one I'd associate with." She explained to her father how her allies had been tricked by Virginia into helping to cause the attacks.

"Damn, that's cold."

"But how did she know what to do?" Ernie asked.

Redmond shook his head. "That's one thing I never could puzzle out, no matter how much research I did. No one really knows where the Forger's domain is or what goes on there. We know a Forger can make the cards and plenty of other things, too—those rune tiles, the Cortalaza blade, the Forger's Marks, the Sunrise—"

Ernie groaned. "Yeah, and most of those things are gone now. Or at least, all the things that I could have used to stop Virginia." They'd used the Marks to try to get favors for Kot, who'd wanted to restore Nuria to her mind and body, and for Tarlae, who'd wanted Trey back. Only one of those favors had been granted, but the Marks had been used up with the requests. The Cortalaza blade was gone as well—it had been ruined, melted and warped after Virginia had used it to stab Andy and take his throne. And the Sunrise . . . Virginia had it, and god only knew what she'd do if she got the key from Ernie. Maybe the best and only option, then, was to lie low and make sure the key stayed hidden.

"We don't know every single artifact the Forgers made," Redmond said. "So you don't know that there's nothing that would help defeat her." He slumped. "But unless you can find something in my notes that I don't remember, I'm pretty much at a loss. I wish I could help, Weed. I really do. But now I'm just a useless old man."

"Stop it. You're taking care of Mom, and you've done all you can to help. So right now, just stay safe, okay? Maybe avoid large gatherings of people until I can figure out what Virginia's planning?"

Redmond nodded. "I don't suppose I could ask you to do the same?"

"For now, I'm going to help Gabe and a few others save as many lives as possible, and we'll go from there."

"And that's the part I'm worried about." He reached out and clapped a hand on Ernie's shoulder. "Listen to me—the Forgers, they're not much different from each other. Something about that gig kind of ruins a person, I think."

"I think Andy and Virginia were misfit toys even before they took the job," Ernie said.

"My point is, Andy'd been Forger for a century or two, and the world didn't explode. Virginia's doing damage, sure, but once she settles in, she'll make the usual hash of things. But that's not going to be the end of the world."

"*That's* your standard?" Andy had presided over wars like nothing the world had seen before. The Holocaust. Stalin's purges. Millions and millions of innocents murdered, and to them, it *had* been an apocalypse. When she thought of it that way, her course seemed clearer. "I'm not ready to be all shrug emoji about this, Dad."

He scowled and squeezed her shoulder. "I'm not asking you to shrug it off! I'm telling you not to take on a minor god, because she's not anything special, as far as I can see, and anyone who takes her place is likely to be just as bad."

Ernie considered that, remembering how, in the moments before Virginia had shown up and ambushed Andy, it had looked like Gabe was about to defeat the Forger and take his place. "I'm not so sure, Dad. I think some people are incorruptible."

"Absolute power corrupts absolutely, Weed. I wouldn't wish it on anyone." He gave her a hard look. "Including my daughter."

"I'm not angling to be Forger, Dad. I just want to stop Virginia from destroying the world, and I'm starting to wonder if that's what she has in mind."

"How are you going to stop her, if you don't actually kill her?"

The enormity of Ernie's task hit her, along with its improbability. "I'm glad you and Mom are okay." She brushed off his grasp on her shoulder. "I'll check in on you again soon."

Ernie transported herself back to her apartment, where she realized she'd left the television on. She turned it off before she could find out whether there had been another terrorist attack, because she didn't want to know. It didn't change anything, just like the conversation with her father hadn't changed anything. For a long time, Ernie had believed Virginia needed to be stopped. Even before she'd become the Forger. And now she was more convinced than ever. She didn't agree with her father that anyone who became the Forger would be corrupted by the power, and even if she did, she wouldn't just be able to sit back and throw up her hands while a feckless and heartless being killed hundreds of thousands on a whim. There had to be a better way to run things.

But she was at a loss for how to make that happen. She knew of no way to force Virginia onto her turf, and no weapon that could kill her if she did. The only thing she could do was draw together the allies who had been with her on the mesa in Utah when they'd united to try to defeat Andy and felt his wrath—and when Gabe had almost succeeded in becoming the Forger, with a little help from his friends. Minh was iffy, though. She recalled a conversation with him around Christmastime when he'd been a bit c'est la vie about the nature of good and evil. Ernie had no idea where he'd stand now. Kot might join them, but with Nuria to look after, he might not. Alvarez was unreliable as far as Ernie was concerned. And Tarlae? Ernie wasn't sure whether the Dealer of the Coconut Octopus deck was on their side at all, but it was worth trying.

It was always worth trying. Giving up was not an option. Not one she could live with, anyway.

Newly energized, Ernie conjured herself a veggie wrap and a protein shake. She changed into a Spartan jersey, jeans, and boots. Then she sat down on her living room floor and thought through her cards. She knew that Tarlae would never be trackable or seeable using the Revelation card—the Coconut Octopus Dealer was clever and had expressed disdain at the idea that one Dealer would even try to find another using that obvious method. But she'd said there were other ways.

Ernie pulled her Wisdom card and crossed it with her Ally card, thinking hard about Tarlae and how, despite the woman's prickliness, she'd fought at Ernie's side time and time again. Ernie admired her strength and fierceness. She knew Tarlae's pain at losing Trey was deep to the point of unfathomable, but she also knew being alone couldn't be good for the woman. She thought about all of that and peered hopefully into her cards.

Nothing. Of course.

Ernie pulled her Draw card. Most often, she used it to pull objects toward her—but could she use it to draw the attention of an ally? Maybe . . . *if* she lowered her own conjured shields and concealments. The Conceal card and the Shield card were almost always active for all the Dealers, maintained by their animal spirits, blocking attempts at surveillance and hiding them from enemies, keeping channels open for allies only. Except Ernie wasn't sure whether Tarlae was an ally anymore.

She still needed to find her. She pulled her Shield and Conceal cards and mentally opened all channels. She crossed Inverse over Shield and Ally on a whim, focusing on Tarlae one more time, asking her whether she was open to meeting. She held her breath and waited.

Nothing. Dammit.

This might be a pointless effort. Ernie put her concealments back in place, pocketed her deck, and drew her Transport card. As much as she didn't want to, it was time to return to Herestford and see whether there was anything she could do. After that, maybe she could fall into Gabe's arms for a few hours before deciding what to do next.

She was thinking about him when the arm wrapped around her throat. For one crazy moment, she thought it was him, but the smell of cigarettes and sweat was all wrong. By the time she realized it, though, she was already in the void, pulled through space and over miles by someone who was choking the living daylights out of her. Panic struck at the same time her feet hit solid earth, and she jabbed her elbow back and stomped her foot onto steel-toed boots. Her captor hurled her onto a dirty cement floor, but Ernie rolled and jumped up quickly, drawing her deck as Legs burned fiercely on her arm.

She was in some sort of warehouse, wooden pallets stacked on one side of the space, oil-stained concrete beneath her feet, glaring lights overhead revealing her captor. Ernie's stomach clenched as she took in the rangy figure standing about ten feet away. He had his own deck drawn.

Spiked hair—formerly magenta, now platinum blond. Narrow face. Permanent sneer. "Hyena," she said, working to keep her voice level. Rupert had been dead determined to murder her for months, and he'd probably just taken advantage of the moment she'd dropped her concealments to reach out to Tarlae. "You really should have called first."

"Diamondback." He wore a tight smile as he fanned his cards. "We have a few things to discuss."

CHAPTER SEVEN

Ernie didn't wait for him to "discuss" anything with her—the warehouse he'd dragged her to wasn't exactly a cozy place to chat. She palmed Strike and Accelerate, then shoved her hand forward with Escape already rising from the rest of the deck. Rupert had been ready, though. He played Shield and Capture simultaneously, blocking her strike and sending heavy chains flying toward her. They hit her with the force of a bus, taking her to the ground with her cards scattered everywhere.

Legs was off her arm and growing in less than a second, the sound of her rattle echoing ominously in the cavernous space. While Rupert cursed and unleashed the hyena from his left forearm, Ernie's Strength card glowed and jumped into her hand from a few feet away, filling Ernie with the power she needed to toss off the chains. She flicked her wrist, her cards flew toward her palm, and she tossed Amplify toward Legs, who grew abruptly to the length of a subway car and the girth of a five-gallon bucket. The hyena yelped and backtracked, its hackles up, but Rupert sliced a card, probably Inverse, toward the diamondback, shrinking her down to size.

"Stop fighting me," he shouted.

"Are you freaking serious right now?" hollered Ernie as she played Tool, Enemy, and Clay, causing a stack of wooden pallets next to Rupert to turn into about a swimming pool's worth of wood glue, which splashed over and around him and the hyena with viscous force, leaving them flailing and yelping in the goo.

Ernie drew her Escape card again, planning to get as far away from her enemy as she could, but as soon as she pulled it, Legs shot up in the air, hissing and rattling, and ended up slung over a steel beam about thirty feet overhead. Before Ernie could bring her down, Rupert, who had freed himself from the glue using his own cards but was still coated in the substance and looking pissed as hell, hit Ernie with a hard strike to the gut, sending her flying. Her back struck a stack of the pallets, which crashed down on her with bone-breaking momentum. Pain rocketed up her right leg and spine, drawing a tortured cry from her throat, but fury and adrenaline kept her in the duel. She played Weapon and Air, conjuring hornets that surrounded the blond enemy Dealer in a dark, angry cloud.

"Bloody hell, would you just listen to me?" shouted Rupert, his cards glowing from within the swarm. And then he disappeared.

Her hands trembling and her left arm pinned, Ernie finally managed to play Escape, and it was just enough to pull her from the crushing wreckage of the pallets. She found herself lying next to it and played Air and Warp to float poor Legs down to her. The serpent swirled in the air and alighted gracefully on Ernie's arm, a tattoo once more. Groaning, Ernie played her Healing card, pressing it to her body and letting her eyes fall shut.

What the hell had that been about?

Before she had a chance to form even a wisp of an answer, a hard hand clamped around her throat. Her eyes flew open to see Rupert again, his face flushed, his eyes narrowed, his jaw clenched. With his other hand, he snatched several cards from her deck and released her, jumping backward. "I'm not here to fight," he said, breathing hard.

Ernie stared at him—no longer covered in wood glue, he was drenched from head to foot, water dripping from the tips of his spiky hair. "Then give me back my cards," she said slowly, her heart racing.

Rupert must have seen the panic in her eyes, and he looked down at the cards in his grip. The blank white card was on top. "What in bloody hell . . . ?" He plucked it from the rest. "What's this?"

Ernie lurched to her knees, and Rupert skipped back, the blank card between his fingers. "Make a move and this one gets torn in half."

Ernie froze. "What do you want?"

Rupert flipped the blank card, examining it. His eyebrows shot up when he saw the hybrid winged snake on the back. "Holy hell. You and the Kestrel?" He grinned. "I think I'm keeping this."

He moved to pocket it, but Ernie played her Draw card, pulling the blank to the tips of Rupert's fingertips before he blocked her with Shield. "Nice try, Diamondback." Their eyes met, and his glinted with an intensity that gave her pause. "I'm serious. I'm not here to fight you. I just want to talk."

"We don't really have much in common."

Rupert's lip curled. "For which I'm bloody thankful." Then his look of contempt sagged. "I want an alliance."

"You're really bad at this, you know that?"

"I was born in Herestford," he snapped. "That bitch leveled my hometown." Ernie was shocked to realize that the glittering sheen in his eyes was actually unshed tears.

"My condolences." Ernie kept her eyes on the blank card that connected her to Gabe. She wondered whether he could sense that it was in the hands of another Dealer. "But isn't Virginia the horse you bet on? I thought she was your ally."

"She's no one's ally." His hands fell to his sides, Ernie's stolen cards still clutched in his right one. "It was a mistake to think she'd favor the blokes who got her where she is. She killed Lawrence like he was nothing."

Actually, Ernie had killed Lawrence—Virginia had just used the strike as a chance to grab the Brahman Bull Dealer's cards—but Ernie wasn't about to remind him. "Yeah, loyalty doesn't seem like her thing. But you know what? Doesn't much seem like yours, either."

Rupert looked down at Ernie's cards in his hand. With a jerk of his own deck, the Diamondback cards flew toward her, along with the hybrid card, zooming back into the deck held in her left hand. Ernie flinched with surprise. "Thanks?"

"I'm trying," Rupert said roughly. "I help my allies."

"By not stealing their cards? Not really that helpful."

"You attacked me!"

"Dude. You showed up in my apartment and kidnapped me. Not a great way to start a friendship."

"I'd been trying to find you for weeks," he grumbled, not making eye contact. "I knew Virginia was planning something. She had talked about what she would do if she ever became Forger. She bragged about it. And then after she became the Forger, she brought me to her new digs."

Ernie gaped at him. "You've been in the Forger's lair?"

"Wiggiest place I've ever been—I can tell you that much. The old bird wanted to impress me, I think."

"What was it like?"

"Looks like an old Greek temple, only floating in the middle of space." He shuddered. "The whole place smells weird. Anyway—she told me she was gonna run things differently, kick things off with a bang."

Ernie narrowed her eyes. "You *knew*?"

"Not everything, obviously."

"Oh, so if the massive and devastating terrorist attack had been in my hometown instead of yours, you'd still be her lapdog?"

He flinched. "I'm offering to help you."

"Help me *what*, Rupert? Why on earth would I ever trust you? I'm totally aware that you would love to see me die a horrible death—how am I supposed to believe you're not using this fake alliance thing to make that happen?"

"These attacks are only the beginning," he said.

"The beginning of *what*? Is she going to start another world war or something?"

"You could say that." He shuffled his cards with one hand, deft and deadly. "She's rewriting the rules."

"There are written rules? No one told me that."

"I'm just saying she's got more up her sleeve than these attacks! God, woman, I had no idea you were this bloody dense."

Actually, Ernie had just been enjoying making his face turn red with frustration, but she'd also been trying to buy herself time to think. Rupert had never been anything but a threat, so he must be seriously spooked if he was coming to her now. "You say you want an alliance, but that tells me exactly nothing. What. Do. You. *Want?*"

"I can help you."

"Help me *what*? Why me? Why not Akela or Ruslan? Isn't he your pal?"

His mouth twisted, as if he was biting the inside of his cheek. "They're gone."

"Gone where?"

"How the bloody hell should I know?" he shouted. "Ruslan was pissed after she killed Lawrence, and he said so when she first came to us as Forger. He said he wouldn't help her with her plans, and she bloody disappeared him!"

Ernie frowned. "Did she take his deck?"

Rupert shook his head. "I was there. She just . . . pointed some rune tile at him and said he needed a time-out."

"She banished him to another dimension? Huh."

"Akela, too, I think. Usually I can find the Wolf Spider, but she's just . . . gone." Rupert looked haunted. "I took the assignment so the evil old bat wouldn't banish me, too."

Ernie considered—was that how Virginia was handling disobedience from her Dealers? If Ernie had turned down the bank assignment, would Virginia have banished her, too? "What did she want you to do?"

Rupert wouldn't meet her eyes. "Cloak a few people."

Suspicion pulled taut inside her. "In London?"

"And in Munich." He registered the fury on her face. "I had to, all right? I didn't know how all the pieces fit together!"

Ernie didn't, either. "It doesn't matter now. What matters is that Virginia gets stopped."

For the first time in the last few minutes, their gazes locked. "She'll be expecting it," he said.

"Are you actually willing to help?" Ernie wondered whether she was signing her own death warrant. "How do I know this isn't another assignment for you? How do I know you're not a spy who'll run back and tattle as soon as we make a plan?"

"I can help you," he said, shifting his weight from foot to foot. "But you have to come with me."

"This sounds hazardous to my health."

"I won't hurt you." He seemed to be working to keep that habitual sneer off his face. "I swear."

"Where are we going?"

"To get something you want."

"Jeez, Rupert. What's with the cryptic?"

"I'm not telling you a thing until I know if we're allies."

"And I'm not agreeing to be your ally until you prove that you're not leading me into a freaking ambush!"

Rupert jammed his deck in his pocket and raked a hand through his hair, re-spiking his wilting do. "I know where it is, okay? That egg thing."

She went still. "The Sunrise?"

"No idea what it's called, but Lawrence never gave it to her. He hid it after we took it from you and the Kestrel in Marrakech. The idiot wanted to make sure you all wouldn't be able to steal it back. He meant to give it to Virginia after we ambushed you lot in Ireland, but he never had the chance."

Ernie thought back to that night, when they'd laid a trap of their own and their allies had come to their aid in the fight against Virginia and the Dealers who had aligned themselves with her—the Komodo Dragon, the Brahman Bull, and the Hyena. Now one was dead, one was banished, and one was standing right in front of her, telling her that the artifact she and Gabe had fought for was still in play. And come to think of it, Lawrence's final exchange with Virginia had been kinda weird . . .

It's-it's in my—Lawrence had said to his former ladylove as she stood over his crumpled body.

He'd been begging her for help, and she'd told him he was as useless as tits on a bull. And then she'd taken his cards and said, *And that's for failing me twice.*

"Holy crap," Ernie muttered. "She never got hold of it?"

"She was pissed, too, but then it didn't end up mattering. You handed her the weapon she needed to kill the Forger and take his place."

"For the record, I didn't *hand* the Cortalaza to her."

Rupert waved away her comment. "That gold egg thing. Will it take her down?"

Ernie had no idea. They'd never been able to figure out what, exactly, the Sunrise did. But Virginia had wanted it, and others had wanted it before her, so it had to do *something*. For a second, Ernie paused. Doing *something*—like killing four thieves on a crowded Munich street—had resulted in disaster before.

But doing nothing? How could that possibly be better, when Rupert had told her that Virginia was only getting started?

"Yes," Ernie said firmly. "The Sunrise will take her down. If you tell me where it is, then I can just—"

"Oh, you'll need my help to get it. Lawrence was a tricky *bastard*."

"What, is it in a safe or something? Do you have the—" She stopped as Rupert shook his head. "Is it in his haven?"

Rupert nodded, but there was something in his expression that made Ernie hesitate. "If you know where it is," she said, "then why haven't you retrieved it yourself? Why would you need me?"

"Your deck," he said. "I used to hang out with Duncan." His eyes flicked to Ernie's arm, where Legs lay quiet but ready. "When she was his, she was a force to be reckoned with."

Ernie arched one eyebrow. "You're an idiot if you think that's changed."

"I bloody don't, you ninny," he snapped before clapping his hand over his mouth. His nostrils flared as he took a deep breath and then started over. "Look—I know what your deck can do. When Duncan was Diamondback, he devoured the Cardinal deck and the Crested Ibis deck just in the last few decades since I became a Dealer." He caught Ernie's puzzled expression. "He had a thing against birds," he explained. "Virginia never really trusted him."

A thing against birds. Probably because Duncan's brother was none other than the Kestrel. "Okay, so Duncan was a jerk who went after other Dealers. And his deck ate theirs. I knew that already." Although honestly, it was pretty disturbing to think about it in detail, and knowing the specific decks that had been devoured by her diamondback gave her no joy. Legs was tingling fiercely on her arm, but Ernie didn't know whether it was an apology or an expression of pleasure. She was, after all, a predator. "What does this have to do with anything?"

"Your deck is strong. Your cards are strong. It's why you can hold your own against Dealers who have a lot more skill than you do."

Ernie bit back the urge to shout *Screw you!* Deep down, she feared he was right. "Okay, fine. My deck is awesome, and I generally kick ass. So?"

"So you have to be the one who goes after that Sunrise egg thing. I can't."

"Why?" she asked warily. "Where exactly is Lawrence's haven?"

Rupert crossed his arms over his chest. "It's in the Challenger Deep."

CHAPTER EIGHT

"The what-what?" Ernie asked.

Rupert groaned. "The deepest part of the goddamn ocean, you reptilian twit. The Mariana Trench? In the goddamn Pacific, almost seven miles down."

"Seven miles? Whoa." She knew enough to understand that the pressure would be crushing, the darkness complete. "Why did he put his haven there?"

"How many people do you know who could attack a fortress seven fucking miles deep in the middle of the ocean?"

"Seems like overkill."

"Seems like it doesn't bloody matter!"

Ernie couldn't help it; she enjoyed pissing Rupert off. "So your hyena can't swim, I take it?"

Rupert took a few steps toward her, looking like he'd love nothing more than to strangle the life out of her. "If I tried to get down there, my Shield would crumple instantly, before I had a chance to nick the bloody egg."

"Ah." Ernie nodded. "So you'd like to send me in there to fetch it so that you can mug me as soon as I surface. Got it."

"Can we go?" asked Rupert. "She's got spies, you know."

Ernie thought of the guy who looked like Trey, the one she'd seen in Munich. Was that guy a spy? Was it *Trey*? She supposed she'd have to figure that one out later. "We can go, but I want Gabe to—"

Rupert put his hands up and shook his head. "We're doing this now, and we're doing it alone, or else I'm not doing it at all."

"Because that seems totally aboveboard and not worrisome at all."

"You think I want to be outnumbered and ended by the two of you? I saw what you did to Duncan."

That put a warm feeling in Ernie's chest, knowing other Dealers might fear her and Gabe together, but it also didn't help her right now. She supposed she could insist that Gabe come along, except . . . maybe she needed to just handle this. Gabe had his hands full, doing the thing he cared about most—rescuing and protecting the vulnerable. He might not want to be part of yet another scheme to take on Virginia, especially one as harebrained and doubtful as this one. But if she could get the Sunrise and figure out what it did—assuming it did enough to give them something to use against Virginia—then he might feel better.

"Okay," she said. "I'll go. And I'll try. But if you turn on me, Gabe's going to know. And he won't like it."

Rupert pulled out his deck and turned his Transport card face up. "You have your concealments back in place? Very sloppy to let them slip, Diamondback."

Ernie sighed as she let Rupert move closer to her. She wondered whether Tarlae had gotten her message and whether she would respond, but that, too, had to wait. "I put them back up right before you found me."

"Here we go, then. I hope you don't get seasick." His fingers closed around Ernie's wrist, and he yanked her into the void. She stumbled against him and grabbed onto his bony shoulder for balance. They wobbled awkwardly, trying to maintain a stiff distance from each other, until their feet crunched over gray volcanic rocks as the sun rose off to their left over a vast and endless ocean.

Ernie blinked and tried to get her bearings. She must be facing south. "Where are we?"

"Guam," Rupert answered, conjuring a boat with a wave of his cards. "I wasn't about to drop us in the middle of the bloody Pacific."

Ernie eyed the boat he'd pulled out of thin air. It was a large canoe, basically. "You're kidding me, right?"

"Oh, how I wish. I can get you right over the haven, but you have to do the rest."

"God, this seems like a trap."

"Only a total pillock would lay a trap like this—what a bloody waste of time." His hair had begun to curl at the ends and was blowing stiffly in the humid, salty breeze. Ernie redid her own ponytail, pulling it tight, and climbed into the canoe while complaining about how the thing didn't even have a sail. Glaring at her, Rupert swung his leg over the side and climbed in, too, then played the cards to summon the right current to propel the boat into the ocean. They moved swiftly over the deep blue water, which began to swell and dip the farther out they went.

"I don't suppose you have any Dramamine on you?" Ernie asked.

Rupert muttered something under his breath and rolled his eyes.

"How far is it?" She really didn't want to be seasick.

"About three hundred kilometers."

"Dear god," Ernie said with a groan. She did some quick math— almost two hundred miles!

"There was a reason I wanted to get going," he sniped. "I didn't want to dunk us straight into the ocean, and it's not as if there's a handy yacht hovering right over the spot."

Ernie played her Accelerate card, and the boat surged forward. Rupert gave her a curt nod of thanks and turned his face to the horizon. They bumped along in silence for a while, the boat slicing through the increasingly choppy waves while the sun rose like a laser over the ocean. Ernie wanted desperately to use her Shield card to get some shade, but she knew she would need every drop of power she had to create a barrier that could withstand the forces at the bottom of the sea. "Hey—how will I know what I'm looking for down there?"

"Since Lawrence is gone, his concealments have faded. I guess nobody thought to look but me."

Including Virginia, she supposed. But how long until the Forger realized that the treasure she'd been hunting was out in the open once more?

Ernie pulled out her Revelation card and thought about how much she needed to find Lawrence's haven. Only darkness lay beneath the card's omega symbol, but as Ernie squinted, one part of the image seemed a little inkier and denser than the rest. "That's it?" she asked. "His haven?"

"No idea how he set it up without getting himself trapped down there for an eternity, but he was a strange old bloke. More powerful than he got credit for." He gave her the side-eye. "Taken down by a deceitful twat he could have bested with one eye closed on most days."

Ernie wasn't sure whether he was talking about Virginia or herself. "Seems like he had both eyes open and a serious issue with underestimating his enemy, if you ask me."

"I'd be careful down there and not underestimate *him*, if I was you," Rupert said. "But if you add me to your allies, I'll be able to watch you with my Revelation. I might be able to help if you get into trouble."

Ernie wasn't quite sure how that would work, but at this point, did it matter if he could track her for a little while? She drew her Ally card and looked over at him. "Fine. We're allies. For now."

"Sure as hell won't be forever," he said, all surly, and perhaps a bit green.

Ernie didn't feel too good herself and decided she was antsy and queasy enough to launch from there. She drew her Shield card, along with Prolong, Endurance, Strength, Light, Amplify, and Air, as well as Tool. She thought about what she required—an encapsulated space, an oxygen supply, and something to let her grab hold of the Sunrise when she found it. "Wish me luck," she murmured as she examined the Revelation card again. Legs burned on her arm, almost certainly a warning. Her diamondback didn't like this one bit, but the temptation of the Sunrise was too much. She needed it. She needed the hope it provided. It was so much better than surrender.

Ernie closed her eyes and played the cards, crossing them one over the other, then brought the Revelation card close to her face. Usually her cards emanated heat, but this one was emanating frigid air. She clutched her cards tightly and stepped over the side of the boat.

Immediately, she was encased in a clear, thick bubble, and it surrounded her completely before she was submerged in the ocean. She descended rapidly, the hull of the boat becoming a sliver of brown in the light blue above her before disappearing entirely as she sank into the abyss. At first, she felt relaxed, but the longer she sat there in her bubble of darkness, the more stifling and close it became. She played Nourishment and asked Legs to keep the pressure levels stable so that she could stay conscious, breathe, and not be crushed by the ferocious pressure of the depths. She kept as still as possible, meditating silently and trying to keep her thoughts calm and her strength up.

Her deck was strong. Legs was strong. She was strong. She was. Every time a doubtful thought tried to worm its way into her head—how she didn't have the steely will it took to master her deck and wield it as forcefully as the Diamondback Dealers before her—she shot it down, reminding herself that she was the Diamondback Dealer now, so that meant she was definitely strong enough. She'd won Legs's loyalty and defeated Duncan, and yes, Gabe had helped, and so had the blank card that joined them, but Gabe had been right when he said she would have been powerful enough on her own. She was. She definitely was.

She definitely hoped she was.

She pulled up the sleeve of her Spartan jersey and looked at Legs. "Hey. We don't trust Rupert—I know that. But this is still a good idea, right?"

Legs continued to burn her skin but didn't give any other signal. Ernie summoned light as the darkness became complete, and worked on keeping her heart rate low. She would feel better if she could run now. If she could climb a wall or a rope, if she could hurl a javelin or leap over a barrier. If she could move, in other words. But right now, her mind was getting all the exercise. Using the dim glow provided by her Light card, Ernie peered into the Revelation card and willed herself to the haven. The bubble accelerated, and Ernie hoped she was only imagining the strange, constricting pressure pressing in on her lungs and ears and eyes as she sank ever deeper.

Long after she'd lost track of time, her little bubble, no more than four feet wide and high, hit the ocean floor and began to slide along. Ernie shone the light from her card in the direction she was traveling, and a wall of rock appeared. As she approached, her light glancing along the stony crags and curves, she spotted a pile of debris. A shipwreck?

Or Lawrence's collapsed haven?

Ernie willed her contraption closer to the pile, slabs of rock and splintered timber jutting out at odd angles. The light from her card only beat back the darkness a few feet in front of her, with the impenetrable unknown closing in like a tightening noose. There were no fish here, only the occasional floating shrimp, and no plants, only a flat expanse of beige sludge. The closer she got to the wreckage, the more concerned she became. It was the size of a house. How was she supposed to find the artifact? And more importantly, could she find it before the cards she'd played lost their power?

And when her cards did fizzle out, would she be able to play Transport fast enough to get herself out of there? Ernie felt a flash of resentment toward Rupert and then toward herself. She was the one who'd let him talk her into this.

With a rumble and a squeak, her bubble contracted, the walls bowing and pressing in. Ernie yelped and willed herself closer to the wreckage. She played Rend and Shelter, crossing them and sighing with relief as the splintered timbers fell to either side, then groaning as they kicked up a swirl of sludgy murk around her when they hit the ocean floor.

She turned back to her Revelation card, asking it to show her the Sunrise, but it revealed nothing but a brown fog. "Come on, you old weirdo. Where did you hide it?" she whispered. As the bubble scooted right up to the collapsed haven, her diamondback tattoo pulsed with a sick heat, and Ernie looked down at it. "What's up?"

Her only reply was a constant throb that matched her galloping heartbeat. Her bubble shuddered and shrank again. Sweat trickled between Ernie's shoulder blades. It felt like a fist had closed around her heart. Legs appeared to be freaking out, sending searing jolts up her arm, but she didn't pull herself off Ernie's skin. Ernie couldn't blame her.

She had to find the Sunrise *now*.

The Draw card wriggled up from the cards clenched in Ernie's damp palm. She'd intended to conjure a set of metal arms to dig through the rubble to find the precious artifact, but if this worked, it would be much faster, and time was of the essence now. Legs must be warning her that the bubble protecting them from the crushing ocean depths was about to give out. Ernie plucked Draw and concentrated with all her might on the Sunrise.

The top of her bubble dipped inward, brushing the top of Ernie's head. The walls were barely wide enough to accommodate her shoulders now. And all that lay in front of her was dense, silty fog. "Come on," Ernie growled through clenched teeth. The Sunrise might help her stop Virginia. The Sunrise might be the only thing she needed to save the world from the Forger's murderous plans.

Light glinted off something hidden by the swirl of sediment kicked up by the displaced timbers. Ernie pressed her Light card, its beams fading to a dim glow, to the skin of her bubble, only to have it groan and bulge inward against her palm. She cried out when the gold-veined egg floated out of the brown haze, even as her only protection from permanent drowning pressed in on her.

Ernie's head swam with a wave of dizziness. Was her oxygen running out? She hoped the vision just outside the bubble, the Sunrise gliding toward her, wasn't a hallucination. Her tattoo of the diamondback was so painful now that she could barely move her arm, but as the Sunrise pushed itself against the wall of her bubble, Ernie willed herself upward. She glanced in the Revelation card at her destination—the boat, Rupert waiting—and prayed that the walls would hold until she made it.

Wishful thinking. A sudden, deafening pop was the only warning she had. Ernie's fingers spasmed around her cards as the ocean smashed in on her. Agony enclosed her in its merciless vise. Her bones were being pulverized, her cells smashed flat. Pure instinct and determination were all that allowed her hand to shoot out, her fingers to close around the Sunrise. A glowing card ripped itself from her deck. Transport.

Her world went black. She was in the void. Alive. The Sunrise was clenched in her fist.

Gasping, Ernie hit the deck of the canoe like a rag doll, boneless and flailing. Rupert leaned over her. "Did you get it?" he asked.

Ernie sucked in a breath. She looked over to see the Sunrise in her right hand, a small hole in the bottom showing the place the key was supposed to be inserted. Legs still throbbed fiercely on her arm. "Yeah." Everything hurt. Everything. But she'd done it—her shield had lasted long enough, and her plays had been fast enough. She smiled, then let out a weak laugh.

Rupert held out his hand. "Give it to me."

Ernie pushed herself up to sitting, which took every ounce of will and concentration she had left. "I think I'll hold on to it, if you don't mind." She looked around, taking in the ocean around her, the blond

Dealer standing over her . . . and a bloody hand poking up from the other side of the farthest bench seat in the canoe, near the prow. "What the—"

"Was hoping you wouldn't notice him," Rupert said.

Ernie's head whirled around as his voice shed its Cockney accent. She gaped as her companion's face morphed, as his shoulders broadened and his frame grew an extra few inches, as his skin darkened from pasty to olive.

He had become someone very familiar. Ernie swallowed hard. "Trey?"

CHAPTER NINE

He tilted his head. "How do you know my name?"

"You-you're dead," she stammered.

"Obviously not," he said. "Unless that was a threat. Was it a threat?" He sounded amused as he took in her bedraggled appearance.

Ernie blinked at him and turned to lean over her own bench, toward the prow. There, on the soaked floor of the boat, lay Rupert, bleeding from a massive gash to the side of his head.

"He's kind of an annoying guy, isn't he?" Trey asked. "Slow reflexes, too."

She turned back to him and gasped at the pain shooting along her legs and arms. Trey sank onto his own bench and watched her as the canoe rose and fell with the waves. "How—" she began.

He put out his hand, palm up. "Last chance to hand it over all friendly like."

"What are you doing here?" Ernie said, though her words were strained. The pain was unrelenting; her joints were on fire.

Trey looked her over. "Ever hear of the bends? I think you've got a case of 'em."

The bends. She hadn't considered what instantly surfacing from almost seven miles down in the ocean might do to her. As the pain surged, she looked down at her deck, needing her Healing card. Trey's hand shot out, and he grabbed the Sunrise, yanking it from her weakened fingers. "Better handle that before it gets worse," he suggested.

Struggling to breathe, Ernie clumsily snatched for the precious artifact. Confusion over the who-how-why of Trey and what he was doing spiraled inside her, but the pain zapped the questions right off her tongue.

"Thanks for doing the heavy lifting on this," Trey said as he admired the treasure in his palm. "I wasn't sure I could do it myself." He gave her a mischievous smile that had a strange coldness to it, completely foreign to the Trey whom Ernie had once known.

She tried to speak, but only a moan escaped her mouth. Trey stood up and pulled his deck from his pocket. On the backs of his cards lay a raccoon triumphantly holding the world between its paws.

It was really him. Trey. He wasn't dead. He was, however, stealing the Sunrise. Ernie lunged for it, but Trey shoved her backward. Her head slammed into the bench behind her as she scrabbled for her cards. Strike jumped into her hand, and she slashed it through the air. Trey let out a grunt.

When she raised her head, he was gone.

Ernie drew her Healing card and pressed it to her chest as the terrible agony consumed her. For several minutes, it was all she could do to breathe, but each inhalation became a little easier as the sun beat down on her from high in the sky and the ocean tossed the boat up and down.

And then the canoe abruptly disappeared, and she splashed into the water. She surfaced quickly, coughing and spluttering. Her cards were still in her hand, and Legs had calmed down a little. Too late, Ernie realized that her diamondback had probably been trying to warn her about what was happening in the canoe while Ernie had been on the ocean floor, trying to get to the treasure.

Treading water, Ernie spun in place and realized that Rupert was gone. Dread shot through her, and she plunged underwater to see him floating a few feet below the surface, eyes closed, arms and legs akimbo.

In a few strokes, she made it to him, and she pulled his limp body against her as she edged her Transport card up with her thumb. A moment later, she'd gotten them back to her apartment, and she dumped the dripping Hyena Dealer onto her couch. His body convulsed, and he vomited up a splash of ocean water all over her throw pillows.

"Ugh," she said, sinking down onto a kitchen chair.

Hacking, Rupert pushed himself up to look at her. "Ambush," he said between noisy breaths. "He—"

"I know." She frowned. "Actually, I don't. What the hell just happened?"

"Did you get the Sunrise?" he asked.

"Yeah, but then he took it."

Rupert cursed. "I tried to warn you." He shoved his hand into his pocket and yanked out his deck. Fanning his cards, he scanned their faces. "Bloody hell. That bastard stole four of my cards!"

"You're lucky he didn't take your entire deck."

"He just appeared in the boat," Rupert said as he pressed his Healing card to his head. The wound on his temple began to knit itself together instantly. "Slammed me in the head with a pipe."

"He disguised himself as you."

Rupert arched an eyebrow. "Why would he need to do that at all? Weren't you guys mates?"

"We were. But he's supposed to be *dead*."

"Crazy old bird must have resurrected him."

"She can do that?"

Rupert frowned. "Only if he never died in the first place, I'd imagine."

Ernie thought back to the last time she'd seen Trey—he'd shoved her out of the way as Virginia had tried to strand her in the splinter dimension yet again. He'd gotten trapped there instead, with only half his deck. "We knew he might survive, at least for a while," she said slowly. "But he didn't know me just now. He acted like a stranger."

"A stranger who happened to know exactly where we were and what we were doing." Rupert ran a hand through his hair. "A stranger who has our bloody relic!"

Ernie shuffled her cards, which were already dry. "Which cards did he take from you?"

"Why would I tell you?" he grumbled. "You'd probably use it against me."

"Dude. I thought we were allies."

"Doesn't mean I trust you."

"Clearly you've had sucky allies."

He looked away. "Ruslan was all right, the bloody fool."

Ruslan had been as mean as they come and as dumb as a post, but Ernie thought it wise not to make those observations out loud. "Trey only took four cards from you," she said. "So he didn't want to kill you. He wanted to be more powerful, and maybe in specific ways. So which cards did he take?"

Rupert heaved an exasperated sigh. "Revelation, Wisdom—"

"My guess is that one didn't get much use anyway."

Rupert gave her the dagger eyes. "He also took Strike and Dreams."

Her throat tightened. "I have to find him."

"Now he'll bloody use that damn egg, I'll wager," Rupert said. "And he's *not* on our side."

Trey couldn't use the Sunrise even if he wanted to—that much Ernie knew. He didn't have the key, though she wondered whether he'd shown up in Munich in an effort to find out whether she had it with her. She didn't—it was hidden in her haven in the dream realm, and that was why it didn't particularly please her to hear that Trey had stolen the Dreams card from Rupert. "I have no idea whose side he's on. But I have a few ideas." She rose from her chair. "I'll contact you once I know what's going on."

Rupert scowled. "Wait a minute—" he began.

Ernie played Ally, Transport, and Nourishment, and sent Rupert to the London pub where she and Gabe had found Alvarez. It hadn't felt right to leave him sitting in her living room, and she needed to concentrate.

Was Trey working for Virginia, doing her bidding?

Virginia and Trey had hated each other. Like, *hated*. She'd been almost gleeful as she'd absorbed a stack of his cards into her deck. While Tarlae had screamed and raged, Virginia had crowed in triumph as she vanquished the Raccoon Dealer.

Tarlae. Did she know Trey was alive?

The questions flew around her mind like debris in a tornado. She could grasp only a few shreds of thought: she had to get the Sunrise back, and she had to make sure the key was safe. She peered into her Revelation card and pictured the Sunrise. Where had Trey taken it?

Nothing in the card except fog. "Dammit," she whispered.

"Hard day?"

Ernie whirled around so fast that she lost her balance and stumbled into the kitchen table. The Forger was sitting on her living room couch. A trickle of frigid terror slid down Ernie's back. For a moment, she stood frozen like a rabbit in the sights of a hawk. "Yeah," she said breathlessly. "You could say that."

Virginia was watching her with a sly, searching expression. "Anything you'd like to tell me, little snakey?"

Legs burned on Ernie's arm, reminding her that even though she had no hope of single-handedly taking down a Forger, she was anything but helpless prey. "Honestly? You're kind of a dick."

Virginia smirked. "I knew you'd stop the robbery, of course. But killing the thieves?" She guffawed. "You really think you're better than me?"

Ernie clutched the table's edge, both to hold herself up and to keep herself from reaching for her cards. "You used us."

"That's my *job*, dear. And I must say, I did it well. You were the perfect person for the task in Munich. You have just the right level of righteous arrogance that I needed, and all I had to do was send you off to save the day." Her eyes flashed with triumph. "And you most certainly did. Would you like to know, Ernestine? Do you want to understand your part in all of this?"

Ernie's stomach turned. "No," she whispered.

"Oh, don't be a chicken." Virginia winked. "One of those thieves was having a crisis of conscience. If he hadn't been caught, he would have turned his buddies in. He would have stopped the IGA bombing in Munich. And where would the fun be in that? It had the highest body count of any of the attacks so far!"

So far . . . Rage made Ernie tremble, melting her fear. "This is your idea of fun?" Her voice was shaking.

Virginia stood up. "You're hiding something from me, Diamondback. I sensed it just now. It's why I came to see you." She eyed Ernie. "Where have you been?"

Ernie forced herself to stay very still. She wasn't sure of the Forger's power, how much she knew or how she knew it, but clearly Virginia wasn't as all-knowing as she wanted to be. Ernie's mind was a cascade of hastily formed and discarded lies, all meant to keep Virginia in the dark. Ernie knew she looked like a bedraggled mess, her hair and clothes stiff with drying seawater, and she decided to go with that. "I was trying to rescue people from the bombed cruise ship."

Virginia grinned. "I thought that particular attack had a lot of flair." Her smile dropped away. "I don't believe for a moment that you've just been out there playing hero. I sensed something else from you."

"Probably how much I hate you."

"Well, bless your little heart." Virginia rolled her eyes. "If you think I care how you *feel* about me, then you haven't got the good sense God gave a goose." She rose slowly, her gauzy white dress floating around her on a nonexistent breeze. "What I care about is power, Ernestine. Having it. Wielding it. Keeping it. And if I wanted to, I could rip that snake right off your arm, little girl. You make it very tempting."

The fear was back, but Ernie stomped it down. "Does that mean you think I'm a threat, boss?"

Virginia snorted. "You're adorable." But her eyes darted away.

"You do. You came here from on high because you're afraid."

The Forger's eyes bled from gray to black. "Watch yourself."

"If you take my deck, the others will see you as weak," Ernie said, praying she sounded more certain than she felt. "They'll *know* I was a threat." She held up her arms. "Little old me. Haven't even been a Dealer for a year."

Virginia's spindly fingers clenched into fists. "Defy me, and I'll crush you."

"All I was doing was sitting here in my living room! Do I look particularly defiant to you?"

"You're hiding something. You're planning something."

"Paranoid much?" snapped Ernie. "Look—you tricked me into doing something that I'll have to live with for the rest of my existence. And okay, I thought I could make a difference. I thought I knew the right move. I thought I was saving lives, and instead I helped cause a freaking catastrophe." Her voice broke, and it wasn't an act. "You taught me how foolish I was." Ernie dropped into a chair like a marionette whose strings had been cut. "Am I mad? Yeah. Do I wish I could stop you?" She chuckled. "Of course. But do I think I'm powerful enough to take you on?" Their eyes met, and relief filled Ernie's chest as she saw that Virginia's were already fading back to gray. "No," she said quietly. And honestly. "I don't."

Virginia's eyes narrowed. "I'll have another assignment for you soon."

Ernie's stomach turned. "I'm sure you will."

"Refuse it, and I'll—"

"Banish me to a splinter dimension? Been there. Done that."

"I was going to say I'll take your deck. You're too much trouble to banish."

Ernie put her hands up. "Weren't you the one who told me threats were boring? You won, Virginia. You're the Forger. You've got the tools and the power. The only reason I can think for you to be here in my living room is that you're scared."

Virginia's face was unreadable, and Ernie's heart pounded as they stared at each other. The Forger shifted her weight from foot to foot, and it looked for all the world as if she was anxious. As if she had somewhere she knew she needed to be. It gave Ernie hope. Finally, after what felt like a solid minute at least, the Forger's face crinkled with a tight smile. "Whatever you're hiding, whatever you're scheming, it won't stop me. Nothing can."

"And yet you're still here playing bully, when all I want to do is take a shower, drink a beer, and watch a Tar Heels game."

"You'll hear from me soon," Virginia growled. Then she vanished.

Ernie lowered her head into her hands as her entire body shook and her skin rippled with goose bumps. The sudden rush of adrenaline made her eyes water and her bones ache. She'd held it together, though. She'd fooled the Forger.

Maybe.

After a few plays to strengthen her concealments, followed by a lightning-quick shower and a change into fresh clothes, Ernie drew Dreams and Haven from her deck. Virginia had given something away—she knew a lot, but she didn't know everything. And she wasn't as certain of her power as she wanted everyone to believe. That made her more dangerous, but it also gave Ernie hope. Maybe there really was a way to stop her—and maybe the Sunrise was it. She needed to go after Trey, but seeing as he'd stolen Rupert's Dreams card, she needed to secure the key first. She sank onto her bed, pushing away the temptation to summon Gabe, to invite him to lie with her there, to pretend like the world wasn't falling apart for a few minutes.

But Gabe was out there, trying to hold everything together. Remembering how he'd basically helped her cheat in the Spartan race, she wondered whether this was better anyway. She'd always had someone to help her. Gabe. Minh. Kot. Her deck was strong, and in traveling to the deepest part of the ocean, she'd just done something major with it. She'd also stood her ground against a being that could end her existence. But she still had something to prove. And besides, even though Virginia had seemed like she had her hands full, Ernie wasn't eager to get anyone else involved, in case the new Forger was paying the slightest bit of attention.

She crossed Dreams and Haven and let herself fall into the realm of the mind, appearing in the forest clearing and breathing in the fresh, fragrant air of spring blooms and new growth. The tent with the broken zipper looked undisturbed, and Ernie gingerly opened the flap and climbed inside. The lockbox she'd created as a case to conceal both her father's writings and the key to the Sunrise sat next to her sleeping bag and a grease-spotted paper towel wrapped around a crispy, still-steaming Hot Pocket. Next to it sat a cold bottle of Yoo-hoo.

Ernie smiled and shook up the bottle, then downed the chocolaty goodness and took a careful bite of the Hot Pocket. It burned the roof of her mouth anyway, but she barely cared as her body awakened to the realization that she was freaking ravenous. A minute later she had blisters in her mouth but a slightly happier belly and, probably as a result, a slightly more optimistic state of mind.

She opened the lockbox and sighed with relief as she pulled out the jagged black key the length of her pinkie. Cold to the touch despite the muggy air, the key almost looked like one of the runes Ernie had seen on the tiles, with pointy, triangular teeth. It seemed too large to fit in the hole she'd seen in the Sunrise, and for a moment, she wondered whether the man who'd given it to her—Belkacem, the Moroccan whose family had hidden the artifact for over a century—had handed her the wrong key. She really hoped not, seeing as it had been his final act before dying.

Her hand closed over the key, and it pulsed with cold, as if signaling that it was special. Powerful. Enough to help her stop Virginia from using the world as her personal sandbox—as long as Ernie was able to get the Sunrise back from Trey.

The snap of a twig outside told Ernie she wasn't alone. Virginia? Or someone else? With a smooth flip of her Case card, Ernie created a necklace chain and fastened the key around her neck, where it lay cold and sharp on her breastbone. "Hello?" she called out, receiving nothing but silence in return, which made her think it probably wasn't the mouthy old Forger. And in the dream realm, it could be anyone or anything—and it wouldn't be the first time Ernie's mind had conjured something just to screw with her. Most recently, it had been Gabe, who had singed her with his touch and promised her more pain before melting like ice cream on a hot summer sidewalk. Before that, her brain had signaled her with a tank that blew her shelter to bits.

She palmed her deck and figured she should be ready for any kind of weirdness, but that didn't stop her from gasping when she lifted the flap of her tent and saw Tarlae standing in the clearing.

The Dealer of the Coconut Octopus deck had her cards drawn and was watching Ernie with heavy-lidded eyes. Her deep-brown skin had lost its lustrous look, as had her thick ebony hair. Ernie sighed. Was her brain simply trying to remind her not to forget about Tarlae? She'd sent out a signal and immediately gotten distracted by Rupert and her pursuit of the Sunrise—and her little one-on-one with Virginia.

"Hey," Ernie said as she climbed out of the tent. Her cards were at the ready; just because this was a figment of her imagination didn't mean it was harmless. "How are you?"

"How do you think?" spat Tarlae.

Ernie took in the way Tarlae's thumbs stroked her fanned cards, tracing their symbols. It didn't escape her that the Strike and Death cards were on top. "That was a stupid question. Sorry. I don't suppose Virginia gave you an assignment?"

"None of your business." Tarlae's gaze streaked around the clearing as if she expected an ambush. Then her dark eyes settled on the key around Ernie's neck. "You summoned me. Why?"

"I was worried about you." Ernie tucked the key into her shirt.

"Liar." Tarlae began to pace back and forth. "You want to use me again. You want an ally."

"Of course I want an ally! We're in the fight of our lives here. Surely you can see that."

Tarlae shook her head, her messy hair falling over her face. The long maxi dress she was wearing was torn along its hem, and it dragged through the rotting leaves that covered the forest floor. Tarlae's muddy bare feet peeked out with every stride. "You are the reason he's gone," she muttered.

Ernie felt a pang. She hoped this sad, disheveled Tarlae was merely a product of Ernie's brain, a message from her subconscious. "I never meant for that to happen," Ernie said. "But remember that it was Virginia who pushed him into that splinter dimension. She's the one who stole his cards."

"You're the one who started the fight with her in the first place," Tarlae shouted, her cards giving off an eerie glow, the octopus tattoo on her forearm undulating and glimmering. "You never cared about the casualties."

Tarlae had never wanted to fight in their alliance—she'd done it only because Trey had been loyal to Gabe, in part because he'd once saved Tarlae's life. "Why are you here now?" asked Ernie. "Did you come to tell me something? To warn me?"

Tarlae whirled so fast that Ernie's fingers could only tighten over her deck before she was hit with a strike that sent her flying backward. She landed on her tent, which collapsed with a snap of its frame and a rip of canvas. Ernie rolled out of the way in time to avoid a ball of fire that sent the tent up in flames with a sudden whoosh and a wave of heat. Ernie got to her feet, stunned and squinting through the smoke. "That was totally rude!"

Tarlae, hair wild and eyes wilder, stalked forward. Ernie instinctively threw up a shield to block the next strike—a curved dagger that was devastatingly similar to the Cortalaza, which Virginia had used to kill Andy. It bounced off the barrier Ernie had conjured, which disappeared quickly. She supposed she should be happy her Shield card had worked at all, given the amount of energy and power she'd drawn from it in order to survive the Challenger Deep, but right now she needed it nearly as much. Tarlae sliced a card through the air, and lacerating pain cut across Ernie's shoulder and chest. The chain that held the key to the Sunrise snapped, sending the key to the ground. Ernie cursed and dove for it in time to dodge yet another strike. She scooped the key up in a handful of wet leaves and ran for cover behind the nearest tree.

Tarlae was seeming less and less like a figment of Ernie's imagination. Ernie used her Strike card, sending a twelve-pound weighted ball flying across the clearing, where it struck Tarlae square in the belly and sent her staggering. "Is that really you?" Ernie called out.

"You are an *idiot*," snarled Tarlae.

"It seems like it might actually be you."

A net dropped from above and wrapped around Ernie's body, but she managed to pull her Escape card and ended up across the clearing again, behind the smoke screen from the still-flaming tent. "I don't actually want to fight you," Ernie hollered.

"No, you want to co-opt me in another useless and deadly quest. I won't let you hurt everyone else the way you hurt me."

This time, the ropes came up from the forest floor, coiling around Ernie's legs, then her arms. The bonds dragged her to the ground as she struggled to keep her grip on her cards, but one of the braided strands coiled up her wrist and knocked them from her hand. They scattered across the clearing, blown by an ill-timed breeze, while the ropes around Ernie wrapped around her neck and squeezed.

With spots floating in her vision, Ernie flung out her arm. She'd been trying to reach her cards, but instead, Legs came crawling off her skin, her rattle silent. She slithered toward Tarlae as the vengeful Dealer strode around the tent to where Ernie lay fighting the ropes holding her to the ground.

The rope around her neck had pulled taut, leaving Ernie struggling for breath. The ropes around her arms were now so tight that her hands were going numb, and her grip on the Sunrise key was loosening. Her cards were close, but not close enough to reach, and Ernie couldn't summon her concentration as her consciousness faded. Legs had gone off somewhere, but she didn't seem to be attacking Tarlae, who approached Ernie warily, her expression tight. "I'll kill you first, then Gabe," she said. She was breathing heavily, and tears shone in her eyes.

Ernie wanted to speak, but she couldn't. A glimmer of white behind Tarlae caught her attention. Legs had coiled herself around the blank card that connected Ernie's deck to Gabe's. She hoped that meant he'd feel what was happening here. She hoped that meant he'd come. But right now, she was on her own, so she made her best play.

"Trey," she croaked.

"What?" snapped Tarlae as she leaned down to pick up Ernie's scattered cards. If Tarlae allowed her deck to absorb those cards, both Ernie and Legs were dead.

"*Trey,*" rasped Ernie. Her eyes met Tarlae's. "He's alive."

Tarlae's eyes flew wide, and then everything went black.

CHAPTER TEN

Ernie flickered back into consciousness slowly, and her new reality clicked into place one piece at a time. She couldn't move her arms or legs, but her limbs throbbed with pain. She was tied to a chair, with ropes wound thickly around her chest, holding her upright. She slowly raised her head, inhaling warm, briny air. She appeared to be in some kind of hut, sea-weathered gray wood and a view of a dark-blue sea just outside the window. A messy bed, crumpled sheets and dented pillows, lay off to her right. To her left was a hallway.

"Say what you said before," Tarlae muttered from behind her.

Ernie flinched at the sound, wishing she felt the familiar warmth of her cards in her pocket. "You're going to have to be more specific." She squirmed and looked down at herself, realizing with dread that her left forearm was bare. Where the hell had Legs gone?

"Looking for these?" Tarlae trudged between Ernie and the bed and plopped down in a chair, one of two at the small table near the window. She set Ernie's deck in a neat stack on the tabletop. "I could end you right now."

"Why haven't you, then?"

Their eyes met. "You know why," said Tarlae. "Say what you said."

"About Trey, you mean."

Tarlae's jaw clenched.

Ernie regarded her cautiously. She didn't know exactly where she was, but she was guessing it was Tarlae's haven, somewhere on a beach. It could have been Barbados or Fiji for all she knew. Not that it mattered at the moment. What mattered was Tarlae's state of mind, which seemed pretty shaky. "He might be alive," Ernie said, thinking on every word.

"I would know if he was alive," Tarlae said with a dismissive flick of her wrist. But her eyes gave away something else. Doubt. Need. Grief. And hope.

"Have you had any indication that he might be around?" Ernie asked.

"*Around?*" Tarlae scoffed. "You do remember where she left him? You remember how she destroyed the rune tile that was the only way to get to him? You remember all that, or was it too unimportant to you?"

Ernie groaned, both in frustration and discomfort. The ropes were *really* tight. "I saw him, Tarlae. In Munich. And he showed up in Guam, too."

Tarlae held up her deck, with the Revelation card on top. "If you were telling the truth, I'd be able to see him."

"Not if he's cloaked."

"Trey would never conceal himself from me," she said, her voice breaking. "Unless he was off getting me a surprise." Her beautiful, strained face crumpled. "He did that often."

Ernie swallowed the lump in her throat. "Because he loved you. But there's something different about him now."

Tarlae scowled down at her Revelation card as if she expected her lover to appear. "It wasn't him," she muttered. "You're lying to me."

"I'm not," Ernie said. "I mean, sure, I guess it might have been his identical twin, who happens to answer to the same name—"

"Trey didn't have a twin."

"I was being facetious."

The Coconut Octopus Dealer pinched one of her cards between her fingertips, and the ropes around Ernie's chest constricted. "I do *not* like facetiousness." Tarlae's voice was flat. Her face was impassive as she watched Ernie's eyes bulge. "You say it was him. Tell me what he wanted. Because he wasn't interested in *you*."

She almost sounded jealous, which was laughable considering how deeply Trey had loved her, but because she looked so fragile, Ernie decided it was best to be cautious. "No, of course he's not interested in me," she said with a wheeze.

Tarlae's eyes narrowed, and she held up her own deck and dealt a card, laying it face up on the table, next to Ernie's deck. "Tell me what he wanted, then."

Ernie eyed the card. "Honestly, I'm not sure."

A second card leapt into Tarlae's palm, the one she'd pinched between her fingertips before. She waved it at Ernie. The ropes tightened yet again. "You're lying."

That upturned card on the table must be Discern, dammit. "He stole something from me."

Tarlae slid her hand inside the neckline of her dress and came up holding the Sunrise key. "Does it have something to do with this?"

Double damn. She'd hoped the key had remained in the dream realm. "Yep."

"Explain."

"We used to be friends."

"We were never friends." Tarlae looked away. "I don't even like you."

"I think you do, just a little."

Another flick of that damn card, and the ropes pulled a bit tighter. "Tell me what this opens."

"It's an artifact," Ernie mouthed, a desperate idea forming in her head.

"What?" Tarlae leaned forward, frowning.

Ernie repeated the words silently, speaking the truth without sound. Tarlae would know she wasn't lying, but she would also have no idea what Ernie had said. Ernie mouthed the words again. Tarlae growled with frustration and drew her hand back, causing the ropes to loosen a smidge, but not enough. Ernie wheezed and shook her head.

The ropes loosened some more. She wriggled back and forth, taking big gulps of air as if she'd been underwater for days. She bowed her head, her shoulders heaving. "Artifact," she whispered.

"Speak up," Tarlae said irritably, rising from her chair and leaning forward. It was exactly what Ernie had needed her to do. She launched herself up from the chair, the ropes loose enough to allow her to tear one arm from the bonds. She barreled into Tarlae, head-butting her and knocking the woman's cards out of her hand. The Sunrise key hit the floorboards with a crystalline plink as Tarlae staggered back, and Ernie charged, snatching her cards off the tabletop and crushing Tarlae against the cottage door, which opened and sent both women spilling out onto the porch. While Tarlae cursed and kicked Ernie off, Ernie groped for the card she wanted. Even with Legs absent from her arm, the cards responded, and Tool pulled itself from the rest. Frantically, Ernie thought of what she needed, and the card morphed into a pair of gardening shears, which she used to snip a thick section of rope, causing the rest of the coils to go slack. She stumbled off the porch and landed in the sand in front of the cottage, untangling herself from the bonds while keeping one eye on the spitting-mad Coconut Octopus Dealer.

As Tarlae gathered her own cards, Ernie played Shield to protect herself. "I don't want to duel, lady," Ernie said. "You need to understand that something's wrong with Trey."

Tarlae stood in the doorway to the cottage. "Tell me what it is, or else I'll kill you."

"Nothing's wrong with Trey," said a male voice. Trey had appeared a few yards away, standing next to a cluster of palm trees.

Tarlae's skin went ashen. "Raccoon," she whispered.

"Yup," he said. "And you are?"

Tarlae gaped at him. "Trey. It's me."

He tilted his head, his brow furrowing. "Not ringing a bell. But I think you have something I need."

Crap. The Sunrise key. If he had that, he could get the Sunrise to work, and who knew what he'd do with it? Hell, how did he even know about it? "Tarlae," Ernie said. "This is what I was trying to tell you."

Tarlae had eyes only for Trey, though. It was as if Ernie hadn't said a word. "How are you alive?" Tarlae asked him, her voice trembling. She took a few tentative steps onto the porch, eyeing her lover hungrily.

Shedding the final stretches of braided rope, Ernie secured her footing in the sand and watched the two Dealers as they slowly moved toward each other.

"Do we know each other?" Trey asked her.

"Better than any two people have a right to, you damn Raccoon," she replied. Tears welled in her eyes.

"Huh," said Trey. "I'm really just here on an errand."

Ernie played Draw and Tool behind her back and was rewarded quickly as the little black key came zooming out of the cottage and landed neatly in her palm. Trey cursed and drew his cards, but as Tarlae came forward, he took a step back and swung a card toward her, hitting her with a blast of air that threw her against the cottage.

"Tarlae, if we capture him, we can—" Ernie began, only to be tackled by Trey in the next instant. He was lean but strong as hell, and as he crushed her to the ground, she realized he'd probably played his Strength card to make sure he could take her out. His hand closed around her wrist as he groped for the key. She played her own Strength card and bucked him off, only to have him broadside her yet again. The key flew from her hand and landed on the porch.

Ernie charged at the Raccoon Dealer, playing Draw and Accelerate, willing the key toward her. To her surprise, the Sunrise itself came zooming out of one of Trey's pockets and flew toward her, but hit an invisible wall midair and plopped to the ground. Trey dove for it but was thrown backward—but not by a strike from Ernie.

It had come from Tarlae. She stalked forward, her cards fanned. Ernie scrambled out of the way as the Coconut Octopus Dealer and the Raccoon Dealer faced off, with the Sunrise key on the porch and the Sunrise itself half-buried in the sand at Trey's feet. He struck at Tarlae first, sending a wave of smoky fog toward her, leaving her coughing and doubled over, but then Rika, the spirit of Tarlae's deck, came sliding off her mistress's arm, promptly grew to the size of a small car, and wrapped one of her tentacles around Trey's ankle. She yanked him off his feet as he shouted with alarm and clawed at his cards.

Sensing her chance, Ernie dodged a flopping, heavy tentacle and made for the Sunrise. Her fingers closed around its smooth, gold-veined surface. She pulled it from the sand, but then her foot was jerked out from under her by the octopus. With that choking fog Trey had conjured drifting around them—tear gas, Ernie realized as her eyes and throat began to burn—Tarlae and Trey continued their close-quarters war, each making the other disappear only to have the victim reappear after just a few seconds, madder than before.

It seemed personal—for Tarlae, at least. Coughing, with tears streaming from her eyes, Ernie scanned the porch, which was now splintered on one side, looking for the key to the Sunrise. She played Draw again, trying to bring it toward her, but got nothing.

Brimming with frustration, Ernie took advantage of the fact that the other two Dealers seemed to have forgotten she existed. She played Land, Shelter, Ally, and Transport in Tarlae's direction, then played Sea and Enemy in Trey's. Both Dealers disappeared—Tarlae to a hotel Ernie had once stayed at in Kiev, and Trey to the spot where he'd dumped her and Rupert into the Pacific. Ernie leapt onto the porch, scanning every inch of it for the key to the Sunrise. It had been right there.

Trey stumbled out of thin air and onto the porch, not three feet from Ernie, and landed a solid kick to her side, sending her sprawling. He played a card, and the Sunrise attempted to slide out of Ernie's pocket and fly toward him, but she dove on top of it.

"I'll kill you if I have to," Trey said. "I promised her I'd get it for her."

Her. Ernie could think of only one person that could be. *Virginia.*

Trey conjured a sword. Ernie cursed and jerked to her feet, barely dodging his first swipe. She had to get out of there, but her energy was fading and her Shield card was weakened from so much use that day. She tried to play Strike, but Trey blocked it, then charged her, with the sword leading the way.

Ernie played Escape, picturing the mesa in Utah where she and the allied Dealers had faced off against Andy, the former Forger. She knew Trey had been able to find her before, so it would have been lousy to run to Gabe or to her apartment in Asheville, only to have Trey suddenly show up.

Hunted and panting, Ernie pulled her Conceal card as Trey appeared on the mesa with her. Before Ernie could play the card, Trey hit her with a gush of seawater that knocked her off her feet and carried her toward the edge of the table rock as she desperately tried to keep her grip on her cards and the Sunrise.

Glancing behind her at a sheer drop of hundreds of feet to the rocky ground, Ernie shoved all her cards except two in her pocket and put her hands up. Trey extended one hand, aiming a few cards at her, and held the other upturned, fingers grasping. "Give it," he said in a flat voice.

Ernie took a deep breath. Then she threw herself backward and played the cards she'd held on to—Conceal and Transport. As the ground rushed up to meet her, she flew into the void at terminal velocity, thinking hard about the one place she wanted to be right then. The darkness folded around her like a suffocating blanket—oppressive, but a hell of a lot better than being smashed to bits on the red slickrock of Utah.

Dizzy but whole, she appeared in the small living room of Gabe's seaside cottage in the north of Ireland, with the wind rattling the windowpanes and the pale curve of the gray beach visible beyond the glass in the moonlight. Arms closed around her from behind, and a familiar smell filled her nose. Whiskey and salt. Gabe. As she relaxed into his arms, he whispered, "I've got you."

CHAPTER ELEVEN

For a moment, Ernie let the solid, reassuring realness of Gabe sink into her consciousness. He bowed his head and kissed her shoulder, and she leaned in to feel the scrape of his stubble against her cheek. His clothes carried the scent of smoke and sweat, and the hair at his temples was damp with exertion. "I knew you were in trouble," he murmured.

"More than I thought possible." Ernie's forearm tingled and burned, and she glanced down at her wrist in time to see Legs's rattle materialize there, peeking out from under the edge of her sleeve. "Did Legs come to you?"

"I was in the midst of a tricky rescue when she came to me, maybe an hour ago. She brought me a present." He pulled the blank card from his pocket. "I could tell you were alive, and as soon as I could, I followed the thread of you."

"The . . . what?"

His arms tightened around her. "It was this way when you were trapped in the splinter dimension. The card doesn't just tell me whether you're alive in that moment. It also tells me a bit about your intentions, and in this case, I felt you coming here. I got here a few seconds ago. Didn't even have time to light a fire." He slipped two more cards from his pocket and waved them at the woodstove in the corner. Flames burst from the logs and kindling inside the stove's chamber, glowing merrily.

"I have so much to tell you," she said as exhaustion threatened to pull her to the floor.

Gabe guided her to a squashy chair, pressed a tumbler half-full of whiskey into her hand, and sat down across from her.

She pulled the Sunrise from her pocket and cradled it in her palm. The golden veins that ran across its surface reflected the firelight. Gabe's blue eyes went round. "I thought Virginia—"

"Lawrence never gave it to her," Ernie explained. "He stowed it in his haven, and Rupert came to me, wanting me to fetch it." She told him the story of where the precious artifact, created by Phoebe, the Forger before Andy, had been hidden.

Gabe listened in apparent awe as Ernie described her trip to the deepest spot in the ocean. "Not many Dealers could manage that, I'll wager," he said. "Please tell me Rupert didn't try to pull a double cross when you made it back up to the surface."

"He didn't. Trey did."

Gabe sat back as if Ernie had shoved him in the chest. "He's alive."

"I guess. But something is *really* wrong with him." She told the rest of her story, starting with Virginia's surprise appearance in Ernie's living room. "She knew I was hiding something. She just didn't know what."

"Fair play, if you got out of that with body and soul still together." He seemed shaken to hear that she'd had such a close call.

"I convinced her that she'd look weak if she got rid of me." Ernie slumped in her seat. "She's going to have more assignments for us soon, though. She's not done."

Gabe glowered. "If that hag thinks for one moment that I'll go along—"

"She banishes people who don't, Gabe. And she threatened to take my deck."

"Then we'll have to stop her before she has a chance."

It was heartening to hear him confirm that he was still in the fight after all the horror they'd experienced, and knowing that gave her the energy to relate the whole back-and-forth with the Sunrise, the key, and Trey and Tarlae.

Gabe looked like he could scarcely believe what he was hearing. "So he doesn't seem to remember any of us, not even the woman he loved more than life itself." His fists clenched. "Virginia did this."

"I'm thinking you're right." Ernie looked down at the Sunrise in her hand. "He said he'd promised to get this for her."

"Like when she gave me my Wild card back," Gabe said. "Soon as she became Forger, she probably went to the splinter dimension and saved him."

"But didn't Andy say he'd given Trey's deck to another Dealer?"

"Maybe. It would have been easy for Virginia to return it to Trey, though."

"Wouldn't Trey be dead at that point?" Ernie asked. "Alvarez was dying fast when Virginia stole all but a few of his cards. He had minutes to live, not hours. And when I separated Lawrence from the Brahman Bull using the Cortalaza blade, he died within a few seconds."

"But that was without Forger intervention," Gabe said. "Remember that we really don't have a handle on what all the Forger is capable of."

"Something which she's been only too happy to remind us of in the last few days." Ernie took a large swig from her tumbler and savored the burn, the smoky taste, the hint of sweetness. "She obviously doesn't know everything, but she has a sense of the future." And perhaps that was why she'd appeared to Ernie earlier—she'd sensed that Ernie was up to something. "She knows enough to be able to mold events into the shape she wants."

"Only if she's got a group of willing Dealers to do her bidding." Gabe shook his head, looking disgusted. "We played right into her hands. A hundred thousand dead, and that's just the official count so far." He covered his face with his hands, all hunched over with his elbows on his knees. "My soul is soaked in that blood, Ernie."

Ernie set down her glass and dropped to her knees in front of him. She pulled one hand away from his face. "She did use us, Gabe. And that means we have a responsibility to stop her."

Gabe wouldn't meet her eyes. "That's what I said to Minh and Alvarez, but they're done."

"Done? How is that even—"

"People die, Minh says. And he's right. Every day, thousands and thousands reach the end of it. Snuffed out. Today is more than usual, but . . ."

"Minh is trying to keep himself from feeling too much," Ernie guessed.

"He doesn't want to fight Virginia, love. Alvarez doesn't, either. He wants to lie low and hope to God she forgets he exists. Both of them headed off after a few hours in Herestford. Like it was too bloody depressing for them to stay and deal with the catastrophe we caused."

"You probably thought I was doing the same, didn't you?"

He tucked a stray lock of Ernie's hair behind her ear. "I know you better than that, darlin'."

"We have to find Tarlae," Ernie said. "I'm almost sure she's got the key to the Sunrise. If we can convince her to give it to us, we can figure out how to use this against Virginia."

"Neither of us have been able to track Tarlae, not since Trey died." Gabe took the Sunrise from Ernie and examined it. "Why was she after the key?"

"She wasn't," Ernie admitted. "I summoned her. And I think she wanted to punish me. She's not . . ." Ernie sighed. "I don't think she'll ever forgive me for the fact that she lost Trey because of me."

"It has to be worse now that he's back and not remembering her, though. Perhaps she'll align with us just to stop him."

"Or she'll help him, because she still loves him," Ernie said. "For a minute outside her haven, I was afraid she was going to do exactly that. Then Trey pissed her off, and she fought him like she meant it."

Gabe was frowning. "Never in my wildest dreams would I have imagined they'd be enemies."

"Dreams," Ernie murmured. "Hey—you know how we've been unable to really find Tarlae, no matter how hard we tried? What if she's been escaping into the dream realm?"

"Could be. If a Dealer's spirit and deck are there, her body would probably be undetectable with the cards."

"But if we were both in the dream realm?"

Gabe rubbed his jaw with the back of his knuckles. "I would think it would be like it is in the waking world. Possible, if you know your way around the cards."

"And maybe easier, if one Dealer doesn't think to conceal herself, because she thought she was alone," Ernie said, rolling her eyes. "She appeared to me in the dream realm, Gabe. She found me there because I assumed almost no one could, not without a lot of effort."

"Tarlae is cleverer than most with her combinations," Gabe reminded her. "Don't beat yourself up about it. But you might find a new location for your haven."

Ernie thought about the haven she'd had since she became a Dealer, the tent that connected her to her father and had maybe even been his haven before it had been hers. Legs had guided her there when she'd been brand new. Legs had known where to take her. She looked at her arm. "I wonder if our animal spirits know their way around the world of dreams better than we do."

"Seeing as they're not as grounded to the physical world, it would make sense." Gabe rubbed his own forearm and smiled down at the image of the Kestrel. "Caera guided me to the cave where I hid the Marks."

"She appeared to me once in the dream realm, too," Ernie told him. "I thought it was a product of my own mind, but I think it might actually have been her. She was trying to keep me focused on saving you, and it was during a time when Duncan had blocked her from getting back to you."

"And you just told me Legs left you in the dream realm—and came to warn me in the waking realm." He arched an eyebrow. "Shall we step into the bedroom, love?"

Ernie couldn't help it—her cheeks went warm. "When you put it that way . . ." She leaned back and accepted Gabe's hand. He pulled her to her feet and led her into the small, cozy room where his bed lay, the pillow still dented from where Ernie had laid her head to rest. After using both their Case cards to conjure a lockbox of thick steel that would keep the precious Sunrise from being detected, they lay down and drew the cards that could carry them from sleep into an infinite realm that connected mind to mind. Ernie laid her head in the crook of Gabe's shoulder, and he threaded his fingers into her hair. They crossed their Dreams cards, peered at them, and willed themselves into the dream realm.

They appeared in a vast plain, with waving grass stretching for miles under a striking sapphire sky. Ernie squeezed Gabe's hand and let it go, then knelt and held out her left arm. Legs came slithering off her skin immediately, and Caera flapped onto Gabe's wrist. "We need to find the Coconut Octopus," Ernie said to Legs. She glanced over to see Caera staring at her with beady predator's eyes. "Can the two of you help us search for her?"

Caera let out a shrill cry and fluttered down into the grass next to Legs, who shook her rattle slowly. Ernie knew her well enough to understand that it was more a greeting than a threat. The two powerful animal spirits regarded each other for a moment before looking up at their Dealers. Gabe reached over and took Ernie's hand.

Legs and Caera stared at them for a moment, then disappeared.

"What do we do now?" Ernie asked.

Gabe looked around. "I wonder why we ended up here. Is this a place you know?"

"Not even remotely." Ernie turned in place and paused as she realized a storm was in the distance, a dark, churning mass of thunderheads, lightning flickering within. "But I'm thinking that might be something we should pay attention to."

Gabe turned to look. "Could be anything. But since we've got nothing else . . ." He laced his fingers with hers, and together they strode through the grass. As they walked, the strands of pale green parted a few steps in front of them, creating a path to ease their way.

"Sometimes I wish the waking world was this nice," Ernie said quietly. "It feels safer somehow."

"Ever dreamed that you were in a real jam?"

She laughed. "All the time. I dreamed I was in a crashing plane once. And another time, I dreamed I was trapped on a sinking ship. I fall a lot in my dreams. Like, off buildings."

He gave her a funny look. "You ever hit the ground?"

"Not even once."

"Probably why you feel safer here. You've always awakened before the collision. Doesn't mean there can't be one."

"But our bodies are safe in your bed, aren't they?"

"Your mind is here, though. So who's to say it isn't real?" He paused and turned to her, running a finger down her cheek. "I feel the softness of your skin beneath my fingertips, and it melts me down, just like it does when we're awake."

Ernie shivered as the caress traveled down the side of her neck. "I wish we could stop everything for a while," she blurted out. "It feels like something bad is coming, like there's *always* something bad coming, and we've never had a chance to get started."

He bowed his head, bringing his face close to hers. "What would you like to start, love?"

She placed her palm on his chest. "I want us to have a chance. To see if this can work out. But it feels like we can't quite get our timing right."

"It might be easier than you think, to find our own rhythm," he murmured, his gaze falling to her mouth. "We don't need to wait for the world to give us permission. We wouldn't ever get it, anyway." His lips curved into a half smile. "I'm beginning to believe that happiness in this life is the purest form of defiance."

Ernie rose on her tiptoes and kissed him, her lips parting, her tongue meeting his. Eager and hungry, she explored his mouth as he pressed her body closer, as his hand slid up under her shirt and met the skin of her back.

Thunder rumbled on the horizon, a distant warning, or maybe only a swirling thought, the whim of another dreamer or perhaps the collision of two, a cold front and a warm front, a whispered yes and a frightened no. Ernie had no idea, and when a soft bed of silk rose up from the plain, conjured from their mutual desire or maybe just Gabe being practical, she decided she didn't care.

"Tell me this is real," she murmured against his ear as he steered her onto the plush expanse, an island of luxury in the middle of the undulating and seemingly infinite grass. The buttery sun shone above them, warming her skin as Gabe stripped off her jacket.

"We're both here, and we're alive, and this is real," he said as she unbuttoned his shirt. He guided her hand over his heart, which hammered against her palm. "It doesn't matter what comes next. Right now we burn for each other."

Truer words had never been spoken. She didn't have time for the usual worries about what he'd think of her body, about whether she could make him feel good. His admiration for her was apparent with every brush of his fingers over her bare skin, with the heat of his gaze as he undressed her. She didn't need to ask whether he loved her. She didn't need him to promise her a future. All of that seemed foolish. In this moment, they were beyond that. Here in this endless plain, there was a storm on the horizon, but there was peace in each other. She tasted his skin and savored the heat of his body, the hard lines of him, the way he gasped when she touched him, the way he groaned when she stroked.

When he entered her, she pressed her face to his neck and held on as the feeling consumed her. She'd never had this—no stray thoughts, no niggling anxiety, no distraction, only the way he moved against her and his harsh breath against her ear. Only the taut muscles of his arms, his chest, his hips.

She opened her eyes when a shadow passed over them, and realized that the storm was fast approaching, bringing with it the whisper of rain, but she and Gabe were locked together, and not even the thunderclouds overhead could steal her joy, or the wish that this would be all there was for the rest of her days.

When the first drops hit his bare back, Gabe flinched and began to raise his head, but Ernie took his face in her hands, wanting him to see only her, only her eyes. He'd never looked this way, lost in passion, dazed by the feeling, and she had never felt more powerful. It ratcheted up her own pleasure until the sensation broke over her like a wave. Ecstasy carried both of them toward the edge, over that edge, while lightning struck around them and thunder made the ground tremble.

With the warm rain pouring down, Gabe collapsed onto her, and she wrapped herself around him and held on tight, unsure whether the drops on her face were from the rain or tears. "I don't want this to be over," she murmured.

"It will never be over," he said, his heart pounding against her chest. They lay there for a few minutes as the rain poured down, soaking them while the sky swirled and the wind blew. Despite the storm, Ernie felt safe, as if the danger couldn't quite reach her here. She knew they had to go, though. They couldn't stay here—they had to find Tarlae. They had to find the key.

"Gabe—" she began, but he was already pushing himself off her and turning his face to the sky. The rain was dwindling, and slants of sunlight were reaching toward the plain, brushing the waving grass.

He held his hand out and pulled her up to sitting. When he looked down at her, the warm slide of his gaze down her body sent a shiver of happiness through her. "Are you all right?"

She laughed. "Are you kidding?"

He grinned. "Need anything?"

"Apart from dry clothing . . ." She trailed off as Gabe dug inside the pocket of his discarded pants and pulled out his cards. With a few plays, he conjured a colorful canopy and an outfit.

"I wouldn't mind if you ran around naked as the day God made you, but I suppose it would be rather distracting," he said with a sigh, pulling another set of dry clothes from thin air.

As the rain faded to a silvery mist, the thunderheads rolling into the distance, carrying the lightning with them, Ernie and Gabe got dressed. She took the time to peek at her Revelation card and saw her and Gabe lying on his bed, him holding her tight against his chest. The way his arms stayed wound around her, even in sleep, made her heart soar. That was real, and so was this, the way he opened his arms to her as she climbed off the already-dry bed and stepped back into the vast plain, the way his head bowed over hers as she encircled his waist with her arms.

"Where to now?" she asked.

"Legs and Caera are off searching, so perhaps . . ." He released her and turned in place, then pointed off into the distance.

Ernie peered in that direction, which was where the storm had come from. Now, with the clouds and rain gone, she could see a mountain range. "Okay . . ."

They set off, hand in hand, the grass once again flattening and parting to create an easy path. The mountains seemed to creep toward them as they hiked, and what Ernie had assumed was a hundred miles became only a few, and the craggy, snowcapped peaks loomed over them.

"Is this a creation of your mind or mine?" Ernie asked.

"It might be both or neither. I've spent a lot of time in this realm, and I think that sometimes, what's here to see is a bit of the collective consciousness, you know? It's all connected, even though the ways we share this particular realm aren't always clear."

"So is it a bit like another dimension? Is it another world, or are there splinters?"

He squeezed her hand. "That," he said, "is a very good question."

The waving grass had thinned out as the ground became rockier, and they began to pick their way along a stony path that wound up into the mountains. Ernie wasn't sure where they were going, but the sun seemed to shine along the ground in an undulating river of light that hugged the curves of the trail in a way that made her sure this was where she was supposed to be heading and gave her hope that she'd find Tarlae and the Sunrise key there when she finally made it.

Ernie let go of Gabe's hand as the trail narrowed and grew ever steeper, crossing patches of scree that required a bit of scrambling to negotiate. She focused on her footsteps and handholds, pulling herself up and letting the breath whoosh from her lungs, with an odd curiosity and eagerness beating against her rib cage. Behind her, she could hear Gabe's heavy breaths, too, and she looked over her shoulder to see his sweaty face, where a few tendrils of his hair, having escaped his ponytail, were stuck to his temples. "Maybe we should work out together sometime," she said in an amused voice.

He let out a groan and a laugh and raised his head to look up at her, but his gaze skipped from her face to something above her. "What the hell?" he asked, smile fading.

Ernie turned to look in time to see a flowing bit of pale, gauzy fabric disappear behind a large boulder a few dozen feet above them on the steep trail. Her stomach clenched, and she immediately reached into the pocket of the track pants Gabe had conjured for her, grasping for her cards. "Was that Virginia?" whispered Ernie.

"Why would she hide?" Gabe's voice was quiet and wary, though, and when Ernie looked back at him, she saw he had his own deck out, cards fanned. "Do you want to go back?"

Ernie shook her head slowly. "If she wanted to attack us, she could. Hell, she just shows up—in my car, in my living room . . ."

"So she might not have seen us yet."

"Then let's go see what she's up to." Holding her deck in one hand and using the other for balance, Ernie negotiated the steep climb as quietly as she could, with Gabe right behind her. When they reached the boulder where they'd seen the fabric, they peeked around it to see a long, narrow path with sheer rock faces on either side.

"Not where I'd want to be caught if this is a trap," Gabe muttered.

"We'll be ready." Ernie struck out along the path, jogging with light footsteps, every cell in her body on high alert. She could hear the scrabble of rocks tumbling against each other up ahead, out of sight. When they reached the bend in the path, the sound was louder, as were the gasps and grunts of someone unseen but near. It sounded like the person was displacing rock after rock, or maybe digging?

Ernie braced herself, nudging up the cards she might need from the rest of her deck—Strike, Shield, Escape. If she had a choice, she wouldn't fight at all, not now, not without a weapon that might give her a chance, but she'd learned to be prepared. And on that thought, she stepped silently around the corner, Gabe right behind her.

The woman, wearing a flowing white gown that was now smudged with dirt and smeared with mud, had her back to them as she grabbed rock after rock from a massive pile in front of her, where it looked like a passageway had collapsed. Her long black hair hung tangled and limp down her back. Ernie watched her slender arms shoot out and her hands, fingernails short and crusted with grime, grab yet another rock. Ernie stared at the woman's left forearm, confusion spiraling. She cleared her throat, and the woman spun around, her dark eyes wide.

Ernie offered her a smile and spoke in gentle tones because the woman looked so alarmed. "Hi, Nuria."

CHAPTER TWELVE

Nuria looked down at her hands and then back up at Gabe and Ernie. She shook her head.

"What are you doing here?" Ernie asked as she and Gabe approached.

Nuria opened her mouth to speak. "Fuh," she said. "Fuh-fuh—" Her jaw clenched.

"It's all right," Gabe said gently. "Are you in trouble? Do you need help?"

Nuria stared at him, her brows drawn together. Then her hands became fists, and she let out a growling shout that conveyed a frustration so desperate that it shook the entire mountain, it seemed. The ground vibrated beneath Ernie's feet, and all around them, rocks broke loose and cascaded down, cracking and crashing at their feet. Ernie yelped and conjured a shield in time to save herself and Gabe from getting slammed in the head.

"Stop it," she shouted to Nuria. "Whatever's going on, let us help you!"

But it was as if Nuria couldn't hear her at all. She continued to rage until Gabe rushed forward and grabbed her by the shoulders, calling her by name in an apparent attempt to snap her out of her fit. After a few moments of that, Nuria shoved her face close to Gabe's and roared, "Must. Find!"

Then she vanished from between his hands.

Ernie slumped, filled with a numb sort of confusion. "What do you think she was trying to find?"

"No *feckin'* idea."

"It began with an *F*, though," Ernie said. "In the past, she's tried to say Kot's name, and it just came out as 'kuh.'"

"Maybe it's a person she's trying to find? Know anyone whose name starts with *F*?"

"What if it's not a name? What if she was trying to say 'Forger'?"

Gabe shook his head. "It's useless to speculate. After we're done here, we'll go pay Kot and Nuria a visit."

Ernie peered at the giant pile of rocks in front of them. A sizable number had been moved to either side—at least a few tons. "Do you think her cards burned out? Was that why she was moving rocks by hand?"

"Could very well be." Gabe held up his deck. "Should we see if we can clear it, maybe see what she was trying to get to?"

Ernie cast a wary eye all around them. The air stirred against her skin as if it carried an electric charge. It felt like a warning. "I'm wondering if this is a distraction. We came here to find Tarlae."

"True, but I wonder if we were meant to find Nuria." Gabe gestured at their surroundings, the rocky path behind them and the blocked passageway before them. "Of all the places we could be in this realm and all the moments we could have chosen, how did we manage to run into her?"

Ernie scanned the heap of rocks Nuria hadn't managed to clear away. "Maybe it's connected. Do you think she was looking for the key, too?"

"Maybe. Or maybe she was looking for Tarlae, though I didn't think they knew each other well."

"Or maybe she was looking for a way to stop Virginia," Ernie suggested.

"Could be, but why wouldn't Kot be with her? The bloke barely leaves her side, yeah?"

"He might have been at her side just now, Gabe. Sleeping right beside her. We're in a whole different realm."

"Seems odd that she'd sneak off, though."

Ernie couldn't disagree with that. She'd seen Kot and Nuria together—the Grasshopper Dealer had always looked at her man with pure adoration in her eyes, and she'd been distraught when they'd been separated. "Let's try to move these rocks, I guess," she said, putting her musings aside for the moment. "Unless you have a better idea."

Gabe winced and looked down at his left forearm. "I don't," he said, rubbing his bare skin, "but Caera might."

The words had barely left his lips when Ernie's arm started to burn, a stinging pressure that seemed odd since Legs wasn't even on her arm at the moment. "Are they signaling us or something?"

"Must be. Let's . . ." He pulled his Revelation card, gave it a quick glance, and cursed. "They found her."

Ernie drew her own Revelation card, thinking about how she needed to see what Legs had found. What she saw made her mouth drop open. "What the hell is she doing?"

"Let's ask her." Gabe pulled his Transport card, and Ernie folded herself against him.

"How does Transport work in this realm?"

"You have to know exactly where you're going, or you could end up almost anywhere," he answered, looking pained. "It's happened to me a few times over the years. Look at where we need to go—see the spot on the shore?" He held his Revelation card up so she could see—as worrisome as it was. A cave, stalagmites rising in spikes from the ground, and beyond that a glimmering lake of black water. The cavern seemed the size of a cathedral and was lit by a rainbow of light from the gems that crusted the walls and by light streaming from overhead.

It was breathtakingly beautiful, save for the sight of Tarlae standing before one of those glittering walls. The shore of the lake, as Gabe had suggested, would put enough space between her and them that they'd be able to deal with a bit of distance and maybe draw her away from the man shackled to the wall, his arms spread and his head hanging. Gem-flecked rock had grown over his hands, holding him in place.

Tarlae had gotten the best of her former lover, and it looked like she'd been making him pay.

Ernie stared at the spot on the shore that Gabe had indicated, her palm sweating as she held her cards tightly. "Ready when you are."

She teetered against Gabe as they entered the void, consumed by doubt and terrified that she'd be pulled away from him. She'd been used to the close quarters of the void, the way it seemed endless but pressed against her at the same time. Here, in the dream realm, the void didn't press at all—it pulled, tugging at her hair, her cards, her conjured clothes, her flesh, her marrow. She let out a cry and clutched at Gabe, whose arms were steely around her. When they appeared on the eerie shore a moment later, Ernie reeled with dizziness.

Gabe pulled her down, hiding them from view. Tarlae stood perhaps a hundred yards away with her back to them, completely focused on Trey.

In her hand was some sort of baton, and its tip glowed with a pale-blue light. "Don't think I'll have mercy on you," she said. Though her voice was low, the sound bounced off the walls of the cavern, filling the space with sound.

Trey groaned. His olive skin was way too pale. "Just trying to keep a promise to a lady," he said. He raised his head to look at her.

"You made promises to me, too, Raccoon." This time, Tarlae's voice was choked with pain. Her black hair was wild and loose, and she was wearing a colorful dress that seemed to have been conjured to perfectly match the walls of the cave, off the shoulder with a flowing skirt of swirling metallic hues. Like everything in this eerie place, she emanated danger. "Promises I always feared you would break, and now I know I was right to be afraid."

Trey grimaced. "I'd apologize if I knew what you were talking about."

Gabe nudged Ernie forward, pointing to a gap between stalagmites large enough to allow them to creep through. He put his finger to his lips, and Ernie rolled her eyes. She didn't need to be told to stay quiet.

"Tell me why you want this," Tarlae said, pulling a necklace over her head and holding it out, revealing the jagged black Sunrise key. "What is it to you?"

"It's just a favor for a friend," he said wearily. "I already told you that."

Tarlae took a few stiff paces toward Trey, the necklace in one hand and the glowing baton in the other. "Then you know I want more than what you've told me! Who is this *friend*?"

"Jealous?"

She shoved the glowing blue tip of her baton in his face. "Tell me who she is," she hissed.

"We must have really been something together," he said quietly.

"None of that matters now." But Ernie heard the barely suppressed sob, the effort of each word. "You have become a different person. Maybe a person who serves the same evil that took my love away from me."

"I don't know her name," Trey shouted, the side of his face pressed against the wall of his prison to keep from being singed by the glowing end of the baton. "She's old, okay? White hair, wrinkles, the whole bit. All I know!"

Ernie felt Gabe's hand on her back, a warning to be still, but Ernie had already frozen.

"And her accent?" Tarlae asked.

"Yeah? I mean, she has one, I guess." Trey rolled his eyes. "And she's the only person who's ever been nice to me," he muttered.

Tarlae thrust the key in front of his face. "I want to know what this does and why she wanted it. Is it Virginia? Is she the one who did this to you?"

"I already told you that I don't know her name, goddammit!"

Ernie flinched as Tarlae hurled the glowing baton away with a scream of frustration. The weapon clattered to the ground, its cold light bouncing off the gem-encrusted walls.

Trey let out a weak chuckle. "I knew you wouldn't shock me with that thing."

Tarlae regarded him silently for a few long seconds. "I don't need to. You will stay here until you remember something."

His eyes narrowed. "You wouldn't."

"Obviously you don't know me."

"Maybe I wish I did," he said with a sigh.

"Stop it," she snapped. "If you try to play me, I'll leave you here to die."

"You don't understand." Aggravation dripped from every word. "I've got nothing, all right? I don't know who the hell you are or where I'm from or where I've been. All I know is that I woke up, and she was there. She took care of me. She brought me back to life."

Ernie and Gabe looked at each other with incredulity—it hardly sounded like Virginia, but then again, she was so conniving and manipulative that it was hard to tell.

"So when she asked me to get the Sunrise and its key for her," Trey continued, "damn if I wasn't going to do that and anything else she asked, okay?"

Ernie had used the cover of Trey's shouted words to adjust her footing, but she hadn't counted on the damn echo. The reverberated words ended a split second before the crack of a few misplaced stones beneath her feet. Tarlae swung around, pulling her deck from the pocket of her dress in one deft move.

Ernie rose with her hands up. "Don't shoot." She felt Gabe's solid presence behind her.

"How did you find this place?" Tarlae asked.

"Easier to do in the dream realm," Gabe explained. "And we were searching for the Sunrise key, not you."

"That, and you've been so focused on Trey that you didn't conceal yourself well," Ernie added gently. "But we don't want to fight you, Tarlae. It's obvious that you want to get to Virginia as much as we do."

Tarlae looped the chain holding the Sunrise key around her neck again. "I'm not giving it to you."

"It's how she lured me to her," Trey said. Despite his precarious position, hanging by his rock-covered hands against the wall, he managed a self-deprecating smile. "It was actually a pretty clever trap. She knew I'd come after it, and she pretended she was going to give it to me. Just as I lowered my guard, she must have played a few cards that put me right to sleep. Dragged me here, stole my deck, chained me up, threatened me with torture—you know how it is."

"I didn't *steal* your deck," Tarlae grumbled as Gabe and Ernie wound their way through the maze of waist-high stalagmites toward the former couple. "I took them for safekeeping because you are obviously not capable of using them responsibly."

Trey laughed. "Lady, have you taken a look in the mirror lately?"

Tarlae looked as if she'd been slapped. She turned away so he couldn't see her face, giving Ernie a full, heartbreaking view of the tears in the Coconut Octopus Dealer's eyes. It sent a bolt of rage through Ernie. She stalked forward, glaring at Trey.

"Dude. You do know why she looks like that, right?" snapped Ernie. "She once told me that her greatest fear was that she was going to lose you. It took every ounce of courage she had not to chain you up then to protect you!"

"I told you that in confidence," Tarlae said irritably.

Ernie ignored her—she was too pissed at the Raccoon Dealer, who looked startled. "But she *loved* you, Trey. She loved you enough to let you be the brave man you were, to fight by our side against a woman so evil that she thought nothing of killing you, and of killing a hundred thousand people in the last few days alone." She paused, glancing at Tarlae, who was staring off into the vast black lake on the other side of the cavern. "When you were taken from her, do you think she should have just been able to shake it off?"

Trey directed his gaze at the ground and didn't respond.

Gabe cleared his throat. "May I suggest a truce?"

"Not if that truce involves allowing this damn Raccoon to help that bitch of a Forger," Tarlae said, jabbing her finger in Trey's general direction without turning around.

"Tarlae, can we speak with you for a moment?" Ernie asked. She pulled out her Conceal card and waved it in Trey's direction—she needed him not to hear what she was about to say. As the chained-up Raccoon Dealer squinted at them through the dense fog Ernie had conjured around him to keep him from reading their lips, while he strained to hear over the white noise meant to hide their words, Ernie drew Gabe and Tarlae closer. "What if we do give it to him?" she suggested. "What if we use it as bait?"

Tarlae frowned. "He could Conceal himself as easily as you can."

"Not if we take his Conceal card," said Gabe. "It's the core of any cloaking action."

"He is wily." Tarlae tossed Trey a suspicious glance. "That much hasn't changed."

"What if we conjured a fake key?" Ernie asked.

"It couldn't fool Virginia," Tarlae said. "We should conjure a fake Conceal card instead. That way, he can have the real key, and we can follow him." She pulled the Raccoon deck from the pocket of her gown and held the two decks—his and hers—out. The back of the Coconut

Octopus cards showed the octopus with its tentacles wrapped around the world. "It will have to be convincing. But I know the feel of his deck." She sighed. "I know Terrence almost as well as he does."

"Does he still call the Raccoon Terrence?" Gabe asked. When Tarlae nodded, he smiled. "That's a hopeful sign."

"Seems like he has the same preferences he did before. He's not a completely different person," Ernie said.

"I can't think about any of that now," Tarlae replied grimly. "If I do, I'll want to protect him." She squeezed the decks. "I'll want to keep him here forever and never let him go."

Ernie wondered whether that was why Tarlae had brought Trey here in the first place. She clearly hadn't intended to actually torture him. "I know this hurts, Tarlae."

"He's *alive*," she whispered. "I may have lost him, but he is alive. I will accept the hurting."

The sorrow in her voice put an ache in Ernie's chest. "Maybe Virginia put some kind of . . . I don't know . . . spell on him? One that can be broken if we defeat her?"

"That's something out of a storybook," said Tarlae. "As strange as all of this is"—she waved her card-filled hands at the cave, its gem-encrusted walls, its gleaming ebony lake—"it's still real life. And in real life, I'm not sure there are spells or anything quite that easy."

Ernie laughed and held up her own deck. "You're kidding, right? Come on, T. Absolutely anything is possible. Admit that, pull your hope up around you like a pair of big-girl pants, and let's conjure a fake ID."

Tarlae squinted at her. "There are so many things wrong with that statement."

"Oh, man. Just go with it. I have no freaking idea how to conjure a card that could fool another Dealer, so—"

Tarlae waved her concern away. "I've done it before."

Gabe's eyebrows shot up. "You *have*?"

She half shrugged. "I stole a few cards from Akela once and left fake ones behind to allow me to escape. The Wolf Spider is not one to trifle with."

"Remind me never to drink with you," Ernie muttered.

"The Wolf Spider is aligned with many bad Dealers," Tarlae said matter-of-factly. "I only steal from miscreants."

"Actually, I think their ranks might be a bit fractured." Ernie explained what Rupert had said to her about Akela and Ruslan refusing orders from Virginia and being banished for it.

"Where would she banish them to?" Tarlae asked. "She destroyed the rune tile to the splinter dimension where she stranded Trey."

"Doesn't mean she couldn't make more rune tiles," said Gabe. "Or that there aren't others out there somewhere, made by past Forgers. I mean, why would there be only that one dimensional rune tile?"

"A very good point," Ernie said, frowning as she considered how many splinter dimensions might be out there and wondered how many disobedient Dealers could be stranded if Virginia set her mind to it. "She could take Dealers' decks, but why do that when she can really make them suffer?"

"Means she'll maybe try to bring them back later, once they've served their time," Gabe said.

"That is a terrible way to gain someone's loyalty," Tarlae said.

"Yeah, but Virginia's a Nazi," Ernie replied, putting up her hands to forestall the objections she always got when she pointed out that fact. "Look—she's using fear and threats of punishment and death to maintain her power and secure support. *Like the Nazis did.* So say what you want, but she seems kinda fond of their playbook."

"That is difficult to argue with," Tarlae said.

Gabe nodded. "And it means that it's only a matter of time before she does something even more heinous."

"Like kill a few million innocent people?" Ernie asked. "I'm almost sure that's exactly what she's planning—and she wants to use us to make it happen. So let's make that fake card and trigger a freaking bomb on her doorstep."

"You don't know what the Sunrise will do," Gabe warned.

"But she wanted it," Ernie replied. "And she wasn't the only one. If she was after it—or is still after it, considering how she showed up in my living room right after I tried to get it—then it's probably something pretty devastating."

"If it's devastating," Tarlae said slowly, "how do you know it won't *be* the thing that kills those millions of people?"

Ernie swallowed hard, remembering how her well-intended attempts to stop the deaths of innocents in Munich had ended up causing so many more. "I don't. But I think the Sunrise was made by the Forger before Andy—he definitely didn't make it. His predecessor's name was Phoebe, and Minh told me she was gentle. That she made the Marks to encourage contact and to empower Dealers. Whatever the Sunrise does, I doubt it will kill innocent people. But it might be enough to take down a Forger."

"This is a leap of faith I'm not sure I have in me," said Tarlae. She looked down at Trey's cards. "But perhaps it is the only chance I have to get him back."

"If we control the Sunrise, we can make it work for us," Ernie said with more confidence than she felt. "Can you conjure the card and keep his?"

Tarlae was staring through the fog at the man she loved, who was banging his head lightly against the wall behind him and appeared to be singing to himself to pass the time. "All right. I—"

A sudden tremor jolted her mouth shut, and all of them reached for stalagmites to keep their balance as the ground shook. Chunks of sparkling stone tumbled off the walls from high in the cave. "What the hell was that?" cried Ernie as the rumbling subsided.

"Could be a warning," Gabe said, warily eyeing the slabs of rock all around him. He pulled his Revelation card and peered at it. "I can't . . . Could be on our end? Not sure."

Ernie looked at her own card and saw herself in Gabe's arms, but her brow was furrowed even in sleep. "We should go."

Tarlae held up a Conceal card and slid it into Trey's deck. "I'll handle this. I will let him take the key from me and run. I'll let you know when it's done."

Ernie nodded. Then, on impulse, she touched Tarlae's arm. The Coconut Octopus Dealer stiffened at the contact but didn't pull away. "I promised you that I'd do everything I could to help you get Trey back," Ernie said to her. "I don't intend to break that promise now."

"Same," said Gabe. "We'll see this through, Tarlae. If there's any chance we can get him back, we'll be at your side until it's done."

Tarlae's gaze had returned to Trey. "All right."

Ernie took that as a thank-you from the proud Dealer. "We'll wait for your signal," she said as the ground began to shake again, sudden jerks of the earth in a clear rhythm.

Gabe took her hand. "Time to wake up, love."

Ernie turned away as the fog around Trey cleared and Tarlae began to walk toward him. She focused instead on rousing herself, on departing this strange land of dreams and arriving in her equally strange waking reality. She awoke with a start in Gabe's bed. Gabe was already sitting up and rubbing his eyes. A loud banging had followed them from the dream realm—or was possibly what had caused the tremors.

"Someone's at the door," Gabe said, swinging his legs off the bed.

Blinking away sleep, Ernie followed him into the living room to see a familiar figure looming on the other side of the cottage's front door. Gabe swung it open, and Kot stepped inside, his expression strained. "I need help," he said, breathing heavily. "I have no one else to turn to."

"What is it?" Gabe asked. "What's happened?"

"It's Nuria," Ernie guessed.

Kot turned to her. "She's gone, and I cannot see her in my cards, no matter what I deal. She should not be hidden from me, of all people!"

He pulled a crumpled piece of paper from his pocket and added in a choked voice, "She left this behind." He flattened the paper on the nearest wall, and Ernie moved closer, expecting to see some sort of note—but there were no words to be seen.

Drawn on the paper in a childish hand was a woman. Wrinkles on her face. Wild hair. And a long, gauzy dress.

CHAPTER THIRTEEN

"Is that Virginia?" Gabe asked.

Ernie drew back. "Isn't it obvious?"

"Well . . ." Gabe gave Kot a cautious look. "I'm sure Nuria has many skills and talents, but—"

"Drawing is not one of them," Kot said as he stuffed the paper back in his pocket. "However, it looks like only one person I know."

Gabe gestured to the squashy chairs that occupied his living room. As Kot sank into one, Gabe poured him a tumbler of whiskey and handed it over. "Has Nuria been off lately?"

Kot threw back the whiskey in a few gulps, as if it were apple juice. "I think so."

Ernie frowned. "You *think* so?"

"Was she upset by the news about the terrorist attacks?" Gabe asked.

Kot bowed his head. "I have shielded her from that."

Ernie took in the defeated slump of his shoulders. "So you've been dealing with all of it alone."

"I have tried to help," he said quietly. "If I hadn't gotten those security guards fired . . ." He sighed. "I do not like to leave Nuria alone, so I transport to the attack sites when she is sleeping."

Gabe gave Ernie a look—Nuria hadn't exactly been staying put while her lover was trying to save lives.

Kot raised his head and held out his cup, and Gabe provided a refill. "I love her," Kot said. "That feeling is so deep that it is embedded in my bones. But for both of us, things are . . . different."

"Now that you're in this dimension," Ernie guessed. "You were both in the splinter dimension for so long."

"I was there my entire life," Kot said quietly. "I have forgotten so much of that life. I have some memories. Of my mother. My father. And of Nuria. But I feel as if I am getting to know her all over again." He paused. "She is not quite what I expected."

"Nuria was actually from this dimension," Ernie said. "She must have memories of the life she had before Virginia banished her."

He nodded. "Not just memories, I think. Nightmares as well. She had no part in these terrible attacks, but even before then . . . she seemed haunted. And even though the grasshopper is not inside her mind anymore, she seems possessed all the same. She has not had a restful sleep in weeks."

Ernie looked over at Gabe, who nodded. "We saw her, Kot," said Ernie. "In the dream realm." She explained where they'd found Nuria and what she'd been doing. "She seemed really frustrated, and maybe a little confused. She wasn't able to tell us what she was trying to do, even when we offered to help."

"The dream realm is vast," Kot said. "How is it that you came to be in the exact place she was?" He downed his second whiskey but waved away the offer of a third. "Should I look for her there? Can you take me?"

"Maybe," said Gabe, "but if she went into the dream realm, she— her body, at least—would likely still be in your cabana, slumbering away."

"Perhaps all the nightmares of late were not merely inside her head." Kot rubbed his thighs, looking as if he wanted to jump up, to spring into action, to do anything he could to find and save the mysterious woman he had loved for so long. "In the last few days, I feel as if we have all been living a nightmare."

For a moment, they were all quiet, overwhelmed by the damage done, the lives lost. Slivers of memory sliced through Ernie's mind: the little girls whose parents had been killed, the screams of a woman who'd lost her husband, the smoke filling the sky and Ernie's lungs and . . . She shook her head, trying to pull herself away from the horror, knowing she could do more to prevent further catastrophe if she shoved away thoughts of what had already happened.

"Was Nuria able to communicate anything to you about what she was going through?" Ernie asked.

"She was becoming more and more distant," Kot replied. "Sometimes I would touch her, and she didn't even seem to be *there*." His jaw clenched. "She can't speak. She can't write. She has no way of relating her thoughts apart from a few signs. She shared her mind with an insect's for so long that I know it will take a long time for those things to come back, if they ever do. But it has made me feel so helpless." His fists clenched. "I would kill anyone who threatened her. I would get anything she needed. I thought she knew that!"

"She might," Gabe said, his voice low and soothing, as if he were speaking to a skittish horse. "But perhaps we can figure out what she was after, and what it has to do with Virginia, before any killing is necessary."

"How?"

"She was looking for something, and it might be connected with the woman in that drawing," Gabe said, locking eyes with Ernie. "Trey was looking for something, too."

"But we know what Trey was looking for," Ernie said.

"Trey?" Kot tilted his head. "The Raccoon Dealer? Isn't he dead?"

This time, Gabe did the talking, bringing Kot up to speed. By the time Gabe had finished, Kot looked like he'd been smacked upside the head. "He is back, but he is in the thrall of the evil Forger," Kot said. "And you think Nuria is also being controlled by this woman?"

"Has Nuria made any other drawings?" Ernie asked.

"She has been drawing things for days. Mostly the scribbling of a child, along with the tantrums of one."

In Ernie's interactions with Nuria, she'd seemed a little primitive but never simpleminded. Instead, she'd seemed keenly aware of some things, enough for them to eat at her. "She sounds frustrated to me. Like she's trying to make herself understood—or to understand something herself—but she can't."

"I have failed her," Kot said. "I do not deserve her."

"She's lucky to have you," Gabe replied firmly. "Because you won't give up until she's safe again."

"And we'll help." Ernie realized that this was the second time in about an hour that they'd made such a promise, but there was no way she was walking away from Kot. Her memories of the splinter dimension were just that—splinters. But she knew Kot had saved her life more than once, and she felt a bond with him that wasn't tied to any particular recollection. "We're already working on a plan to lure Virginia out and deploy a weapon against her that might allow us to take her down before she inflicts more devastation." Ernie offered a few details. "Once we receive the signal from Tarlae, we'll track Trey and see if Virginia appears to collect the Sunrise key, which is only half of what she needs."

"While we're waiting, why don't we take a look at Nuria's drawings?" Gabe suggested. "Could be there's one treasure among the trash. Maybe a clue that gives us a glimpse into her mind."

Kot put his hand over the drawing in his pocket, the one of the old woman, wrinkles drawn in harsh lines down her face, on either side of the triangle nose and triangle eyes. Then he stood up. "Come. I will take you."

Ernie didn't feel comfortable leaving the Sunrise behind, since Tarlae might give the signal at any moment, so she pulled the relic from its conjured case and pocketed it. Then Ernie and Gabe each put a hand on Kot's shoulders, and he pulled them into the void. When they emerged, they were on the same beach where Ernie had visited Kot and Nuria before, with the cabana facing the ocean. Kot climbed the steps and walked over to a waste bin positioned next to the bed. It was brimming with wads of crumpled paper. "This is what she was doing for days before the attacks. I would wake up at night, and she'd be there, scribbling in the moonlight." He pointed to one side of the bed. "And because I am an idiot, I left her to it and went back to sleep every time."

"And after the attacks?" Gabe asked quietly. "Did she change? Either because she knew somehow or because she could tell you were hurting?"

Kot squeezed his eyes shut. "I don't know. I was too—"

"Don't beat yourself up," Ernie said, plopping down on the bed, not wanting to get buried in grief again. Action felt so much better. "Let's take a look and see if we can find anything that might give us a hint at what's been going on." She reached for a piece of paper at the top of the brimming wastebasket and smoothed it across her thighs. The drawing seemed a little frantic, much like the one of Virginia—harsh, thick lines, with smudges where Nuria's hand had brushed across the page. Ernie tilted her head, trying to make sense of the sloppy squares, circles, squiggles, and lines, squinting in an effort to bring all the disparate parts into a cohesive whole.

"Perhaps there's a pattern we can recognize?" Gabe had seated himself on the floor with a few drawings flattened out in front of him.

Kot, who was also sitting on the floor, pulled yet another drawing from the pile, causing a few wadded-up papers to scatter across the wooden planks. There had to be at least a hundred discarded drawings in the basket. "I should have looked at these sooner," he muttered as he scanned one paper, then another. He frowned at both of them. "I'm not sure she knew what she was trying to convey. These drawings look similar to each other."

Ernie leaned down to examine the two, which looked a lot like the one in her lap, but maybe a little more focused. Squares with circles drawn inside, lines connecting them, some drawn so thickly that the pencil had pierced the page a few times, leaving gouges.

Gabe compared several to one another and the ones Kot was looking at. "Do you think it's a map, with all these arrows and connected lines?"

"Maybe a map to whatever she was looking for?" Ernie grabbed two other papers from the wastebasket, with arrows pointing to different squiggly shapes inside rows of squares. "Or maybe not," she added quietly.

Honestly, it looked pretty random, but she didn't want to say that, not yet, not with Kot grabbing a massive handful of the crumpled drawings to examine one by one. Instead, she snagged a few paper wads and settled in, searching for clues to what Nuria had been thinking before she disappeared.

"These might be symbols," Gabe said. "And look at these lines going off the page. It looks like she ran out of room maybe."

On the drawing in her lap, a few lines went all the way across the page. "What if each drawing is part of a whole?" She slid one paper alongside another, aligning two of the arrows.

"You might be right," Kot said with naked hope in his voice. "Could be if we discover the way to put all of this together, we can see what she was trying to understand. Or to find."

It seemed like a good strategy, in that it felt more purposeful than the nonstrategy they'd had before. First, they tried to consult their decks. Legs had helped Ernie sort out the puzzle of her dad's postcards the year before, so the strategy seemed solid to her. However, their cards showed them each only one specific drawing—Ernie's and Gabe's appeared to be of the same thing: chaotic sketches with a cluster of squiggles at the center and lines shooting off the page. But Kot's was different, showing a curving line ending in a very small scribble. They found those pictures among the rest and peered at them closely, but their cards revealed nothing more. If there was a pattern to the drawings, their animal spirits didn't know it.

For the next hour or two, they laid out the papers all over the cabana, arranging and rearranging, lining up arrows, arguing over which squiggles matched or were distinct. Some drawings really did seem to be different versions of each other, and that only made it harder. Ernie did her best to stay hopeful, but puzzles had never been her thing. They'd always been more of her dad's.

"Hey," she said, waiting until Gabe and Kot stopped their most recent discussion about whether one drawing was actually a continuation of another, even though the lines on the second drawing were straight instead of spiraling like the ones on the first. "I think my dad might be able to help."

"Redmond Terwilliger is the one who cursed Nuria in the first place," Kot thundered. "He has never done anything but hurt her."

Ernie sighed. "He feels terrible about that, and I think he might be eager to try to help her now. He knows a lot." She gave Kot an imploring look. "I think we should bring him here and let him try."

Kot crossed his arms over his chest. "If you think it will help."

Ernie moved fast before the Dragonfly Dealer could change his mind. She transported herself back to the Woodfin shop, interrupted her parents eating breakfast in bed in their birthday suits, endured the awkward shuffling and murmuring as they made themselves decent, and then hauled her father off to Mexico with a promise to her mom that he'd be safe.

Ernie's dad stepped from the void, unsteady and wary. "Ernie wanted me to come take a look," he said, blinking at the mosaic of drawings spread over the cabana. "Don't y'all have cards to help you solve this kind of thing?"

Ernie explained how their decks had shown them only one drawing each, and how Ernie's and Gabe's had seemed like two drafts of the same image. Redmond's eyebrows nearly reached his hairline. "This is fascinating," he murmured. He held out the drawing from Kot's Revelation card. "You got one that was different from theirs." He inclined his head toward Gabe and Ernie. "You know why, right?"

They all stared at him, and he rolled his eyes. "Because he's not from the same dimension as you are," he said loudly. "And look at it! Kot's drawing is a lot smaller and simpler than the ones for the two of you."

"Because the dimension Kot came from is a splinter, and we come from a complete world," Ernie said. "But what about the squiggles?"

Redmond looked at her as if she were a disappointing pupil. "Her handwriting isn't the best, but I think it's pretty damn obvious that those aren't squiggles. Or not random ones, at least."

Ernie gaped at the assembled drawings, and so did Gabe and Kot. "How could we have been so thick?" Gabe asked. "They're *runes*."

"So this—" Kot waved his arm at all the drawings. "This *is* a map."

"Or a diagram," Redmond said. "Of the dimensions. Of the multiverse. Unbelievable." He dropped to his hands and knees, his eyes narrowed as he pored over Nuria's work. "Truly fascinating."

"Will it tell me where she has gone?" The words burst from Kot after a solid minute of tension as all of them waited for Redmond to tell them more. "Because if it won't, then it is useless!"

"You're kidding!" crowed Redmond, not bothering to lift his head to address them. "How could this be useless? It's brilliant!"

Kot glared at his back, then wrenched Redmond up, lifting him by the back of his old flannel shirt. "Where. Is. Nuria?"

The smile disappeared from Redmond's face as he flailed and finally got his feet back beneath him. He cleared his throat and pulled away from Kot. "I have no idea," he said quietly, pulling at his collar.

Ernie stepped between the two men, her eyes on Kot. "He got us a step further," she warned. "He did help."

Kot turned away. "We are no closer to finding her."

After exchanging glances with Gabe, Ernie took her father home. "Wish I'd been able to take a picture of that," Redmond said as he staggered out of the void and into the driveway of Terwilliger Antiquities. "How did she come across all that information?"

"Knowing that might help us figure out where she ran off to," Ernie said. "But we barely have a place to start."

"If you figure it out, let me know. Put that together in one map and you'd really have something."

Ernie shrugged. "Maybe. But right now, I just need to help Kot find Nuria."

"Don't assume that map can't tell you," Redmond said.

Ernie nodded, mostly to placate her dad. "Thanks for trying. I'd better get back." And after giving her parents one last hug and kiss and a promise to visit soon, Ernie drew her Transport card, preparing to travel back to the Mexican cabana. She was half-tempted to check the news, to reconnect with the world if only to see whether Virginia had broken another piece of it, but then she decided she just . . . *couldn't* right now. She had to worry about what was coming next, especially if it meant saving a friend from Virginia or moving a little closer to stopping the Forger once and for all—so their next stop had to be the dream realm. Nuria had been there, trying to dig her way through that collapsed passage. She'd wanted to get through or to find something beneath the rocks—there might be actual answers there.

But when Ernie emerged from the void, when her boots hit sand and the salty sea breeze caressed her face, she could already tell Kot and Gabe had different ideas. They were waiting for her with urgency written in the taut lines of their shoulders. "Tarlae sent the signal that Trey is in the wind—with the Sunrise key and the fake Conceal card," Gabe said, looking down at his Revelation card. "You'll never believe who's with him."

Ernie rushed forward and sandwiched herself between the two men, peering at Gabe's Revelation card while Kot leaned over her shoulder. "Oh my god," she whispered.

There, in the card, slightly hazy because it was another Dealer's deck, Ernie saw Trey. He was on his knees, his back to them, with a vast desert in front of him, rolling dunes for miles.

Nuria knelt at his side, her long sheet of black hair cascading down her back. She was turned to Trey, revealing her profile. Trey held something up, and the sunlight glinted off the jagged black surface of the Sunrise key.

"What is Nuria doing with Trey?" Gabe asked. "They don't know each other."

"Maybe they're—" Ernie began, then paused as a figure in white appeared at the peak of the nearest dune. "Oh no."

"We have to get there," Kot barked. *"Now."*

"I'll send a signal to Minh and Alvarez," Gabe said. "If they're at all willing, I want them there when we face her. You have the Sunrise?"

Ernie swallowed hard and nodded.

"This could be it," Gabe said. "You're ready?"

"I'm calling Rupert," Ernie said. "He said he wanted to be my ally. This is his chance to prove it." Her heart was slamming against her ribs—this really could be the crossroads. Nestled in her pocket, the Sunrise felt like it weighed a thousand pounds instead of a few ounces. She—and every single one of her allies—had placed a lot of faith in that little artifact. If it didn't deliver, they could all be dead by the end of the day. Or in the next few minutes.

Gabe and Ernie each played a few cards, summoning their allies, drawing them to the specific signature of their decks so that wherever they were going, their allies could meet them there. To Ernie, it all felt risky and rushed and harebrained. She hadn't wanted it to be like this. She hadn't had time to think it through. Panic simmered beneath her skin, ready to burst forth. Gabe reached out and touched her shoulder. "Hey," he said. "Is your head in this?"

Maybe too much. "If people get hurt, I'm going to feel responsible."

He gave her a gentle smile. "Are you really *that* powerful, love, that you must carry the whole universe on your back?"

"This was my idea," she whispered. "The Sunrise, Virginia—"

"Bollocks," he replied. "It's the best chance we've got. We almost had Andy over a barrel when we confronted him as a group, and he had more experience than she does."

"She's more vicious." Ernie's dread hollowed out her voice. She clutched at Gabe's arm, remembering Tarlae's anguish during Trey's final fight with Virginia. "If she hurt you—"

"Hush," he said, pulling her into his arms and kissing the top of her head. "We have to see this through. If we let her continue to rampage, who knows how many millions she'll kill?"

"We must go," Kot said, peering at Gabe's Revelation card. "Virginia's getting closer to them, and Nuria's kneeling like a lamb before a butcher! Why doesn't she have her deck drawn and ready?"

Kot and Ernie hitched a ride with Gabe as he carried them to the place where Nuria and Trey knelt in the sand while their doom approached. They arrived at the same time Tarlae did, four Dealers behind two. Ernie squinted at the figure in white, whose gauzy dress was billowing as she made her way down the sand dune and stalked toward the group.

"Here she comes!" Trey said cheerfully, and he and Nuria smiled at each other.

"Nuria," said Kot.

She looked up at her lover with a radiant expression. "Fuh," she said, gesturing toward the lady in white. *"Fuh."*

The figure disappeared abruptly, drawing a wrenching cry from both Trey and Nuria. Gabe cursed, and Kot crouched next to his love, trying to cajole her into leaving with him.

"You scared her away," Trey said, jumping to his feet and turning on the group.

"Nothing scares me," said a familiar voice, southern accent dripping with mischief. Virginia, her wild white hair a cloud of fluff around her head, her white dress billowing and gauzy, appeared several yards in front of them. She smiled as she surveyed the gathered Dealers, and grinned when Minh appeared.

The Dealer of the Pot-Bellied Pig deck took in the scene, rolled his eyes, and drew his cards. "All for one and one for all," he muttered, sarcasm tainting every word.

Rupert appeared next, looked around, cursed, and disappeared.

"Ugh," said Ernie. "At least he showed up? Alvarez didn't even bother."

"The Hyena and the Emperor Tamarin are smarter than the rest of you," Virginia said, her eyes settling on Trey. "Now, this is interesting."

Ernie braced herself, waiting for Trey to offer Virginia the Sunrise key, hoping she could use her Draw card to snatch it from him before he could give it to her. The electric tension rolling off the other Dealers sent goose bumps rippling across Ernie's skin.

The moment must have lasted only a second or two, but it felt like a year. Trey stood facing the Forger, the Sunrise key in his fist. And then he said, "Who the hell are you?"

CHAPTER FOURTEEN

"Wait," said Tarlae. "Virginia is not the old woman in white who brought you back to life?"

"Nope," Trey replied, his focus still on the Forger. He shoved the key in his pocket and drew his cards. "Never seen her before in my life."

Virginia witnessed their interaction with a shrewd glint in her gray eyes. "Andy was such a softie. I knew you were still in circulation, Trash Panda. I sensed you a few days ago. But how on earth did you escape the splinter where I stuck you?"

The allied Dealers all stared at Trey and, like Ernie, were probably wondering the exact same thing.

"So you're saying that Andy did this to him?" asked Tarlae. "Andy stole his memories?"

"I knew he looked stupider than usual," Virginia said. "No brain, no memories, just a bundle of dumb in an admittedly attractive package."

"Ew," Ernie muttered.

"You're the Forger?" Trey asked. He hadn't taken his eyes off her.

"You're behind the times," Virginia answered, smoothing her puff of hair. "And I think I'm going to enjoy this new phase in our relationship. You can bow to me if you want to."

Trey scoffed. "This isn't what I came for. I'm out of here."

"You're not going anywhere." Virginia's eyes had gone from gray to black, the obsidian taint bleeding across the whites. "I sense a relic near, and I want it. Anything any Forger made belongs to me now."

"You're making stuff up as you go," said Minh. "No artifact is yours once it's sent out into the world."

"You really want to fight with me?" the Forger asked, her voice filling Ernie's ears, echoing painfully inside her skull. Judging from the other Dealers' expressions, it was having the same effect on them. Nuria clamped her hands over her ears and rocked while Kot whispered to her, trying to pull her up from the sand.

Ernie nudged up her Draw card from the rest as Legs tingled on her left forearm. Gabe's shoulder brushed hers as he stood next to her, his deck drawn. "We aren't going to let you destroy our world," he said loudly. "And we're not going to let you use us as your pawns. Those days are over."

Virginia bared her teeth. "I've got a lovely splinter dimension I've been saving especially for you, dirty birdie."

"Tell us why," Kot shouted, abruptly rising, while Nuria continued to cover her ears. "Why do you use us to commit atrocities? Why?"

The ferocity of his voice seemed to startle even Virginia, but she regained her bravado in the space of a breath. "Because I needed to keep all of you busy," she said simply. "You think I haven't expected a little ambush like this?" She grinned, revealing her yellowed teeth. "What better way to distract you than with your own bloated consciences?" A bitter chuckle burst from between her lips. "You've all been so funny. So *anguished*. 'I thought I was doing good in the world, but the mean Forger twicked me, wah-waaah!'" She balled her fists and rubbed at her eyes like a baby crying, then pulled her hands away from her face. "You should be thanking me, you ungrateful brats. I've given you a free lesson in how the world really works. No right or wrong, only predator and prey, power or surrender. But sadly, it looks like the lesson didn't take. I guess I need new teaching aids."

141

Virginia raised her arms as a brutal blast of hot wind thundered over them, sand hissing against their skin. The gale died quickly, and Ernie raised her head, the Sunrise heavy and hot in her pocket, her cards at the ready.

When she saw what was facing her, she froze.

A line of twenty people had appeared shoulder to shoulder in front of Virginia, who was barely visible as she paced behind them. Ernie didn't recognize a single one—they appeared to be a diverse bunch in terms of age, race, and wardrobe—but they all had something in common: each held a deck of cards, fanned and ready to be dealt.

Minh cursed. "You've been busy," he called to Virginia. "Making yourself a little private army?"

"As is my prerogative," Virginia hollered back. "Too many of you were getting too big for your britches, and my new Dealers understand that loyalty will be rewarded."

"Rewarded with *what*, exactly?" Ernie asked. "The chance to blindly cause misery and suffering?"

"The chance to do what Dealers were always meant to do," said Virginia. "To be gods among sheep. To make the world their playground and its inhabitants their slaves." She smirked. "And to do whatever I say. It's really not so bad, right? All I asked you to do was a few simple tasks. Wasn't it you, Diamondback, who always wanted to be on a team?"

"You deceived us to gain our cooperation," said Gabe. "Which shows that you have no respect."

"Respect?" spat Virginia. "Give me a break. I'm the Forger, you idiot. You are supposed to respect *me*. And if any of you would like to step off this train that's headed straight for a cliff, this is your chance. Come over here and join us, and you'll be welcomed back into the fold. Stay over there, and I swear, I will *unmake* you, card by card and piece by piece." Her face had flushed now, and her jowls trembled. "Don't think it's going to be an easy or painless death, and don't think I won't enjoy every single minute of it."

Ernie glanced around at her allies. Not a one of them looked like they were even considering Virginia's pathetic offer of leniency. She scanned the faces of the newbie Dealers. Some of them, like the baby-faced young man near the center, looked scared. Others, like the wiry lady with prominent cheekbones and deep-set eyes on the far left, looked a little too eager. But all of them looked like they'd come to duel.

"They're inexperienced," said Kot. "They will make mistakes."

"There are seven of us and twenty of them, so they've got a lot of room for error," Minh said drily. "And Virginia herself backing them up."

"At least you can count," said Virginia, peeking over the shoulder of the baby-faced lad. "So—no takers?"

She waited. Ernie, Gabe, Minh, Tarlae, Trey, Nuria, and Kot stood motionless and silent. Ernie knew she was signing her own death warrant and that the others were doing the same. But the alternative, selling her soul into the service of evil, would be worse than death.

"Listen up, troops!" shouted Virginia, her voice low and terrible and echoing. "The Raccoon has something I want." She shoved her face forward, black eyes glinting and ghoulish. "And so does the Diamondback."

Ernie flinched as Virginia revealed her awareness of the weapon in her pocket, but she forced herself to hold Virginia's gaze instead of looking away. No fear. No surrender.

Virginia nodded slowly, as if she saw the determination in Ernie's eyes. "Whoever fetches me my prizes gets a prize of their own—a full set of extra Wilds. Go!"

That was all the warning they had. Several things happened at once. Ernie dealt her Draw card with every ounce of focus she had, ripping the Sunrise key from Trey's pocket to cause it to zoom into her open palm. At the same time, the new enemy Dealers began to make plays, so Minh disappeared several of them while Tarlae sent a few more flying backward. Nuria jumped to her feet and drew her deck as if she hadn't been moaning and rocking a moment earlier.

Gabe conjured a giant domed shield over the group of seven allies. His jaw clenched as he held his Shield card high. Axes, knives, a wrecking ball, and a substance that might have been acid all collided with it a moment later. Ernie looked down at the key, which was hot to the touch.

"Give it back," shouted Trey.

"She's trying to help you," Tarlae said as she pushed between Trey and Ernie.

Outside the dome, the Dealers were doing everything they could to take Gabe's shield down, and Ernie knew it couldn't last much longer. Once it burned out, Gabe would be left without protection as he tried to duel, and they were woefully outnumbered.

She pulled the Sunrise out of her pocket. Its golden veins glinted under the desert sun. She looked over at Gabe, who was sweating with the effort of protecting all of them. Minh added his strength to the barrier, pressing his own Shield card against it. "What's the play?" he asked. "Are we bugging out or taking a stand?"

"You don't have to be here," Ernie said. Her heart had never raced like this. She could hear it pounding in her ears. "I don't know what this relic is going to do once I activate it, and I wouldn't blame anyone for getting out of here."

"Then Nuria and I will go," said Kot. "Lower the shield and let us go."

"Don't be a fool," Tarlae snapped. "Virginia knows we are the enemy now. You heard her. She will never let us rest until she or her minions have hunted us down. This is only the beginning."

"Have to admit, she's right, man," said Trey. "Not that I want to be stuck here with any of you . . ." He gave Tarlae what Ernie believed might actually be a regretful look, but it was hard to tell in that moment. "But that old bag definitely has murder on her mind."

"Use the Sunrise," said Gabe, his voice strained as he willed the shield to hold. "Do it."

"I don't know—"

"Don't back down now," Gabe shouted. "You're a warrior, and it's time to fight!" The shield bowed under the latest blast from a Dealer with curly red hair and freckles, a woman in a wrap dress and heels who looked like she'd stepped out of a boardroom.

"Lower the shield, then," Ernie said. "Otherwise we might get cooked alive when I use the key and set it off."

"Lower the damn shield, man," Trey urged. "I say we scatter and pick them apart." He rolled his shoulders and neck, loosening up for the fight.

"Damn Raccoon," Tarlae said. "You're going to get yourself killed."

"You know a better way to die than to go down fighting?" he asked her. Their eyes met, and Trey winked.

Tarlae growled, but Ernie saw the tiny smile on her face. Her chest ached. This might all be over in a few moments, and she would have liked to see them get back together. But she guessed a happy ending was out of their reach now.

"I'm ready," she said, holding the Sunrise and its key in one hand and her deck in the other.

"Ready, aim, fire, then," said Gabe, grimacing as he fought to keep the shield up.

But already Ernie could see that it wouldn't be easy—they were surrounded by enemy Dealers, and Virginia had withdrawn to the top of a dune to watch the fight. Her gauzy white gown billowed in the desert wind. Rage spiraled up Ernie's back; this was a game to Virginia. She was enjoying herself while she used them all as pawns. "I'm going after her. You guys can—"

"Go with you," said Minh.

"No," said Kot. "We will—"

The shield popped with a blast that deafened Ernie. The Dealers on the outside of the bubble stumbled back. Ernie played her Transport card and vanished herself just as some sort of weapon whooshed by her face, kissing her with its blade. Her cheek stinging, she spun out of the void on the dune next to Virginia. Immediately, Gabe, Minh, Tarlae, and Nuria appeared around her. The Grasshopper Dealer's delicate face was stiff with determination as she whipped around and put up a shield of her own to block the incoming strikes from the enemy Dealers who had realized what had happened.

Virginia seemed to notice that the battleground had shifted, and she turned toward them. Gritting her teeth, her blood singing, Ernie shoved her deck into her pocket. She stuck the key into the Sunrise and turned it, one twist of her wrist to seal her fate, one little click that shook her world. The gold-veined egg seared her palm with a blast of molten heat, and Ernie screamed.

Virginia's eyes went wide as the Sunrise rose from Ernie's burned hand to float above the group of allied Dealers. The Forger held out her hands as the egg-shaped relic began to glow, filling the sky with streaks of orange and yellow and pink. With a vicious snarl, Virginia swept her clawed hands toward the ground.

A solid dome slammed down over Ernie and her allies. She could hear their voices bouncing in a mad cacophony off the walls of their prison, but she couldn't see a thing. Not because of darkness, though. Instead, the glow of the Sunrise was in there with them, shining so brightly that it blinded Ernie instantly. Her eyeballs burned with light as the terrible realization hit her—the Forger had shut them inside some sort of structure with the weapon Ernie had activated. "Oh, god," she whispered, her hand in her pocket, her fingers groping for a card that would bring escape or protection. Legs throbbed on her arm. A strange humming vibrated against her skin.

146

"This is bad," Minh shouted. "Escape won't work. My Transport card—"

"*Nothing* is working," Tarlae shrieked. "I can't see!"

The hum became louder. Ernie's world was white, and all she felt was regret. "I'm sorry," she wailed.

Gabe's arms closed around her. "I love you," he whispered.

I love you, too, Ernie thought as despair washed over her. The humming became a storm of noise that filled every corner of her mind, leaving no place to hide.

And then everything exploded, and Ernie's world went from white to black.

CHAPTER FIFTEEN

At first, the darkness was complete and silent and heavy. It lay over Ernie like a lead blanket, pressing her down, filling her ears and nose and throat. But slowly, it pulled back, receding with each breath until a soft glow behind her eyelids brought her into awareness. A lilting sound trickled into her consciousness, liquid and soft, like a flute. Birdsong—a thrush, maybe? She inhaled, breathing in the scent of green, sharp and pungent, soft and fragrant, all at once.

Her eyes fluttered open as a cool breeze fluttered through her hair. Branches dotted with buds and leaves waved overhead, framing a brilliant blue sky. She tried to sit up but found she couldn't move. In fact, she couldn't feel anything below her chin. She was breathing; she knew that. And thinking. But she couldn't so much as scratch the itch on her nose. Unease slid through her. Was this permanent? Was she paralyzed? She lay still and focused on moving her fingers but wasn't even sure she was still connected to them, and she couldn't raise her head to check. And then another realization struck her:

She couldn't feel her heart beating. She wasn't sure whether it even was.

Oh, god. She was certain she'd tried to say that out loud, and certain her lips had moved, but she hadn't been able to make a sound. Her unease was rapidly morphing into fear. What the hell had happened? How had she gotten here?

The Sunrise. She'd tried to use it against Virginia. It had been their last hope. But the Forger had easily thwarted her brilliant plan *and* destroyed the relic Ernie had traveled to the deepest part of the ocean to retrieve. It had taken a mere instant for Virginia to conjure a sort of blast dome. A mere instant for her to trap Ernie and her allies: Gabe, Nuria, Tarlae, Minh—the ones who had been determined enough to join her, brave enough to risk everything. And it had taken only a few seconds after that for the Sunrise to detonate right next to them, like a nuclear blast.

When she and Gabe had first talked about the Sunrise and what it could do, Ernie had thought it might mean a new beginning, and Gabe had said that it might bring an apocalypse. Now it seemed that he'd made the better guess. The world hadn't ended, or at least, it seemed like it hadn't, but something had. Ernie felt it with a certainty that didn't make sense, considering that she wasn't even sure where she was or whether she was actually alive.

Legs? Was her diamondback still with her, or had they been separated? Ernie closed her eyes and sent a silent prayer heavenward. *Please let Legs be okay.* Her arm had burned right before the end. It might have been a goodbye, for all she knew. Just like the one she'd gotten from Gabe, the one that had broken her heart and filled her with a fierce joy all at once.

Gabe. Was he here, too? She couldn't turn her head. She couldn't hear anything except the birds and the breeze. The sun seemed to be fading fast, too, faster than it should, as if a few hours had passed within the last few minutes. The fear grew into a panic as Ernie contemplated lying in these woods all night, waiting for a predator to find her. Tears welled in her eyes as she struggled against the numbness, the paralysis, the utter helplessness, the despair. Had Virginia condemned them to this for daring to stand up to her? The Forger did seem fond of torture, and as peaceful and beautiful as this spot was, it gave Ernie no solace. Especially as she considered that Virginia was still out there, with her new army of Dealers, maybe making good on her promise to make ordinary people like Ernie's parents their slaves, and there wasn't a single damn thing Ernie could do about it.

The sun had set now, and the branches overhead were blending with the darkening sky above to become one blank black slate. Ernie stared up at the ebony nothing, trying to move, trying to speak.

She had no idea how long she'd been lying there when a dim glow filled her periphery. It was to her right, a clean white sort of illumination that painted the branches overhead with a glittering phosphorescence. Ernie squinted at the skeletal fingers dotted with buds, marveling at how they sparkled. Were branches supposed to sparkle?

The light became brighter, and Ernie felt warmth against her cheek. She sighed at its caress, wishing she could feel that kind of comfort in her entire body.

This was what she was thinking when the woman leaned over and let Ernie see her face. A maze of wrinkles so thick and numerous that it was difficult to look at the whole without getting lost in the fractal madness of all those lines and curves.

For a brief, painful second, Ernie remembered Nuria's drawing of the old woman.

The woman, her flowing white hair hanging down from her face like a pair of curtains, tilted her head and smiled a wide, toothy grin. She reached for Ernie with gnarled white hands.

Ernie screamed. Her eyes flew open as she awakened, tearing herself from the nightmare and bursting back into the waking world, her hands fisted, her legs jerking. Pain as deep as the Mariana Trench filled her chest, and a buzzing rattling filled her ears. She jerked her head to the side to see Legs coiled on the coffee table in Ernie's West Asheville apartment, her tail high and her head higher, her fangs bared, undulating in a way that conveyed pure agitation and rage. Ernie couldn't feel fear anymore, though—she was too preoccupied with the pain in her chest, right in her breastbone. She put her hand up to cover the spot and flinched as she touched a warm, hard object occupying the space. As soon as her fingers brushed it, sharp bolts of agony shot along her ribs and down her spine, drawing another scream from her and a violent hiss from Legs.

"Calm down," Ernie ordered her diamondback from between gritted teeth.

Instead, Legs struck. Ernie shrieked with surprise and pain as Legs's head collided with the object lodged in her chest. Legs hissed and rattled even louder but withdrew quickly, and when the red splotches of hurt cleared from her vision, she saw that Legs was coiled beside her—and one of her fangs had snapped. Ernie blinked at her, and then raised her head to look down at her own body.

Blood had crusted all over her chest, emanating out from the thing sticking up about two inches right from her breastbone. It looked to be made of stone—and veins of gold ran over its surface.

The Sunrise. It had exploded, and this shard was lodged in Ernie's freaking chest. "Oh my god," she wheezed, but even in her agony, it was a relief to hear her own voice, no matter how weak it sounded. With trembling fingers, she reached toward the stone splinter embedded in her sternum. Legs had probably been trying to get it out of her, and Ernie needed it gone. She knew all the conventional medical wisdom about not pulling out the knife if you'd been stabbed, but all of that seemed ridiculous and small in the face of her desperation to rid herself of the foreign object lodged in her body. She clenched her teeth to stifle a groan as her fingers closed around the exposed end of the shard. The Sunrise had been the size of an egg, so it couldn't have penetrated that deeply if this much was protruding from her skin. She was breathing, and her heart was beating. How bad could it be?

With those self-reassurances, she wrenched the stone splinter upward. It slid free after a moment of resistance, filling Ernie with so much pain that her world turned black for several long moments. By the time she was fully conscious again, Legs had stopped rattling and gone quiet.

Ernie lifted her head and stared at the wound. Her shirt was stiff and bloodstained, with a ragged hole where the Sunrise piece had hit her. Shaking, she managed to slide her shirt up, as well as her torn, crimson-soaked bra. She'd need to heal the wound, assuming she still had her cards. But when she ran her fingers over the spot, she felt only a smooth, raised welt of a scar. Ernie narrowed her eyes and stared at it.

It wasn't red or pink or even white. The scar was gold. She glanced over to see how much of the Forger-made artifact had been lodged in her, but all that was left of it was a little pile of ashes on the rug.

Frowning, Ernie sat up. Legs rattled quietly and slithered a bit farther away. "Hey. It's me. I'm still here." She reached into her pocket and sighed when she felt her deck right where it should be. She held her left arm out, offering it to her diamondback, but Legs hissed and bared her one and a half fangs. Ernie pulled her Healing card from the deck, whipped it out of her pocket, and held it out to the reptile. "Come on. We're a team, and you're hurt."

Legs stared at Ernie with her lidless eyes, as if considering the offer. She didn't move any closer to Ernie, but she also didn't withdraw when Ernie crept toward her. Moving slowly seemed to work, and it was also about the only speed Ernie had available to her at that moment. Her entire body ached like she'd just done three Spartan Beast races back to back. Her hand was unsteady as she brushed Legs's snout with the card, but Legs obligingly stayed still, and both of them let the card do its work. Legs's fang elongated and grew back to its original form.

"Now we're all back to normal," Ernie said with a smile. Then she looked down at her blood-covered chest and cringed. "Mostly, anyway."

Legs didn't seem ready to slither back onto Ernie's arm, so Ernie got up to take a shower. Her mind felt stuffed with cotton batting, and perhaps a shower would clear out the cobwebs and allow her to focus and think. She knew what had happened, sort of. And she could feel the dread and anxiety of a million terrible thoughts clawing at the insulation of her mind to reach her consciousness. She was supposed to be somewhere. She was missing something. Things had gone wrong, and she had to fix them. Everyone she loved was in danger. But she couldn't quite make sense of any of it, and all she wanted was to be clean.

She stripped off her filthy clothes and stepped under the hot water, letting it massage her knotted, weary muscles and wash the grime and gore from her skin. She peered down at the scar on her chest. It was between her breasts, a small, raised golden starburst with jagged tendrils that extended in strange, sparkling veins almost up to her collarbone. She scrubbed gently at it, wishing it would wash away as easily as the blood, but it seemed to be under the skin. Like a bruise, maybe. Perhaps it would go away with enough time.

For some reason, the thought of it marking her for good made her want to throw up. It was a stark reminder of what she'd done to her allies.

Her allies. Ernie cursed softly and twisted the faucet, killing the water. She needed to find out what had happened to the others. Had Virginia gotten them? Had they escaped? Ernie had no idea how she'd gotten back to her apartment, or how she'd managed to sleep deeply enough to have a nightmare about an old woman, but she hoped that the others had been that lucky. Well, not the nightmare part. She just hoped they hadn't been maimed or injured by the supernatural grenade she'd detonated so close to them.

A shout from the living room set her heart racing. Ernie grabbed a towel as a familiar Irish voice cursed fluently and loudly. Wrapping the towel around her body, she stumbled out into the living room to see Gabe facing off with Legs, who was hissing and rattling like she had earlier. Without looking over at Ernie, he said, "Call off your serpent, Ernie. I'd hate to lock her in a box, but I'll do it if it'll save me from being fanged into oblivion."

"Legs!" Ernie made her way across the living room with aching limbs, reaching out to the agitated diamondback. "Lady, what the hell? He's our favorite guy, remember?"

Legs stopped hissing, and her rattling subsided but didn't stop completely. Ernie turned to Gabe—and gasped.

The entire right side of his face was laced with the same veins of gold that decorated her chest, emanating forth from a starburst scar on his jaw, near his ear. One vein ended just beneath his eye, while another undulated along his temple. A third wound across his cheek to the bridge of his nose, and another ended at the corner of his mouth. "Looks like it hit you, too," Gabe said, eyeing her chest.

"I'm sorry," she whispered.

"We all chose it," he said. "We chose to fight back and stand with you." He moved toward her. "And we're still standing, love."

Legs rattled louder as Ernie stepped into his arms. She laid her head on his chest and felt his heart beating, wishing that it was the only sound she needed to attend to. "I don't know what's wrong with her," Ernie said.

"Caera's the same." Gabe held out his arm and pulled up his sleeve, revealing nothing but a stretch of tanned skin. "She's near—I can feel her close. But she doesn't want to be on my arm right now."

"It's the Sunrise, right?" Ernie looked down and traced her fingers along the glinting veins of gold on her chest. The skin above them was numb. "I hope it's not going to make us sick or turn us into zombies or something. God, that would figure, right? It was a relic meant to bring on the zombie apocalypse, and we accidentally made ourselves patient zero."

"You've lost me."

She squeezed her arms tighter around his waist, drawing a groan from him. "I forgot that you're an old man. Someday, when all of this is behind us, we can binge-watch *The Walking Dead*."

"Sounds . . . fun?" He kissed her forehead. "I'm so glad you're alive," he murmured against her skin. "For a while, I wasn't even sure I was."

"Me too. I woke up in the woods, and I lay there for hours until a super creepy old lady came along and terrified me awake. Turned out the whole thing was a dream."

Gabe pulled back so he could look down at her. "Creepy old lady?"

Ernie nodded. "All in white, long hair, and more wrinkles than a shar-pei."

He took her by the shoulders. "Did she say anything to you?"

"I screamed myself awake before she had a chance."

"But it wasn't Virginia."

"Similarities aside, it definitely wasn't her." She tilted her head as she took in the perplexed look on Gabe's face. "What is it?"

"I think I might have had almost the same dream." He released her and backtracked away from Legs, who was still rattling softly from across the room. "I was on a cold beach. I could hear the waves crashing close by, and the tide was rising. I couldn't move to get myself out of the way, and the water was covering my face every other wave." He looked down at the floor and shook his head. "I couldn't save myself, and it was happening so fast, like every second was a minute, every minute an hour."

"And you saw her?"

He shrugged. "I saw someone. I had water in my eyes and my nose, and I couldn't breathe. But there was this light, and then she leaned over me. I think she might have said something, but the water was in my ears and the waves were crashing . . . I woke up before I could hear anything she said, and I was in my cottage. Awful pain in my face."

"You had a piece of the Sunrise embedded in your jaw, I'm guessing."

He gave her a crooked smile. "Better than right between my eyes."

Ernie looked down at herself. "Or right between your breasts."

He arched an eyebrow. "Now, that's not so bad, either. At least, from where I stand."

She pulled her towel higher but couldn't suppress her smile. "I'll go get dressed."

"No rush," he called out as she headed to her bedroom. She slapped on a pair of jeans and a long-sleeved Tar Heels T-shirt, then grabbed a pair of warm socks and went out to the living room.

Gabe was sitting at the kitchen table, having a staring contest with Legs.

"She's unbeatable," Ernie said as she sat down and pulled on her socks. "She never blinks."

"Just making sure I'm ready to escape if she goes for me. Not like it hasn't happened before, but I thought we had a truce." He winked at Ernie. "I figured I had an in."

"You're acting so calm."

"You're not exactly hysterical yourself. I wonder if we're both in shock."

"Have you heard from any of the others?"

"No. Since you and I are all right, save our new"—he waved his hand at his face—"whatever this is, I'm hoping they are, too."

"Do you think those marks will go away?"

"Maybe? But they don't hurt. A little numb is all. I have other scars, so this one fits right in." He traced his finger over the old scar above his eyebrow. "I think our bigger worry is being found by a pack of new Dealers with a mind to take us out and curry favor with Virginia."

"God, I didn't even think of that. I guess I shouldn't hope she's too busy destroying humanity to come after us. Do you think she knows we're alive?"

Gabe shrugged. "Won't take her long to figure it out, I wager."

"She can't focus on everything at once. She's not omnipotent."

"Which is why she kept us all busy brewing up a catastrophe so she could spend her time creating dozens of new decks and Dealers that will obey her without question."

"While simultaneously trying to crush our spirits, apparently." She rose to fetch each of them a glass of water. As she drank hers, she realized how desperately thirsty she was, and Gabe seemed to feel the same. They both ended up at the sink, filling and refilling their glasses, drinking at least four or five apiece before sitting back and staring at each other.

"I guess we built up a thirst," Gabe muttered.

"I'm starving," Ernie blurted out. She'd have thought her stomach would be all sloshy now, but a fierce hunger had replaced the thirst.

Gabe nodded, swallowing hard. "We need to eat."

She almost whimpered in agreement. Gabe pulled out his deck and whipped out his Nourishment card, but all that appeared on the table was a bowl of squirming night crawlers. "What does it say about me that I'm considering eating those?" he asked quietly.

"That you're as hungry as I am," she said, playing her own Nourishment card, imagining roasted vegetable sandwiches, corn bread, sweet potato pie, the works—and receiving a pile of dead mice in return. "And that our animals are in a bad mood." She lunged for the pantry and pulled out a jar of peanut butter and another of Nutella.

A few minutes later, both jars were empty. Ernie clinked spoons with Gabe. "Remind me to take you out for really good pie at Buxton Hall sometime. A time that is not now. We need to find Minh, Tarlae, and Nuria before Virginia does."

"I think—" Gabe whipped out his deck and turned toward the door as someone banged on it, then he dove in front of Ernie as the door exploded inward, showering them with splinters.

CHAPTER SIXTEEN

Ernie drew her cards and fanned them as Gabe stepped to the side, revealing three of the new Dealers from the desert fight. The red-haired woman in high heels was wearing a sleeveless shell and a pencil skirt, and on her forearm lay a scorpion. Next to her was a rail-thin young man with glasses, and he was standing close enough to Ernie that she could see some kind of bear devouring the world on the backs of his cards. On his other side was a person who seemed to defy the whole gender binary altogether, with close-cropped pink hair and a shadow of stubble on their jaw, wearing lace-up boots and a miniskirt.

On their forearm lay a hippo, mouth wide to reveal its enormous teeth.

"Oh, crap," Ernie said as she realized what Virginia had done—she'd chosen the most dangerous and lethal animals to power her new Dealers.

"You knew you couldn't run for long," said the red-haired woman, pacing deeper into the room, strutting as if she were the freaking landlady. "She knows you survived, and she wants the Sunrise."

Ernie laughed. "You're a little late for that." She took a few steps back, closer to the hallway. She clutched Gabe's hand and tugged him along. The Dealers from Virginia's new crop came forward, holding their decks. "The Sunrise is gone."

The Hippo Dealer smiled. "Then it's time to surrender. We're taking you to her."

"Tell her to run her own errands," Gabe suggested. He squeezed Ernie's hand.

A deafening rattling shook the walls, and the three Dealers spun around to see Legs, who had grown herself huge, with her head, the size of a gallon of milk, brushing the ceiling. "Legs," Ernie shouted. "Get over here!"

Ernie played a few cards—Weapon, Accelerate, and Enemy—to toss her furniture at the enemy Dealers as she ran along the side of the room and held her arm out. As the intruders hurled strikes at Legs, Ernie's Shield card jumped into her hand, and she flung up a barrier to protect the diamondback. Legs shimmered in midair and twisted herself onto Ernie's arm, where she throbbed and burned. Gabe, who had flattened the Scorpion Dealer against the wall and pinned the other two beneath the couch, grabbed Ernie's hand and yanked her into the void. She clung to him as he dragged her through the darkness, and they both hit concrete and staggered. They were outside in the parking lot. Ernie's arm was killing her—and so was the scar on her chest.

"Caera," Gabe roared. "I'm not going without you, ya geebag!"

The Kestrel spiraled through the air and dove toward them, pecking hard at the top of Ernie's head before slamming onto her Dealer's arm. He grunted at the impact. The windows of Ernie's apartment blew out, and glass rained down on them. When the enormous hippo shoved its head out of the opening and bellowed, Ernie wrapped her arm around Gabe's waist and spun them into the void again. They arrived in front of his old haven, the stone cottage on the rocky Irish bluff overlooking the ocean. Gabe played his Conceal card and Ernie followed suit, and then they were off again, this time with Gabe leading. When they emerged from the void, they were in an alley right at the edge of a busy city street. "Where are we?" she asked, breathless.

"Bangkok," he said, leaning against the wall, his chest heaving. He winced and rubbed his arm, then his jaw. "Christ, but this hurts."

"I know," she said, grimacing. Legs did not seem happy to be on her arm, but she wasn't emerging right now, either, perhaps sensing that Ernie needed her to stay put and come along for the ride. A terrible thought hit her. "Did I just lead those Dealers to your haven?"

He stroked her arm. "It's okay. I built myself a new one after everything that happened."

They'd had a massive battle with Virginia right on his doorstep, so that made a lot of sense. "Where are we going now? And can they follow?"

"Not as long as our concealments hold up. We won't be able to run forever, but maybe we can find our allies and find a way to help each other." Gabe pulled out his Revelation card. "And it might not be as hard as I was thinking. Kot's signaling me."

Ernie drew her own Revelation card and peered beneath the omega symbol. "Whoa." There was Kot, his arms around Nuria, trying to hold her back as she reached frantically for the papers that Ernie and Gabe had helped her lover assemble. Spread across her right palm was a very familiar-looking gold starburst mark. "I guess that's where we need to be."

Gabe pulled her against him, and she looked up at his face. The golden veins along his cheekbone glinted under the nearby neon lights, and she traced her fingers along them. "Someday," he said, "we'll be able to breathe. We'll be able to rest."

"And go to Buxton Hall for pie?"

He lowered his head and kissed her tenderly. "And biscuits and all the rest of it." Then he crossed his Transport card with Revelation and Conceal, and they traveled to the Mexican cabana, where Kot was wrestling with Nuria. He'd pinned her to the bed, their bodies writhing among the papers, but it was not in the least bit romantic—he looked absolutely tortured, and she was sobbing, clawing desperately for her scribbled drawings.

"Kot," Gabe said roughly, striding up the steps. "Is she going to hurt herself?"

"She is making no sense, and she will not calm down," Kot cried. "She's been getting more and more upset, and I don't know how to soothe her."

Nuria thrashed beneath the heavier body of the Dragonfly Dealer, tears streaming down her face, her scarred hand splayed on the mattress. On impulse, Ernie crawled onto the bed and pulled down the collar of her shirt to reveal the golden veins emanating from the starburst scar. Nuria went still.

"Gabe?" Ernie said. "Come over here where she can see you."

He obeyed, leaning down and turning his face so she could see his scar. "You're not alone, darlin'," he said gently. "We're in it with you."

"Fuh," Nuria said by way of reply. "Fuh?"

"The Forger is an evil bitch who's going to come after us with all she's got?" Ernie nodded. "If that's what you're saying, then the answer is yes."

Nuria's brow furrowed, and she shook her head. *"Fuh."* She said it slowly, deliberately, as if Ernie were being thick.

Ernie lightly touched Nuria's hand, then poked Kot. "Get off her. I know you're trying to protect her, but I really think she needs to figure all this out, or else she'll never settle down."

Kot jerked his head toward a small table near one of the billowing silk walls of the cabana. There, about the size of a house cat, was the grasshopper. "Her animal is unsettled, too, and they seem to be at war." He winced and swallowed as if there were a terrible taste in his mouth. "I am afraid they are going to merge again," he added in a strained voice.

"Not what's happening," Gabe said. "Unless it's happening to us, too. Caera's none too happy to be with me right now, and I don't think Legs is giving Ernie an easy time of it, either. Not to mention Legs nearly bit my head off when I showed up tonight."

Kot lifted his body off Nuria's, allowing her to sit up. Instead of diving for the drawings, she seemed content to trace the lines of her new, golden scar and croon to it softly. "I was so relieved to find her alive," Kot said, watching her closely. "When she transported away from my side, I thought that was the last time I would see her. And when I saw Virginia put that dome around all of you, I knew I was watching all the people I cared about die, and there was nothing I could do. Although I did try. I fought to get to all of you. But when the dome exploded, it sent a shock wave over the entire desert. I was knocked flat, and the only thing I could do was play Escape." He hung his head. "I was a coward."

"You were a survivor," Ernie said. "And so is Nuria. So am I. So is Gabe. We need to find Minh and Tarlae and make sure they are, too." She had no idea what to think about Trey, though—but that would have to wait until they found Minh and Tarlae, who'd been under the blast dome. "We'll keep each other alive and figure out how to turn the tide in our favor. There's no way Virginia's got what we have."

"And what's that?" asked Kot.

"An actual team. She's created a bunch of newbies who'll operate with blunt force and only for themselves." She looked back and forth from Kot to Nuria, and then at Gabe, who met her gaze with a fond smile. "We actually care about each other, and we've got something worth fighting for."

Kot chuckled, a deep and desolate sound. "You are either admirable or insane, and I have not yet decided which."

Ernie lifted her chin as Nuria tugged down the collar of Ernie's T-shirt to view her scar again. Humming happily to herself, Nuria traced the veins, all the way to the starburst scar. Ernie cleared her throat and took Nuria's hand in hers. Nuria reached out with her left and picked up one of the drawings that lay within reach. "Fuh," she said. She touched her own temple. "Fuh." She bowed her head and made a little snoring noise, then feigned popping awake. "Fuh?" She touched Ernie's chest where the scar lay, then poked her in the forehead.

Ernie turned to Kot. "Where was Nuria when you found her?"

"She was here," he said. "I couldn't believe it. She was sleeping in the sand, right next to the cabana."

"I wonder if our animal spirits whisked us off to the safest places they knew as the Sunrise exploded that dome that had trapped us," Gabe said.

Kot shrugged. "She awoke happy, and she seemed even happier when she saw the scar. But then she became agitated again and returned to all those papers!"

"What was she doing with them?"

"Assembling them in some order, drawing more indecipherable figures on each sheet, then rearranging them. But the longer she did it, the more agitated she became, and then the grasshopper attacked her, and I had to tear them apart." He sighed. "I can't make sense of any of this. But I have taken her cards and locked them away, for now." He angled his head at a small, locked trunk sitting on a wooden table nearby. "I do not want her to disappear again."

Ernie picked up one of the papers, one she remembered trying to find a place for earlier that day. Next to one of the squiggles that her father had said was a rune, Nuria had drawn something else, a stick figure of a creature with an oval for a body, four lines for legs, and two dots for eyes. "Is this an animal?"

"I suppose?" Kot said. "She's been drawing things like that all over the place."

"It seems like Nuria had a different kind of dream than we did," Ernie said slowly. "Hey—do you have that drawing she did right before she disappeared last time?"

Looking weary, Kot pulled the crumpled paper out of one of his pockets. "Here it is."

Ernie took it and spread it across the bed, then touched Nuria's shoulder. "Who is this?"

Nuria grinned. She scooped the paper up and hugged it against her chest. "Fuh."

"Are you thinking this old woman she drew isn't Virginia at all?" Gabe asked.

"Nuria was willing to fight Virginia to the death, but now she's all lovey-dovey with that drawing. Something tells me it's not of our Forger."

"You think it's the woman in both of our dreams." Gabe turned to Kot and offered the condensed version of his and Ernie's dreams, ending with the woman in white.

"But who *is* it?" Kot asked when Gabe had finished. "That description fits Virginia."

"And yet," said Ernie. "I think that's something we'll have to figure out as we go along, as all we know is that Nuria is drawing animals now instead of an old lady."

Gabe shrugged. "We also know . . . fuh."

Nuria grinned and nodded eagerly, showing him the starburst scar on her palm yet again.

Gabe had pulled his deck and was peering at his Revelation card. He frowned and crossed it with a few others. "I've got Minh," he said. "He's not concealed as well as he usually is, but he's also not responding to my summons the way he usually does."

Ernie looked over at Gabe's cards to see a blurry view of Minh curled up on the bed in his haven. "Is he okay?"

"Let's go find out." Gabe flipped his Transport card up and crossed it with Revelation, Ally, and Aid.

"I will stay here with Nuria and the grasshopper," said Kot, his face lined with strain as he watched his love shuffle through her papers again, then reach for a pencil to make another drawing.

"Nuria hasn't named the grasshopper?" Ernie asked, then pressed her lips closed. "I guess that would be kind of hard, right?"

Kot shrugged. "She may have named him, but she is not able to tell me. The animal likely knows either way, but right now they are at odds."

"Tell me about it," Gabe muttered, rubbing at his left forearm. "Come on, love."

Ernie took his hand, and together they were transported to Minh's haven in the Vietnamese jungle. From deep within the woods came a squeal and a bellow, along with the sound of something crashing through the brush. Ernie eyed the undergrowth. "Bao?" she asked softly.

"I'm thinking yeah," Gabe said, looking wary. "Let's get inside."

The door of the simple hut hung open, and the sight awakened Ernie's uneasiness. She peeked through the doorway to see that the spare furnishings inside had been destroyed, pottery broken and furniture smashed. Minh was curled up in a fetal position on his pallet, and Ernie rushed to his side. He was bare from the waist up, and his ripped and bloody shirt lay crumpled on the floor. He clutched at his head and mumbled to himself in another language, most likely his native tongue.

"How are you faring, mate?" Gabe asked gently as he leaned over his ally. "Bao seems a bit restive, huh?"

Minh didn't show any indication of having heard him. His knees were pulled almost to his head, and he lay on his side, rocking gently. Blood stained the sheets beneath him, and Ernie pointed to a large splotch beneath his waist and ribs. "He's hurt."

"Probably a piece of that damn relic," Gabe said. "He's going through the same thing we did."

"But you, me, and Nuria are all okay," she replied, pulling at Minh's shoulders to try to see his chest and belly. Minh didn't fight her—he was too focused on holding his head. His eyes were squeezed shut, and he dripped with sweat. When they got his legs straightened a little, Ernie could see the problem—a large piece of the Sunrise had embedded itself in his abdomen, above his belly button and below his rib cage. The shard protruded up perhaps an inch, telling Ernie that more lay beneath the surface—his wound was deeper than hers had been. "I'm going to pull it out."

Gabe made a worried face. "You sure that's the right play?"

"Mine healed instantly as soon as I removed it—did yours?"

Gabe nodded. "But it didn't look *that* bad."

"Which is probably why he hasn't been able to do it himself yet." Ernie knelt at Minh's side and stroked his thick black hair away from his face. He groaned and kept muttering to himself, whispered syllables of heartbreaking desperation, almost a prayer. Given that Minh's default demeanor was smooth and sardonic, and usually gave away few of his innermost thoughts, this display made Ernie's chest hurt, sending pulses of pain along her starburst scar and the golden tendrils that emanated from its center.

When she touched the Sunrise shard embedded in Minh's body, those pulses coalesced into a sudden burst of agony. She yanked her hand back, shaking out her fingers. "Crap." She looked around the hut. "Is a pair of pliers too much to ask for?"

Gabe arched his eyebrow and held up his deck. *"Really?"*

Her cheeks heated. "I'm under a little bit of stress here, okay? Florence Nightingale I am not."

Gabe played his Tool card and produced a large pair of pliers. "I'll hold his shoulders. In my extremely limited experience, pulling one of those out hurts like a bitch."

"No argument here." She accepted the pair of pliers and waited as Gabe positioned himself behind Minh. Gabe pulled the smaller man's shoulders against his back, and Minh struggled a bit, every muscle taut, but without his deck and his usual wiry and focused strength, he was no match for Gabe. Ernie swallowed hard, offered a silent mental apology, and positioned the open pliers over the splinter of gold-veined stone. Gritting her teeth, she closed the pliers over the Sunrise shard and pulled. It slid free quickly, sending bolts of heat up through the plier handles and into Ernie. Minh screamed, his eyes flying open and his entire body shaking. The pliers fell to the wooden floor and so did the Sunrise piece, which spurted blue and green flames that faded to reveal only black ash in the space of a few seconds.

Ernie rubbed her throbbing hands over her thighs. Minh had collapsed onto Gabe, his chest heaving with each labored breath. The wound in his abdomen closed. A starburst scar formed rapidly, and veins of gold grew up along Minh's chest and down along his abs. Minh's brown eyes scanned the room, and Ernie expected them to settle on her or Gabe. She expected a sarcastic remark to escape his lips. But instead, his eyes fell shut again, his hands rose to clutch at his head, his knees rose to his chest, and he began to mutter in that same frantic, pained way he had before. "Why isn't he better?" she asked.

Gabe shook his head. "Maybe we can figure out what he's saying, though." He drew his Translate card, and so did Ernie, and they listened.

"It's *there*, it's there in the rocks in the tunnel in the place, the place, the place where it's waiting, four lengths away and a left turn at the third fold in the place, the place, the place where it's been stuck."

"Gibberish," Gabe said, shaking his head.

But Ernie wasn't so sure. She used the Translate card to speak in Vietnamese to Minh. Even though his English was perfect, it seemed like his first language was the only one available to him right now. "What is it?" she asked. "The thing that's waiting?"

"To the seventh fold, four lengths away," he said.

"Thanks for clarifying," Ernie mumbled. She looked over at Gabe. "Any ideas?"

Gabe shook his head as Minh continued, "And the eleventh fold, nine lengths. And the fifth, a thousand lengths. And the second, five hundred and ninety-seven."

"He might need some time to come back to himself," Gabe said. "We can ask him—"

Bao, Minh's pot-bellied pig, crashed into the hut with thunderous force that belied his compact size. He careened off the walls, squealing and grunting. Ernie dove on top of the beast, hoping to keep him from hurting himself, but he threw her off and ran at Minh. Gabe scooped Minh off the bed, as it was obvious that Bao was raging, definitely not in his usual affectionate mood. Bao slammed into Gabe's legs, sending him stumbling backward with Minh in his arms. As soon as he ran into Gabe, though, Bao paused and sat down, looking up at him as if awaiting a command.

Gabe's eyes flashed as he glared at the pig, who suddenly seemed entranced. "Take a nap, will ya?"

Bao collapsed to the floor, already snoring.

Ernie's mouth dropped open. "Gabe . . . how the *hell* did you do that?"

CHAPTER SEVENTEEN

"No idea," Gabe muttered. "Might be he exhausted himself. But I'm glad he listened. Let's take them back to Kot and Nuria. I think we've got a bit of safety in numbers."

"Yeah, and two seriously impaired Dealers whose animals aren't exactly cooperating right now." She leaned down to pat Bao's bristly hair.

"You'd never leave Minh here," Gabe said, "and if we need to go find Tarlae, at least Kot and Nuria might be able to watch him. Bao would have space to rampage on the beach if he wakes up."

It seemed as reasonable a plan as any, so Gabe traveled with Minh, and Ernie brought the snoring pig. Legs wasn't fighting her, but she wasn't making it easy, either. Ernie's forearm burned like she'd laid it on a hot griddle, and her fingers twitched with the hurt. And as soon as Ernie alighted on the Mexican beach, Legs slithered off her arm and made a beeline for the seagrass. Ernie watched her rattle disappear into the brush, shamefully glad to have her gone for the moment. Not only did her arm feel better, but so did the starburst scar on her chest.

A shriek from the trees drew Ernie's gaze upward in time for her to see Caera take off from a palm tree. Gabe had already gone into the cabana with Minh, so Ernie left Bao slumbering on the beach and trudged through the sand to the open, silk-walled structure that seemed like it had become a makeshift psychiatric hospital. The grasshopper was nowhere in sight, but Nuria seemed pleased to have Minh there. As he lay on the bed mumbling, she was arranging her drawings around him, her expression serious and focused, while Kot eyed them both with naked alarm. Gabe put his hand on Kot's shoulder. "Compared to Minh, I'd say she's in pretty good shape," he said.

"Is that really supposed to make me feel better?" snapped Kot as he watched Nuria place one of her drawings over Minh's face. He barely seemed to notice, and the paper rippled and shook with every mumbled word that flew from his mouth. Ernie decided Kot had a point, because Nuria seemed to be getting more agitated with every passing second. She repeated that same syllable—*Fuh*—saying it to Minh as if she expected him to know what she was talking about, and she seemed more frustrated with him than she had been with Ernie and Gabe when he didn't respond with recognition. When she began to tug on Minh's arm, Kot intervened, gently pulling her hand away and speaking to her with a fond care that temporarily concealed his frustration and fear.

"Are there cards we can play to fix the two of them?" Ernie asked. "Wisdom? Aid?"

"We can try," Gabe said. He turned, expertly pulling his deck and fanning his cards, as a dark figure appeared in the sand next to the still-sleeping pig. Gabe's face brightened. "Tarlae."

She strode toward them, looking clear-eyed and pissed—but wonderfully uncrazy. A cloth bag was slung across her body, hanging by a strap.

"You're okay," Ernie said, smiling as the Coconut Octopus mounted the steps and entered the cabana.

"I am not okay." Tarlae pulled up the skirt of her maxi dress to reveal her right thigh, where a golden starburst scar decorated her brown skin, along with the same sparkling veins that emanated from Ernie's, Gabe's, Nuria's, and Minh's scars. "Rika has turned on me, and when she is on my arm, everything hurts."

"Where is she, then?" Gabe asked.

Tarlae stroked her bag and the bundle within. "I played Rest on her and put her in here."

"Now that was pretty damn smart," Ernie said, wondering whether Legs would forgive her if she did the same.

"Of course it was smart," Tarlae sniped. "But those damn new Dealers came after me, and we had to escape quickly."

"Did you play Conceal?" Ernie asked.

Tarlae gave her a look suggesting she was insulted at the mere inquiry. "There were three of them. A bright-blue frog—"

"Poison dart frog!" Ernie was happy that she knew that but shut her mouth again instantly. Tarlae was the freaking *queen* of throwing shade with a single glance. "Please go on."

"Some sort of snail, and a shark," Tarlae continued. "They are dangerous, with much raw power, but as Kot observed in the desert, clumsy."

"I think Virginia's bequeathing the most dangerous animal spirits to her new minions," said Ernie.

"What's wrong with the two of them?" Tarlae had turned toward the bed, where Minh lay and Nuria sat next to him. The Grasshopper Dealer had snagged a paper and a pencil from the bed and was scribbling yet another stick-figure animal next to one of the rune squiggles. She held it up, glared at Kot, and jabbed her finger at the page.

Kot put up his hands. "I wish I knew," he said to Tarlae.

"Minh was hurt with a large chunk of the Sunrise and hasn't recovered yet," Ernie said.

Tarlae nodded. "I awakened in my haven and had to pull a piece of it out of my leg."

"So you were asleep, too?" Ernie looked down at Tarlae's bag as one of Rika's tentacles emerged and whipped back and forth.

Tarlae nodded. "I had a nightmare. For weeks I have dreamed of Trey and how I lost him, but this was different. There was a woman in—"

"White?" asked Gabe. "Ernie and I saw her, too, and we think Nuria may have as well."

"And Minh?" Tarlae tilted her head and listened to him muttering. "I suppose he can't tell you."

"He's talking about something that's hidden somewhere," said Ernie. "But he's not saying what, and everything else is just . . . stuff about folds and lengths."

Nuria was struggling in Kot's grip again. "She's trying to get to her cards," he said as he held her.

"You're keeping her from her cards?" Tarlae's lip curled. "I would never be with a man who treated me like that. You must respect her."

Kot gave the Coconut Octopus Dealer a withering look. "If you knew what she could do with her cards, you would know it is a sign of my towering respect that I do not let her get to them right now."

"She isn't a child." Tarlae slapped at Rika's tentacle, which slapped her back on the wrist.

"She and I have been together for nearly twenty years," Kot snapped. "I cannot remember all we have been through, but the truth is written in my bones and defies dimensions. I have been her guardian and protector and worshipper for all that time, and she gave me the privilege of keeping her safe when she is not able to do that for herself. You," he added, his voice loud enough to cause Minh to clap his hands over his ears, "would know nothing of that kind of love."

Tarlae drew back as if Kot had rammed his fist into her middle. She turned away and stalked out of the cabana.

"That was harsh, Kot," Ernie said softly. "She's still mourning the loss of Trey, and I think it's even harder that he's back now but doesn't remember or seem to even want to."

"Perhaps I will apologize one day," Kot said drily.

Ernie was opening her mouth to reply when Tarlae screamed from outside. A dozen of the new enemy Dealers had appeared near the shore. They'd hemmed Tarlae in. One of them, a muscular, bald white guy with tattoos down either side of his neck, lunged for her, but Tarlae disappeared. She reappeared closer to the cabana, but the cloth bag containing Rika had been torn from her body, and the enemy Dealers had gathered around the Coconut Octopus. With a cry of rage, Tarlae fanned her cards and attacked, one Dealer against twelve.

"Gabe," Ernie shrieked, but he had already charged for the beach, along with Kot, leaving Ernie to protect Nuria and Minh. Three enemy Dealers were already peeling off and heading for them, so Ernie pulled her deck. With a glance at Nuria, she played Inverse and Lock, and the trunk containing the Grasshopper deck sprang open. Nuria yelped and jumped over Minh to get to her cards. She scooped them up and shouted something unintelligible. The grasshopper jumped down from one of the folds of silk, tiny but shimmering, and swirled into a glittering tattoo on Nuria's forearm. Nuria grimaced and rubbed at the tattoo, then fanned her cards and played two, making the three attacking Dealers disappear.

Nuria glanced at Ernie, pointed at the drawings scattered across the bed, then at Minh. "Fuh," she said.

Then she played another card and disappeared, too.

Ernie stared at the place she'd been. "Great. Kot will be so pleased."

The three Dealers Nuria had vanished appeared again, right at the front of the cabana. It was the Scorpion, the Poison Dart Frog, and the baby-faced young man from the desert, who turned out to be the Snail. As they struck, Ernie flung up a shield and ran to Minh's side. "Now would be a great time to wake up, friend," she shouted.

Minh blinked and hollered, "The eighty-eighth fold, sixty-nine lengths!"

At least it was in English this time. As her shield started to bow inward under the savage attacks of the three Dealers, Ernie looked toward the beach, where someone had kicked up so much sand that she could barely see the scrum inside, just a few grappling silhouettes and an occasional charging animal. At the sound of a rattle, Ernie turned to see that Legs had slithered back into the cabana and coiled herself at Ernie's feet. She lowered her arm, and the diamondback shimmied up onto her skin, awakening that same burning pain in both the tattoo and the scar, but also lending power to Ernie's plays.

She leapt onto the bed, stood protectively astride Minh, and faced off with the three Dealers. "You guys bet on the wrong horse," she yelled as her cards glowed and warmed her fingers. "Virginia won't do anything but use you and throw you away."

"We're going to rule at her side," said the Scorpion, tossing her red hair over her shoulder and playing Strike, sending knives flying at Ernie and Minh.

With a flick of her wrist, Ernie played Warp to alter the path of the blades. As soon as she thought of a play, the cards flew up to match it—Weapon and Shelter to encase the Poison Dart Frog, a wiry Indian man with an elegant nose and sharp brown eyes, in a small iron box. She played Draw, and several of the Snail's cards flew from his hand into hers. He yelped and clutched his cards to his chest, staggering backward and falling on his butt in the sand.

The Scorpion rolled her eyes and held out her arm, letting her animal scuttle off her skin. The red-haired Dealer played Amplify, and the creature became twice the size of the cabana, splintering the floor with its weight. Ernie knew her Shield card was going to be useless if she didn't give it some time to recharge, and she also knew Minh was helpless at the moment. The bed listed with the collapsing floor, and she played Aid and Ally to create a cushioned pocket, which Minh, at the mercy of whatever was going on in his head, rolled into as Ernie played Enemy and Sea, hoping to transport both the enormous scorpion and its unpleasant Dealer to the middle of the Pacific. But the Scorpion Dealer, clearly faster and more vicious than the other newbies, threw up a shield of her own to successfully block the strike.

The stinger of the giant scorpion rose, the hooked barb hanging over Ernie like a sword. "I don't know much about gambling," the

Scorpion said as she watched her animal prepare to attack. "But I think the odds are in my fav—" Her words were cut off by her scream as she went flying into the trees, tossed by an unseen force.

Gabe landed on the giant scorpion's back a second later. Ernie gaped—she expected that the animal would try to buck him off, that it would fight, but instead, it turned toward the red-haired woman, who was charging back toward them through the seagrass with her cards at the ready. With his hand on the scorpion's back, Gabe whispered something to the beast, and its barbed stinger shot downward and speared the woman in the chest. Her eyes went wide, and the fierce look dropped from her face, replaced by pure shock.

Gabe looked just as surprised. He jumped from the animal's back right before it shrank to its normal, diminutive size, its stinger pulling from its Dealer's chest as it did. The woman sank to her knees, and Gabe strode forward. He snatched her cards from her limp hands. The scorpion crawled up his boot and pant leg.

"It's on you," Ernie blurted out before using her Strike card to throw about five hundred sheets of flypaper at the Snail guy.

Gabe allowed the scorpion to crawl onto his hand as if it were the most natural move in the world. Ernie watched in awe as it sank into his palm, disappearing into his skin. The red-haired woman let out a helpless cry and aged before their eyes, withering to a hunched, skeletal crone before disintegrating into dust. Gabe raised his head and locked gazes with Ernie. He looked as shaken as she felt, but they had no time to analyze what had happened—there was a battle raging on the beach, and the Snail fellow and the Poison Dart Frog, who had finally managed to free himself from Ernie's box, had headed down there.

"Kot and Tarlae—" Ernie began.

"Were holding their own," Gabe said. "When I saw that thing standing over you, I couldn't—"

"I love you," Ernie said. "I didn't get to say it before, but—"

Gabe smiled. "I know." He ran toward the beach. Ernie thrilled at the sight, remembering a time when he had been ready to give up the fight, even to give up his deck. To see him now, protecting his allies, fierce and strong and unstoppable, was not only a relief but a triumph. She was proud that he'd held on, grateful that he'd made it this far . . . and more than a bit puzzled by the new ability he seemed to have acquired. How the heck had he gotten that scorpion, which by all rights should have flung him off and tried to sting him in order to protect its Dealer, to do his bidding?

No time. Ernie glanced at Minh, who was sitting up now in the cushioned wreckage of the bed, rocking back and forth, seemingly lost in his own world. Then she peered across the sand, where Gabe, Tarlae, and Kot were battling eleven inexperienced but strong Dealers.

Her allies were surrounded, and although they were fighting with skill and finesse, Ernie could see that they were being overpowered—the strikes were coming from too many directions. The newbies even sometimes hit each other in the chaos of the onslaught. A weak shield around Ernie's allies was fizzling and fading. Kot was bleeding from a shoulder wound, and his dragonfly, now the size of a delivery drone, had gotten shot out of the sky and was flitting and flailing in the sand several yards away. Tarlae was disappearing Dealer after Dealer, but they always reappeared quickly, and four were now focused on her. And Gabe, clearly the most dangerous, was having to fight a half dozen.

Ernie conjured a bomb shelter for Minh, hoping he would be out of sight and out of mind, and ran down to the beach to help Gabe. At least one newbie Dealer had gotten the idea that the Kestrel couldn't deal if his left arm were torn from his body, and for all Ernie knew, that could be a thing. Furious at the dirty fighting, she kicked up a ferocious sandstorm around a few of the newbies, then played Lock, Sea, and her Alchemy Wild. The swirling sand zipped together and formed a thick coating of concrete around the enemies, temporarily trapping them inside a stone skin.

Gabe pressed his Healing card to a deep gash in his shoulder and dealt with his right hand to hold off the two remaining Dealers who'd been trying to take him out. Figuring he could hold his own against novices, Ernie ran to help Tarlae while Kot dueled with the Poison Dart Frog.

The Coconut Octopus Dealer was hunched over Rika. The Dealers attacking her had figured out that Tarlae would do anything to protect her animal. Rika had shrunk herself down to her normal size, but she still presented an easy target for strikes, and she had already had a few of her tentacles severed. Blue blood spattered the sand. Her face alight with rage, Tarlae flung out a series of cards, twisting two of her opponents into terribly contorted shapes. Even with the noise of the battle, Ernie heard the pop of bones being torn loose from sockets as she ran.

Ernie was readying a play when she got hit from behind with ropes that wrapped tightly around her, winding around her throat and cutting off her air. She flopped onto the sand and watched helplessly as a thrown object, maybe a stone, slammed into Tarlae's head, knocking the woman to the ground. Two enemy Dealers, an Asian woman and a white woman with platinum-blond hair, closed in on her.

"Gabe," Ernie tried to shout. Tarlae needed help. She was bleeding from the head, and her cards were scattered in the sand. Rika thrashed impotently nearby. But the rope around Ernie's neck had cut off both voice and breath.

Smirking, the blonde played two cards, slashing them through the air, but before she'd completed the downward motion, the cards flew from her hand and landed in the palm of a man who'd appeared between Tarlae and her attackers.

It was Trey. His face rigid with focus, his hands nimble, he played a few cards and knocked the two enemy Dealers together. Ernie heard their skulls crack against each other, but she couldn't see anymore, because the stars in her vision were turning everything white and bright. The scar on her chest burned like the sun itself, and Ernie felt something she never had before, a need that she had no idea how to extinguish—although oxygen would probably have done the trick. Her thoughts turned fuzzy and bemused as unconsciousness dragged her under.

The ropes fell away and disappeared from around her body, and Ernie gulped air like a drowning woman, unclear about how long she'd been out. She shoved herself up and spun in place to find the beach empty of everyone except her allies, but all of them were gathered around Trey, who was convulsing on the beach.

Ernie stumbled over. Gabe and Kot had their Healing cards pressed to Trey's body, and Tarlae knelt next to his head with tears streaming down her face.

"What happened?" Ernie asked as she knelt in the sand and pulled her own Healing card.

Gabe looked grim as he tried to keep his card pressed to Trey's heaving form. "Bastards teamed up and managed to get most of his deck as he tried to defend Tarlae and Rika. Then someone hit him with a strike as they fled."

"He is dying, Tarlae," Kot said in a low voice. "Our Healing cards are only prolonging his suffering."

"He sacrificed himself for her," Ernie said quietly.

"I never asked him to do it," Tarlae wailed. She pressed her face close to his. "You idiot," she spat in a desperate whisper. "How dare you."

Trey grimaced as the convulsions subsided. "My choice, babe," he mumbled.

"Do you remember, then?" she asked him.

He groaned. "Call it instinct." He tried to wink, but his face pulled into a mask of pain that made it impossible. His olive skin had gone gray, and his handsome face was turning more gaunt by the second.

Tarlae flinched and put her hand over her thigh, right at the spot where Ernie knew the golden starburst scar lay. "I refuse to accept this." Every word was a harsh burst of defiance.

"Tarlae," said Gabe, reaching over to touch her shoulder. "If he's going, focus on giving him the best goodbye you can."

"Yeah," Trey croaked. "Kiss me for my trouble, maybe."

Tarlae jerked to throw off Gabe's hand. She bowed her head, her fingers curling tight over her thigh. Ernie felt a pang of sorrow. Tarlae had already lost Trey twice, once when Virginia took his deck, and once when he came back without his memories. Now it looked like his feelings were coming back—or forming anew—but it was too late. She couldn't imagine what Tarlae was going through.

Trey let out a shuddering breath, his jaw and cheekbones way too prominent in his skeletal face, his eyes sunk deep in his skull. Ernie stared at his chest, willing it to continue its rise and fall, overcome with dread as it remained still.

Tarlae raised her head abruptly, and Ernie lurched back. The woman's eyes glinted with gold, maybe a trick of the setting sun, but startling nonetheless. "I will not accept this," Tarlae shouted, flinging her arms wide.

Her hands were *glowing*. Golden tendrils grew from her fingertips and snaked down toward Trey's few remaining cards, which had been discarded in the sand as the others had fought to keep him alive. The delicate, liquid-looking golden strands picked the cards up and carried them to Tarlae, arranging them in front of her.

The allied Dealers gaped. Ernie had never seen any Dealer do anything like this. Tarlae's hands glowed like a blacksmith's forge, orange with golden veins flowing beneath. Tarlae scanned the arranged cards with her gold-streaked eyes, and the skin of her palms cracked and bled liquid gold.

Something began to emerge from her split flesh, sliding forth and plopping to the sand, flecked with blood.

It was a card.

CHAPTER EIGHTEEN

As one of the golden tendrils that had sprouted from Tarlae's fingertips reached down to pick the new card up and place it in the array in front of the Coconut Octopus Dealer, Ernie caught a glimpse of the back— it bore the Raccoon holding a globe in its hands. And as it rotated to face her like all the rest, it was revealed as a Revelation card, its omega symbol glowing.

By the time Ernie processed this, Tarlae had produced three more cards. Her blood fell in gold drops but hit the sand crimson and dark.

"Am I seeing this?" Kot murmured from Ernie's side.

"Shh," said Gabe. His eyes were on Trey, *who was breathing*.

"My god," Ernie whispered. "How—"

Gabe reached up and laid his finger across her lips. Ernie nodded and pressed them together. He was right not to distract Tarlae, whose face was turned to the sky as her hands birthed card after card. A dozen. Two dozen. Three dozen. Not one duplicate—each card was part of the deck, each one necessary to make Trey whole again. As the cards filled the gold-veined space around Tarlae and hovered a few feet above the Raccoon Dealer, his features filled out again. His hair went from wispy and white back to black. His skin went from pasty to dark, sickly to radiant with health.

Finally, fifty-four cards floated in front of Tarlae, held there by a maze of gold threads, capillary thin and all coming from the Coconut

Octopus Dealer's fingertips. Trey opened his eyes and blinked up at his luminous new Raccoon Deck, and then at his equally luminous savior. Every muscle in Tarlae's body had gone taut, and her ebony hair floated around her as if she were suspended in the depths of the ocean. Her eyes were open, but whatever she was seeing with her gold-streaked pupils, if anything, was beyond the senses of a normal human, or even a normal Dealer.

"What. The. Hell?" Trey's tone was quiet and bemused as he stared up at Tarlae. He reached up hesitantly and touched one of his cards, sending a tremor along the web of golden veins connecting them to their maker. Tarlae gasped. The veins retracted, drawing back into her body with an audible snap. Tarlae collapsed into the sand, her eyes closed, her limbs slack, and the cards that had hovered in front of her fell onto Trey and littered the space around him.

With a flick of his wrist, Trey summoned his cards, and they leapt into his palm as if they were eager to serve. He yanked his Healing card from the rest and scrambled over to Tarlae. Gabe, Kot, and Ernie beat him there, but Trey shoved Gabe aside to get to her head. "What happened to her?" the Raccoon Dealer demanded. "What did she do? Did she just give me her deck?"

Keeping an eye on Tarlae's face, Ernie cautiously felt the pockets of Tarlae's sand-crusted, sea-damp maxi dress. When she was conscious, there was no freaking way the Coconut Octopus Dealer would tolerate someone reaching for her cards. Right now, though, Tarlae seemed dead to the world but fortunately . . . not actually dead. Her cards were safe and sound in her left pocket, but her left forearm was bare.

"She didn't give you her cards," Ernie said. "Her deck is right here. But Rika—" She scanned the beach and spotted the forlorn creature inching forward on her damaged tentacles, trying to make it to the ocean. Drawing her Healing card, Ernie made for the creature. She touched Rika gently with the card, and the wounded octopus stopped moving and reached up with one of her tentacles to wrap it around

Ernie's wrist, holding the card to her body. Ernie scooped up the beast and carried her over to the group as Rika's tentacles regenerated.

Gabe sat back on his knees and brushed sand from his palms. His long hair had pulled loose from its tie and blew around his face in a gust of salted wind. "We saw the cards coming from her palms," he said, nodding at Tarlae's hands, which were a mess. Each palm bore a gash that seemed to go to the bone. With a look of anguish, Trey cradled Tarlae's head and took her left hand in his. He pressed his Healing card to the wound while Kot used his own Healing card to heal her right.

"We can't make new cards for ourselves," Kot said, peering at the terrible injury to Tarlae's right hand that was now rapidly pulling itself together.

"Then what did she just do, Kot?" Ernie asked, setting Rika down next to Tarlae and Trey. She hoped that being close to the coconut octopus would help Tarlae recover, but the unconscious woman gave no sign that she knew Rika was there, even when the octopus stroked the tip of a tentacle across her cheek. Next, Rika stroked Trey's hand.

He gave the animal a strained smile. "I think she likes me."

"She probably loves you," Gabe observed. "She knows you, even if you don't remember her."

"You still don't remember?" Ernie asked.

Trey shook his head. He was holding Tarlae close, though, and was hunched over her protectively. Ernie couldn't help but hope that this behavior would last well past when Tarlae woke up—as tough and fierce as the Coconut Octopus Dealer was, Ernie had a feeling she badly needed to bask in that affection and care after being without it for so long.

"Then why did you return?" asked Kot. He laid Tarlae's healed right hand across her middle and sat back.

"I regretted abandoning you guys before, okay? And she—" He glanced down at Tarlae and his jaw clenched. "It didn't feel good. So

182

I looked for you. All of you. She was the only Dealer who wasn't concealed from me."

Gabe got to his feet. As he pulled his hair back to keep it out of his face, he said, "She still had hope you would return to her."

"She really loves me?" Trey asked. "Because I don't know who I was before, but I'm thinking I'm kind of a jerk."

"You were never a jerk," Ernie said. Then she looked at Gabe for confirmation—Trey had been so friendly that it was easy to forget she hadn't known him that long.

"He was never a jerk," Gabe confirmed before turning to Trey. "But you seem to be serving a different master now, and I'm thinking I won't trust you until I know who it is." Gabe alone seemed to be reflecting back on the moments before the battle in the desert, when both Trey and Nuria had disappeared to bring the Sunrise key to the figure in white. "Was that the old woman who brought you back to life?"

Trey nodded. "The Grasshopper Dealer—that lady who can't talk? She knows her, too, I guess. Not sure how."

Kot looked around. "Where is Nuria?"

Ernie's heart sank. She'd almost forgotten. "She's gone again, Kot."

"What? How? I locked up her cards!"

"And she was helpless without them. We were battling a dozen Dealers, and we needed all the help we could get!" Ernie knew she sounded defensive, but the Dragonfly Dealer had thunder in his gaze. His eyes raked the beach and spotted Pol the dragonfly, who had shrunk down to normal insect size and was thrashing in the sand nearby.

He rushed over to the creature and healed it with a card as he stalked back over to the group. "I trusted you," he said to Ernie. "I left her in your protection."

"Based on what you said," Gabe argued, moving closer to Ernie, "Nuria is more than capable of protecting herself when she needs to."

"But she has not been stable or in her right mind," Kot snapped.

"I think she might be more stable and sane than you believe," Ernie said. "It's easy to misinterpret her behaviors because she struggles so hard to communicate with us. But I heard her in the dream realm—she spoke. Two words, but they were clear as a bell. She was looking for something. We thought it might have been the Sunrise and its key, seeing as she seems to know this mysterious old woman in white who Trey was trying to get the relic for."

"Wasn't that artifact destroyed in the desert?" asked Kot.

Ernie nodded. "But Nuria's still looking for something. Maybe she went back into the realm of dreams to find it."

"The realm of dreams," said Trey. "Seems like that's the place everyone wants to hide stuff." He rose, scooping Tarlae into his arms and bringing Rika, who had been sitting on Tarlae's stomach, with him. Tarlae's head lolled against his shoulder. "Why isn't she waking up?"

"It might be that she simply needs a bit of a kip after what she did," suggested Gabe. "It looked like it took a load of energy."

Kot stormed ahead of them toward his destroyed cabana, anger practically oozing from his every pore. Ernie and Gabe walked on either side of Trey as they followed. Wordlessly, Gabe waved a few cards—Mercy, Ally, Shelter—and another cabana appeared next to the wreckage, identical to the first *before* it had been the scene of a giant-scorpion attack.

As Ernie remembered the battle, her thoughts alighted on her puzzlement as she'd watched Gabe instantly tame the scorpion and turn it on its own Dealer. "Gabe," she said, her footsteps slowing. "The Sunrise."

"Hmm?" He turned to her, and the others did as well.

"It did something to us."

"I feel fine." He looked down at himself, then stroked his fingers along his jaw and cheek. He made a pained face. "Uglier than I used to be—"

"Not true at all," she interjected drily.

"—and Caera seems a bit pissed at me, but otherwise, I feel good."

Ernie arched one eyebrow. "You had Bao willing to do anything you asked," she reminded him. "He was on a tear one minute, and then suddenly, he was acting like the best-trained dog in the world." She thought back. "It was after he ran into you. After he touched you. He fell into a deep sleep because you told him to take a nap!" She gestured toward the beach, where they'd left the pig, but his bristly black figure was nowhere in sight.

She frowned and resumed her trek toward the cabana, recalling that she'd left Minh in a very vulnerable position. "And during the fight just now," she continued, "you did something to that scorpion."

Kot looked over at Gabe, eyeing the golden veins that laced the right cheek and jaw of the Kestrel Dealer. "You made an enemy Dealer's animal obey you? How?"

Gabe shrugged. "In the moment, all I cared about was protecting the people I love. I wasn't thinking much at all, to be honest."

"You got that thing to kill its own Dealer," Ernie said quietly.

"I was angry." He sighed. "I was thinking she didn't deserve to be a Dealer in the first place."

"And with that thought, you somehow got the scorpion to carry out your wish? That's a little scary, if you think about it." Trey hefted Tarlae a little higher in his arms. "I gotta put her down, man. She's all muscle and weighs as much as a sack of bricks." He glanced up toward his own forehead—in the time they'd been talking, Rika had climbed off Tarlae and was now perched atop Trey's head, her tentacles hanging down either side of his face like a bad wig. He let out an exasperated breath, turned, and carried his burdens to the newly conjured cabana.

Gabe and Ernie joined Kot next to the original, the roof of which had collapsed over the rest of it. Kot played Air, Amplify, and Strength, levitating the thatched roof right off its base and moving it to the side. Minh lay within the bomb shelter Ernie had created, safe and sound and, unfortunately, still catatonic. Ernie disappeared the shelter and sat down next to him, brushing bits of straw and splinters of wood away from his face and body and hair. "We need to find a way to help him."

"We don't even know what's wrong with him," Kot replied, collecting the few drawings Nuria had left behind with agitated swipes of his hands.

"We have a solid clue." Gabe pointed to the right side of his face. "When the Sunrise exploded, each of us got hit with a piece of it. And Ernie's right—seems like it was more than a bomb."

"It didn't kill us or even hurt us, really," Ernie added.

Kot gestured at Minh's body. "I doubt the Pot-Bellied Pig Dealer would agree."

"Okay, but look at what Tarlae did," Ernie said. "She created cards! They came right out of her body, like she was giving birth to them!"

"Well," Gabe said, a wry look on his face. "Not *exactly*."

She rolled her eyes. "And you—you've got the animal spirits eating out of the palm of your hand. Also, literally *sinking* into the palm of your hand."

"Tell that to Caera, would ya?" he asked, scowling at his kestrel tattoo. "She's aching something fierce, and she only does that when she's mad or scared or hurt."

Ernie glanced over at the other cabana. Trey had laid Tarlae on the bed and was sitting next to her, holding one of her hands and watching her face with a conflicted yet tender kind of expression, as if he couldn't decide whether to lie down next to her or run for his life. Ernie would have thought Rika the coconut octopus would have felt no ambivalence about being close to Tarlae, but instead of returning to her Dealer's arm, Rika was curled at the foot of the bed, a few of her tentacles hanging off the end.

"They don't like it," Ernie murmured, looking down at her own arm, where Legs throbbed painfully. "Our animals don't like what's happened to us. That's why Bao was rampaging around like a crazy pig, too."

"But what actually *happened*?" Kot asked. "Does Nuria have some new power? If Tarlae can now conjure cards and Gabe can now charm or control animals—"

"Not completely sure *what* I can do yet, mate," Gabe interjected.

"—then what can Nuria do? What about Minh? And Ernie?"

Gabe and Kot both looked at Ernie, who put her hand over the spot on her chest where the Sunrise had penetrated her breastbone. "No idea," she said.

"Nothing different during the fight?" Gabe asked.

Ernie considered it. She'd fought like she always had, a focus on disabling but not killing, on protecting her allies and repelling her enemies. She'd battled well—and had three of the Snail Dealer's cards to prove it. There had been one moment, when she'd been tangled up in ropes trying to strangle the life out of her, during which she'd felt a pure, powerful kind of need growing inside her, like something desperately wanting to emerge from under layers and layers of restraints, but that could have been a product of her air-starved mind, so she didn't mention it. "No," she said. "As much as I wish I could magically control the elements or stop time or something nifty like that, I think I'm pretty much free of superpowers."

"Or you haven't figured out what your power is yet," said Gabe, watching Ernie's hand as it rubbed over the scar between her breasts. He tore his gaze away and looked over at Kot, who was staring at his cards, most likely searching for his wayward lover. "And maybe whatever new power Nuria has, it's driving her to do . . . whatever she's doing."

"She was doing odd things before, though!" barked Kot, shoving his cards back into his pocket. "And once again, I cannot find her anywhere."

"Maybe the odd things she was doing before had something to do with finding whatever the lady in white wanted," Ernie said.

"I'd feel more comfortable with that if I knew whose side the lady in white was on," Gabe said.

Ernie took in the rage written in the lines of Kot's face, the clench
of his jaw, and the tension in his shoulders. "We should find Nuria first.
Let's get somewhere safe and concealed, and then I'll help find her."

"Not without me, you won't," Gabe said.

"I will accept your help with gratitude," Kot said, his head bowed.

Ernie put her hand on his shoulder. "You're our friend, Kot. I know
how much you love her."

After a brief conference with Trey, who agreed to protect Tarlae and
Minh while Kot, Gabe, and Ernie searched for Nuria, the six Dealers
traveled at Gabe's suggestion to the steppes of Mongolia, cloaked with
ample concealments. Before departing, Gabe summoned Bao with a
simple call of his name, and, keeping his hand on the pot-bellied pig's
back, he transported the animal without difficulty.

Ernie stood with her allies at the edge of an overlook. Beyond them
sprawled a scrubby grassland free of buildings or trees or roads. There,
the Kestrel, Diamondback, Dragonfly, and Raccoon birthed a joint
haven, a large yurt that could comfortably house all of them and be used
as a home base. With no structures or forest to obscure an approaching
enemy, with no nearby settlements with a vulnerable populace, it gave
them the ability to respond to any attack quickly and without holding
back—if their enemies could even find them. Of course, it could be that
Virginia could locate them at any time, but for now, it seemed that she
was content to let her newly appointed minions chase them around the
globe, running them to ground.

Ernie worried that Virginia had more on her mind than their team
of rebels—the Forger seemed intent on world domination and human
suffering—but she also knew they could do little to stop her until they
pulled themselves together and figured out what the Sunrise had done
to them.

After the group settled Tarlae and Minh on opposite cots and conjured a simple meal, which Trey, Kot, Ernie, and Gabe shared around
a stone-enclosed campfire at the edge of the overlook, Kot, Ernie, and

Gabe lay down on pallets of their own, side by side. They crossed their Ally cards and their Dreams cards and journeyed into the realm of the mind.

With Gabe and Ernie's shared memories of the place where they'd first seen Nuria, they arrived at the base of the mountain rising up from the vast prairie. Ernie looked out across the grass, remembering the storm and the rain and the passion. Gabe took her hand as he stood next to her. "One day, love," he murmured.

She squeezed his hand. They released each other and led Kot up the trail. "Can you see her in your cards now?" Ernie asked him.

He peered at his Revelation card and shook his head. "Why would she conceal herself from me?" His voice betrayed his hurt.

"Could be she's driven by something beyond herself, mate," Gabe said.

"For years, I trusted that she loved me back." Kot strode ahead, maybe so they couldn't see his face, maybe because he was desperate for answers and the forward movement was the only hope he had. "But sometimes I wonder—"

"She loves you," Ernie said firmly. "Sometimes there are . . . things, you know? Things people are dealing with." She was thinking of her mother, the grief and guilt Mara Terwilliger had carried for all the years of her husband's absence. "Sometimes those things kind of overwhelm even the most powerful love. Sometimes they're too heavy. Too much. But that doesn't mean the love isn't under there, trying desperately to come out."

"I want to believe that," Kot said. "I will give my life for her if that is what it takes to free her. But I would like to know . . ."

"I know," Ernie said, her throat tight. She exchanged a quick glance with Gabe and looked away. They had no time for sentimentality now, no time for softness or wishing or anything but determination and focus. "It was this way." She pointed.

They had reached the passageway where she and Gabe had followed the white-gowned Nuria. Ernie took the lead as they strode quickly along the stone corridor. Above them, clouds had begun to gather and swirl, as if this was the spot where storms were born. Even as darkness gathered, so did Ernie's hope. They rounded the final corner before the blocked passageway, and there she was.

Nuria had clothed herself in the same white gown as before, and now it was streaked with blood and dirt. Her hands were covered in open blisters, seeping and grime encrusted. She whimpered as she tried to move a particularly large rock to a pile. Her cards lay discarded nearby, and the grasshopper leapt from rock to rock, its wings clicking and buzzing.

"Nuria," Kot cried as he rushed toward her. She yelped and pushed him away as he tried to take her in his arms. "Please, my love, why are you doing this to yourself?"

Nuria clawed at his arms until he released her, then she went right back to attempting to move the rocks. Gabe grabbed Kot's shoulder as he moved forward to restrain her again. "We can help her, mate," he said. "You can't get her back by keeping her from her goal."

"He's right." Ernie pulled her deck and selected a few cards. "She's been trying to clear this passageway. She's worked so hard that she's burned out her deck."

Kot sighed, his fingers twitching as he listened to Nuria groan with strain while she moved a smaller rock, leaving bloody handprints across its rough face. He drew Strength, Prolong, and Endurance. "Tarlae was right. I have been so focused on protecting her that I haven't respected her as I should."

Ernie drew the blank card that connected her deck to Gabe's. She showed it to him. "Think this would help?"

He smiled. "I think we're more powerful together than apart, if that's what you're asking."

She played it, along with the cards Kot had, while Gabe played a few she hadn't even thought of—the Alchemy and Clay Wilds. With those, he transformed many of the rocks to a porous foam that they could simply kick to the side.

You're a genius, she thought, knowing he would hear.

I'm just old, he replied. *But I suppose age has its benefits.*

Ernie's scar throbbed, but this time it was a deep pang of happiness. A few months ago, Gabe had felt cursed with age, condemned by a list of sins and the weight of his own conscience, so much so that he had considered giving up his deck and ending his existence. Now she could sense his acceptance, his peace. The deep well of goodness inside him was there, too, something she knew on faith but felt keenly when they were connected by the blank hybrid card that joined their decks.

But there was something else there as well, something new and hidden but huge, electric, and dangerous. She could sense its potential, its power . . . and its threat. Even as she focused on it, whatever lurked inside of Gabe seemed to lurch toward her, sharp and grasping. She stumbled forward as a wave of dizziness threatened to lay her out.

I feel it in you, too, he murmured into her thoughts, halting and hesitant. *It's . . . reaching for me.* Their eyes met, and Gabe swayed, turning pale. As her heart skipped unsteadily, Ernie shoved the hybrid card back into her pocket, shutting down their connection.

"These rocks won't move themselves," Kot called out, his back to them as he bent to work, unaware of what had transpired between Ernie and Gabe.

Shaken and sweating, Ernie played a few cards to blow the light foam chunks out of the way. She didn't want Gabe to see how upset she was at having to terminate their connection, at realizing that something so good and reassuring had suddenly become dangerous and threatening. Gabe seemed focused on the task as well, playing Air and Accelerate to levitate dozens of stones away from the passage.

Ernie had thought that they were clearing a blocked passage, but as they worked, it became obvious that the corridor did not continue past the rockfall. Instead, they uncovered a cleft in the ground, and as soon as the last rock was cleared, Nuria climbed into it. Kot didn't try to restrain her this time—he offered her a hand to steady her as she descended. She rewarded him with a look of relief and adoration, and Ernie could almost hear the Dragonfly Dealer's heart pounding with joy.

Playing her Light card, Ernie followed Kot and Nuria into the hole, with Gabe's solidly reassuring presence behind her. The cleft narrowed the deeper they got, forcing them to descend one by one. Ernie's hands slipped along the slick, wet rock faces, but the opening wasn't wide enough to allow her to fall far. Below her, Kot was grunting and struggling as he tried to force his broad shoulders and chest between unforgiving stone walls, and above her, Gabe cursed and groused, occasionally pelting Ernie in the head with pebbles jarred loose beneath his boots.

The lower they climbed, the darker and colder it became, until Ernie's teeth chattered and her hands became numb. Doubt crowded her thoughts—she and Gabe had told Kot that helping Nuria was better than trying to pull her away from her goal, but seriously, what if they were following the Grasshopper Dealer into a trap? Ernie had felt fairly certain that Nuria's behaviors weren't completely irrational or demented, but what if she'd been wrong? What if all those years of being melded with the grasshopper spirit, of having a living deck of cards embedded in her soul, pricking and torturing her, of being taken over piece by piece by a primitive, language-free being really had taken a permanent toll on Nuria?

Ernie blinked as she looked below her. Was that a light? In the cracks not blocked by Kot's and Nuria's bodies, brightness seeped up from the depths. Something was down there. Ernie could hear Kot asking Nuria what it was, as if she could answer him—but to her surprise, Nuria *did*.

"Here," she said.

In the dream realm, Nuria had a few words, but that was more than she had anywhere else. Ernie smiled as the light became brighter. Nuria had found what she was looking for.

The space below her opened up as Nuria and Kot made it to the bottom. Her heart racing, Ernie quickened her steps, and judging from the number of stones pelting her from above, Gabe sensed the end of the interminable descent coming as well. When Ernie's feet hit level ground, she wanted to cheer. She dropped to her hands and knees to crawl from beneath a shelf of rock, emerging into a warmly lit chamber of jagged crystals.

After Gabe emerged next to her, giving his torn shirt an exasperated look, Ernie scanned the chamber and found Kot and Nuria on the other side of a jutting wall of quartz, standing in front of a diamond- and ruby-encrusted box. Nuria began to reach for its lid.

"Wait," said Gabe. "I'm reminded of Pandora's box here."

Nuria looked over her shoulder at him and tapped the box. "Good," she said.

"Can we talk this over?" Ernie said, eyeing the box. She and Gabe started forward as Nuria began to open it.

Kot barred the way. "She believes this is the right thing, and we will trust her."

Gabe and Ernie had time only to exchange one last worried glance before Nuria's fingers closed around the box's lid and pulled it upward. Blinding white light flooded the chamber, bouncing off every crystalline facet in prisms and gleaming, star-bright pinpricks. Ernie shielded her eyes, her hand dipping into her pocket for her cards.

"You have nothing to fear from me," said a gentle voice. The light softened and dimmed, and Ernie lowered her hand.

Standing before them was the woman in white. Her long hair hung in spiraling curls over her shoulders, and her skin was nearly as pale as her hair and dress. So were her eyes. Her wrinkled skin was virtually transparent, revealing a maze of pale-blue veins flecked with tiny particles of black just beneath the surface.

Ernie swallowed. She didn't know whether the woman in white was beautiful or something out of a horror movie she'd seen once.

Nuria had dropped to her knees and was stroking the hem of the woman's silky white gown, similar to the one the Grasshopper Dealer had conjured for herself, only pristine and clean instead of streaked with grime. Kot knelt next to Nuria. Ernie couldn't tell whether he was in awe of the woman in white or simply wary, but she guessed it was a bit of both. And Gabe stood shoulder to shoulder with Ernie, his face unreadable.

The woman spent a moment looking at each of their faces. "Hello there," she said. "I didn't expect so many of you."

"Who are you?" Ernie asked.

The woman gazed down affectionately at Nuria. "You know who I am, don't you, my darling? Tell them." She reached down to stroke Nuria's black locks, and her hand passed right through Nuria's head. "Go ahead—tell them," she said again, her voice tinged with pleasure.

Nuria turned to Kot, then looked back at Ernie and Gabe. "Fuh-fuh . . ." She pressed her lips together, then gazed up at the woman in white and smiled. *"Phoebe."*

CHAPTER NINETEEN

Kot's brow furrowed as he scanned the awestruck expressions on the faces of his allies. "You all know this person?"

"She was the Forger before Andy," Gabe said. "And, I'm guessing, the Forger who made Nuria a Dealer."

Phoebe nodded. "Nuria, my fierce warrior, only wanted to save her village from destruction at the hands of invaders. I gave her the power to do so, in return for her service as one of my Dealers. I gifted her with the Grasshopper spirit, a creature at once implacable and nimble, hardy and determined and ruthless." Phoebe gave Nuria a look of concern, as though she could tell something had changed.

"How are you here?" asked Ernie. "Didn't Andy kill you so he could become the Forger?"

"There is something of the infinite inside all of us, especially a Forger, and that part of me lives on." Phoebe's opalescent gaze returned to Ernie. Her smile was the one Ernie remembered from her dream after the Sunrise had exploded. "Diamondback," she said. "An old deck with a new master." She stepped forward, her nearly transparent body passing right through Kot's and Nuria's kneeling forms.

"She's a ghost," Gabe muttered.

"More or less, Kestrel," Phoebe said as she stood in front of them. "Hopefully less than more."

Ernie looked up at Gabe. "Is this real, or is one of us dreaming this?"

"We all dreamed of her separately before today," Gabe said.

"The dream realm is where my spirit has been dwelling for centuries. And until recently, I was unable to roam at all, locked in this prison as I was." Phoebe swept her hand toward the jewel-covered box that Nuria had freed her from. "Am I correct in assuming that Andy met his match?"

"There's a new Forger who defeated him, if that's what you're asking," Gabe replied.

Phoebe nodded. "And that change was enough to allow me more freedom, for his will no longer dominated. I recently discovered that I could project my spirit beyond my prison for short periods of time. Longer in the dream realm than in the waking world, but I've been getting stronger."

"And you appeared to Nuria," Kot said. His expression was somber as he rose and pulled his lover up with him.

"I asked her to find my prison," Phoebe replied, giving Nuria a fond look. "She has a will of iron and a strength of spirit that is unparalleled." Her brow furrowed. "Though you are different than I remember, my child."

"She was merged with the spirit of her deck, using a Forger-created rune tile," Kot explained. "For many years, she and the Grasshopper were one."

Phoebe let out a distressed cry. "It is a wonder that she survived at all." She brushed her ghostly fingers along Nuria's lips.

"Get better," Nuria said, pointing at herself. "Better."

Phoebe nodded. "Better with every moment. You will be what you were, and even more."

Gratitude and awe were written all over Kot's face. "You can give her back her words," he said softly.

Phoebe shook her head. "Not all of them, Dragonfly. In this form, I can only do a little of what I was once capable of."

"How can you do anything at all?" Ernie asked. "We saw Andy die. He turned to ash, and what was left seemed to be absorbed by Virginia." At Phoebe's questioning look, Ernie added, "She was the Chicken Dealer. She defeated Andy."

"The Chicken. That's new. He must have created the deck specifically for her." Phoebe sounded amused. "What you saw was his power traveling into the new Forger. That power is too great to hold inside one Dealer, a former mortal who already holds within himself the fantastic power of a deck. And so the deck and the spirit must be sacrificed to make room for the greater power of the Forger, yes?"

Remembering the sight of Luigi, the leghorn rooster that had embodied Virginia's deck, flailing and dying after the Forger's power had entered Virginia, Ernie nodded. "So most of the power goes into the new Forger." She waved a hand toward Phoebe's pale figure. "But something survives?"

"Like I said, we all have a piece of the infinite inside us. And that piece of me was imprisoned here, in the dream realm."

"By *who*?" Gabe asked.

Phoebe's fingers trailed along a line of rubies on the box's lid. "Andy created this prison for me. Pretty but cruel, like him, you see?" Her quiet laugh dripped with ruefulness. "Most likely, Virginia has discovered that she must find and contain Andy's spirit as well, for if she doesn't, he might be strong enough to cause trouble for her. Perhaps she has contained him by now, or perhaps she is still struggling to complete the task."

"Another reason for her to keep us distracted," Ernie said. "But she's doing more than distracting—she's already killed maybe a hundred thousand people." Ernie's thoughts flicked back to Munich and the thieves and the moment Ernie had ended their lives in the desperate hope that she could save others. "She tricked us into helping her."

197

Guilt bubbled up inside of Ernie—she'd played God, and Virginia had seemed to know she would.

Phoebe interrupted her thoughts by saying, "The beginning of a Forger's reign is usually tumultuous."

Gabe tilted his head. "Was yours?"

Phoebe's gaze was wistful. "I was given the throne. The transition was peaceful, and my time as Forger was peaceful, though of course I struggled to find my feet at first. The spirit of my predecessor guided me until he decided to become one with the universe." She swept her hand toward the ceiling of the cavern as if it showed a map of the galaxies. "But after a few centuries, one of my own—the Lynx Dealer—decided that he craved my power too much." Her face radiated distress. "I never imagined he would be so brutal," she whispered.

Nuria reached toward her maker, clearly wanting to comfort her, but her hands passed through Phoebe's shoulder.

"I'm fine, darling," Phoebe said to her. "You have been so kind and steadfast. You have freed me, and I hope you will restore me."

"Restore you?" Gabe's knuckles brushed the back of Ernie's hand.

Phoebe nodded. "The Sunrise," she said. "The Sunrise would restore me to my body. When I rescued the young Raccoon Dealer from the splinter dimension, I asked him to get it for me."

"The Sunrise is gone," said Kot.

"We tried to use it against Virginia," Ernie explained, "and it . . . exploded."

"What?" Phoebe's serenity dropped away like a cloak. "You used the Sunrise on the one who is already Forger? That is very bad."

"*She* is very bad," said Ernie while Nuria nodded emphatically. "And I have a feeling she's only getting started."

"But now the Sunrise has made it worse. Oh, this is tragic." Phoebe covered her face with her hands, but her sorrowful expression was still visible through the maze of pale-blue, black-flecked veins and the film of her transparent fingers.

"Didn't you create the Sunrise?" Gabe asked her.

"I created many things for my beloved Immortal Dealers," Phoebe said, lowering her hands. "The Sunrise was never meant to be used against a Forger. I certainly wouldn't have wanted my Dealers to use it on *me*."

"It didn't exactly come with an instruction manual," Ernie mumbled as her cheeks grew warm. "What did you mean it to be used for?"

Phoebe drifted backward as if she hadn't heard, looking despondent. "With the power of the Sunrise, the new Forger will be unstoppable. In trying to defeat her, I am afraid you have made her infinitely powerful."

"Or not—we *tried* to use the Sunrise against Virginia," said Gabe. "But it backfired on us."

Phoebe's pearly eyes widened. "Backfired . . . ?"

"Virginia saw what we were doing and trapped us inside some sort of blast dome." Gabe turned his face and pointed at the starburst scar on his jaw, from which the golden veins emanated like sunbeams. "It detonated with us inside."

"And it hit you." Phoebe's trembling, transparent fingers drifted toward Gabe's face as if she was desperate to touch him. "*You* have the power of the Sunrise," she whispered. "You are the one." Her smile returned. "I had always hoped . . ."

"Actually . . ." Ernie pulled down the collar of her shirt to reveal her own scar. "It got five of us, not just him."

Nuria proudly held out her palm to show Phoebe her golden scar. Phoebe touched it with the tip of her index finger. Then she peered at Kot. "And where is your scar, Dragonfly?"

Kot shook his head, looking sheepish. "I was not under the dome when the Sunrise detonated, and I have no scar."

Phoebe looked around the crystal-filled chamber. "Then where are the others? You said there were five."

"Don't you know?" Gabe asked. "We all saw you in our dreams right after it happened."

"It is possible you met an echo of me," Phoebe answered. "Once I was able, I sent projections of my spirit out into the dream realm, seeking Dealers who might help me find the Sunrise and return to physical form. Perhaps those echoes sensed each of you in that moment."

Ernie was more interested in the problem at hand than in the nightmare she'd had. "What was the Sunrise, Phoebe? What does it do?"

Phoebe's thin lips formed an incredulous smile. "I should think that would be obvious, Diamondback." She reached out and brushed Ernie's chest with the blunt fingernail of her ghostly pointer finger, leaving a cold, tingling sensation in her wake. "The Sunrise was the power of the Forger, or most of it, at least. Being the Forger is a lonely existence, and I created the relic in the hopes that the Dealer who found it would become a companion." Her gaze flicked toward Gabe. "But I wanted that Dealer to have the right spirit and desire, and for it to be a choice, which is why I created the key to activate it."

"Whoa. I have as much power as the Forger now?" Ernie looked down at herself.

"You have the part of it contained in the fragment that struck you when the power was released," Phoebe explained. "But apparently the Kestrel also has a piece, and the Grasshopper has a piece."

"That's why our animals are pissed at us," Gabe guessed. "Because this new power is taking up space inside."

Phoebe looked down at Nuria's forearm. It was smooth and tattoo-free, but Ernie heard the annoying buzzing that told her the creature was nearby and agitated. "It would be unpleasant for them, yes," Phoebe said, "but because it is not all the power of the Forger, all at once, perhaps they will grow accustomed to it in time . . . or decide they will seek a new home."

"Wait. That can happen?" Ernie asked. She covered her burning, throbbing tattoo with her hand. The idea of Legs leaving her hurt a lot more than the pain the diamondback was causing her now. "They can decide they want to leave and go find themselves a new Dealer?"

"I think that's part of what made you a Dealer, love," Gabe said, tucking a lock of Ernie's hair behind her ear. "You fought for Legs, but I believe she chose you first, in a way."

Phoebe arched an eyebrow as she watched their exchange, but apparently decided to let it go. "Nuria, my child, tell me of your new power." She gestured toward Nuria's gold-veined palm.

Nuria squinted at her scar, then she tapped her temple. "Feel . . ." She looked up, meeting Phoebe's curious gaze. "Dealer?"

"Ah," said Phoebe. "The spirits of the decks call to her."

"That's why she started drawing animals," Gabe said, giving Nuria an inquiring look. "Yeah? You know where all the Dealers are now. You feel them?"

Nuria nodded, patting her chest above her heart, then touching her temple and splaying her fingers out in front of her, as if to show a projection.

"She was drawing some sort of map before," said Kot. "Of the dimensions?"

"I have been showing it to her in dreams, little by little," said Phoebe. "I hoped it would help her find the Sunrise, as I didn't know in which dimension it could be found."

"And now she can sense which dimension each Dealer is in," said Ernie, her stomach sinking. "She drew so many animals in so many different dimensions."

Phoebe's brow furrowed. "That is strange, unless Andy created them there—or banished them."

"My guess is the latter," Gabe said.

"He was always a bit of an imp." Phoebe brushed a few white spiral curls over one shoulder. "A dangerous one, but an imp nonetheless."

"A generous interpretation for the guy who basically killed you," Ernie observed.

"I've had hundreds of years to contemplate what went wrong there." Phoebe moved between them like a breeze, until she was close to the spot where they'd emerged into the hidden cavern. "So Nuria has the power to sense the Dealers, a power that is difficult to wield but controllable. What power have you gained, Kestrel?"

"Nuria may be able to sense animal spirits, but Gabe can control them," Ernie said even as Gabe opened his mouth to respond.

Phoebe cast a glance between the two of them. "The Kestrel must have the power to bond and unbond," she explained. "The animal spirits sense their master in him. Like Nuria's, a power difficult to wield but controllable, I would think. And you, Diamondback?"

"I don't know."

The former Forger's eyebrows rose. "You don't know? Have you sensed nothing that is different?"

Ernie half shrugged. "Maybe something's a little off, but I haven't busted out with any fancy new abilities."

"What about the other two?" Phoebe asked.

"Tarlae can create cards," Kot said, holding out his arms, palms forward, as Tarlae had when she was producing an almost completely new deck for Trey. "They slid right out from beneath her skin."

"Ooh." Phoebe clapped her hands together. "She has the heart of the Forger's gift. Together with the Kestrel, she can create new Dealers. But you must have both, working in harmony."

"Not sure I've ever worked in harmony with Tarlae," Gabe muttered. "Try as I might."

"I'm good with you keeping your harmony to yourself," Ernie replied.

"And the fifth?" Phoebe asked. "Who is the fifth Dealer gifted with power?"

"Minh," Gabe answered.

Phoebe's expression lit up with joy. "The Pot-Bellied Pig," she said. "He was a special one."

"He's not doing well," Ernie said. "He got hit with a big piece of the Sunrise, and he hasn't really regained consciousness since the event."

Phoebe's ghostly face fell. "My poor Minh."

"Tarlae isn't doing all that well, either," Kot added. "She seemed overcome after creating almost a whole deck for the Raccoon when he lost most of his cards during a battle."

"Two Dealers overcome," Phoebe murmured. "Great gifts come at a high price."

Ernie crossed her arms over her chest. She supposed she'd gotten only a small sliver of the Forger's power, and it sounded like she should be grateful for that. "How do we help Minh, Phoebe? And why is he in such a bad way? When Virginia got the entire Forger's power all at once, she'd never looked better. It was like a face-lift and a gym membership all in one."

Phoebe blinked at her, and Ernie realized the old ghost might be a little behind the times. Despite that, she did seem to grasp the thrust of Ernie's question. "The Forger's power is meant to be taken as a whole," she said. "Think about your own body and all the things it does without you even being aware of it. Your heart beats, your thoughts fly, your eyes blink, your lungs inflate, your blood flows, and all of it without a conscious intention from you. That is the power as a whole." She cocked her head and came forward, staring at Ernie's chest. "But what happens when you receive only a sliver, and that is all you have? When you do not have all the pieces working in concert? In some cases, you have the power working beneath the consciousness, and in others, it appears to have *overwhelmed* the consciousness." A smile formed on her lips. "But this could work to your advantage."

"Why?" asked Gabe.

"Because, Kestrel, a Forger was once a human, with the capacity of a human." She brushed her fingers down her own transparent, veiny body. "A Forger must focus to feel her own heart beating. She must concentrate to localize one stray thought. In just this way, she must focus to isolate and locate a stray Dealer, a rune tile she created, an animal spirit she wishes to summon. She cannot do all things at once—there is not enough of her to manage! No, she must focus. But you—" She gestured at the three scarred Dealers. "You have one power to focus on, and only that."

"We can work as a team to beat Virginia," Ernie said. She bit her lip. "Assuming we can figure out our abilities and use them properly." Then she thought of Minh. "And assuming we're actually able to function in spite of those abilities." She pulled out her deck. "We should get back and see how Tarlae's doing, then see if we can't help bring Minh around."

Nuria frowned and pointed at Phoebe. "Help."

"We'll be able to help her a lot better once we've figured ourselves out," Ernie said.

Kot put his hand on Ernie's arm. "She's saying Phoebe might be able to help us. Guide us. Yes?" He looked at Nuria for confirmation, and his lover beamed at him and nodded.

All of them looked at Phoebe, who had drifted closer to the box from which Nuria had released her. "If you want me to help, I will," she said. "But I do not go where I am not wanted. My policy with my Dealers was to invite, not to compel."

"Can you come back with us into the waking world?" Gabe asked. "Didn't you appear to Trey and Nuria in the desert?"

"I was able to project myself there for a short time," Phoebe said. "But only for a moment or two."

Ernie thought back to how Phoebe had vanished after her brief appearance amid the sand dunes. "We can come back into the dream realm and talk to you."

"There is another way," Phoebe said, looking down at her hands. "One way to give me a stable presence in the waking world, even without the Sunrise." She raised her head. "But I do not think any of you would want to do it."

"Tell us how, and we'll decide," said Ernie. "Because we'd appreciate your guidance, especially if it will help Tarlae and Minh."

The others nodded, and Phoebe inclined her head. "The Kestrel called me a ghost—but I am a spirit, and my physical body perished centuries ago. To inhabit the waking realm for more than a few moments, I must have a body, and it must be strong."

"Can we create a body for you?" Ernie asked. "Is that a power one of us has?"

Phoebe shook her head. "The more complex the machine, the more difficult to conjure, and the human body is perhaps the most intricate machine of all." She looked at each of them in turn. "No, in order for me to be in the waking world, I must possess one of yours."

CHAPTER TWENTY

"When you say *possess*," said Ernie, "are we talking a friendly little passenger in someone's brain, or an *Exorcist*-level takeover?"

Gabe translated for the others, who were, for obvious reasons, not quite as hooked on pop culture. "Would the person you possess still have control over his or her body?"

Phoebe clasped her hands together. "I'm afraid not. I would need to occupy the consciousness almost completely in order to be able to really help you, to think my own thoughts and act on them. But if they were able to speak, Nuria and Minh could attest that I treasure life, and especially those of my Dealers. I would treat any body I occupied with reverence and protect it with all my power."

"Do you *have* power?" Kot asked. "You are not the Forger anymore, nor are you a Dealer."

"You are astute, Dragonfly," Phoebe said, giving him a respectful nod. "I believe I retain some of the magic of the Forger in my veins." She ran her fingers along her throat, calling attention to the pale-blue veins flecked with black. Then she leaned forward, opening her eyes wide and revealing similar black grains glinting in the opalescent orbs. Ernie remembered that whenever Andy was getting ready to deliver a Forger smackdown, his baby blues had turned obsidian, and occasionally his veins had run black with that magic.

"So you still have some power, and that's how you got Trey back to this dimension, even without his memories," said Gabe. "I wondered how that could be done."

"It took nearly all the energy I had, particularly because I was only able to send an echo out to retrieve him. I wish I had been able to restore his memories."

"Me too," said Ernie, "but something tells me he knows who he is even without them." It had given her hope, seeing him defend and care for Tarlae, as if his heart were able to hear the cry of hers, even under layers of forgetting.

Phoebe smiled. "It seems as though Andy chose well when he selected new Dealers for such venerable decks as the Diamondback and the Dragonfly."

Ernie glanced over at Kot. Neither of them had been chosen by Andy—and neither of them had intentionally become Dealers—but here they were, fully committed to their paths. "What about the Kestrel?"

Phoebe looked Gabe up and down, and Ernie would have had to be blind not to see the glint of feminine appraisal and admiration in the ghost's gaze. "I can tell that the Kestrel deck was created especially for this man," she said softly. "And indeed he bears it well."

Gabe cleared his throat, and his cheeks darkened as he impatiently brushed a tangled lock of hair away from his face. "It seems we must decide who is willing to take a back seat in their own mind and allow Phoebe to take over if we wish to have her help."

Ernie glanced at Nuria, who was staring at Phoebe with somber focus. She seemed like the most obvious candidate. But Kot stepped between them, glaring at Ernie, then at the rest of them. "Not *her*. For the first time in nearly twenty years, this woman is finally the only one residing in her own body, and I will not let anyone possess it but her." Then he seemed to catch himself, and he looked over his shoulder at Nuria. "Unless . . . she wants to allow it." Every word was full of dread, as if Kot had to force each syllable past his lips, a testament to his new commitment to respecting Nuria's independence. She rewarded Kot with a stroke of his arm, then leaned her head on his shoulder. She might have been willing to do almost anything for her maker, but her relief at not being singled out for possession was palpable.

Ernie put her hands up. "You're right. I'm sorry."

Ernie and Gabe looked at each other. The idea of sacrificing control of her body and mind was abhorrent, even for a good cause, but the idea of Gabe having to do it was almost worse, because she'd be looking at his face, his body, and still be unable to reach him. She opened her mouth to offer herself, but Gabe shook his head. "We need to discuss this alone," he said to Phoebe. "If you don't mind."

She shook her head. "I wouldn't have blamed you if you crammed me back in that box and left me to molder. I understand how precious one's independence is. Please go discuss it amongst yourselves and let me know of your decision. You all have a goal, and I would like to think of myself as a counselor, here to help you further that goal. I am at your service, as I was when I was Forger." She bowed her head. "Once that goal is reached, I will leave the body I possess." And with that, she vanished.

"We shouldn't talk here," said Gabe, looking around the cavern in the silence that followed. "Especially with Virginia and her horde on the hunt for us. We need to see how the others are faring and talk this over with everyone. Agreed?"

In answer, all of them pulled out their Revelation cards. Although it was possible to wake oneself without cards, it was easier if you located yourself in the physical world first. Ernie could see herself sleeping on a cot next to Gabe. Their fingers were intertwined, drawing a secret smile to Ernie's face in the dream realm that was mirrored by her sleeping self. And that was how she woke up, her cards in one hand, and the other still holding Gabe's.

Minh was on his cot, curled into a ball and muttering to himself. Tarlae was sitting up on her cot, looking wan. Trey was in the process of handing her a cup of steaming liquid. One whiff told Ernie it was hot chocolate, and her stomach growled. "If you're serving up snacks, I guess it's safe to say Virginia hasn't shown her face?"

"Nothing yet," said Trey. "And not that I want her to crash our little party here, but I can't help but worry about what she's out there doing."

Ernie had the same fear but also a sliver of hope. "We may have found something to help. Or, really, someone." As Nuria, Kot, and Gabe awakened, rubbing their eyes and pocketing their cards, Ernie explained the situation—how each of them had a slice of the Forger's power, how they'd found Phoebe, her offer to guide them, and the cost of that wisdom. Tarlae's reaction to the idea that Phoebe's spirit would possess one of their bodies was as Ernie would have expected—complete revulsion and a firm statement that she would not be the one offering up her body and mind.

"We don't have to take her up on her offer," Gabe said to all of them. "But I'm not mad about the idea of fighting alone. That bird knows things. At the very least, she might be able to guide us to use the new powers we've got."

Ernie got up and seated herself next to Minh. Sweat beaded his brow. His eyes were open, but he didn't seem to be seeing any of them. Ernie knew that beneath his clothes, he bore the biggest scar of all. Whatever power he'd gained when the Sunrise had pierced his flesh had overwhelmed him. "I doubt Minh would let anyone possess him under normal circumstances, but what if Phoebe could fix him?" she asked. "She's wielded these powers before, and if she were in his head, she would feel them and know what they are, right? She'd know what to do, and maybe she could get him back to normal?"

"I'm hesitant to make the decision for him," said Gabe.

Ernie glanced at Kot and Nuria, who had conjured themselves a meal of noodles and tea. In the dream realm, Nuria had been slightly more capable of communicating. *What if . . .* "I'm going to ask him." She pulled her Dreams card, then dug in Minh's pocket for his. Next, she slid her arm under his head so they were cheek to cheek. She guided his unresisting hand to his Dreams card, then crossed his card with hers and leaned forward with him in her arms, feeling the pitch and fall as they entered the realm of the sleeping mind.

They were lying in a meadow speckled with wildflowers. Minh blinked up at the sun and shielded his eyes. Ernie's heart leapt—it was already more conscious movement than he'd managed since being hit with the relic shard. "Hey," she said quietly. "How are you?"

"What happened?" Minh's face was drawn and somber as he looked her way. "I . . . it's been like standing in the center of a storm. I know I'm with you guys, but I can't . . . I can't . . ." His voice rose with apparent panic, and he sat up suddenly. "Where *am* I?"

"The dream realm. And you're safe." Ernie explained some of what had happened. "You're in a bad way in the waking world, but it looks like your mind is intact."

Minh ran his hand through his shiny black hair, leaving it sticking up in places. "I don't know about that, but thanks for bringing me here. It's quiet in my head for the first time in . . . I have no idea."

"You have some sort of new power from the Sunrise, and whatever you got was big. It overwhelmed you. Bao is okay, but he's not able to be on your arm right now. We've kept him close, though."

Minh gave her a nod of thanks. "How did you figure all this out?"

Ernie began to tell him, but a white glimmer to her left drew her gaze. Phoebe had appeared under a copse of trees. Ernie waved. "There you go."

Minh turned toward the spirit of his maker, and his smile eased any sense of anxiety Ernie had. "Phoebe," he said, his voice full of awe as he got to his feet and jogged unsteadily toward her. Ernie caught up and grabbed his arm to keep him from falling. "Are you real? I've been dreaming about you, but—"

"I am as real as you are, my darling child," she responded.

He opened his arms to embrace her but ended up almost running into a tree after staggering through her transparent body. Ernie steadied him again and turned him toward the former Forger. "She's a spirit," Ernie explained. "And she can't be with us in the waking world unless she possesses one of our bodies."

Phoebe looked regretful. "A difficult decision, I know."

"I'll do it," said Minh.

Phoebe cocked her head back. "Are you sure, child?"

"Something's wrong with me," he told her. "I don't want to go back into the waking world, not when I can't control my own mind. It was like torture."

"I'm so sorry," she said, her voice breaking. "I hoped the Sunrise would bring me a companion, but it turns out I've only caused suffering to Dealers who never wanted the power in the first place. I should have found a way to leave something—a myth, a map—to reveal what it offered. But I was afraid that kind of thing would lure only the greedy."

"It did anyway," said Ernie, remembering how eager Virginia had been to get her hands on the Sunrise. "But without intending to, you might have given us a way to stop Virginia," Ernie said. "So all you're gonna get from me is thanks."

"Agreed," said Minh. "But I . . . I guess I can't handle whatever I got."

Ernie touched his arm. "Dude. You got hit with the biggest piece." She pointed at his belly, and he lifted his shirt, unveiling the large golden scar.

"That's rather alarming," he said weakly.

"I think it looks kinda cool," Ernie said, showing him her own scar, which was nearly as large but, for some reason, hadn't affected her mind at all. She was definitely glad, but at the same time, she felt a pang of regret—she wanted to be able to help fight Virginia, and she couldn't even figure out what she'd inherited. "Gabe got it right in the face."

Minh guffawed. "Did it make him any prettier?"

"I think he is a fine specimen," Phoebe said, then offered Ernie a girlish smile. "I may be old, but I'm not blind."

"No argument here, lady," Ernie said, determined not to be weirded out, not when Phoebe could offer critical help. "I'm pretty fond of his face myself."

"So how do we do this?" Minh asked. "Can you tinker with my brain and sort it all out?"

"I will certainly try," Phoebe replied.

"Will I feel it?"

"You will dwell here in spirit, as I do now." Phoebe gestured at her own transparent body. "I will do my best to restore your mind and to help your allies defeat this new Forger, who sounds like a scourge."

"Scourge, Nazi, tomayto, tomahto," Ernie muttered.

"Have you thought about who will take her place, though?" Phoebe asked.

Ernie bit her lip. "Oh. Um, no."

"Maybe we can talk about it later, once I'm not catatonic?" suggested Minh.

"Seems reasonable." But already, Ernie's thoughts were spinning.

"The possession," Phoebe said. "Are you sure, Minh? I do nothing without your full consent. For this to work, you must welcome me."

Minh looked down at the scar on his abs once more, then dropped his shirt. Concern flickered in his dark eyes. "What happens to Bao?"

"Gabe can probably help, right?" Ernie looked at Phoebe for confirmation.

Phoebe nodded. "Gabe could sustain the deck and the spirit. He can maintain the bond it has with you. I will instruct him."

Minh elbowed Ernie. "Will you visit me?"

She grasped his shoulder. "You're not going to be here long, okay? We'll get this done and get you back. No one gets left behind."

Phoebe spread her arms. "You are my child, Minh. I will care for you and deliver you back to your body as soon as I can."

Minh ran his hands up his arms as if he had a chill. He looked uncertain, maybe even a little afraid, so different from his usual casual confidence. On impulse, Ernie leaned over and gave him a firm hug. "*No one* gets left behind, okay?" she whispered.

Hesitantly, Minh returned her embrace. "You're maybe the only Dealer in the universe who I can trust to mean that." He chuckled. "Except maybe Gabe. I've always thought the two of you made sense, as foolish as it is."

"I know, I know," Ernie said, releasing him. "We'll see you soon."

Minh nodded, swallowing hard. He turned to Phoebe. "Go ahead."

She moved forward. "Don't fight it," she said as she drifted close to him. "Just let it happen." Then she drifted *into* him, and his entire body shuddered. His eyes sought Ernie's, and for a moment, it was all Minh, and he was scared. Ernie's stomach clenched. But then the fear disappeared, and his deep-brown eyes flowed with streaks of white and ice blue and flecks of black. His fingers twitched, and his mouth opened and closed.

A transparent shadow of Minh drifted out of his solid body's left side and fell to the ground, floating a few inches above its grassy surface. "Whoa," Minh's ghostly form said, looking breathless and pained.

Ernie sank to her knees next to him. "Are you all right?"

"No idea," he murmured, holding up a hand between them and peering through it, right at Ernie's face. "It feels like I'm about to fly apart."

"You'll get used to it." It was Minh's voice, but it came from his solid body, which was now occupied by Phoebe. "You're not contained by flesh and bone any longer. But you're in no danger, my child. Your spirit is whole and strong."

He nodded, looking a little relieved and a lot uncertain.

"We should go back to the waking world," Phoebe-Minh said.

213

It was so weird hearing her words coming out of his mouth, in her friend's voice. Ernie turned back to the real Minh, the transparent, floating spirit before her. "I don't think I want to leave you alone."

"They'll need you in the waking world," spirit Minh said. "And I'll be fine, as long as you don't leave me here forever." He let out a laugh that was tinged with nervousness.

"You know I would never," Ernie said.

Phoebe-Minh knelt before Minh's spirit. "And you know I would never, either."

"Go, then. I'll see you soon."

Her chest tight, Ernie took the hand of the solid Minh, the body containing the spirit of the former Forger, possibly the one person who could help them save the world from Virginia. "Let's wake up, then."

Phoebe-Minh smiled, not quite Minh's smooth and confident smile, but close. Ernie showed her Revelation card, which revealed Ernie sleeping with her head tilted against Minh's, her arm under his shoulders. "You care about him," Phoebe-Minh murmured.

"You bet I do." Ernie blinked her eyes open in the real world and looked over at Minh's body as Phoebe made his fingers rub his face.

Phoebe-Minh sat up on the cot and looked around the yurt. "This is lovely. All of you here together."

Gabe, who had been sitting on his cot and consuming a bowl of noodles with the desperation of a starving man, whipped around at the sound of Minh's voice. His face lit up. "Minh!"

"Not quite," Ernie said as she moved to her own cot.

Gabe lost his smile. "She possessed him."

The others had all stopped what they were doing and were peering at Minh with assorted expressions—horror, hope, curiosity.

"Refer to me as Phoebe," the former Forger said in Minh's voice. "I won't pretend to be him, or the true owner of this body."

"This is weird," Trey mumbled.

"Agreed," said Tarlae.

"He chose it of his own free will," said Phoebe. "He could not control the power, and he asked for my help."

Gabe looked to Ernie, and she nodded. "He trusts Phoebe, and we'll restore him to his body as soon as we can."

Phoebe pulled the Pot-Bellied Pig deck from Minh's pocket and offered it to Tarlae. "He needs you to hold this while I occupy his body, as you are the custodian of the cards."

She hesitantly accepted the deck. "I would never let another Dealer take possession of *my* deck."

"But you are more than a Dealer now," said Phoebe. "And Minh is trusting you." She turned to Gabe. "You will need to use your power to sustain Bao and maintain the bond until Minh is in control again."

"You'll show me how?"

Phoebe nodded. "I will personally instruct you. And I am happy to tell you, I can feel the powers he received from the Sunrise." She ran Minh's fingers down his lean ribs and over his abdomen. Ernie couldn't help a shiver at the strangeness of knowing Minh hadn't chosen to do that himself. *He consented to this,* she reminded herself before focusing on what Phoebe was telling them. "Minh can sense every relic ever created by a Forger." She touched his temple. "Nuria can sense the Dealers, but Minh can sense the artifacts. There are other powers here, but that is the one that overwhelmed him, because of the relics' sheer number and power."

Ernie's fingers closed around the edge of her cot. "Does that mean you can help us find them?"

Phoebe nodded, smiling Minh's smile. "I know exactly which ones we should retrieve first."

"And which would that be?" The question came from Tarlae. It was the first time she'd spoken since Minh had woken up. Her voice was harsh with suspicion.

Phoebe gestured at Nuria. "She knows where the Dealers are, scattered across dimensions." She touched Minh's chest. "And I know where the dimensional rune tiles are."

Gabe grinned. "We can bring them home. That's brilliant."

Phoebe-Minh's responding smile radiated pleasure and pride. "Thank you, Kestrel."

Hope pushed aside the discomfort Ernie felt at seeing Phoebe-Minh look at Gabe like that. It also eased some of the ache of having left the real Minh behind. "If they're willing to come back and stand with us," Ernie said, "maybe we can build an army to match Virginia's."

CHAPTER TWENTY-ONE

Dimensional rune tiles had apparently been some of Andy's favorite toys. He'd created a trove of them, each one a doorway into another slice of the universe. According to Phoebe, who could sense them with Minh's mind, most of them opened into splinters, incomplete dimensions that had been shaven off one moment in time. The splinter dimension where Kot had been born and in which Virginia had trapped Ernie—and Nuria and Redmond Terwilliger in the decades before— had been only a few hundred miles in each direction, ending in dead brown oceans where no fish could live and no boat could sail, at least not if the sailors wished to make it back home. Some dimensions were even smaller, more specks than splinters, made up of only a few square miles, the perfect places to imprison rebellious or disobedient Dealers.

According to Nuria, who had returned to her map of the dimensions to point out the rune symbols she'd drawn and the Dealers located within each place, many were locked in those pockets of the universe. Only the Forger could retrieve them—or a Dealer wielding the exact rune tile that connected her world to that precise dimension.

And according to Phoebe, settled into Minh's body and mind and firmly in control, most of the dimensional rune artifacts were hidden in one spot. "Biggest bang for the buck," Ernie said when Phoebe gave them the news. She received only a blank stare in return.

Gabe mussed the top of Ernie's hair. "She means we should go get them right now," he said with a smile.

Phoebe beamed at him, and once again, Ernie couldn't help but pause at the utter weirdness of seeing Minh look at Gabe in that way . . . with an expression that said he wouldn't mind at all if Gabe mussed *his* hair. Ernie cleared her throat and moved a little closer to Gabe. "So where exactly is this treasure?"

"Edo," said Phoebe.

Gabe nodded. "So we go to Japan."

"Never heard of it—is it a small town?" Ernie asked.

"The opposite. It's called Tokyo these days." Gabe reached down to pat Bao, who had snuggled against his leg. Phoebe and Gabe had spent over an hour huddled together that morning, during which time Ernie had done her best not to note the frequency with which Minh's hand had brushed Gabe's body. Apparently, Phoebe had explained to Gabe that his touch and a few focused, intentional thoughts could keep Bao calm, the deck stable, and both connected to Minh's spirit. Knowing she was being petty and ridiculous, Ernie had pressed her lips shut to keep from asking whether Phoebe was looking for an excuse to get Gabe to touch *her.*

"How close can we get to the actual rune tiles?" Ernie asked. "Phoebe doesn't have the power of a Dealer, so she can't exactly find it in a Revelation card, right? My guess is that Tokyo doesn't look quite the same as it did when Andy buried his treasure."

"A very good point," Phoebe said with a frown. "I have an image in my head, but I don't know if this is a portrait of the place as it was when the rune tiles were hidden or the place as it is today." She gave Gabe a wink. "I'm older than I look."

Gabe smiled. "But you have a youthful spirit."

"So does Minh," Ernie reminded them.

Phoebe smoothed out her flirtatious expression, turning Minh's face serious again. "If you can get me close, I think I can lead you to it."

"Should we all go?" asked Kot, looking up from the cushioned space where he and Nuria were enjoying a siesta. Trey and Tarlae had gone outside for a walk and, Ernie hoped, a heart-to-heart.

"Stay here and get some rest," Ernie suggested. "You guys can take the next mission." She couldn't remember the last time she'd slept, and the noodles she'd downed had been the first meal she'd had in at least a day, but for now, her body was abuzz with energy and the need to move. Perhaps it was the new, mysterious power inside her, or maybe it was simply her natural tendency and long-standing habit to exercise hard when her mind was unsettled, but right now, all Ernie wanted to do was get something, anything, accomplished. The idea that she and Gabe might be on the verge of finding the rune tiles that would bring dozens of stranded Dealers home? Perfect.

Gabe had circles under his eyes, but he seemed to feel the same way as Ernie. He listened intently to Phoebe describing where in Tokyo the rune tiles were located—north of the port, to the east of the Imperial Palace, either left there by Andy like a mystical Easter egg or stolen and hidden by some mortal middleman. Gabe, who had been to Tokyo more than a few times, volunteered to get them to a safe landing spot, and with concealments applied, he and Ernie linked arms with Phoebe and stepped into the void. Minh's lean body trembled against Ernie in the darkness, and Phoebe murmured "I'd forgotten what this feels like" as she clutched at Gabe's chest.

They arrived in a quiet corner of a busy subway station. Ernie pulled Phoebe away from Gabe, trying to make the movement casual and not at all like a sudden yank. The clock told Ernie it was one. Judging from the crowds in the place—or more accurately, the lack thereof—it was probably the middle of the night instead of just after lunch hour.

After giving Phoebe a few moments to pull herself together, they trooped into the open and headed up to street level, where they emerged into a maze of mammoth skyscrapers. "It's that way," Phoebe said confidently, pointing up the street toward one of the smaller skyscrapers, though Ernie supposed it was probably at least four times as tall as the tallest building in Asheville.

As they drew nearer, Gabe's expression darkened. "It's a bank," he said. "Not good."

Ernie peered at the building, its windows dark but its sign lit up red. "Andy hid the rune tiles in a bank?"

"Someone else got them and hid them, more like," Gabe said. "Hope it wasn't Virginia."

"Could be someone who didn't even know what they'd gotten their hands on," Ernie said. "Like someone who found them in some ruin in the middle of the Amazon and is planning to sell them. You never know."

"You'll have to get me in there," said Phoebe. "I can feel all of those rune tiles, all their power. And I can tell you—they're below ground. But I can't tell you exactly where they are."

Gabe sighed. "They're most likely in a vault." He strode right up to the building and peered through the glass front doors at a security guard sitting behind a desk in the lobby, a petite woman with her hair in a bun, wearing black pants and a long-sleeved green button-up, with a badge pinned to the right side of her chest and a Taser holstered on her belt. "Come here, love," he said, and both Ernie and Phoebe approached. Gabe's eyes met Ernie's. "We can hide ourselves, but we should disguise Phoebe, too, in case our concentration lapses. Can you conjure a uniform like hers?" He flicked a finger toward the guard inside the building.

"Sure thing." Ernie dealt Conceal to hide them, then played Alchemy and Ally to change Minh's designer pants and T-shirt into the drab stylings of a bank security guard. When they'd done that, Gabe transported them inside, near the elevator banks. Ernie pressed the down button. Phoebe looked calm and collected, which made her appear more like Minh than she had since they'd come back from the dream realm, but once they were in the elevator, she laughed and shivered. "This is so very strange," she said. "In so many ways."

"Like?" Ernie asked as they descended to a sublevel and Gabe bypassed the keycard requirement with a simple play of Inverse and Lock.

"This body, for one," Phoebe said.

"Oh, you mean being a man when you're usually a woman? I totally get that."

Gabe arched one eyebrow. "You do?"

Ernie shrugged. "I've done it before. Weird to have dangly bits when you're usually streamlined."

Phoebe giggled, a strange sound coming out of Minh's mouth. "I rather enjoy the . . . dangly bits." She glanced at Gabe, setting Ernie on edge. "But also," Phoebe continued, "his youth, his strength, and his mind. Fascinating to be inside another person."

"Just don't get too comfortable, okay?" Ernie gave her a bright smile.

Phoebe reached out and squeezed Ernie's hand, then Gabe's. "He is lucky to have such friends. It means a lot to him—I can feel it in his heart. And it brings me joy. Minh lost almost his entire family— parents, sisters, wife, sons—to a terrible sickness in his village. He was on the verge of death himself when I appeared to him, but still he was trying to gather fresh water and food to save the family of his sister, who had already lost her husband. I gave him the power to restore their health and his own, but after watching so many of his loved ones die, he shied away from human connections. I think they frighten him."

"Did you know that about him?" Ernie asked Gabe as the elevator doors opened onto a pristine world of metal and white concrete.

Gabe shrugged. "Most of us have pasts we're happy to leave behind. I always assumed it was the same for him, no matter how he played it."

"It's that way," Phoebe said, pointing down the hall to their left. A shudder passed through Minh's uniformed body. "There are so many," she added in a whisper, leading them down a narrow corridor lined with alcoves, each one home to at least a hundred electronically locked safes complete with fingerprint scanners.

"So who exactly are we robbing?" Ernie asked quietly, glancing up at a glossy black pod hanging from the ceiling, beneath which she knew lay a security camera. She and Gabe wouldn't appear on any surveillance displays, and as long as their concentration held, Minh wouldn't, either.

"Smuggler, middleman, fence, take your pick," said Gabe.

"Not an archaeologist or historian? My dad would have given his left arm to get ahold of a set of artifacts like that, even if he didn't know exactly what they were."

Gabe arched an eyebrow. "Archaeologists and historians are unlikely to use a bank like this one to store their treasures. Think more yakuza or Bratva and less Indiana Jones."

"Then I guess it's good that they won't know who stole from them."

Gabe smirked. "Honestly? Might be fun."

Phoebe marched along confidently, until she let out a gasp and took a sharp right into one of the alcoves. She pointed at the third little safe up from the ground on the left side, in the fourth column from the hallway. "It's in there," she announced. "All of them are in there together." Minh's handsome face was covered in a sheen of sweat.

"You okay?" Gabe asked as he considered his cards. He put out a hand to support her.

"It's overwhelming," Phoebe said in a strangled voice, clutching at Gabe's fingers while steadying herself with a hand on one of the safes' screens.

Gabe abruptly raised his head. "She just set off an alarm." He played a few cards, then swiped two—Lock and Inverse yet again—over the safe Phoebe had pointed to. Its door popped open, and Ernie reached in and grabbed the only thing within: a small but bulging canvas sack.

She had her hand in the safe when Gabe shouted and flew backward, knocking into Phoebe. It was a domino effect: Phoebe crashed into the safe door—which slammed over Ernie's wrist—then into Ernie herself as the hallway lit up with a bright light.

"Here they are," shouted a female voice.

"Dealers," Gabe said from between clenched teeth, yanking a knife from his shoulder and scattering droplets of his blood across a few safes and the pristine floor.

With searing pain devouring her right arm, Ernie yanked out the bag with her left. Phoebe groaned and grabbed at Ernie's waist to pull herself up from the ground. "I can't defend myself," she said, Minh's voice high and tremulous with fright. "I'm immortal because of the Forger power inside this body, but without a deck—"

"I've got you." Ernie jostled Minh's body until it was behind hers while Gabe blocked the entrance to the alcove and sent strikes in both directions.

Gabe glanced over his shoulder, his gaze lasering to Ernie cradling her mangled wrist. "Go now. I'll be right behind you."

"No," Ernie snapped, shoving the bag at Phoebe and wrestling her own cards from her pocket.

Gabe threw up a shield to protect them from some type of sizzling liquid, which hit the clear barrier and ran down its outer surface in viscous rivulets. "*Now.* Make sure you keep concealed. I'll lead them on a little chase, maybe teach them a lesson or two."

Ernie glared at him. "If you're not home within half an hour, I'm coming after you."

Pressing his Healing card to his shoulder, he winked. "Yes, dear."

Ernie spun around, the pain almost drawing a scream from her mouth. "Hang on to me tight, got it? I can't hold on to you."

Looking at her with Minh's wide eyes, Phoebe lunged forward and wrapped her arms around Ernie's waist. Ernie played Transport crossed with Conceal and twisted them into the void. Her last glimpse of the corridor was of Gabe's shield exploding outward and him stepping forward with glowing cards fanned in both hands. Her last thought was that those newbie Dealers didn't stand much of a chance, especially if Gabe deployed his new power. Love mixed with pride mixed with fear spiraled inside her as she carried Phoebe through the void. Her wrist throbbed, sending jolts of pain up her arm to her shoulder, but she stayed focused on getting Phoebe back to the Mongolian haven safely.

They arrived outside the yurt, but even as Ernie put her foot forward to keep her balance, she was yanked back into the void, spinning and out of control. Minh's leanly powerful arms remained locked around her waist while they plunged through the darkness. "It's the Forger," Phoebe called out. "She's got hold of us!"

Ernie's heart lurched in her chest. The fingers of her left hand spasmed over her deck, and Legs throbbed like a burst of flame on her forearm. The bottoms of her feet hit solid ground with a force that reverberated up from her heels to her hips to her head, exploding inside her mind in a flash of red agony as Ernie and Phoebe fell to the floor. Crashing and shouting echoed all around her. Light flickered above, and as her vision clicked into focus, she realized they were back at the bank. Virginia, her gauzy white gown floating around her, stood several yards away, grinning as her newly created Dealers dueled with Gabe at the opposite end of the hall. They'd gathered in a cluster around his alcove.

Down the hall, Ernie could see bodies strewed. The newbies or maybe Virginia had slaughtered the guards who had come down to investigate the tripped alarm.

"The Forger has kept him from transporting away," Phoebe said from Ernie's right. She was already sitting up and reaching over to help Ernie to her feet.

Virginia walked forward, her white hair bouncing around her shoulders, her wrinkled face stretched by her smile. "I have no idea how you three are alive—I suppose the Sunrise was a dud, after all that fuss." She rubbed her hands together, the friction giving off a few blue sparks and raising the hair on the back of Ernie's neck. "I knew you greedy idiots wouldn't give up, though. Did you think you'd get away with *this* treasure?" She tilted her head and looked over Ernie first—and then Minh. Her brow furrowed. "Why can't I sense you, piglet?" she asked him.

Phoebe smiled. "You have a lot to learn, young lady," she said, and Minh's voice was both friendly and deadly. "Gabe!"

Virginia cocked her head back, for a moment resembling the rooster she'd so coldly abandoned on that mesa in Utah. "He can't help you now, and all of you have grown a little too tiresome to tolerate." As she spoke, her eyes turned an inky black. "Say goodbye to your animals—and your decks." Her hands glowed with blue strands of electricity.

Just as Ernie went for her deck, several of the enemy Dealers shouted and fell away from Gabe's alcove, and he charged out. Ernie gasped—and so did Virginia. Gabe's eyes were streaked with the same gold that radiated across his face. All around him, the enemy Dealers' animals jumped off their arms and began to race down the corridor after him as he ran toward Ernie and Phoebe.

Virginia's face twisted with rage and confusion, and she drew her hand back, perhaps to throw the blue bolts at Ernie and her allies. But as Gabe reached them, Phoebe shoved Ernie to the side and stepped between her and the Kestrel. Phoebe grabbed both Ernie and Gabe by the wrist—Ernie's broken bones crunched in her grasp, forcing Ernie to bite back a scream. The skin of Minh's hands had gone almost transparent, and the veins lying beneath that thin veil ran with flecks of gold and blue and black. Gabe grunted and jerked forward with the impact of the animal spirits that had abandoned their Dealers and dived into his back, but he managed to stay on his feet as the Forger sent her power hurtling toward them. Phoebe pulled their joined hands upward.

The ropes of blue lightning suddenly disappeared as if they'd hit a wall of icy water. "Transport now," Phoebe shouted in Minh's voice.

Ernie's Transport card leapt from her pocket to her good hand, and Gabe's shot into the air, where he caught it before throwing his arm around Ernie as they dove into the void once more. "How—" Ernie began as they traveled with the universe pressing in on them.

"I was Forger for centuries," Phoebe said, voice rising to be heard through the whooshing darkness. "I might have learned a few tricks in that time."

A moment later, they arrived on the steppe, with the yurt haven on one side, the steep overlook on the other, and the wide open space lit by only the stars and the moon. Caera exploded off Gabe's arm in a flurry of shrieks and feathers. She soared into the air and was out of sight in seconds. Gabe fell to his knees with Phoebe leaning over him, her hands on his back. "I'm fine," he said, sounding winded but not pained.

Trey came rushing out of the yurt. "You look—" he began, but Ernie shook her head and played Shelter, instantly creating another yurt for herself adjacent to the other. Normally, she would have wanted to be the one taking care of Gabe, but her heart was still pounding with mortal fear, and her right wrist hurt so much that speech was beyond her. She ducked inside her conjured shelter, collapsed to the stiff grass at her feet, and drew her Healing card with frantic desperation. She sighed with relief as warmth radiated out from the card.

Legs tingled along her arm then slithered off her skin. The diamondback rattled gently and coiled herself next to Ernie, as if to say that she still liked her, even though her Dealer's arm was the last place she wanted to be. Ernie looked away from her, eyes fixed on the rippling fabric that covered the yurt's entrance. Would Legs really adjust to being with Ernie now that she had part of the Forger's power, or would she decide to seek another person to be her Dealer? The idea awakened a pain inside Ernie that had nothing to do with her rapidly healing wrist.

When she turned to look over at Legs, the snake had already slithered away, perhaps to hunt, perhaps to ponder the existential dilemma in which she found herself, whatever the reptilian version of that was. Ernie waited until her Healing card had gone cold to slip it back into her deck, and tested her wrist. Outside, she could hear Trey, Phoebe, and Gabe discussing what had happened, with an occasional monosyllabic comment from Nuria, who must have come out of the yurt to see what was going on. Ernie knew she should go talk to them, but even though her body was restored, her thoughts were unsettled.

Gabe poked his head through the doorway, glanced at Ernie's now-healthy wrist, and entered the shelter. He played a few cards, and a large, soft mattress appeared, complete with silky-looking sheets and fluffy pillows. Ernie gave him a weary smile. "How are you so full of energy? A minute ago, you looked like you'd just finished a marathon."

He collapsed on the bed. "That was something, wasn't it?"

"Which part?" She crawled up onto the mattress, into his waiting arms.

Gabe slid his fingers into Ernie's hair and began a gentle massage along her scalp. "We fought back against a Forger and *won*, love. Phoebe channeled our power, and boom! She was amazing, wasn't she?"

"We didn't win," Ernie said, sighing as she laid her head on his shoulder. "We pissed Virginia off and gave her another reason to come after us."

"She was doing that anyway. I think she came to enjoy the show. She certainly got more than she bargained for. Probably all she can do right now is clean up the mess."

Ernie rose up on her elbow and looked Gabe over. "Mess?"

Wearing a sly smile, Gabe lifted his shirt, the fabric sliding up over his belt and revealing the taut skin of his abdomen. There, decorating his tanned skin, lay what appeared to be several small tattoos, each one only two inches or so across.

One was a scorpion. There were four others: a bright-blue frog, a bald eagle, a black snake of some type, and a snail.

"Oh, that poor guy," Ernie said, stroking her finger over the snail. "I never did quite get that one, compared to all the others. A snail? Really? I thought she was going for deadly."

Gabe pulled her hand away. "*That*," he said, pointing at the snail, "is a cone snail. Poisonous enough to kill a grown man."

Ernie cringed. "Can you feel them?"

Gabe nodded. "I didn't exactly mean to take them. I only meant to draw them away from their Dealers. But I don't think they were happy with where they were."

Ernie thought of Legs. "I hope that doesn't mean that *our* animals will—"

"No, love. Phoebe told me that I do have to call to them in the first place." He sighed. "Caera's none too happy about any of this, but *she* can't leave unless I release her, since I've got the power to control the animal spirits. And I'm not willing to let her go quite yet—not until we get this sorted. So she's stuck unless Virginia got ahold of me alone, I suppose. She's still the Forger, with all the power I have and a lot more."

"How come we just knocked her back a step, then?"

"Surprise, I imagine. She'll probably be ready for us next time. My guess is that she's realizing the Sunrise wasn't the dud she thought it was." He covered Ernie's hand with his own, pressing it to his heart. "She won't stop now until she's taken each of us out. Wouldn't be surprised if she tries to pick us off one by one. Best shot we have is to stay together and rally around Phoebe."

Ernie considered the canvas bag they'd swiped from the bank. "We might be able to do more than that, if we can bring banished Dealers home. But I'm not sure what the end game is. Say we defeat her . . ." She looked up at Gabe, taking in the gold veins running down his neck and up his jaw. "Do you want to be Forger?"

He stared at the roof of the yurt. "Being truthful?"

"Yeah."

He turned and kissed her forehead. "No."

She squeezed her eyes shut. "Same. It seems like a freaking lonely job. I think you have to want power more than you want connection to other people."

"Not sure it was that way for Phoebe—she seems to care for us. But I wouldn't wish it on anyone—Trey or Tarlae, Nuria or Kot."

"And Minh?"

Gabe shook his head. "Do you really think he'd want that?"

"Right now, I think all he wants is to have his body back, and his mind." She already felt guilty for leaving him alone in the dream realm for so long.

"What if . . ." Gabe paused to look down at Ernie. "Do you think Phoebe would want her old job back?"

CHAPTER TWENTY-TWO

When Ernie didn't give an immediate response, Gabe's brow furrowed. "What?"

"I don't know," Ernie said slowly.

"You don't think she'd take it, or you don't think it's a good idea?"

"I just don't know." She closed her eyes. "Can we go to sleep? I'm so tired."

"Someone has to be Forger."

She sighed. "I understand, Gabe. But I don't know Phoebe, okay?"

"She's done nothing but help us, with some risk and no benefit to herself." His tone had taken on an edge.

"I'm not so sure about that—she can't seem to keep Minh's hands off you," Ernie said drily.

Gabe tensed. "You've got to be kidding me. This is jealousy?"

Ernie scooted back, putting space between them. "I only said I wasn't certain she was the right person, and now you're all mad."

"You said more than that." He sat up. "I've just realized I'm not so tired after all. Get some rest. I'll see you later." He got up and walked out of the yurt.

Despite her exhaustion, it took Ernie a long time to fall asleep. Gabe's faith in Phoebe was so clear, and Ernie knew she had been a bit petty with her comment about Phoebe's roaming hands. She couldn't

shake what her father had said about how power could corrupt anyone . . . but then again, Phoebe may have been different. Was her hesitation about the old woman really just coming from the fact that Phoebe
seemed to have a thing for Gabe?

Maybe. Ernie was worn thin, and it didn't take much to bother her.
She needed to brush it off and get back in the game.

With all the Dealers' concealments around them, their power
pooled, her slumber was restless but blessedly dreamless. Slowly, her
guilt and worry slipped off like a heavy cloak in a hot room, leaving her
with only relief. She awoke with the dawn, slowly, and found herself
warm and snuggled in against Gabe's solid, relaxed body.

Not wanting to rekindle the tension from the night before, Ernie
stayed quiet as they rose, dressed, and exited their private shelter. Her
arm tingled and burned—at some point during the night, Legs had
returned to tattoo form, but she seemed as unhappy about her situation
as before. Gabe explained that Caera had done the same, but the Kestrel
had positioned herself in a distinctly threatening pose. With a chuckle
and a wince, Gabe showed Ernie how, when his arm was hanging by
his side, the image of the Kestrel actually seemed poised to attack the
animals tattooed across Gabe's stomach. Ernie laughed, too, but she
couldn't stifle all her unease. How long could this go on? Would their
animals and decks abandon them completely? And if so, would they
have any warning?

Kot and Trey were chatting over a hearty breakfast of rice porridge
flavored with slices of fruit and fresh ginger, raising a heavenly scent
that made Ernie's stomach growl. Kot handed Ernie and Gabe bowls
of their own. "We're going to start this morning," he said, inclining his
head toward the pieces of the map Nuria had created, which were now
laid out in several rows and columns, with rocks weighing down each
sheet. "Nuria will guide us, and Phoebe will choose the rune tiles to
take us where we need to go."

Nuria and Phoebe walked hand in hand along the perimeter of the map, and the canvas bag they'd stolen from the Tokyo bank dangled from Minh's fist. Phoebe had clothed his body in a flowing white shirt and loose linen pants; it was so different from Minh's usual stylish, silky, and slim-fitting wardrobe that Ernie stared for a few moments, wondering what Minh would think of his body being attired that way.

Gabe touched her shoulder to draw her attention. They had seated themselves on a few conjured chairs near the merrily crackling and magically contained campfire, the flames of which licked harmlessly at the surrounding stiff grass without setting it alight. "Care to venture to another dimension today?"

Ernie shrugged and spooned a few mouthfuls of the porridge into her mouth. Then she swallowed and said, "I think I need to visit a different realm today—dreams."

"To see Minh," he guessed. "You worried about him? Seems like Phoebe's taking good care of his body. She was trying to protect it last night. It's obvious she thinks of him like a son." His voice carried the slightest challenge, as if he were expecting her to disagree.

"Not exactly worried," she said, sidestepping the issue. "But I promised him I wouldn't leave him alone there."

"Looking after your teammates."

"Always." She nudged his shoulder with hers, needing the connection, hating the tension she felt in his body when they touched. "Are you going?"

He nodded. "I was talking with Kot and Trey last night after you were snoring away—"

"Oh, god. Really?"

"We're going to go in pairs in order to be efficient. I was going to go with you, but if you'd rather stay, I'll go with one of the other teams, maybe with Phoebe. Our goal is to send a signal to the banished Dealer in each realm upon entering the dimension, so we don't have to spend too much time looking about for them."

"Are we sure these people are friendlies?"

"Well, they were banished for a reason, but given who was in charge, I'm thinking they're more likely to be independent minded than criminally inclined." He swallowed a bite of his porridge. "I'm also thinking we'll go ready to defend ourselves if it's necessary, while hoping the banished will be grateful for a rescue."

Tarlae exited the yurt gingerly, rubbing her palms together as if they still smarted. Trey was at her side instantly, offering a bowl of porridge that she waved away. She cast a wary glance in the direction of Nuria and Phoebe, then met Trey's gaze. He tilted his head, perhaps reading her expression, because he announced in a loud voice, "We're down to six, guys. Tarlae needs another day to get her strength back."

"It's five," said Gabe. "Ernie's got herself a different mission."

When she saw the others' frowns, she said, "I don't feel good about leaving Minh alone."

Phoebe laid her hand over Minh's heart. "Oh, dear. You think he's been alone this whole time?"

"Isn't he?" Ernie could feel the gazes of her allies on her. "*You* were alone in the dream realm, weren't you?"

Phoebe smiled. "But I feel Minh in *here*, dear." She patted the chest of her borrowed body. "And it keeps me connected to his spirit. I assure you, he's quite all right, although he'd like to return to himself as soon as possible. I wish you trusted me." Her eyes met Ernie's. "We should gather the banished quickly, before the Forger regroups and focuses her energy on finding and eliminating us one by one. You can stay if you want, but your presence will be missed. Gabe, are you accompanying me?" She held out Minh's hand to him.

"I'll go with Gabe," Ernie said quickly. "If you're sure Minh's okay."

Phoebe blinked at her. "You think I would lie to you?"

"Maybe Ernie should not venture off alone in the dream realm right now anyway," said Kot. "Virginia may be looking for a way in." His gaze met Ernie's. "And you don't even know what power you received from the Sunrise, do you? You are a mere Dealer like me, for the time being."

"'Mere' isn't really a word I'd apply to either of us," Ernie said. "But I hear you. And I'll go with Gabe." She tried to keep the edge from her voice but didn't quite succeed.

Gabe stood up, giving Ernie a look that said he'd registered that edge and he thought she'd been rude, but he didn't contradict her.

Phoebe closed the distance between them, gracefully stepping over the corner of the pieced-together map while its pages fluttered in the grass. "Diamondback, you are a true friend. Minh feels your loyalty, and it warms him. But he needs your help now, to gather the allies that will help us secure a tomorrow."

Feeling like a jerk, Ernie simply nodded. Phoebe and Nuria began to pull out rune tiles and lay them on the corresponding spots on the map, next to the animals the Grasshopper Dealer had drawn. In some cases, they could only guess what each animal was, as so many had four stick legs, a stick tail, and oval heads with dots or slashes for eyes and mouths and ears. But in others, it was obvious the creature was a snake or a fish. At least one was a completely unrecognizable mass that none of them could even guess at. Another was definitely a spider—a circle with eight stick legs—and Ernie was pretty sure that was Akela, the Dealer of the Wolf Spider deck.

Once several of the rune tiles from the bag were matched to locations with animals, Phoebe handed the remainder of the tiles to Tarlae, asking her to keep them safe until they returned. Tarlae accepted them with the eagerness with which one might receive a venomous snake and disappeared back into the yurt. Phoebe, Kot, and Nuria conversed in primitive sign language over one of the tiles and its corresponding animal drawing—"It's a cat, no, a wolverine! A bear? A camel?"

While they tried to figure it all out, Ernie approached Trey. "Is she okay?" she asked, jerking her head toward the yurt.

Trey's black-brown eyes skated over the shelter. "I'm still getting to know her, but if I had to guess, I'd say she's not exactly comfortable with this situation. I've told her Phoebe's on the level, but she doesn't seem to trust easy, man."

Gabe, who had come over to listen, laughed. "Seems you know our Tarlae as well as you ever did. She's one of the least trusting people I've ever known."

Trey gave them a crooked smile. "I kinda like it. I mean, she's complicated, but . . ."

"You like the challenge," Ernie guessed.

Trey's cheeks darkened, but he said, "I can't resist one of those."

"Shall we go?" Phoebe asked. "Nuria and Kot have volunteered to go after this apparently aquatic animal." She pointed at an image with the toe of her sandal. "Trey, would you accompany me to retrieve this one?" She knelt next to the snake. "I think this might be the Eastern Indigo Snake, and if it is, she'll want to see me."

"But you're not really you," said Ernie.

Gabe let out an exasperated breath. "We all knew what she meant, Ernie."

Phoebe gave them a gracious smile. "The Eastern Indigo Snake knew Minh, as I made them both."

Ernie's cheeks warmed. She felt more like a jerk than ever.

"Sounds like the snake is your first stop," said Gabe. "I assume you'd like Ernie and me to try to fetch someone, then?"

Phoebe nodded, then reached over and touched the unrecognizable drawing, a blob of scribbles with eyes. "Maybe this one?"

"Any idea what that is?" Ernie asked.

Minh's brow furrowed as Phoebe considered the drawing. "It may be the Black Bear, but Nuria couldn't say. But if that's him, he should be easy to bring home." She gazed upon the drawing with fondness. "He's a jolly old dear. An old scholar—Italian Renaissance."

"He specialized in the Renaissance? He and my dad would probably get along."

"No, child, he was mortal during the Renaissance."

"Ah." Ernie accepted the rune tile from Phoebe, then turned to Gabe. "Where shall we go to open up the portal?"

Gabe took her arm and transported them maybe half a mile away from the camp, which was still visible at the top of the low, sloping rise of the steppe. "How about here?"

Ernie scanned the land beyond the overlook and saw two small figures she assumed were either Kot and Nuria or Phoebe and Trey. "Welp. Let's go get the Black Bear, shall we?" She tried to sound friendly, like all was well, and hated the air of disapproval around Gabe as he stepped toward her, even though she probably deserved it.

She held up the rune tile and focused on opening the portal. The sky darkened. Ernie glanced around, inhaling a scent she could understand only as burning meat. "What the hell?"

She reached into her pocket and drew out her deck as she took in the sight in front of her: a row of cows and pigs and sheep, lying slaughtered in a dirt clearing, their blood flowing into the red earth and turning to mud. A jungle of tangled vines and gnarled trees leaned in on them from either side, but within the greenery, lantern lights bobbed, and a distant drum throbbed like a heartbeat.

Gabe pulled out a few of his cards—Revelation, Inverse, and Ally. "I'll send out a summons for any Dealer in the—" Before he could finish, he was blown off his feet by a blast of fetid black liquid.

Ernie turned to see a blur of a dark creature sprint by on all fours and dive into the trees. An inhuman, hitching howl echoed out of the brush. She held her Shield card at the ready and kept her eyes on the spot where the thing had disappeared while she sidestepped over to Gabe, who was coughing and gagging. "Are you—" she began.

"Watch out," he shouted, and Ernie whirled around. A lean, muscular woman with pale eyes, dark skin, and dreadlocked hair stood with cards fanned at the edge of the trees. She was clad in a high-necked, long-sleeved, fitted leather shirt and leather pants. One hand held a single card, as if she was poised to strike.

Ernie threw up a shield as another blast of the black liquid poured forth from the card. The stuff splattered against the clear barrier, and Ernie took the chance to play Translate. "We come in peace," she yelled. "We're here to take you home."

The woman cocked her head. "I am home," she said. "Leave now." The translated words were only just louder than the woman's native language.

"You're an Immortal Dealer," Ernie shouted as Gabe reinforced her shield. "We were sent by Phoebe to bring you home as an ally." She wrenched up her sleeve to reveal the tattoo of Legs. "I'm the Diamondback, and that"—she indicated Gabe, who was cleaning the sticky black gunk off his face—"is the Kestrel. What may we call you?"

The Dealer had gone still. "Phoebe," the woman said slowly.

Ernie's brow furrowed. "Your name is Phoebe, too?"

The Dealer smiled, revealing teeth studded with what appeared to be glittering stones. "No, but I will come with you." She began to walk toward them, her gait smooth and strong, her fingers shifting her cards one over the other with practiced ease.

Ernie looked around them, taking in the blood and death. "Do you . . . I don't know—do you have a family or possessions you want to bring?"

The Dealer's smile grew. Her pale gaze swept over the slaughtered animals, lying in a long row of at least fifteen, and then toward the distant lanterns and sounds of drums. She let out a deep, resonant laugh. "They will believe their sacrifices finally worked if I go away."

"Sacrifices?" Ernie asked weakly, blinking at the carcasses. She exchanged glances with Gabe, who had one eyebrow arched and was looking past the woman.

"That is *not* a black bear," he muttered as something huge rustled in the brush and let out another howl.

Ernie leaned toward the sound in an effort to see the animal, but the banished Dealer turned and held out her arm, blocking the view. Ernie caught a glimpse of a shimmer of obsidian spiraling over the carnage and sliding up the Dealer's sleeve, presumably onto her arm. "How should we address you?" Ernie asked.

"You wouldn't be able to pronounce it," the Dealer replied. "Call me Mhambi."

"Cool." She swallowed back uncertainty and decided that friendliness was the best strategy. "I'm Ernie."

Gabe raised a hand—the one that held his deck of cards. "Gabe."

Another jewel-studded smile. "Let us go." Mhambi pocketed her deck and came over to stand next to Ernie in the patch of earth that was still covered with stiff grass, the connection point to their home dimension.

With one more quick glance at their new, eerie friend, Ernie clutched the tile in her palm, and the jagged rune carved into its surface glowed an electric blue tinged at the edges with red. The dark, bloody world disappeared, replaced by the steppe spread out before them, with scrubby green grass, mountains in the far distance, golden sun in the sky. Mhambi shaded her eyes with her cards and turned in place. She muttered something in a foreign language and smiled her jeweled smile.

Ernie and Gabe led the glitter-toothed Dealer toward the camp. As they drew near, Ernie spied two other newcomers sitting near the fire—a woman who looked to be in her twenties with light-brown skin, dark-brown hair, and blue tattoos decorating both cheeks, and a man with gray hair and a hawk nose. The allied Dealers sat next to them, and everyone seemed rapt, listening to Phoebe regale them with some tale of the past, judging by her sweeping gestures and animated expressions. When Ernie, Gabe, and Mhambi drew near, she stopped midsentence, her spread arms slowly lowering to her sides. Or, rather, Minh's sides.

Phoebe, her face unreadable, spoke in some foreign dialect, and Ernie pulled her Translate card again, tucking it into her bra, against her skin, so she could understand what was being said without having to hold the damn thing.

"—to this camp and peaceful society of allies," Phoebe was saying in Minh's voice.

"I recognize you even if you do not wear your old skin, Forger," said Mhambi.

Phoebe inclined her head. "You have always been clever. We have a new enemy to fight *together*."

Mhambi's pale eyes widened slightly. "Do we? I look forward to this honor."

Phoebe gave her a smile, but Ernie knew Minh's face, and she recognized a certain detached coldness he had deployed only when things got distinctly hairy. Phoebe raised her arms again and announced, "Come, children—we can feast together tonight, but now we must go out into this universe and bring our brothers and sisters home!"

The other Dealers, including the newcomers, got to their feet, and Mhambi clapped loudly. "Let us begin!" she shouted, loud enough to make Nuria flinch.

For the rest of the day, Ernie and Gabe put the tension between them aside, selected rune tiles, and stepped from one dimension to another, inviting the Dealers trapped within to come with them. None of them were quite as weird as Mhambi, and all of them, usually wary at first, seemed delighted when Ernie or Gabe mentioned that Phoebe was the person coordinating the effort, making Ernie feel like even more of a jerk for questioning her motives.

The Jackrabbit, the Wood Wasp, the Stingray, the Horned Lizard, the Badger—the first four had been banished by Andy for pissing him off, and the last one had been ambushed by Virginia and stranded in a splinter dimension so small that it was little more than a shack on perhaps an acre of grass, surrounded by inky black darkness that the

Badger Dealer called "the nothing." He seemed especially grateful to be rescued and eager to join in an effort to fight Virginia. He also greeted Gabe with a careful reverence that made Ernie wonder exactly what Gabe had been like in his early days as a Dealer.

By the time the sun set over the flatlands of Mongolia, the group of allies had grown from seven to nearly thirty, including Akela the Wolf Spider and Ruslan the Komodo Dragon, both of whom Gabe had vowed to keep a close eye on, given their history of aligning first with his evil brother and then with Virginia. Akela and Ruslan seemed subdued and wary rather than defiant, though, and both indicated that they were willing to be part of the effort to depose the former Chicken Dealer. However, both seemed to want to avoid their former enemies and instead conversed quietly with other previously banished Dealers.

Soon, a party was underway. The fire grew in size and heat as Dealers conjured plates of roasted vegetables, bread, and all sorts of delectable spreads. The only exception to the vegetarian tendencies was Mhambi, who conjured herself a fire several yards from the group and promptly produced a spit of roasted meat that wafted bitter, fatty fumes over the rest of them, earning herself many dirty looks and not seeming to care about it at all. The woman merely smiled to herself as she watched fat drip and sizzle while she turned the spit.

With Legs once again off slithering through the steppe—she'd slipped off Ernie's arm only a few minutes after they arrived back in the home dimension—Ernie spent time talking to a few of the newcomers, learning their histories and tales, sympathizing with what they'd gone through, and silently assessing what kind of ally each might really end up being. If she was going to be on a team with the formerly banished, she wanted to know they weren't going to stab her or any of her allies in the back and hand her over to Virginia on a platter in the hope of getting a sweet deal for turning.

All of them, though, seemed willing and even happy to join together to take down a rogue Forger, and a lot of that had to do with Phoebe, who seemed to have boundless energy for encouragement, empathy, comfort, and kick-ass pep talks. Ernie had to admit, of all the trainers and coaches she had ever had, the former Forger was definitely one of the best. It took the pressure off Ernie, who for once wasn't the only one trying to convince people that working together was the best thing for everyone.

Long after the sun had set and everyone had settled in around the fires to imbibe whatever, Ernie conjured herself some Wedge Iron Rail IPA and a comfy lawn chair. Gabe was off playing some complicated-looking game with hoops and throwing knives with a few of the others, and Ernie gasped as the Serow Dealer (who had sternly told Ernie that his fluffy-faced animal was a goat antelope native to his homeland of Japan) sent a blade spiraling between Gabe's legs. Gabe made an exaggerated, comical sound of relief, and suddenly Ernie felt like she could almost be at a late-summer barbecue with friends, their only purpose to kick back and relax. And when Gabe glanced over at her and smiled, she couldn't help but relax.

Minh sat down on the grass next to her, and Ernie almost asked him why he hadn't conjured himself a chair—then she remembered it was actually Phoebe, who wasn't a Dealer at all. Ernie played a few cards and created a lounger identical to her own.

Phoebe grinned as she stretched out her borrowed legs and accepted an Iron Rail from Ernie. "This is marvelous, isn't it?" she said after taking a long sip, gesturing at the gathering. "I never thought I would see the Dealers gathered this way, though I always hoped."

"What's Mhambi's deal?" Ernie glanced over at the lone fire set apart from the rest, where Mhambi was tearing meat from bone with her bejeweled teeth.

"She is an anomaly, I am afraid. And to my shame, if I had known it was she you were retrieving, I might have told you not to." Phoebe sighed. "I will only say that she is one you should keep an eye on. You

241

already seem to know you can't trust her. She is not, as *you* would say, a team player."

Ernie looked over at Phoebe, who smiled and added, "As I told you, I have access to some of Minh's memories. I know you, of all people, understand the importance of working together. It seems the Dealers have moved away from that in recent centuries."

"But they worked together before?"

"I tried to encourage camaraderie, not rivalry," Phoebe explained. "I take it Andy was different?"

"Minh always told me Dealers work alone."

"Minh is a wary sort." Phoebe gave Ernie an assessing glance. "I've been wanting to ask—have you been able to access and understand the power you received from the Sunrise?"

Ernie closed her eyes. Without Legs on her arm, the starburst scar on her chest throbbed every once in a while but mostly felt like what it was—a scar. "Not yet. I'm not sure exactly how to go about it."

"Perhaps you're avoiding it," Phoebe said gently. Her gaze fell on Ernie's hand as it rubbed over Ernie's empty left forearm. "You miss her. You miss what you were together. And right now, it's hard for her to be with you."

Ernie nodded, feeling an inexplicable lump in her throat. "I haven't been a Dealer that long, honestly. But she feels like a part of me."

"Good Dealers always feel that way about their animals." Phoebe patted Ernie's arm. "But the only way to move forward is through, yes? You must access and master that power."

Ernie looked down at Minh's hand on her arm—Phoebe's hand—and knew it was time to put her doubts aside. "Can you help me out? You had all these powers at one time."

Phoebe smiled. "I was hoping you'd ask. Since I began occupying Minh's body, I've been pondering how different it feels to have only one power as opposed to all of them working together like organs in a body. Certainly it is not easy." Minh's dark eyes skated over the Dealer gathering. "There are five pillars to the Forger's awesome powers. Five pillars to hold up the roof that should shelter all these magnificent beings. Like the five senses, in a way. And each of you was hit with a piece of the Sunrise—I assume each of you got one."

"So being able to sense rune tiles and relics is one of them?"

Phoebe nodded. "As is the ability to sense the Dealers themselves."

"And Tarlae—she can make cards."

"Yes. And the Kestrel has been gifted with a bond to the animal spirits, so he can call them and command them."

"I think he's enjoying it," Ernie said as she watched him take a swig from a bottle, his long hair hanging loose, his face bearing an easy smile.

"It suits him," Phoebe murmured. "I think that power may have chosen him specifically."

"So what's the fifth pillar?" Ernie asked, wanting to move on quickly. "Wouldn't that be the one I have?"

Phoebe tilted her head, looking bemused. "Come now. You seem like a smart young lady. Think about what a Forger can do and what is not represented among your cadre of friends, and that will be your power."

The obviousness of the whole thing struck her like a bat to the head. "Oh my god," she whispered, setting her beer down and peering at her hands. Her starburst scar tingled as her conscious mind slid over the realization, and her palms ached with potential. "The ability to *create* relics and rune tiles."

She looked at Phoebe for confirmation and found the former Forger smiling Minh's smug smile. "Now," Phoebe said, "perhaps you should ask yourself, What can you create that will turn the tide of this war?"

CHAPTER TWENTY-THREE

Ernie clenched her hands into fists, trying to wrap her head around the idea that she could be the one to create the weapon that could beat Virginia. She remembered other Forger-made relics: the Marks, used to demand a favor from a Forger, and the Cortalaza, a blade that could cut through anything, even dimensions, even the Forger himself. Those two relics had been the combination Virginia had used to undo Andy, though she'd manipulated Ernie and her allies into unwittingly helping with her plot. And then there was the Sunrise, which all of them had believed was some sort of weapon that could be used against a Forger, even though Phoebe had apparently created it so that she could find herself a companion . . . or maybe a mate? Despite her intentions, the Sunrise had turned out to be a weapon after all, though a complicated one. But hell, Ernie would take what she could get. "Phoebe?"

Phoebe had been sipping her beer as she chuckled at the cavorting Dealers, some of whom were dancing while Kot plucked an instrument that resembled a homemade mandolin. "Hmm?"

"How am I supposed to access the power?"

"How did Gabe? How did Tarlae?"

Ernie considered it. "I guess both of them were under some stress. The first time, Gabe was being attacked by Minh's animal, and the second, he was trying to protect me from the Scorpion Dealer's. As for Tarlae, Trey was dying. I'm not sure she even knew what was happening."

"Sometimes great gifts come naturally." Phoebe polished off her beer and stifled a burp with the back of her hand, such a Minh thing to do that Ernie once again felt a pang of guilt. Despite Phoebe's reassurances that staying focused on unseating Virginia was the best thing, Ernie missed Minh. "Others only come with intention and practice." She gave Ernie a sly wink. "Though my guess is that if Gabe were under attack, you would produce a relic quickly that could save him. I know I would certainly want to."

Ernie ignored the look and the feelings it threatened to uncover. She needed to concentrate on how best to help her team. "Is it like dealing the cards, then? It's about *willing* something into existence?"

Phoebe shrugged. "A bit, though you must do it without the guidance and magic of a deck and its animal spirit."

"True." Legs had been like a set of guardrails for Ernie, keeping her plays focused and effective, and sometimes coming up with ideas of her own. "So it takes concentration."

"And you have to know exactly what you want."

"That's easy: I want to remove Virginia as the Forger. Can I create a relic that will do that?"

"Perhaps, but you would have to know the *way* you would be removing her." Phoebe held up the beer bottle. "For example, thissa beer is making me feel drunk, and you handed it to me. So you are using zomething to make me drunk." Phoebe leaned forward unsteadily. "But for you to create a relic that could accomplish such a thing, you'd have to know how to make the calcofall. I mean, the alcohol. Got it?"

Ernie's brows rose. "One beer, really? I've seen Minh go through a half dozen without losing a step."

Phoebe gave Ernie a tremulous smile. "You're not the only one who's conjured me up a drinkie tonight. And that's the other thing to think about—not only will you need to think of the method by which your creation will do its job . . . you also need to think about how much power to apply."

Ernie watched as Phoebe sagged back into her lounger with a seemingly happy groan. "I assume I'd put everything I had into it, to make sure it would get the job done."

Phoebe giggled. "Careful there—wouldn't be the first time a newly created relic has caused a disaster. My predecessor once told me he'd caused a few earthquakes and volcano eruptions in his day with his botched attempts."

Volcano eruptions? Ernie shivered at the thought of having that much power inside her. "So I have to control it. Moderation."

"Ah, yes." Phoebe put her hand out. "I'll have another of those, if you don't mind."

Ernie played Nourishment to produce another frosty IPA as she thought about a weapon that might kill a Forger. Phoebe took a swig and eyed Ernie. "You're thinking of becoming the Forger yourself, eh?"

"Huh?"

"Well, if you strike the blow to depose the Forger, you're the one who takes the throne!"

"Oh." Ernie frowned and took a gulp of her own beer, once again remembering the look on the doomed thief's face right before she stopped his heart. "No. I don't want to be the Forger. I don't think playing God is my thing."

Phoebe looked surprised. "Really? You seem like an ambitious creature, and you hold a deck that was created to be aggressive and dominant. The Diamondback has been at the peak of the pyramid for centuries!"

Ernie had heard things like this before. "And at least one of its Dealers used it to commit war crimes. Doesn't mean I will." She bit her lip and glanced at Gabe, who was now clapping along merrily as he watched the dancers. He looked over at her, and when he saw that she was talking with Phoebe, he simply smiled and winked, warming Ernie all the way to her toes. "Actually," Ernie continued, "Gabe and I were wondering if *you* were interested in taking the throne again."

Phoebe pulled her white shirt closed at the collar as if she'd felt a chill. When she spoke, she seemed a bit soberer than she had minutes earlier. "Only if there is agreement among you. I am not the sort to grasp for power. I will only take it if it is willingly bestowed."

"Which makes you unique among Forgers, not that I've known that many."

"I only really knew the one before me," she said quietly. "And someday I will join him out there, mingled with the constellations." She leaned back and looked up at the sky. The light of the stars was reflected in Minh's dark eyes. "But perhaps not yet, if there is work to be done to protect the Dealers—and the universe."

"My understanding was that it was the Forger's job to create chaos. Andy said it was basically the fuel that kept the universe . . . I don't know, moving forward?"

"There's always chaos," said Phoebe. "He was right that if everything stopped, if there was complete order, then we would cease to exist. But creating chaos is a perverted version of the true purpose of the Dealers."

Ernie sat up straight. "Which is?"

Phoebe's eyes were still on the sky. "To preserve freedom. And choices. And free will." She blinked. "As well as the consequences that come with action. Those things can sometimes look like chaos, as people follow the many different paths laid down by the thousands of choices we make each day. But that complexity does not require a contribution from the Immortal Dealers. Believing that it does gives us both too much and not enough credit." She put the bottle of IPA to her lips and downed the rest of it in several glugs, after which she let out a loud sigh. "We are justice, Diamondback. That is what we are. Or what you are, to be more accurate."

"We've all believed a lie," Ernie said, thinking with sorrow of how close Gabe had come to ending his existence, all because he believed that his mission as a Dealer was to cause chaos and do harm. Anger followed hard on the heels of that sadness as she considered how twisted the true mission had gotten, all because of the greed and ignorance of Andy. Virginia seemed to have followed in his footsteps perfectly. "I think it's time to right the ship."

"I may end up as captain, but you will be the one with the wheel in your hands," Phoebe said, her words slurring a bit, her eyes drooping. "Steer us well, Diamondback." She let out a soft snore.

Ernie rose from her lounger, her eyes wide and staring at nothing. Gabe, Nuria, and Kot were still with the dancers, and Trey and Tarlae were nowhere to be seen. Ernie trudged over to the yurt haven they'd created together and knocked on one of the wooden beams that formed its frame. Trey pulled the flap open and gestured her inside. As Ernie entered, Tarlae was curled up on a cot, poking a fork at a plate of roasted potatoes, and Trey was sitting opposite her, looking unhappy. "What's up, guys?" Ernie asked. "There's quite a party going on out there."

"They are strangers." Tarlae stabbed at a potato. "I don't like strangers."

"They're allies," said Trey. "And if you go out and talk to them, they won't be strangers any longer!"

"Then you go and talk to them," she snapped. "I'm tired of you hanging around like a lost puppy. Go make friends of your own!" She flicked her fingers toward the exit.

Trey regarded her for a moment, stone-faced. Then he got up and left the yurt.

"Ouch," said Ernie.

Tarlae lifted her head and met Ernie's gaze. Her eyes were shiny, maybe with tears. "I cannot let him close to me again," she said in a choked voice. Then she abruptly wiped her hand across her cheek, set her plate aside, and sat up on the cot, looking weary. "I saved him from losing his deck, but if we go down this path, what else could happen to him?" She displayed her palms, now bearing wide scars that glittered with gold, like the starburst scar on her thigh. "He hasn't been cursed like us. He can walk away."

"He won't, though," said Ernie. "He's the same guy he always was, even without his memory. And I think he's falling in love with you all over again, even though it looks like he really doesn't want to."

Tarlae snorted. "Then I will be cruel."

"I doubt it's going to work, lady. You're not that convincing."

Tarlae's eyes flashed. "Don't test me, Diamondback."

"I'm not the Diamondback right now, Tarlae. I'm Ernie. Your friend. And I know you're terrified of losing him again, but he'll be stronger and safer if he's confident in your love."

"I saved his life. That made it all too obvious how I feel."

"Um, he was unconscious for most of that."

"Obviously *someone* told him about it," Tarlae said, tossing her curly black hair over one shoulder.

"Not quite the same as having the person you love put her arms around you and welcome you."

"He hasn't asked for that."

"He's probably afraid you'd turn him down."

"I *would.*"

"So he's clearly as bright as he ever was. He needs you to go to him, T."

The corner of Tarlae's mouth twitched. "Are you really my friend?"

"Why wouldn't I be?"

"Because I only like you sometimes, and I'm not good at being a friend."

"Never too late to get some practice."

Tarlae's eyes narrowed. "I don't trust this Phoebe person. I don't like what she's done to Minh."

"Minh wanted her to do it. He was overwhelmed by the Forger's magic, and now Phoebe seems to have tamed it."

"Then she should get out and give him back to us."

Sarah Fine

"I really think she's just trying to help," Ernie said.

Outside, someone shouted. Both Ernie and Tarlae tensed—Tarlae even had her deck out. But the yelling was followed quickly by the sound of several people guffawing, and the two Dealers relaxed. Ernie sat down on the cot Trey had been occupying. "She told me some things," Ernie said to Tarlae. She explained what Phoebe had said about the real purpose of the Dealers, and how the ancient being had agreed to become the Forger once more if asked by all.

"Trey had the same idea," Tarlae said flatly. "I told him he was crazy."

"I had my doubts at first, but I think it makes a lot of sense."

"Then you are crazy, too. We don't know her, Diamond—" She pressed her lips shut before starting again. "We don't know her, *Ernie*." She shook her head. "I thought Minh should be the one. If not him, then Gabe. Them, I trust."

"Really?"

"They are good men. I haven't always agreed with their choices, but there was a reason Trey was willing to follow Gabe into hell." Tarlae winced and directed her gaze away from Ernie. "That damn Raccoon is not crazy," she whispered. "Nor is he stupid. He knows what is right."

"Agreed," Ernie said quietly. "And if you believe that, maybe you should think about supporting Phoebe as the person to replace Virginia."

Tarlae shrugged. "We'll see." She gave Ernie a sidelong glance. "You haven't realized your Sunrise power yet, have you?"

"How did you know?"

"You look reasonably well rested." She rubbed her scarred palms over her thighs. "Creating one deck laid me out, and Rika seems to hate me. She only returned to my arm a few hours ago."

"I have the power to create relics," Ernie said. "I just have to figure out how to use it."

"You are good at creating stupid-looking weapons that actually turn out to be useful. You're known for it, in fact."

250

"Thanks?"

"You are welcome," said Tarlae. "Please create something that will not get us all killed."

"Right. Yeah. Will do." Ernie stood up. She suddenly needed some air. "Can I get you anything from outside?"

"You can stop that awful animal killer from roasting her meat downwind from my tent," Tarlae growled. "Or I may have to do it myself."

"You stay put." Ernie couldn't imagine a confrontation between those two that didn't end in bloodshed, as neither seemed the type to back down. "I'll go talk to Mhambi."

Tarlae nodded and lay down on her cot again. "And tell me if Trey dances with any other woman but me, so I can castrate him if he does."

Ernie cringed. "Yeah . . . I don't really want to get in the mi—"

Tarlae raised her head. "That was a joke." She smiled. It looked a little awkward on her beautiful face, as if she were trying a dance move she hadn't practiced in years.

Ernie felt a rush of affection for the Coconut Octopus Dealer. "Good one. I'll see you later?"

"Not if I see you first." Tarlae laid her head back down, and Ernie slipped out of the yurt and into the night.

The party was still going strong, but Trey was hanging at the edge of the crowd, watching his fellow Dealers dance and play and drink. A beer bottle hung loose in his grip as he watched the merriment. As Ernie approached, he turned his head and gave her a stiff smile. "She doesn't think much of me, does she?"

Ernie patted his back. "What do you know about the coconut octopus, Trey?"

"The animal? I don't know. Octopuses are smart, right?"

Ernie nodded. "They're also great at *hiding* when under threat."

Trey looked over his shoulder at the yurt. "She's damn good at it. I wish . . ." He let out an exasperated breath. "I wish I could remember, you know? She's a master class I might have taken once, but now I'm failing it."

"You're not," Ernie said.

"Thinking of dropping out, honestly."

She squeezed his arm. "Don't. It means the world to her that you re-enrolled."

"She doesn't like Phoebe."

"Sometimes it takes time to trust—I know it did for me. You have to wait her out, Trey. It might not be easy, but it's worth it."

"How would you know?"

"Because I knew you before," she said gently. "And I've never seen anyone more in love than you were. Or happier."

Trey's gaze found Gabe in the crowd. He was dancing with a stout old woman with ruddy brown skin and long braids, who was giggling as she held on to his lean hips. "He told me the same," he said. "He's been telling me about some stuff I did, and missions we did together, and me and Tarlae. He's trying to help, but it feels like fiction."

"Gabe wouldn't lie to you," Ernie said. "He's trying to give you your memories back."

"It's not the same," Trey murmured. He blinked and tossed his empty bottle into the air, disappearing it with the swipe of a card. "I'm going for a walk. Later." He strode away as if he couldn't put distance between them fast enough.

Ernie rubbed her hands over her face. She didn't feel like joining the group, but she didn't feel like going to bed, either. She—

"I will share my meat with you if you like."

Ernie nearly jumped a mile at the sound of Mhambi's voice. Somehow, the woman had crept up on her in the dark and was now standing next to her, right where Trey had been. "Gah," she said, clapping a hand over her heart. "No, thanks. I don't eat meat."

Mhambi's eyes narrowed. "You *are* a predator, though."

As if on cue, a rattling emanated from a clump of grass nearby, indicating that Legs had returned from her reptilian wanderings. "Sort of? I mean, *she* is." She waved her hand toward the place where the grass was rustling. "I'm just . . ."

"Are you prey, then?" asked Mhambi, showing her teeth.

Ernie's hand slipped into her pocket, and her fingers closed over her deck. "Definitely not."

Mhambi grinned. "And so."

"Just curious—are you from this dimension originally?" Ernie asked.

"I was once. But not for a long time."

Ernie peeked toward the Dealer's arm, which was still covered by her close-fitting leather shirt. "Who put you in that other dimension?"

"I chose to be there," said Mhambi. "It was a truce, you could say." Beneath the understandable words, Ernie could hear the abrupt vowels and clicks of the woman's true language.

"Who were you fighting?"

Mhambi took in the gathering of Dealers. "She is a liar. Know that and be on your guard."

"Who?"

"If you're not prey, don't act like it." Mhambi gave her a light shove on the shoulder and then loped back in the direction of her fire for one.

Ernie watched her go, then scanned the crowd and found Phoebe still slumbering in the lounger Ernie had conjured. Her new, fragile trust in the former Forger had just cracked, and her uneasiness had returned with compound interest. Drawing her deck from her pocket, she stalked over to her yurt and ducked inside. Lying down on the cot, she crossed Dreams with Ally and Revelation, then tipped herself into the realm of the slumbering mind.

She arrived in the meadow where she and Phoebe had said goodbye to Minh, and looked around. "Minh," she called. "Minh?" She walked toward the line of trees and peered into the shaded depths of the woods, then turned in place.

"Here," said a weak, croaking voice. A gray shadow floated out from behind a tree. Ernie gaped. Her friend had aged visibly—his chest had sunken, and his eyes were dark pits in deep sockets. It looked like he'd lost twenty pounds off his already lean frame, and if possible, he seemed more transparent than he had been when she'd left him last time. "Where's Phoebe?"

"She freaking lied to me," Ernie said, acid in her voice. "She told me you were okay."

"Have you beaten Virginia?" he asked. "Has Phoebe been able to harness the power of the Sunrise?"

Ernie explained everything that had happened, including bringing all the banished Dealers home. "But we need to get you back into your body. Now."

"No . . . she needs it, and I . . . trust her." Every word seemed to be draining him. His face and body sagged toward the ground, as if even his transparent form was too heavy to hold up. The sight made Ernie's throat tight.

"Minh, we can find another way for her to help—I think this is killing you."

"I'll survive," he said, waving her away. "But hurry."

Ernie hesitated. "Minh . . ."

"Go," he wailed, floating back toward the trees with his pale, ghostly feet trailing along the ground.

Determination and urgency winding tight inside her, Ernie did as he asked, lurching herself awake to find Gabe sitting next to her, eyeing her with concern. "You went to see Minh, didn't you?"

"Contrary to what Phoebe told me, he's not doing well." She sat up. "We need to make our battle plan. This party? Waste of time."

"Not a waste at all, if you ask me." He smoothed his hair back and lashed it into a haphazard ponytail. "Phoebe was wise to suggest it." He gave her a disappointed look. "I thought you'd come around on her."

"I can't trust her, Gabe. Minh's in bad shape, and she wanted us all to believe he was fine."

"She's focused on helping us achieve the goal that we set for ourselves, Ernie. We said we wanted to defeat Virginia."

"She's drunk as a skunk right now! How is that helpful, exactly?"

"The Dealers are building bonds that will be useful if we're to fight together. For the first time in fifty years, I had a cordial conversation with Akela. I played daggers with Ruslan, and he didn't try to stab me even once. And I've talked to nearly every Dealer we brought home today—they're fired up and actually believe we could win *because* we're all together here." He reached over and grabbed her hand, giving it a hard squeeze. "And you're part of that, too. I need you to be part of it."

Ernie stared at their joined hands. "I want to be, Gabe. And I know you want Phoebe to be Forger. I know you want to trust her—"

"Don't trust her if you don't feel it," he snapped, then softened his tone and stroked his thumb across the back of her hand. "Give this a chance, fight this fight with us, and then decide." He glanced toward the open flap of the yurt, out to the few dozen immortals whooping it up outside. "Virginia may have created new Dealers, but we've gathered a force strong enough to defeat her."

"As long as we can get her onto the battlefield—she's using her new Dealers as human shields." Their eyes met. "But even if we can't get to her, I think I might be able to do something big. Phoebe told me that I've got the ability to make relics."

"In other words, she was helpful." He said it as a fact, not a question.

Ernie decided that now wasn't the time to pick another fight, not when they had a war to wage. "Yeah. She gave me some tips. But I've realized what I need to do."

His eyebrows rose. "Which is?"

"I'm going to make a relic that brings the fight to Virginia," Ernie said. "I'm going to take us straight to the Forger's lair."

CHAPTER TWENTY-FOUR

"*Into* the Forger's domain?" Phoebe rubbed at her eyes—Minh's eyes—and gave Ernie a bewildered look. *"Everyone?"*

The party was winding down, and the original yurt haven was now surrounded by similar structures where Dealers were bedding down for the night. Mhambi had wandered even farther from the others, setting up a hut for herself perhaps a half mile away, with only a fire to reveal her location. Ernie wasn't sure whether the woman didn't want to be too close to the rest of them or whether she sensed the other Dealers didn't want her there. Either way, Ernie resolved to keep an eye on her. "Nearly everyone," Ernie replied.

"The Forger's domain is sacred," said Phoebe, looking back and forth from Ernie to Gabe. "Taking Dealers there will have consequences."

Gabe's brow furrowed. "I think that's the point exactly—the consequence will be that we have a new Forger at the end of the day. *You.*"

Phoebe gave him a hesitant smile. "But you can only transport yourself accurately to a place you know," she explained. "Any Dealer who goes there will be able to find a way to get there again, if their mind is focused enough. You can't shield a place from a Dealer who has been there before."

"What would be wrong with that?" asked Ernie.

Phoebe looked horrified. "The Forger would never be safe. She would be vulnerable to attack from any Dealers who knew how to transport themselves into her lair."

"If we had a good Forger, who would *want* to attack?"

"Ernie." Gabe put his hand on Ernie's shoulder as he took in the haunted look on Phoebe's face. "Remember that Andy ambushed her, and not because she was a tyrant," he said quietly. "She's been imprisoned for centuries because she granted more access to Dealers."

"I handed him the tools to destroy me," Phoebe murmured, her eyes wide and seemingly staring at nothing. Gabe put his hand on her back, and she—*Minh*—leaned into him.

Ernie crossed her arms over her chest. "Desperate times call for desperate measures. I think this is what we need to do."

"I respect your strength of will, Diamondback," Phoebe said. "But I cannot help you with this."

"Minh is suffering," Ernie snapped.

Phoebe started to shake her head but stopped when Ernie's fists clenched. "It is not easy to be a spirit," the former Forger acknowledged. "But Minh is strong, and he has faith in me, yes?"

"Minh trusts you." Ernie didn't speak her next thought aloud: *I don't.*

Phoebe frowned as if she'd heard it all the same. "I would help you if I could."

"You were the Forger," said Ernie. "You know where the domain is—you occupied it for centuries, right?"

Phoebe nodded. "And this is what I am trying to explain to you—the body I possessed then was the vehicle that carried me back and forth to the Forger's domain and to this world. That body is gone. Minh's body has never been in the Forger's lair, and so I cannot use its connection to the place to help you get there." She swept her arm toward the cluster of yurts all around them. "None of these Dealers have been to the Forger's domain."

"Rupert," Ernie muttered.

Gabe turned to her. "The Hyena?"

"Virginia brought him to her domain after she banished Ruslan and Akela." Ernie laughed. "I guess she wanted to flex her muscles and show off. But he's been there. He told me so himself."

"This Forger seems quite foolish," Phoebe said.

"She doesn't think he's much of a threat," Ernie replied. "And based on the way he ran from her during our confrontation in the desert, I'm thinking she's right. But she didn't count on what we could all do together." Ernie pulled out her deck and drew Revelation and Ally. Crossing them, she located Rupert, who, despite fleeing at the sight of the current Forger, hadn't bothered to conceal himself from Ernie—maybe because he believed she was already dead or banished at the hands of Virginia. "I'm going to go get him."

She gave Phoebe a sidelong glance and took Gabe's hand, pulling him away and leading him outside the ring of yurts. She played her Conceal card to prevent them from being heard and asked, "Keep an eye on her?"

Gabe looked confused. "Who? Phoebe?" His eyes searched her face. "Are we really on about this again? Love, she's only doing what we asked her to do, and she's not taking a thing for herself! Who better to be our next Forger? All the banished Dealers agree. They like the idea of her leading us once again."

Ernie tried to push her doubts away, wondering whether her own anxiety about what she needed to do was making her more negative in general. "I know. I hear you. I just want Minh back in his body, and I'm not going to feel good about this until he's okay."

Gabe drew her into a hug. "Have I ever told you I'm glad you're on my side?"

She returned the embrace, hard. "I'll be back as soon as I can." With one last glance at Mhambi's solitary settlement, Ernie played her cards and set off in search of the Hyena Dealer.

Rupert came without a fight, but that was because Ernie snuck up on him and immobilized him before transporting him to a rise overlooking the Dealers' camp. His blue eyes bulged and his cheeks were red as she pocketed his deck and played Inverse and Lock to free him.

"Bloody hell, woman!" he roared, neck muscles flexing with his rage. "You could have just asked!" He held out his hand. "Give me my deck. Now."

The hyena flopped off his arm and jumped to its feet, snarling.

Ernie fanned her cards. "If that thing bites me—"

"His name is Wellington," Rupert snapped.

"If *Wellington* bites me," she said, fighting a smile, "I'm gonna have to muzzle him, okay? Don't make me do that."

"Come off it, Wellie," Rupert mumbled. "I'm fine. She's an ally. Also a bitch, but we won't dwell on it."

"Hear me out."

"Give me my deck, and I will," he said, his gaze straying to the cluster of yurts in the distance. "And what the hell is that?"

"A gathering of Dealers aligned against Virginia. There are nearly thirty of us, most brought back from dimensions where they'd been banished. We brought Akela and Ruslan home."

"I thought you'd all be dead," he admitted. "Sorry about that."

"I'm going to give you a chance to redeem yourself."

He narrowed his eyes. "Or what?" Wellington sat on his haunches and whined.

"I'm done threatening you, Rupert. I need your help. You told me you'd been to Virginia's domain, and I need you to describe it to me in detail."

He stared at her. "You're bloody crazy, you know that? You want to try to go there?" He shook his head. "She'll strangle you with your own damn snake."

Ernie covered her blank forearm with her hand, missing that damn snake quite a lot. "I'm not asking you to go with us."

Rupert scratched Wellington behind the creature's overlarge ears and snuck a glance at the large camp. "You really think you could do this."

"Me? No. Us? Yeah."

He rolled his eyes. "I already told you what the place was like. Greek columns everywhere, a bunch of fountains looking kind of like birdbaths, the whole thing floating in space."

"And you said it smelled weird. Like what?" Ernie put her hand over her starburst scar. "I need all the details."

"The smell . . . I dunno. A mixture of old lady and space dust."

Ernie groaned. "Take this seriously, will you?" She offered him his Revelation card. "Try to find it in there—since you've been there, you should be able to."

His eyes went wide, and he shook his head. "She'll sense that. I know she will."

Ernie put up her hands in an effort to soothe both Rupert and his animal, who was letting out a series of distressed yips. "Fine!" The last thing she wanted was to alert Virginia to their presence here. "I guess I'll have to go on what you've given me."

"What are you planning to do, exactly?"

"Forgive me if I don't feel comfortable letting you in on all the details," she said drily. "But you seem like the kind of guy who'd buckle under pressure."

"Oh, instantly." He flipped her off. "Can I go now?"

After asking him a few more questions to try to more of a sense of the Forger's lair, Ernie gave up and handed Rupert back his deck. "Are you really going to run away from this?" she asked.

He kicked at a clump of grass. "Not all of us are heroes. Some of us are just survivors."

"Fair enough," she murmured as he played his Transport card and vanished.

Ernie sat down on the grass, facing the camp. She didn't have the luxury of running away. Minh was depending on her. Maybe everyone was depending on her. If they didn't take the fight to Virginia, they'd always be dueling on her terms, whenever she decided to appear, and all she'd have to do to escape was scamper back to her special hidey-hole. But if they could mount a home invasion that brought all of them to her turf and gave everyone the ability to get back there when necessary, maybe they could corner her, and even do it without having to kill the newly created Dealers. Maybe some of them could be redeemed. It seemed likely that many of them hadn't known what they were getting into when Virginia offered them their decks.

It seemed ideal. All Ernie had to do was somehow manage to pull the perfect relic out of thin air. "No problem," she muttered, peering at the completely ordinary-looking palms of her hands.

When Tarlae had birthed all those cards, they'd pushed themselves out from under her skin while she'd seemed caught in some kind of trance. Was that what this would be like? Or would it be easy, like Gabe's power? He seemed to be himself, only with a new ability that made him extra dangerous to other Dealers. That would be nice, she thought. Because if she had to somehow produce something like the Cortalaza from her palms, it seemed like that would *really* hurt.

A rattling nearby signaled that Legs was close again. "Hey, lady," Ernie called. "Probably not the best time to be on the arm."

The rattling grew louder, and Ernie rose to find the source of the sound. Legs was coiled in a clump of grass. As she wriggled her thick body, Ernie spied something in the center of the spiraling shape made by the diamondback. Squatting next to the serpent, Ernie played her Light card to get a better view. Legs shifted so the object was on her back.

It was a crystal, about four inches long and an inch or so thick, deep orange and broken at one end, like it had been snapped right off a larger formation. Ernie picked it up and examined it as Legs stopped rattling. She thought about the Forger-made relics she'd seen in the past. Some were tiles with runes on them, while others were larger objects, like the

Cortalaza blade and the Forger's Marks. "You think I could use this and turn it into a relic?" she asked the snake.

Legs answered with a mild shake of her tail.

Ernie smiled. "You're the best, you know that?"

Legs rattled a little louder and stared up at her with her lidless, cold eyes.

Ernie took a few steps back. "I'm going to give this a try." She sat back down, crossed her legs, and held the crystal cupped in her hands. "A relic that will take us to the Forger's realm. That's what I need."

Nothing happened. Ernie pulled the collar of her shirt away from her body and looked down at the starburst scar and the veins that wound their way across her chest and into the hollow of her throat. The scar throbbed dully, as it always did. Ernie bit her lip. She closed her eyes and tried to picture the place as Rupert had described it, columns and birdbaths and stars and all. She pretended that she was there, descending a set of crumbling steps the Hyena Dealer had mentioned and emerging into a sunken amphitheater where the broken columns stood. Her chest burned, and the golden veins pulsed. The crystal in her hand glowed like a light lay within it, going from cold to hot as the pain in her scar turned sharp. Ernie gasped.

The light died. Ernie squeezed the crystal. Nothing.

She tried again. And again. And again. Each time, she could feel something start to happen. Her chest would tighten and burn as if she were having a freaking heart attack, and the crystal would glow, but at some point, everything would fall apart. She tried to stay focused on the place Rupert had described, but it wasn't carrying through to the crystal. Nothing was. Maybe because she was distracted by the pain, maybe because she was getting the details wrong.

Had she really believed she could create a relic based on a half-assed description from Rupert? "I'm an idiot," she whispered.

"You might be right," said Mhambi from behind her. Ernie whirled around to see the Dealer standing several feet away. Blood was smeared on her hands and her right cheek. At her feet lay what appeared to be a dead sheep or goat or yak—whatever it was, it was really woolly.

Ernie eyed the carcass. "You're hunting?"

"Me?" Mhambi shook her head and grinned. "I don't need to."

"What are you doing up here, then?"

"Collecting my prize." Mhambi tilted her head. "Do I need your permission, Diamondback?"

"It's a big steppe. Plenty of room for everyone."

"You are helping her without thinking about what it means," Mhambi said, throwing the furry carcass over one muscular shoulder.

"How about you just tell me what you want me to know?"

"What do I know? I have been far away for many years, and much has changed. Many Dealers, but none from my time. A new Forger. A new enemy."

"Do you want to go back to where you were before?"

"I was a goddess there. Here? I do not know what I am. But I do know *who* I am. More than you know."

"I wouldn't say that."

Mhambi looked intrigued as she took in the crystal in Ernie's cupped hands. "If you bow to anyone at all, make it the right person."

"And you don't think that's Phoebe?"

Mhambi's pale eyes glinted in the moonlight.

"If you're not going to tell me, how am I supposed to find out?"

Mhambi bared her jeweled teeth. "Ask the ones who know her." She played her Transport card and vanished, along with the dead goat thing.

Ernie suppressed a shudder, and not only because of the slaughtered animal that Mhambi may or may not have taken down with her bare hands. The woman had been right—if they were going to hand the Forger's power to Phoebe, they needed to make damn sure they knew who she was. Minh had vouched for her, so that was a plus. But only one or two of the rescued Dealers had been made by her, so most seemed to be relying on what they'd heard about her generosity and kindness. Apart from Minh, and maybe Mhambi, who had more or less told Ernie that Phoebe couldn't be trusted, who knew the former Forger?

Nuria did, but she couldn't speak. And Trey did. Sort of. For some reason, Phoebe hadn't told him who she was—she was simply the first thing he remembered seeing. Ernie's scar pulsed sharply as an idea occurred to her. With her heart skipping, she plopped back down onto the ground with the tangerine-colored crystal clutched tightly in her hand. Maybe she'd aimed too high at first. Maybe she hadn't had enough to go on. Maybe this was a better first step.

Maybe she needed a few answers before charging in blind.

"Answers," she said in a loud, clear voice. "This will be a tool to find them." She squeezed the crystal as that heart-attack feeling rose once more in her chest, burning and stabbing, making her ribs feel like they were being squeezed in a vise. Her vision spotted and flashed with golden sparkles. She tried to draw a breath but couldn't. The crystal pulsed with searing heat. Ernie gritted her teeth and forced herself to keep holding it, to keep concentrating on what she needed, to keep going until she held the key in her hand.

Suddenly, a power beyond her control streaked up her spine and wrenched her head back. Her mouth flew wide, a silent scream into the golden abyss that was the only thing Ernie could see. Agony crept along her limbs, burning her bones to cinders. The smell of smoke filled her nose, and the sound of distant crackling filled her ears, but there was nothing she could do. Her chest flashed with star-bright pain, and her mind filled with a press of images. She was standing in a pit, trembling as a giant grasshopper devoured a human body. She was bleeding from the shoulder as Kot drove an old jalopy along a bumpy road with her dad in the passenger seat. She was walking along a road while talking to Andy, thinking about how stupid his braided beard looked. She was staring at her cards, willing Gabe to appear. Each memory added to the pressure in her skull until, with a pop, everything went black.

CHAPTER TWENTY-FIVE

Gabe strode toward her across a field of lava, along its black crust, every footstep creating cracks that revealed the molten rock underneath. Ernie wanted to run to him, but she couldn't; she didn't seem able to move at all. Heat rippled up through the air, warping her view of him, but relief filled her all the same. Drops of sweat slid along his temples as he held out his hand to her. "Come back, Ernie," he said, and she heard his voice like his lips were pressed against her ear. "Come back now."

Ernie's eyes fluttered open as she inhaled in what felt like the first time in years, breathing in the scent of whiskey and smoke. Gabe had his arms around her, and he drew back as her fingers spasmed around his wrist. Between his fingers was the blank card, one corner of which was singed. A haze of smoke hung in the air, filling the yurt with its bitter scent. "Thank god," he whispered, pushing Ernie's soaked hair away from her sweaty brow. Outside, people were shouting to each other, but the words slipped away beneath a loud whooshing sound.

She shivered. "What . . ."

Minh poked his head into the yurt, his cheeks smeared with soot. "The others have gotten the fire under control."

Ernie coughed, then whimpered as her entire body objected. It felt like her ribs had been shattered. "Fire?" she croaked.

Minh—or, she remembered, Phoebe—frowned at her. "I warned you," she said.

Ernie's gaze searched her face, then Gabe's. His somber expression was terrifying. "Was it me?" she whispered.

Gabe looked over at Phoebe. "She needs to rest."

"The others are cleaning up, but we're probably going to have to move the camp," she replied, then gave Ernie a stiff smile. "But by some miracle, no one was hurt."

"What happened?" Ernie asked, her voice breaking, her throat raw and aching.

"You're in a better position to answer that than anyone else," Phoebe said. "You were trying to create a relic, I assume? But you didn't control it."

Ernie blinked. Her entire face hurt. Gabe cradled her gently, trembling slightly. "I felt something wrong," he said. "Legs appeared right next to me, rattling like a Kango. Right after, I smelled the smoke, and then the entire steppe was on fire. I found you on the rise, surrounded by flames." He winced and touched her cheek. "I healed you as much as I could."

Ernie looked down at her body and realized she was covered by a blanket and nothing more. Her skin was raw and pink, and her clothes lay in a torn, blackened pile near the entrance to the yurt. "I'm sorry," she said. "I didn't . . . didn't mean to . . ."

What had she been trying to do? What had happened? The recollections trickled in slowly, wisps of thought as fragile as the tendrils of smoke around her. She glanced at her arm—Legs was right there, where she hadn't been before. Gabe touched the tattoo with his fingertip. "She came to you when you needed her," he murmured.

Ernie closed her eyes and swallowed back tears. If Legs had wanted to find another Dealer, that would have been the perfect way to do it, probably. She could have just let Ernie burn.

"Well?" asked Phoebe. "Did you create the relic—the one to transport Dealers to the Forger's realm?"

266

Gabe's blue eyes held something Ernie couldn't quite read. But she answered honestly. "No, I didn't."

"If you want to use the power, you'll have to harness it." She looked Ernie over. "If you'd like, we could allow Minh to reoccupy his body, and I could jump into y—"

"There has to be another way," said Gabe. "Ernie can control this. She's a quick study, and there's no one stronger."

Phoebe transformed Minh's face with a soft smile. "She's so lucky to have you as a protector," she said. "But it's her decision. Like I did with the power to sense rune tiles that was overwhelming Minh's mind, I could help Ernie control her relic-creating power—and keep it from hurting others."

Ernie stared at the wall of the yurt. "I'll think about it," she said.

"You are wise, my child," Phoebe said before withdrawing.

Gabe's embrace tightened. He guided Ernie's chin until she was looking at him. "Did you lie just now?"

"Which part?"

"The relic to reach the Forger's realm."

Her eyes met his. "That was the truth."

Gabe reached into his pocket and pulled out the tangerine crystal. "What's this, then? I was careful as hell with it—I didn't want to end up in Virginia's house all alone."

Ernie took it from him, feeling its power surge beneath its surface, a smile creeping across her face. "This won't take you there. That's not what it's meant to do." With his help, she sat up and conjured herself some clothes: track pants, a sweatshirt, and her favorite trail shoes. "But if it works, it should give us what we need." She stood up, grabbing Gabe's shoulder to steady herself. Her muscles screamed as if she'd run a Spartan Beast.

He rose slowly. "And what do we need?"

"Trust me?"

He paused. "I may not agree with you in all things, but I do trust you."

It was enough. Ernie kissed his gold-veined cheek, and when her lips brushed his skin, her own scar pulsed, as if with recognition. "I won't be long." She headed for the yurt's exit.

"You might want to—" was all Gabe had a chance to say before Ernie emerged into a blackened plain dotted with the wreckage of burned yurts. "Whoa," she whispered.

She might as well have shouted it. A few dozen pairs of eyes seemed to laser straight to her. The rescued Dealers—who did indeed seem to be in the middle of a cleanup operation, with some sucking the smoke down from the sky, others disappearing burned yurts, and a few others healing singed comrades—looked at her with equal parts curiosity, suspicion, and hostility.

Trying to keep her hands steady, Ernie crossed Revelation with Ally, then transported herself across the camp.

Tarlae and Trey were working together to pull the smoke from the sky, having crossed Air with Tool and Nourishment. The black fog swirled and disappeared as they aimed their cards. "Can I talk to you, Trey?" Ernie asked.

Trey lowered his card and turned around, scowling. "I thought you were busy setting things on fire," he said.

Ernie nodded. "Not on purpose, obviously."

"Phoebe said she could fix your power if she took over your body— a lot of us think you should do it."

Ernie looked past Trey to Tarlae, who seemed uncertain. "Is that what you think I should do?" she asked the Coconut Octopus Dealer as she removed the crystal—now a relic, she was certain—from her pocket.

"I would never allow another being to take over my body or my mind," said Tarlae. "And I would not blame you for rejecting her generous offer."

"Even after she nearly killed all of us?" Trey asked, his voice rising.

"I really need to talk to you, Trey," Ernie said. "Somewhere private."

Tarlae tilted her head as she eyed the crystal in Ernie's hand. "What is that?"

"Something that should be able to help him," Ernie replied, moving closer to Trey.

Trey spotted the crystal as it caught the light of the newly revealed sun. "What the hell?" he said, taking a few steps back. "What are you doing?" His fingers began to sift through his cards.

Tarlae played a few of her own, so quickly that the Raccoon Dealer didn't have a chance. He froze, his eyes wide and his limbs stiff. Tarlae approached him quickly, putting her arm around his lean waist as he stared at the two of them with shock and anger. "We can take him somewhere else," Tarlae said. "Come."

Ernie grabbed Tarlae's arm as the Coconut Octopus played Transport and carried the three of them a few miles closer to the mountains, beyond the massive circle of scorched earth. Tarlae touched Trey's stiff face. "You won't hurt him, will you?"

"I don't plan to," Ernie said. She had no room for doubt or hesitation, not now. She pressed the crystal between Trey's palm and hers. The relic pulsed, and the steppe disappeared, replaced by a torrent of images that came so fast Ernie was barely able to stay upright. Her heart pounded, and her breaths came fast and shallow. She could hear Tarlae's frantic questions—what was happening; were they okay—but she couldn't dredge up the words to answer her from under the flood of scenes. And then, finally, came Phoebe's face—her actual face—smiling as she reached inside of Trey's head, her ghostly fingers sliding into his skull.

Trey pushed Ernie away, and she stumbled backward, nearly falling on her ass. "You-you-you—" he stammered, his eyes bulging.

Tarlae grabbed him by the shoulders while shouting at Ernie, "If you've damaged him, I swear I'll—"

Tarlae didn't get to say more. Trey wrapped his arms around her and kissed her hard, his hands sliding over her body with a desperation that quickened Ernie's pulse. When he pulled his mouth from Tarlae's, the Coconut Octopus Dealer gave him a dazed smile. "Damn, Raccoon," she mumbled.

"You ain't seen nothing yet," he said, giving her a light smack on the backside. He looked over at Ernie. "I remember everything."

Ernie grinned and held up her relic. "I thought you might." She didn't mention the other power hidden in her relic—she'd needed to access his memories, all of them, and in doing so, she'd given them back to him. But now she had them, too.

His smile faded. "Phoebe. She took my memories from me."

"I will skin her alive," Tarlae growled.

"You can't," Ernie said. "Not yet, anyway."

"She's right, babe," Trey said. "Andy had restored my deck and dumped me in the dream realm, but then he disappeared. I guess when he was killed?"

"He told me he'd taken your deck," said Tarlae, stroking his face, looking like she couldn't get enough of him.

"He said he ought to, but he was going to give me another chance, because he knew Virginia and I didn't get along. He said she needed someone to smack her down."

"I think he appeared to a few of us," Ernie said, recalling how Andy had come to her in the splinter dimension and told her to keep Virginia from getting the Sunrise. She'd lost those memories when she'd returned to this dimension, but the relic she'd created had brought everything back. "He knew Virginia was a threat, but he didn't want to seem weak by asking for help."

"I was weak," Trey said. "And when Phoebe appeared to me, I thought she was a product of my imagination. She said she wanted me to get something for her, and I told her to get lost. All I wanted to do was find a way back to Tarlae."

"And then she stole your memories?" Tarlae bared her teeth. "*Skin* her."

Trey took her face in his hands. "God, it's so good to have you back. I feel like I've been walking around in a fog for weeks, knowing I was missing a huge piece of who I was."

"You are *mine*," she purred.

"Exactly," he said. He glanced at Ernie. "We can't let her be Forger."

"Agreed." Ernie looked down at her relic. "But I don't think we can announce that. We need to feel out the other Dealers. The last thing we need is to split into factions. We need everyone fighting together."

"I'm going to go back and act like nothing's happened," Trey said. "See what I can find out." He leaned in for another passionate kiss. "You coming?"

"I'll be right there," Tarlae said.

Trey played his Transport card and vanished, and Tarlae turned to Ernie. "You gave him back to me."

"He loves you so much that I don't think you really ever lost him."

Tarlae pulled her deck from the pocket of her dress. "You are a true friend and ally." She produced a card and handed it to Ernie. "And I will fight by your side, whatever comes."

Ernie stared down at the card in awe. "You made this."

"I've been practicing." Her brows rose as she scanned the blackened earth that stretched between them and the horizon. "Perhaps you should as well."

"I know. I have to contain it." She tossed the tangerine crystal up in the air and caught it. "I guess I put a lot of power into this one." As she watched it catch the sunlight, she had an idea, one that made her look toward the camp. "And I think we'd better get back."

They transported themselves to the camp, which the group had largely cleaned up. Someone had even turned the burned terrain back to gold-and-green grass, and a few others had re-conjured yurts arranged in a circle around a central fire. As they had before, most of the formerly

271

banished Dealers gave Ernie some serious side-eye when she appeared, but Gabe, Nuria, and Kot approached immediately. "We've been waiting for you to get back," he said as Nuria stepped forward with an anxious look on her face.

"What's up?"

"Apart from the fact that there are rampant rumors that you don't want Phoebe to be the Forger?" Kot said. "Is that true?"

Ernie glanced around her to see several sets of eyes focused on their discussion. "I want the best person to be the Forger," she said cautiously.

Nuria frowned, so Ernie said, "I know you're really fond of her, Nuria."

The Grasshopper Dealer scowled.

"There are also rumors that you want to be Forger yourself," Kot added.

"What? Who said—" Ernie looked over at Phoebe, who was deep in conversation with a small group of Dealers who kept giving Ernie seriously dirty looks. The group included Trey, so they at least had a plant who could tell them what was being said, but Ernie had enough to go on already. "Let me guess—Phoebe herself."

Gabe put his hand on her shoulder. "She knows you're not with her. Maybe you could meet with her again? She needs to know we're behind her."

Tarlae, who had been listening silently, scoffed. "She took Trey's memories. *No one* should be with her."

Gabe paled as Ernie explained what Phoebe had done. When Ernie had finished, he shook his head. "I can't . . . She's been lying. This whole time."

Ernie ached for him—he'd wanted so badly to believe in Phoebe. "We can still be united against Virginia. But not with Phoebe as our leader."

Gabe glanced around. "It won't be easy to convince everyone else of that, though."

Nuria grabbed Ernie's wrist. "Muh," she said.

"I know she was your Forger," Ernie replied.

Nuria's jaw clenched, and she held up a card—Dreams. *"Muh."*

"Minh?" Ernie asked.

Nuria nodded eagerly and repeated what was, apparently, his name. Kot had watched this interaction with intense focus, and he said, "She wants you to go with her."

Ernie gestured around them. "Right now, I'm not eager to be asleep and vulnerable."

"We'll guard you as you sleep," Gabe said, indicating Kot and Tarlae. "No one will dare try to harm you."

Kot and Tarlae nodded, and with the sight of them looking so fierce and strong, Ernie consented to follow Nuria into the dream realm. They ducked into a newly conjured yurt and lay down side by side on two cots. Solemnly, Nuria crossed Dreams with Ally, as did Ernie. At the last moment, Nuria grabbed Ernie's hand, her slender fingers grasping firmly. Ernie focused on the image in the Dreams card and let herself tip forward into the realm.

She and Nuria appeared in the meadow where Ernie had seen Minh before, but he was nowhere in sight. "Minh?" called Ernie. "Come on out!"

"C-c-can't," Nuria said. She looked relieved to finally be in a place where words came a tiny bit easier.

"He can't? Why?"

After opening and closing her mouth a few times, Nuria gave up, grabbed Ernie's hand, and dragged her over to the trees, where she pointed into the woods.

"He's in there?"

Nuria jabbed her finger toward the trees. Beneath the leafy canopy lay a damp, mossy darkness, presided over by a bit of floating haze. Ernie began to walk forward, but Nuria yanked her back, shaking her head. Once again, she pointed.

Ernie's stomach dropped. She eyed the haze in front of her, nothing more than a pale fog wisping around the trees. "No," she whispered. "Is that him?"

Nuria nodded. She pantomimed grabbing the haze and shoving it into her body.

Ernie stared at the fog. "We need to free up Minh's body so he can return to it before it's too late. Is it too late?"

Nuria touched her head and heart before pointing to the fog. Ernie took a wild guess: "You can still sense him." Nuria nodded, then hesitated. She bobbled her hand, indicating she could *sort of* sense him.

"We're on the verge of losing him forever." Ernie swallowed. "You okay with helping me get him back? It means pushing Phoebe out, if she's not willing to be cooperative."

Nuria met Ernie's gaze—and nodded. Ernie thought she might not be the only one who sensed something off about the too-good-to-be-true former Forger. Ernie took Nuria's hand. "Let's get back, then. We can go talk to her."

But as Ernie awakened on her cot and heard the sounds of a pitched battle coming from outside the yurt, she understood that the time for talking had passed.

Ready or not, it was time to fight.

CHAPTER TWENTY-SIX

Ernie was jumping up from her cot, already palming her deck, when a blast from outside ripped the yurt away. Showered with splinters and shredded cloth, Ernie and Nuria dove in opposite directions. One quick scan of the area confirmed what Ernie had already suspected—the massive fire *she* had caused in her effort to create the relic had allowed the newly created enemy Dealers to locate them. A massive duel was on.

Several of the banished Dealers had surrounded Phoebe, protecting her with their lives and decks as the dangerous but inexperienced newbies attacked. Ernie could hear Minh's voice shouting orders and instructions from within the huddle. She was glad his body was protected, but it also presented a challenge—she needed to get to Phoebe.

Dodging strikes and throwing up her shield, Ernie ran toward Gabe. He was easy to locate—the golden veins of the scar that ran along the side of his face sent off luminous beams of light as he summoned enemy Dealers' animals right off their arms and made them charge the exact people they'd usually defend with all their strength. Kor protected Gabe from strikes, and Caera circled overhead as Gabe used the awesome power of the Sunrise. The Dragonfly Dealer saw Ernie charging forward and blocked a strike—a weighted net with shards of broken glass woven into its mesh—from the Hippo, allowing her to reach Gabe's side.

"Where is Nuria?" bellowed Kot as he dealt his glowing cards.

"She ran that way," Ernie said, pointing. "Go ahead."

Kot, always the protector, sprinted in the direction Ernie had indicated. Gabe gave Ernie a look of relief when he realized she was next to him. "They busted into our camp so suddenly, it was all hands on deck," he shouted as he pulled the hippo off its Dealer's arm with a simple motion. The person screamed as it trampled them. "Did you find Minh?"

"I need Bao," Ernie said.

Gabe's brows rose. "Is that a yes or a no?"

"It's a now," Ernie said, huffing as they were hit with a blast of wind that blew clumps of grass and splintered rock over them.

Gabe didn't question her—gold streaks bled across his irises as he touched his stomach, right where the tattoos lay, and put out his hand. Bao, whom Gabe had sheltered there for safekeeping, emerged in a shimmering swirl that quickly coalesced into his compact, bristly body. The pot-bellied pig looked up at Gabe, as if awaiting instructions. Gabe leaned down and put his hands on the animal's back, then looked up at Ernie and nodded. "Protect him?"

"You know I will," she said. "Stay alive, okay?"

He frowned. "Ernie . . ."

"I love you." She whirled around, throwing a clear shield around Bao. The creature streaked along next to her while Ernie blocked strikes with other cards. They headed across the camp toward the banished Dealers surrounding Phoebe. When the ones on the flank recognized Ernie, a few began to aim strikes in her direction. Awareness of her rippled through the ranks, and the circle re-formed, with some banished Dealers fighting the new enemy Dealers and others focused on Ernie. She used Inverse to cause a few strikes to bounce back, Warp to change their path, and Draw to rip cards right out of their Dealers' hands. Her left forearm pulsed with pain but also a fierce energy. Legs was in the fight with her, no matter that she had to share Ernie's body with her new power. As Ernie dove out of the way of a few deadly strikes, the knowledge that Legs was with her fueled her strides.

But as she drew near to the ranks of Dealers protecting their would-be Forger, she realized she wasn't going to be enough. "I need to talk to Phoebe," she shouted.

The Black Bear and Peacock Dealers stood shoulder to shoulder, their very different faces lit with rage. "Stay back," shouted the Black Bear, a ruddy-faced man with a bushy white beard. He managed to land a hard strike, sending Ernie to the ground with some kind of stinging bugs swarming around her. Ernie rolled and smacked at her face and arms, desperately trying to play the cards that would free her from the thousands of needle jabs filling her entire body with pain and venom. A few yelps and several screams told her that some new threat had entered the battlefield, but it was all she could do to play Sea and Aid to cause a sudden deluge of salty water to crash over her. Bao grunted next to her, still enclosed in a little dome of protection at her side.

By the time Ernie was on her feet again, already pressing the Healing card to her face, the new danger was clear.

Some type of giant *thing* the size of a silverback gorilla was rampaging through the ranks of enemy and supposed ally alike. With shaggy fur and a long snout, the creature ran on all fours but had muscular shoulders, clawed hands, and a bloody set of jagged teeth. Behind it came Mhambi, laughing as she wielded her deck in one hand and a short blade in the other. Her cards swooped around her like raptors, glowing as she caught them and slashed them through the air. The new enemy Dealers fled in terror after the beast sank its teeth into the Hammerhead Shark Dealer and shook the poor guy in its jaws before hurling him to the side in a bloody heap.

"Kill her," shouted someone within the ranks of the banished Dealers—it was Minh's voice. "She controls the monster. Stop her now!"

As if that voice was the signal, the beast launched itself off the bleeding Hammerhead and bounded toward the group of banished

Dealers. Mhambi loped along behind it, and her eyes met Minh's. She grinned. "You gave me my monster, Phoebe," she shouted. "And it is good to taste blood again."

The beast she controlled, which Ernie could swear looked like a werewolf ripped straight from the most terrifying horror movie ever, caught Ernie in its yellow-eyed gaze. It howled. Ernie began to draw cards to strike it, but it sank onto its powerful haunches and propelled itself over her. "Phoebe's head is mine," Mhambi said as she reached Ernie's side. "We can fight together."

"The head that beast will take isn't hers!" Ernie charged forward as the werething reached the banished allies and began to decimate them. Its hide seemed immune to the strikes aimed in its direction. "Call your animal off—those are allies we need!"

"They strike at us."

"Because they've been told lies," Ernie yelled. "If we give them the truth, we can fight the real enemy together!" Ernie pulled the tangerine crystal from her pocket. "Help me get to Phoebe without hurting the others."

Mhambi eyed the crystal. "You want to be the Forger."

Ernie shook her head. "But I have a few gods to kill anyway."

Mhambi nodded in apparent approval. "I knew you were a predator." She let out a sharp whistle, and the werebeast came bounding toward her. It leapt into the air and spiraled onto Mhambi's arm without even slowing the woman down—her cards were fluttering around her before the beast went still on her skin.

Together, Mhambi and Ernie moved forward, driving both the newbies and the banished aside. As the defenses peeled away, Phoebe tried to run, but Mhambi released the werebeast again, and it cornered the former Forger against a yurt. Just as it seemed poised to strike, blue bolts of electricity gathered between Phoebe's—Minh's—fingers. With a clenched jaw and her back to the wall, the power dripped from her hands, and the beast stumbled back. Ernie didn't, though. Gripping the crystal, she didn't even break stride. She dodged around the creature and collided with Minh's body like a pro football tackle. As her brain lit up with agony and electricity, she pressed the relic against Minh's neck.

It seemed like a lifetime passed in the space between seconds. Centuries ticked by inside Ernie's mind like bomb blasts. Memories— Phoebe's memories—piled so high inside Ernie's skull that it felt as if the top of her head were going to blow off. She could see it all. The lies and the truth. The relic Ernie had created had been meant to allow her to mesh her mind with another, and it worked so well that she lost awareness of where she ended and Phoebe began. All she felt was hunger. A hunger for power, for love, for worship. The need was consuming, blurring Ernie's intentions and goals as Phoebe's spirit battled for control.

Phoebe was trying to shield her mind from Ernie's, but Ernie could see it all. The Forger before Phoebe, a young-looking man with a sly smile, had not given up his power willingly as Phoebe had told them. No, she had entrapped him with her body, youthful and, even then, desperate for love and the power that came with it. She'd seduced a god and brought him low, been given a deck—the Asp—and used it to strike him as he slept deep and trusting in her arms. Her reign as Forger spun inside Ernie's thoughts, all the decks that had been birthed with seeming benevolence but that had come with the expectation of worship—but Mhambi hadn't bowed, hadn't been grateful, and hadn't been like any of the others. Phoebe had banished her instead of taking the deck of the were-creature, which Phoebe had created just to see what she was capable of.

The Sunrise relic lay in Phoebe's memories as well, but it hadn't been made with the desire for a companion, a mate, an equal. No, it had been an insurance policy, hidden carefully in case Phoebe ever faced a rebellion and needed more power or to restore power that had been lost. She had no intention of ever ending her reign. Her hunger had mellowed only slightly with age, but the edge was always there, and it had sharpened to a deadly point during the centuries of imprisonment.

She'd lured Nuria and trapped Trey. She'd tricked Minh. Ernie could feel the coldness inside. Phoebe hadn't really meant Minh any harm. She hadn't cared much about him at all. He'd been a way to get back to the waking world. He'd been a tool for her use, a means of getting a bit closer to her goal of regaining the throne.

The throne. As Phoebe's will battled her own, as Minh's hands shocked her with the remnants of a Forger's power, Ernie focused on Phoebe's memories of the peak of her reign. A vision appeared before her, as if she'd stepped right into it. The darkness of space was all around her, indigo black and streaked with cosmic dust. The marble floor was firm and cold beneath the soles of her feet. She stood in a white amphitheater, surrounded by crumbling steps and five towering pillars, each topped with a carved rune.

Gathering her waning strength, Ernie opened her eyes and looked into Minh's. "You can't," Phoebe croaked, even as she wrapped Minh's fingers around Ernie's throat.

Ernie pressed the relic even harder against her friend's skin. "You used all of us," she said, feeling her pulsing golden power coiling at the center of her chest. "Here's how it feels."

The heat exploded from the depths of her, and it was all Ernie could do to control it. She concentrated on what she needed and felt it forming against the palm of her left hand. The relic took shape from bone and earth, a solid lump with an ivory sheen, pushing forth from Ernie's palm in a burst of agony and blood. She was only dimly aware of the skirmishes around her, of Bao nearby, of Mhambi's creature looming over them, of Gabe's voice shouting her name. She'd hoped to have time to make a plan, to bring her true allies together, to confront the threat as a team, but the momentum of what she'd conjured was too great. She caught one last glimpse of the battle on the Mongolian steppe before everything went black and cold. All she could feel was Minh's struggling body beneath hers.

They hit the hard, frigid plane of rock with a force that knocked any remaining breath right out of Ernie. Her vision flashed red and white before her eyes blinked open to the sight of stars and planets. The sound of Minh's groan drew her gaze downward. She was lying on top of his body, and his eyes looked up at her with a blank sort of malevolence. "You've signed your own death warrant," Phoebe whispered. "Minh's, too."

Ernie's fingers clenched around the two relics she'd created, one to meld minds and view memories, and one to carry her to the Forger's realm. A brief scan of the amphitheater in which they lay told her that she'd made it. She looked down at Phoebe again, summoning the power she needed as she peered deep into cold, hungry eyes. "Only one of those things is true," she said. "Minh's going to be just fine."

With her mind and her soul and her power, she reached for Phoebe. Not Minh, whose body was a shell right now, but for the former Forger who had used it for her own gain with no thought for the noble spirit whom it belonged to. Ernie shoved as hard as she could into the massive, icy consciousness that had crowded him out of his own skin. Phoebe clung to his bones, to his marrow, but Ernie was fueled by love, not merely the craving for it. She was energized by loyalty to her friend, not the demand for devotion in return. She felt Phoebe's spirit slip free, wailing and ghostly, as Minh's body heaved and gave it up.

He went still, his eyes closed. Ernie dropped the relics and groped for a pulse. "Come on," she muttered. "Come *on*."

"I knew you were stupid," Virginia said, "but this is pretty impressive, even for you."

Ernie jerked upward. A wisp of white swirled nearby, maybe Phoebe's disembodied and powerless spirit, maybe a bit of cosmic dust. But the former Forger who had gotten her here was no longer the threat—the current Forger sat several feet away, on a grand throne carved from glittering, smooth stone that seemed to glow, lighting the space around it with soft white luminescence.

Virginia smiled as Ernie rolled off Minh's body and crouched over him, wishing he would move or breathe or give some sign that she hadn't just destroyed him. She'd thought this would work, but Bao wasn't here, and she didn't have Minh's deck—Tarlae had taken possession of it just like Gabe had temporarily taken custody of Bao. She had only one of the Forger's powers—creating relics. She couldn't create cards, summon an animal spirit, or locate a human one, so all she had was Minh's empty body, which she'd brought to the most dangerous place in the universe.

"Do you feel powerful, Diamondback?" crooned Virginia.

Ernie's fingers closed around her deck. "Maybe a little."

The Forger's white hair floated around her as she stood up. Sparks of blue electricity rode along the backs of her veined hands, and her dress billowed. She descended the stairs slowly, her steps steady and unhurried.

Ernie tried to jump to her feet but found that she could barely get to her knees. Her entire body shook with what it had been through, the battle, the fight for Minh's mind and body, the epic struggle to keep Phoebe's memories and will from overwhelming her. She felt as if she were staring up at a mountain, with a fifty-pound bucket of gravel held in her arms. She had little left, but she'd only just reached the beginning of the fight.

Virginia put her hands on her hips. "Oh, come on. You've done more than most could have."

Ernie drew her deck with a shaking left hand. Legs tingled on her arm. "I'm not quite finished."

The Forger's eyes went slate black. "That's where you're wrong," she said in a deep, terrible voice. "You got a slice and acted like you had the whole pie, Serpent. But here you are, all alone." She grinned. "And now I'm gonna eat you."

Ropes of searing power shot from her hands and wrapped around Ernie, yanking her off her feet and twisting her upward. Her vision reeled—a glimpse of Minh's body, a glimpse of the stars, all lit with sapphire agony. Her cards flew from her grasp. Legs slid from her arm and hit the marble ground with a sickening slap. Her diamondback was silent and still as the bonds of blue tightened. Ernie's right hand trembled as she groped for her pocket. The urge to give up was rising, along with a wave of hopelessness. But she'd come this far . . .

Her fingers touched the two cards she'd kept separate from the rest of her deck, just a brush of fingertips and a pulse of desperation. Virginia bent her hands into the shape of claws, clearly intending to crush Ernie's body and soul. "I'm not . . . ," Ernie rasped.

"What? Did you have some last words?" The bonds around Ernie loosened slightly, just enough to let her draw breath. "Go ahead." Virginia sounded amused. "I'm feeling generous."

Ernie ripped the cards from her pocket and flipped them both. One a hybrid winged snake, and one a creature Ernie had no name for, a tentacled beast with fangs and a rattle. Her two blank cards, one a gift from a Forger, the other created by a friend. "I'm not alone," Ernie shouted.

The blue ropes disappeared as Gabe and Tarlae appeared on either side of her. Now that they were connected by their hybrid cards, their thoughts filled Ernie's mind as her body hit the ground. Their energy pressed against hers, reaching toward it. The power of the Sunrise was trying to pull together, Ernie realized.

"You're still my Dealers," Virginia said, stepping back while Tarlae and Gabe lifted Ernie to her feet. Both of them had their decks drawn in their other hands. Quickly, Tarlae bent and pressed Minh's deck to his chest, but he still didn't stir.

Gabe and Tarlae each threw strikes at Virginia, working together to hit the Forger with Capture and Death and Pain and Lock, a desperate attempt to hold her back. Ernie dove for her cards, which had scattered across the floor around Minh's body. But Legs lay unmoving next to

Sarah Fine

him, and the cards were cold. Ernie's heart ached, and her bones suddenly felt brittle, as if the slightest strike could shatter them. She looked down at her hands, which had gone veiny and wrinkled.

She'd lost her deck. She'd lost its spirit. Legs lay, eyes open, staring at the stars. A scream birthed from the center of Ernie's soul burst from her mouth. Gabe and Tarlae were both on their backs now, struggling against Virginia's power. Ernie felt their agony, their waning hope. Together, they had three-fifths of a Forger's power. And it wasn't enough.

Tarlae flung her hand out as her body lurched back and forth. The skin of her palm split, dripping gold and crimson. A white card slid from beneath her skin, and Ernie caught a glimpse as it fluttered to the ground and landed, back facing up. It was a creature with a warped combination of angular limbs and curving tentacles, but Ernie knew exactly what it was.

Summoned by the newly created Octopus-Grasshopper hybrid card, Nuria appeared in the Forger's domain, standing astride Minh's body, her face alight with determination and her deck drawn. The cards flew from her hands and floated around her as she dealt them faster than Ernie had ever seen a Dealer play, even Mhambi. Virginia staggered back, releasing Gabe and Tarlae.

They had only a moment, and they didn't use it to attack the Forger. Instead, they ran for each other. Gabe's hand closed around the back of Nuria's neck. His other grasped Tarlae's fingers. Nuria reached for Minh, her palm cupping his jaw. Ernie grabbed Minh's hand.

The Sunrise power flared inside her, inside all of them. Gabe focused on Legs. Tarlae's outstretched palm generated card after card, replacing the Diamondback cards Virginia had rendered useless. Legs suddenly jerked and rattled, Ernie drew a gasping breath, and Gabe turned his focus to Bao, pulling him through dimensions toward them. At the same time, Nuria pulled Minh's spirit toward her. Ernie's relic acted as a homing beacon, and her power amplified everyone else's. Minh's body convulsed as the image of Bao bloomed on his left forearm.

284

His eyes opened, and his fingers squeezed Ernie's. Energy surged between them. Then he reached for his deck.

Virginia struck them all at once, and the air filled with the scent of electricity and fire. "You think you're better than me? You're no different!" she bellowed. "You'll tear each other apart, fighting over who gets to be Forger."

Ernie felt the questions flow between her friends, like the pulse of blood through veins. Which of them would take the throne? Gabe? Tarlae? Minh? Nuria?

Ernie?

"No," Ernie said, because the answer was as clear to her as the stars above. "All of us."

All of us.

Yes.

The thought didn't come from any one of them. It came from all of them at once. Hands clasped, the five Dealers got to their feet, facing the Forger. Virginia sent the blue lightning ropes their way again, but together, the power complete inside them, Ernie and her allies turned it back on its owner. The glowing sapphire bonds spiraled around Virginia and pulled tight. Her pale eyes bulged. Her mouth opened.

Her skin crumbled, black ash chipping off and spiraling. The sparkling obsidian essence whirled and gusted in the windless space, carrying itself toward the group of Dealers. Instead of flying into any one of them, it rained down on all of them. It tingled on Ernie's skin as it sank into her. It flowed between them, as did the understanding that they would never again be completely separate from each other.

With a final gasp, Virginia's body collapsed into dust, and the blue bonds that had held her disappeared. Each of them staggered as the power snapped back into them, but Ernie dropped to her knees, her hands out, her focus already on the next task.

What are you doing? She heard Tarlae's voice clearly, as if the Coconut Octopus Dealer had said the words aloud.

Creating a jail cell, Ernie replied. Already, the little box, wooden and lacquered, was growing beneath her palms—and this time, it didn't hurt. Nuria smiled and reached toward the little fog of dust lingering where Virginia had stood only moments before. She pointed at it, then drew her finger down toward the box when Ernie opened the lid. The fog coalesced and swirled toward the box.

But Nuria wasn't done. As if she felt the spirit nearby, she turned and pointed at something Ernie hadn't even seen—another, fainter cloud that had lingered behind them.

Phoebe's spirit.

With a dark light in her eyes, Nuria pointed with her other hand and drew that spirit toward the box as well.

That's going to be the ultimate battle. The thought came from Gabe, soaked with amusement as they all watched the two spirits bounce against each other as they flowed into the box. Ernie slammed the lid and sealed the box shut with the power that now surged from her hands as naturally as she drew breath.

Ernie slowly got to her feet. She looked at her friends. She felt their emotions—surprise, awe, determination.

She held up her hands and said the only thing that came to mind. "High five?"

EPILOGUE

It had been easier than she'd thought, drawing the rest of the Dealers together. The newly created Dealers settled down as soon as Ernie and the others assured them that they wouldn't be destroyed. The banished Dealers who had been brought back from various dimensions required slightly more convincing, but they seemed more willing to accept the new order of things than they might have been if only one Dealer had taken the Forger's throne. Many of them expressed something along the lines of "time will tell," which Ernie thought was fair. All of them agreed to work together—except Mhambi. The mysterious Dealer came to Ernie and asked to be sent back to the dimension to which Phoebe had exiled her, seemingly understanding that her nature would not allow her to peacefully coexist with the others—particularly after her bloody adventures on the battlefield.

Ernie turned her face to the sky. The stars were dimmer here than in the Forger's domain, barely visible through the smoky haze lit with the glow of bulbs strung overhead. The parking-lot beer garden at Wedge was as crowded as it usually was on a Friday night, but Ernie had managed to snag a table for her and her friends—and hadn't even used magic to do it. She grinned as she carried the tray of pints toward the place where they sat, right in front of the singer who strummed her guitar and crooned about being a Blue Ridge girl. Tarlae had her arm around

Trey as he nodded his head to the beat. Nuria perched on Kot's lap, her fingers in his hair. Minh and Gabe played a straightforward game of gin rummy—they'd transformed their decks for the purpose.

Ernie set the tray on the table, glad to be rid of its weight. "I think I got everyone's order."

Gabe grabbed her hand and pulled her toward him, and Ernie didn't resist. While the others claimed their pints and lifted them in a toast, she took his face in her hands.

"I think it's going to be a quiet weekend," he said.

Ernie grinned. "You think?"

He cast a sly glance toward the others. "I may have pulled a few strings."

They commanded the Dealers now. They made the decks and summoned the spirits. They could reach through the dimensions and build new ones. But not without each other.

The world had kept turning. The universe had continued to expand. They'd begun to mend the damage that Virginia had done, using quiet acts of peace and influence. The possibility of the years to come and the awareness that the awesome responsibility wouldn't be held by any one of them filled Ernie with hope. They would bear the burden together.

"Can we go out for sweet potato pie, then?" she asked, dipping her head to brush a kiss across his lips.

His smile was spring and summer rolled into one. "And biscuits and all the rest of it."

Ernie reveled in his embrace, knowing it wouldn't always be this easy, but also knowing it wasn't all on her shoulders. And with that knowledge, she settled into her seat and enjoyed a beer with her team.

ACKNOWLEDGMENTS

Many thanks to the entire team at 47North for seeing this series through to its conclusion, particularly Adrienne Procaccini, who led the charge and advocated for the books from start to finish. Special thanks go to Tegan Tigani, my developmental editor, for helping me shape *The Warrior* into something I'm truly proud of; Janice Lee, my copyeditor, for helping me keep all my time zones straight during Ernie's and the other Dealers' international and interdimensional wanderings; and Phyllis DeBlanche, my proofreader and fearless typo-zapper. More thank-yous go to Blake Morrow for designing covers that were absolutely perfect for each book, Kathleen Ortiz for being available to provide any needed support, Jena Gregoire for organizing all the outreach for the series, and Debbie Simpson, trainer extraordinaire, for providing me with some insight into the mind of a Spartan racer—any inaccuracies about those aspects of the books are my fault and mine alone.

To my family, thank you for supporting me through sun and storm. To my dearest friend, Lydia Kang, thank you for understanding, for being there, for celebrating with me, and for keeping me sane whenever things felt like they were falling apart. To my dearest love, Peter, the only one with whom I am willing to share my pie and biscuits and all the rest, thank you for everything. And to my fans, thank you for hanging with me and my characters until the end of another series. You are the reason I write.

ABOUT THE AUTHOR

Photo © 2012 Rebecca Skinner

Sarah Fine is the author of more than twenty books and novellas for adults and teens. Her adult books include the Servants of Fate Series; the Reliquary Series; and *The Serpent, The Guardian*, and *The Warrior* in the Immortal Dealers Series. She confesses to having both the musical tastes of an adolescent boy and an adventurous spirit when it comes to food (especially if it's fried). Sarah has lived on the West Coast and in the Midwest, but she currently calls the East Coast home. To learn more about the author and her work, visit www.sarahfinebooks.com.